As Seen on TV!

What Reviewers Say About CF Frizzell's Work

Exchange

"CF Frizzell really knows how to write tension! A great read, a real roller coaster of emotions with a sensational love story." —*Kitty Kat's Book Review Blog*

Night Voice

"CF Frizzell has written a beautiful love story, a romantic tale that will have you cheering on Murphy and the lady who has stolen her heart. …There was just enough angst and plenty of hot sex in this excellent book to keep anyone hooked. Emotions ran high and how all of those involved communicated their feelings made for a very interesting read. I loved it."—*Kitty Kat's Book Review Blog*

"I very much enjoyed it. The main characters felt real and likeable. The connection between them was palpable and the slow build-up was a pleasure to read. The supporting characters were also well developed. …I liked the author's writing style and will keep an eye out for her future works."—Melina Bickard, Librarian, Waterloo Library (UK)

Stick McLaughlin: The Prohibition Years

"[E]xciting reading and a story well told!"—*Golden Threads*

By the Author

Exchange

Night Voice

Nantucket Rose

Measure of Devotion

As Seen on TV!

Stick McLaughlin Novels

Stick McLaughlin: The Prohibition Years

Crossing the Line

As Seen on TV!

by

CF Frizzell

2022

AS SEEN ON TV!

ISBN 13: 978-1-63679-272-9

This Trade Paperback Original Is Published By
Bold Strokes Books, Inc.
P.O. Box 249
Valley Falls, NY 12185

First Edition: October 2022

Credits
Editor: Cindy Cresap
Production Design: Susan Ramundo
Cover Design By Jeanine Henning

Acknowledgments

This is a novel I'll remember writing for many reasons, not the least of which is that my editor called the concept, "quirky." And, of course, she's right.

As Seen on TV! somehow emerged despite Covid dulling my senses with too much television, despite the hangover from my previous book's deep historical dive, and despite losing my favorite aunt to cancer. I acknowledge the powerful, lasting influence of all three.

Some good-natured harping from BSB author Kris Bryant kick-started my brain for this project, and I thank her for helping shove the wheels back into motion. Don't fault her for the "quirky" storyline, however. *That's* the product of too much TV, my wife, Kathy, and I growing addicted to paranormal and cooking shows, respectively.

And I thank Kathy, forever and always, for guiding the wheels as life reconfigured the track. I know that Aunt Fran, who loved my books even more than her Hallmark movies, sends you a heartfelt thank-you, too.

Acknowledgments

Dedication

Aunt Fran
Forever sending you Hallmark movie love,
just as seen on TV.

Kathy
You are proof that incredibly beautiful spirits *do* exist.

Chapter One

Screaming smoke alarms yanked Ronnie off the couch as if she'd been electrocuted. Popcorn went airborne. Being startled ranked right up there with paper cuts and sour milk: freaking awful and usually your own fault. She flew into the kitchen where wisps of smoke leaked from the oven door.

"Shit! Shit! Shit!" She grabbed two potholders just as her best friend burst in out of the rain.

"*Now* what are you burning?" Cheryl shouted over the insistent alarm. Waving her hands at the haze, she rushed to open the window a few inches.

Ronnie kneed the oven door shut as she set the smoking skillet atop the stove. "I lost track of time, dammit." She switched on the overhead exhaust fan and flapped a dish towel at the alarm to calm it. Mercifully, the noise ceased.

"At least the monsoon outside would save us," Cheryl quipped, hanging her slicker by the door. "Were you smoking meat in the oven again?" She peered over Ronnie's shoulder and tried to assess the situation. "Why is the Dutch oven sitting on the chicken? Shouldn't the chicken be *in* it?"

"It escaped."

"Distracted again, huh?"

"Now, I have a *really* crispy chicken recipe." Ronnie removed the cast iron pot and inspected the splayed bird in its pan. "It's not totaled."

"You forgot to set Alexa again, didn't you?"

Ronnie wiggled two spatulas beneath the chicken and lifted it onto a wire rack. She hated to admit that, once again, she'd been distracted by her newly discovered television program, *Aerial America*. Her customized nineteenth-century farmhouse had the design and furnishings she wanted, but not the self-thinking oven she sometimes needed.

"This recipe's for my shoot next week. I've got two days to polish it up and I have one chicken left to start over."

"Maybe the char will add barbecue flavor."

"Glad you think so because it just became our supper." Ronnie scrubbed the pan in the sink. "I used to cook this all the time but just for myself."

"So…let me guess what happened here: Another scenic flight over some state you've never watched."

"Did you come here to nag? The episode was about Montana. It's just as easy on the eyes as that hot ghost hunter Peyton Whatshername you lust over." She loved teasing Cheryl about her fascination with those convoluted ghost shows, particularly *Paranormal Pursuit*, and the fan-crush she had on its popular star.

"There's more to that show than Peyton Stanford, but she *is* attractive and you know it."

"I know. She's drop-dead gorgeous. I *have* seen the show, y'know."

"Yeah, right. You've only seen a few minutes a couple times," Cheryl reminded her as she inspected the chicken. "Remember—and this is from me, the best friend who's also your agent—*Paranormal Pursuit* has done wonders for our network. Peyton's the number one paranormal investigator on television."

"So, I've read."

"And you should catch her show online. In fact, watch your Smithsonian show online, too. Stream them, so you aren't locked into those TV time slots. Or bring your laptop out here, maybe."

"*Aerial America* has to be seen on a big screen. When my laptop grows another sixty inches, I promise I will."

"Well, if you keep watching TV programming while you're cooking, you'll become the number one disaster chef on the network."

"I'm no chef. I'm just a cook."

"Ronnie, don't knock a good thing. I just upgraded my office on your success." She peeled some crispy skin off the chicken and popped it into her mouth. "Your show is—" She turned and stared at the bird in disbelief. "Oh, man, this is fantastic."

"My show is what?"

"A smash. People love *Casual Cook*, and they love you."

"Yeah, well…What I happen to do is what people apparently want to see. I lucked out." She shrugged, humbled. After two years on the air, the popularity of the ridiculously simple show she created still amazed her. "You know I'll never understand all the fan mail."

"God, Ronnie. What am I going to do with you? I know you read everything you get, all that chatter, the Facebook stuff, the tweets. How many times have you joked about covering the living room walls with them?"

"Yeah, the chatter usually is fun." Ronnie gazed out the window as she scrubbed. "But I'll never get used to how much people love the show."

"Well, get used to it. *Casual Cook* flies under the radar of those flashy, big-name shows, and you're establishing your own niche—and it's growing like crazy. Fans relate to you, feel like they have you to themselves. Your numbers have threatened the big guys both years you've been on the air. So, get used to fandom, girlfriend."

Ronnie chuckled at Cheryl's tone. "Easy, tiger. I'm working on it, okay?"

"And to think I blew all that time and money on your wardrobe."

Ronnie leaned back against the sink, drying her hands. "I told you not to. This casual cook wears T-shirts and jeans, inside and outside."

"Just keep doing what you're doing—except use a timer if you *must* cook while bingeing shows."

"*I* don't binge-watch. *You* do. Poor Jeff. Too bad he's just your husband and not a TV ghost hunter."

"Hey, we're happy doing our own stuff. And you're a good one to talk about *my* love life." She snickered. "I should pitch the network *Ronnie's Cooking for One*."

"You keep me too busy working to do any serious dating."

"You'd have *very* sweet dreams if you followed the adventures of a certain gutsy paranormal investi—"

"Oh, yes, I'll have yummy dreams watching people run around condemned buildings, chasing shadows and talking to the air. Right."

"I should take your pulse," Cheryl said, half-turning to face Ronnie. "For Christ's sake, Ronnie, I'm talking about Peyton Stanford. Watching her drink freaking coffee gets *me* hot and I'm straight." She squinted at her. "Do you still like girls?"

Ronnie checked an invisible watch. "Of course. They should start arriving soon, so if you want a good spot in line, you better—"

"You're impossible." Cheryl rolled her eyes. "Such fun lives we lead. Seriously, you really would like *Paranormal Pursuit* if you gave it an honest chance. You know she doesn't go for gimmicks like creepy music or those damn Freddy Krueger subliminal images. And she includes all parts of her investigations, including the behind-the-scenes stuff."

Ignoring Cheryl's fan-girl rambling, Ronnie set the scorched chicken *into* the pot this time and put it back into the oven at a lower temperature to roast. "I'm sorry, hon, but ghosts and shadows and voices? Oh, my! Nope. Not a big believer. It's all a bit much."

Cheryl grumbled something as she plopped down at the island and plowed aside clutter to make room for her laptop.

"Why do you have to be such a skeptic? Peyton gets into some pretty intriguing stuff and she's a real stickler for legitimacy. Somehow, she stays respectful, genuinely studious about the paranormal. Watch more episodes with me and you'll see."

"Cheryl."

"What happened to that intrepid partner-in-crime I had in college? You're missing the fun of paranormal adventure."

Ronnie stopped halving a pile of potatoes. "*Cheryl*." Getting her all riled up was fun, but this always happened when she over-teased about Peyton Stanford. She let her mind drift back to the forty-five minutes of bliss she'd had prior to all this and wondered when she'd see the rest of that episode.

"Just watch a few with me. Come on, Ron." Laying it on heavy now, Cheryl pouted as she clicked through screens. "It's my one vice…well, except for Belgian chocolate and anything Gucci. We'll watch some *full* episodes after dinner, and you'll get into it. I know you will." She looked up to see Ronnie nodding reluctantly. "Really? You're saying you will?"

"If it'll make you stop harping about Stanford, yes."

"I-I can't promise that."

When she didn't elaborate, Ronnie stopped cutting again. "You really suck at keeping secrets. And you can't look chagrined with that stupid grin on your face."

"You need to sit." She waved Ronnie to a stool at the island. "I have a surprise." She seemed suspiciously giddy as she turned the laptop toward Ronnie.

"A surprise I'm going to like as much as you apparently do?"

"Just read this. It came in a half hour ago from the programming department, from Ed Rankin himself."

Ronnie drew a stool closer and read the email, her breath catching after the first paragraph.

"No friggin' way!" She sat back hard.

"No way what? You agree or disagree?"

"Are you shitting me? Do I have a say in this? I've done dumb things all my life, but this…No. Absolutely not. I do not agree with this. It's stupid."

"The network is aiming for something totally new—"

"This is beyond new."

"—and putting you and Peyton Stanford together is *it*. Oh, come on. It'll be fun."

"God. Shit no! '*Fun*'? It's the stupidest idea ever. And what about this?" She pointed at the email's second paragraph. "A *live* finale? *Live*? On *Halloween*? Did I say, 'Shit no'? Well, shit no! Kill me now, please."

"Problem is, girlfriend, this isn't a concept. The wheels are in motion already, Ronnie. Some variation of *Paranormal Pursuit Meets Casual Cook* is happening."

Pushing up the sleeves of her sweatshirt as if for a fight, Ronnie stormed to the stove and turned back. She gestured vaguely to her chest. "Seriously? Me? The network's actually given this its blessing? *This?* Sounds like the result of too many late-night cocktail meetings, if you ask me. Really, could there be a more bizarre combination?"

"At first glance, no, and not just because you two couldn't be further afield from each other. This actually is brilliant."

"This actually is embarrassing, that's what this is."

"No, it's a brilliant stroke. Two fan favorites. Crossover shows are lucrative, so…so we've agreed to it."

"*We* have? Oh, for God's sake." Ronnie stood in the middle of the kitchen, hands in her back pockets, and stared out the window, trying not to snort like a bull. Her heart pounded, adrenaline surged, egged on by possibilities and flooded with questions. *Peyton Stanford?*

"Of all people, of all shows!" she snapped toward the window. "How do you possibly combine two programs like ours?" She spun back to Cheryl and threw up her hands. "Is she supposed to find ghosts in my soup? How do I cook in one of her spooky decrepit locations? What the f—Are we shooting comedy now? Am I supposed to be her straight man or something?"

"The network is dead serious here, Ron." Cheryl using her executive voice meant Ronnie was supposed to calm the hell down and pay attention. Ronnie didn't like it. The voice seldom led to anything fun.

Cheryl cleared her throat.

Here comes the kicker.

"This will be a ratings shot-in-the-arm for both shows. You are going to guest star on her show. Three times. And you have to play nice."

Ronnie steamed as Cheryl went to the counter and came back with a bottle of wine, then poured drinks for them. She obviously knew she needed to soften this blow somehow.

"So," Cheryl began again, "We'll be watching *Paranormal Pursuit* a lot. Starting tonight. And you probably should start researching some really old recipes if you don't want to piss off some really old ghosts."

What about pissing me off?

Ronnie paced back to the window and gripped the edge of the sink with both hands. *Shit. Cooking and ghosts? What a freaking joke.*

Aside from coping with the absurdity of it all, she had a hard time conceptualizing any of this. Just as *she* would never suggest such an arrangement, she could damn well guarantee it wasn't Stanford's idea, either. No way the announcement landed softly in the *Paranormal Pursuit* camp. Stanford had an exacting style, a no-nonsense reputation, and, if gossip in TV land was even half-way accurate, she would never tolerate alterations to her long-running show.

"Oh, to have been a fly on the wall when they dumped this on her." Ronnie returned to the island and downed an indelicate mouthful of wine. "What a circus this will be."

❖

Peyton slammed her cocktail down so hard, alcohol sloshed onto the coffee table.

"Son of a bitch!"

She swiped mussed curls off her cheek as she roiled around the conference room, several stories above network headquarters in Manhattan. Eric, her friend and cameraman for all six years *Paranormal Pursuit* had been on the air, leaned against the tall window frame and brooded over his whiskey. He stared down at traffic, safely out of Peyton's path.

"Did I plant the seed for this damn fiasco?" she asked him. "Did I? Last month with the Pottle Inn investigation?" She stepped closer. She couldn't believe this nightmare may have originated with her and hoped he agreed. "Remember all the energy in that kitchen? The hints of chocolate? The baking bread? Everyone in the crew smelled them."

"Yup and Rankin's people could have picked it up from our discussion after the shoot," he offered. "We did toss around the idea of food from the era, how it can arouse residual spirits. Maybe that did it."

Peyton recalled the Rhode Island site, active during the jaunty 1890s, and the remarkable amount of paranormal activity in that kitchen. Too bad they weren't able to record and convey the fleeting aromas they detected during the crew's three-day investigation. How they had bemoaned that fact during their summary analysis.

"They must have heard us." When Eric nodded, she shoved both hands through her shoulder-length blonde hair. "Argh! That's gotta be it. That's where they cooked up this asinine idea."

"Poor choice of words."

"Dammit. Yes." Peyton exhaled with a huff. She kicked an ottoman out of her way, strode to the windows, and shouted to any deity that could listen. "We turn our operation into a cooking show? *A frigging cooking show*?" She turned to him so sharply, he straightened with a start. "Tell me how this is supposed to work because I have no Goddammed idea. Do you? No, of course you don't, because it won't."

Across the room, crew members Caroline and Brian strolled in, their energetic expressions quickly dropping when Eric flashed a foreboding look. They glanced at each other and withheld greetings, taken by Peyton's march back to the coffee table.

"Have you two heard?" she barked and downed the remnants of her drink.

"Just an hour ago," Caroline said, settling on the couch. "It's a done deal?"

Peyton returned to glaring out the windows, arms folded across her chest. The network toying with their successful format would turn their production and careers, her own image into a nationwide joke.

"Our next case, the house in Eastham on Cape Cod," Eric said to the team, "the one we're leaving for on Wednesday? It'll be a little different now." Peyton sagged into an armchair and dropped her head back, trying not to hear him. "Rankin's people made it clear that the property owners are excited about this 'special episode' and have turned over complete use of the house."

"Including the kitchen?" Caroline quickly looked to her fellow crewmembers. "I mean, Ronnie Sharp's really going to be there? She's gonna cook?"

Eric nodded. "Apparently." Brian snickered as he retrieved a beer from the mini-fridge.

Peyton just stared at the ceiling. "Network's arranged a meeting on Monday for the two of us to break the ice. Should be lovely." She lifted her head and eyed Caroline. "You watch those damn cooking shows. Isn't she the one around the campfire, all Timberlands and flannel?" She let her head fall back again. "Jesus. How does something like that stay on the air?"

"Peyton," Eric said into his glass. "Your privilege is showing."

"I think her show's fun," Caroline said. "You really should watch it. She doesn't cook outside all the time."

Peyton sat up with a snap. "So, she's going to cook God-knows-what while we tiptoe around her, investigating?" She shook her head. "That's not how we work. I won't stand for it, and I'll tell her so."

Caroline bit her lip.

"Peyton." This time, Eric frowned at her. "Blame the network, not Ronnie Sharp. You know better."

"Yeah, yeah." Peyton scrubbed a hand over her face. She had to stop the temper tantrum. "I know she's as entitled to her show as we are to ours, but it doesn't make sense to mess with a good thing. Network threw this together and sold it in a heartbeat. How smart is that?"

"Well, pretty damn smart," he countered, "if sponsors jumped on board. The money people must really believe this will fly. It's supposed to boost ratings all around."

Brian looked from Peyton to Eric. "Yeah, but…damn. We shoot with lights out most of the time, so is she going to cook in the dark?"

Peyton guffawed. "Oh, are we lending her night-vision goggles?"

"You know," Caroline tried, "Ronnie seems like the adventurous type so maybe she'd fit right in. She might even be a fan."

Brian elbowed her. "Crush much? Are you after some celebrity home cooking?"

Ignoring him, Caroline watched Peyton return to the windows. "Of course," she added, "Ronnie could be just as upset as we are, Peyton. Her ratings are very good, so I'm sure this wasn't her doing."

"Well, we may have competition like never before, but we're still on top of our market, don't forget," Peyton stated without turning. "I know our numbers have leveled off for the first time in years and, no doubt, that's what's pushing the network, but I'm not letting *Paranormal Pursuit* take a back seat to anyone. We have too much to lose. I don't care whose emotional breakdown led to this."

Chapter Two

Cheryl leaned into Ronnie's shoulder as the elevator ascended to the twenty-first floor. "Forgive me, because I know you'd rather be home, playing in the garden or whatever, but *I'm* excited to meet her."

"Because you're a groupie," Ronnie answered, watching the floor numbers light. "I'm curious, more than anything." She wondered if Peyton Stanford had a posh condo like the one they were climbing toward, which belonged to Stanford's agent.

"Oh God." Suddenly, Cheryl looked panicked. "What if she's a snob? I mean, she won't be, right?"

"She seems pretty hard-nosed on TV, don't you think? Oh, that's right." Ronnie caught herself and snapped her fingers. "You're too starstruck to notice such things."

"Shut up." Cheryl brushed nonexistent lint off her suit jacket and checked her skirt for more. "I notice everything. Occupational hazard. I think she's nice on the show, cool under pressure. She's…" she gave her head a little shake, "well, if I was so inclined…"

Going into this first face-to-face with the paranormal hotshot, Ronnie wished she had some of Cheryl's passion for the genre, and worried about stifling her own skepticism. *Casual Cook*'s reputation was on the line, so that was a must.

"You're my agent. If you kiss her feet—"

"I can't?"

"No. Even if she's wearing Guccis. I'll be gone."

"The hell, you will. You'll behave yourself. This is serious." She turned Ronnie by the shoulder and gave her the once-over. "And you're looking really fine. We're not going to waste it."

Ronnie snorted, looking down at herself, the buttery yellow V-neck sweater and black slacks. No formal business attire for her. "Right, Mom."

Within minutes, a tiny woman with a silvery buzz cut greeted them at the door. The folds of her flowery kaftan lofted out as she raised her arms, proclaiming their arrival. "Here you are! Welcome. Come in." Smiling broadly, she shook Cheryl's hand with both of hers. "I'm Max, Peyton's agent."

"Pleased to meet you," Cheryl responded, firmly in business mode. "I'm Cheryl McMichael, representing Ronnie Sharp." She lent a nod to Ronnie.

"Oh my. *The* Ronnie Sharp." Max held her hand longer than necessary, her gaze sliding purposefully up Ronnie's frame until their eyes met. "I'm *so* excited to finally meet you. Veronica, isn't it?"

"It is. Well, it's what all the legal papers say."

Max winked. "This way, please." When she finally turned and led them to the living room, Ronnie hiked an eyebrow at Cheryl. "I confess," Max added over her shoulder, "I'm happy that we're all getting acquainted like this before things get serious."

As they entered, a lithe figure with an abundance of untamed blond curls rose gracefully to face them. She stood cool and collected, sleek in beige slacks and modest heels, striking in a fitted and very flattering coppery sweater. Immediately, Ronnie acknowledged that television didn't do Peyton Stanford justice—even though the smile seemed a bit forced.

But she was radiant, with only a slight touch of makeup accenting elegant features, a creamy complexion, and a look Ronnie felt slither down to her toes. Those blue eyes were eerily light and filled with challenge, and they locked onto Ronnie with serious intent.

Peyton looked to be as thrilled as Ronnie about this venture, and her less-than-cordial welcome generated a surprising twinge of disappointment. Ronnie had expected as much professionalism as she had mustered.

"Peyton." She approached, offering a handshake. "Ronnie Sharp. Congratulations on another successful season. Great show."

Peyton relaxed her CEO posture a bit and they clasped each other's hand firmly, a comfortable, if fleeting, moment of fit and feel.

"Greetings to the *Casual Cook*," Peyton offered, exuding all the celebrity confidence Ronnie had predicted. "Thanks, and congrats to you as well. Let's hope you still feel that way after this project."

"No worries." She grinned directly into those luminescent eyes. "This'll be a test for us all, won't it?" She stepped back and gestured to Cheryl. "Cheryl's your number one fan."

"Pleasure to meet you, Ms. Stanford," Cheryl said, shaking Peyton's hand. Ronnie observed carefully, thankful Peyton's penetrating eyes had released her and that Cheryl hadn't swooned.

"Hi, Cheryl. Nice to meet you, too. And, please, it's Peyton."

"Yes," Max injected, "we're definitely on a first-name basis here." She offered them seats and Ronnie chose the opposite end of the couch from Peyton.

"So," Peyton began heavily, "were you as taken aback by this…this concept as I was?" She curled a loose wave of hair behind her ear and delivered a quizzical look.

Ronnie felt it seize her attention like a hand gripping her chin. She almost shook her head to be free of it but managed to counter the steady gaze with a smirk. "I was pissed for days." A hint of a grin appeared on Peyton's lips, and Ronnie wished she could read her mind. "But here we are, aren't we? I mean, come on. Doesn't every ghost show need a cook?"

Peyton's shoulders stiffened. "We investigate the paranormal. 'Ghost show' really isn't accurate." Ronnie raised both palms in concession as Peyton rolled on. "But you're correct. *Paranormal Pursuit* doesn't need a cook. Not by any stretch of the imagination."

"I get it, really, just like I don't need…spirit investigators… romping around my kitchen." Peyton took a breath, about to respond, and Ronnie turned to face her more directly. "I gather you've tried as hard as I have to nix this stupid idea." With a tip of her head, she attributed blame to agents Cheryl and Max. "We really are stuck, aren't we?"

Peyton sent Max a hardened look. "We are. The network knows my concerns about this." Max raised her martini glass. "They all claim to know what's best, leaving me desperate to preserve the integrity of our work. I won't allow this premise to crash our ratings, Ronnie. No offense, of course."

"None taken. We agree on that point. For me, *Casual Cook* is young but successful. Not top dog, like *Paranormal Pursuit*, but inching upward, at least, and I don't want it turned into a comedy. *No offense*."

"Are you saying—"

Cheryl hurriedly inserted herself into the exchange.

"The entertainment value of both shows will skyrocket. Crossovers are proven winners with long-term benefits, and we have an outstanding opportunity here. Too ingenious to pass up."

"Oh, so true." Max gestured with her drink. "Now, we've been over all this a million times. Let's work on some commonality here, shall we?"

Peyton almost laughed. "'Commonality'?"

Ronnie agreed. She was frustrated already, just as irritated by the whole thing as she feared she'd be, and they had just started. Peyton was direct, maybe a bit pompous, but all business and protective when it came to her show. No less defensive than she was. *Damn, this could get heated.*

She poured herself a glass of water from the carafe on the coffee table and leaned back into the couch. "So…commonality, huh?"

Peyton snapped her head around and Ronnie struggled to see past the flawless skin, the delicate glide of her cheek as Peyton readied a response. Those captivating looks alone could have made her famous, but a person didn't maintain celebrity status today without serious smarts, especially if she ran around chasing ghosts.

Ronnie challenged her through a half-smile. "Whatever got you into the gho—the paranormal business?"

"Too many experiences to ignore." Peyton spoke through a crafty smile. "I was in real estate, and the rumors and folklore never bothered me much until I started having my own encounters." She sipped her wine and sent Ronnie a sideways glance. "Resident spirits…residual energy often doesn't appreciate being disturbed, let alone sold to a stranger."

Ronnie wondered if she was expected to take notes. Residual energy probably was a thing she'd be hearing a lot.

"I'm amazed you weren't scared off," Cheryl said. "I mean, early on, you didn't know what you know now. I would've been petrified."

"Well, at first, I just rationalized away all the shadows and noises, but I became ridiculously curious about them. Obsessed, to be honest. Anyway, I found myself spending more time inquiring." She flipped hair from her face and Ronnie tried not to notice how the curls draped over her shoulder and relaxed into easy waves, gold accents on copper.

As if sensing Ronnie's attention, Peyton sat back and crossed her legs. "Nothing really gave me pause until the first time I was pushed down a staircase." Cheryl gasped and Peyton chuckled. "Luckily, just a broken wrist and miscellaneous bruises, but something hard had definitely slammed into my shoulder." Eyeing Ronnie, she added as if to verify, "It left a bruise in the shape of a handprint."

"No way," Ronnie responded. "You said, 'the first time'? How many staircases have you fought?"

"More than I care to recount."

"That first one would have done it for me," Cheryl admitted and received a nod of agreement from Max.

"It seems like it happened in a flash instead of a few years," Peyton told her, "but I went from too much inquiry, to recruiting help, to propositioning the network."

Cheryl stared at her in awe, and Ronnie knew that once back in the car—and probably for the next week—all she'd hear about would be Peyton Stanford.

❖

"We sold our concept on the first try," Max recalled with a distant smile. "The rest, as they say…" She lifted her chin to Ronnie. "And you, Ms. Casual Cook? Are you a foodie at heart? Somehow, I can't picture little Veronica hanging off Granny's apron."

Peyton couldn't picture it either. The image almost drew a snicker. *Bet there weren't even mud pies for this tomboy.* Which made the idea of a thirty-something athletic type cooking on television all the more confounding.

She pivoted where she sat and tried not to reveal her curiosity, justified though it was. After all, this woman and her schtick were being thrust into *Paranormal Pursuit* and God only knew what that would do to her team's routine, its success, and the show's ratings.

"I'm no foodie," Ronnie said, sharing a grin with Cheryl. "In fact, I never spent much time in a kitchen until I hit my twenties. I spent quite a few years as director of a forestry camp for city kids in upstate New York. I learned as much as the kids did—including how to cook."

"So, you're not formally trained?" Max asked. "How remarkable. And your show, how…?"

"I initiated a 'family feast day' for each camp session and we went all-out. Actually, it was a parent who came up with the idea of putting the fun of camp cooking on TV, and eventually, lots of parents started pushing. It took a while before I gave it any serious thought."

"So…You mostly do what, a campfire thing?" Peyton asked. "Like the Girl Scouts?" She dreaded the idea of combining such a show with her own, couldn't imagine how that would fly or how her legions of fans would react. Ronnie was grinning at her, obviously now aware of how unfamiliar Peyton was with her work.

"More inside cooking than outside," Ronnie said. "Sixty-forty, you could say. At first, though, yes, it was the other way around, but we soon thought it wise to reverse the approach for a more universal appeal. But whatever's cooked in the kitchen can be cooked outside, and we prove it often."

"Regardless of weather," Cheryl added with a laugh.

"I've seen all your episodes," Max said, pressing her palm to her chest, "and heaven knows, I'm no cook, but you make everything look so fun, so effortless that even *I* am tempted to try." She flicked a jeweled finger at Peyton. "Even you would be tempted."

Peyton sighed as her cheeks heated.

Okay, so the Girl Scout is a star, but dammit, Max. You're supposed to be on my side. Since when have I ever been the domestic type? I don't even look like one. Hell, Ronnie Sharp doesn't either.

She quickly presented a smile. "Cooking simply never appealed to me. I'm just drawn in another direction, always have been," she added toward a rapt Cheryl, "since I was young."

Cheryl inched forward. "Did you grow up here in New York?"

"Cherry Hill, New Jersey. My father established Stanford Properties in the seventies so I grew up in real estate. The mysteries of historic homes grabbed me as a teenager and one thing just led to another."

"I've heard of Stanford Properties," Cheryl seemed pleased to say. "Huge developer."

The last thing Peyton wanted to delve into now was her affluent upbringing and her father. Only when *Paranormal Pursuit* was renewed for a second season did he finally come around to respecting her work, and she'd had a difficult time appreciating his half-hearted praise. After six seasons, she still did. So today, what mattered most was making sure nothing stifled her success, particularly the network's convoluted scheme with this Girl Scout.

She nodded at Cheryl's observation but turned to Ronnie to redirect the conversation. "How did you end up running a forestry camp?"

Ronnie nestled back into the couch and appeared to be taking all this much too cavalierly. The comfortable posture did look good on her, however. Her eyes were deeply set and extremely dark, and the corners crinkled with a mischief that Peyton might have found enticing under different circumstances. Instead, she was irritated that this woman didn't appear half as concerned for the fate of their respective shows.

"I ran away," Ronnie said and winked at Max.

The wink was cute, but Peyton felt her patience dwindling. "You ran away? What's that mean?"

Max yipped gleefully and clapped her hands. "Oh, little Veronica took off in the dead of night for the woods?"

Now, Ronnie laughed outright. "No, no. Bored Ronnie Sharp picked up a psych degree then jumped ship. Both my parents are shrinks, so they weren't thrilled, especially when I settled upstate."

"Well, now." Max refilled her martini glass. "I see commonality here. Neither of you had your family's endorsement for your ventures."

"I guess we do have that in common," Ronnie said and met Peyton's eyes. "Sounds like your father wasn't too enthused about your line of work. My folks have since come around, but even though they still live in the Boston area, I don't see them often. How about your mother? Brothers and sisters?"

"My parents are…distant. That's true," Peyton said, and caught herself absently swirling the last mouthful of wine in her glass. "My two sisters do stay in touch, though."

"Do they watch regularly?" Ronnie asked.

Cheryl added, "They must be pleased for you, excited to have a celebrity in the family."

Peyton really didn't want to get into it. She hardly ever heard from either socially preoccupied parent and her sisters were supporters, though not really "fans," per se. They didn't let her young nieces and nephews watch.

"They're happy for me, yes," she said. Feeling everyone's eyes on her, Ronnie's in particular, she downed the rest of her wine.

"My younger brother, John, lives in Oregon," Ronnie offered gently, leaning forward. "Big heart, sweet guy. He pontificates, though, about everything from climate change to a daughter's family obligations. He's a shrink, too."

Amused by the term, the confidential tone, Peyton didn't miss the empathy in Ronnie's words. "One too many psychiatrists in the family?"

Ronnie nodded toward the coffee table. She seemed momentarily lost in thought, then surprised Peyton with a dangerously dashing smile. "And I'm happy with the decisions I've made."

Perhaps the only thing we have in common, Peyton thought. She lifted her glass as if to toast. "Likewise."

They shared an uncompromising look, and Peyton hoped it was respect she detected. Something about Ronnie said she was capable of handling whatever came her way, but that devil-may-care attitude could be trouble down the road. Maybe it was her lighthearted spark, the watchful eyes, or that roguish grin juxtaposed against her severe jawline. Whatever it was, *something* said Ronnie Sharp could shake things up.

Peyton exhaled discretely. At least it was a relief to know they were driven in the same way, that each appreciated how much was at stake. Despite their differences, they needed to succeed together, somehow. And yet, it still was damn hard to imagine this outlandish premise *not* failing miserably.

❖

Conversation dropped into a ponderous quiet and Ronnie refilled her glass. As she sat back, she decided they had skirted *real* issues long enough.

"So, you're not Betty Crocker. You don't cook?"

Peyton chortled. "Do you believe in the paranormal?"

"I asked first." *Did I strike a nerve?*

"No," Peyton said, pursing her lips. "I don't cook. Do you believe—"

"No, I don't."

Peyton's eyes faded to an impossibly white-blue. "You don't believe in the paranormal at all?"

Ronnie bit back a grin. "Never had reason to."

Peyton looked sharply at Max. "Oh, now this bodes well, doesn't it? This just might be impossible." She turned back to Ronnie. "You've never had a paranormal encounter," Ronnie shook her head, "or an experience of any kind?"

Ronnie shrugged and a chuckle slipped out. "I'm sorry, but no."

Peyton waved a hand in futility and slumped deeper into the couch. "Jesus Christ."

"Never seen him either," Ronnie quipped, and immediately regretted it.

"This isn't a Goddamn joke." The white-blue look flared hard and hot.

"Come on. Lighten up a little."

"'Lighten up'?" She straightened quickly. "Do you even have a clue about our investigations? This isn't going to be some romp in the woods."

"It isn't?" Ronnie went wide-eyed, feigning surprise. "I must have the wrong house." She stood, pretending to leave.

Peyton growled up at her. "Spare me the smartass routine."

"And you need to chill." Ronnie sat and faced her with a smirk. "Enlighten me, won't you?"

"Honestly, you've really never had a paranor—"

"That's right and—"

"Do you at least believe there's such—"

"As I said before, I've never had reason to."

"Listen. You're going to have to take my work seriously."

"I will—eh, I do."

"Oh, for cripe's sake, Ronnie. For these episodes, you *have* to be a team player."

"I realize that, but my main focus will be pleasing my viewers. I'll join your team, but I won't sacrifice them for it. All this is just as vital to my audience base as to yours, don't forget."

"Agreed, but the whole point of your participation is to help stimulate paranormal activity."

"The whole point is to boost ratings. Yours have leveled off and mine aren't climbing fast enough."

"If this damn premise is to succeed at all, your involvement with our team has to take priority."

"I'll handle whatever comes."

"Uh-huh."

"Look," Ronnie said on a sigh, tired of sparring, "We have to make some uncomfortable adjustments—and we haven't been given a choice."

"I'm well aware of what we're obligated to do, but if you're not going into this with an open mind, well, that's a problem."

Ronnie tamped down her rising irritation. *Excuse me, Your Highness, but ghosts just aren't my thing.* She could feel Cheryl's anxiety from across the coffee table and reminded herself that she'd promised to play nice. "As screwy as this premise is, we'll make it work. We both know how much is riding on it."

"Well, it'll be a challenge, to say the least."

Chapter Three

Ronnie kicked herself for being so wound up about this first day of shooting—her introduction to ghost hunting and Peyton's team. Why the anxiety? It probably was just a combination of anticipation and curiosity. At least the location was a half hour from home. Funny how cruising to the eighteenth-century homestead seemed so much longer this time. Ironically, she'd driven past the place for years and seldom lent it any more than a tourist's gawk, but now, entering the driveway, the property carried far more significance. Nearly three hundred years of it.

She crept along the driveway and eyed the humble cape-style dwelling, meticulously maintained, and dressed in appropriately conservative dark clapboard. It demanded she focus on what lay ahead. She really was eager to see the historic features inside and to meet the challenge of bringing a centuries-old kitchen back to life. *But does the fireplace really work?*

"Hello, ghosts," she called through the windshield. She stopped along the driveway to stare. "Are you in there? You hungry?" She chuckled at herself. "I'm just the cook who's supposed to whet your appetite, so don't pick on me. Go see Peyton. That's what she's here for."

Resigned to focus on "number one," Ronnie returned to concentrating on her own role, her image, and responsibilities. There was just so much to think about. Did she stock enough supplies in the van, wear the right clothes for such an environment? Had it been wise to tackle this by herself, with no production help of her own? Could she take all this seriously and not laugh in the sober faces of these paranormal believers? Hopefully, just masking her skepticism would be the hardest part.

She took a breath to center herself and drove into the adjacent field, slipping her van in among two black Suburbans, a large U-Haul box truck, and a Class A motorhome. She snorted at *Paranormal Pursuit*'s show of strength.

"Guess there's no question whose gig this is."

As she shut off her engine, she recalled the episodes Cheryl had forced her to watch in preparation for this. It had taken a handful of shows to develop interest, but she eventually found some of the investigations intriguing and occasionally intense. Maybe even legit…maybe.

Ronnie sighed. Considering everything the team went through, the legitimacy often was hard to deny. Peyton and her crew relied on an array of scientific instruments and jumped through hoops to rile up, record, and communicate with the paranormal, unable to flinch or relax without their own cameras or the overall scene camera capturing everything. The show's perennial success demonstrated viewers' appreciation, that was irrefutable.

Not for the first time, Ronnie counted her blessings that her own show involved less stress and more fun, because this one came with some trepidation. Having any level of involvement in these investigations made her anxious.

She honestly doubted she'd encounter ghosts in the kitchen. She laughed out loud at the prospect of apparitions sending her running and screaming from the room. Peyton probably had high hopes for such things, but Ronnie certainly didn't.

As Cheryl had advised her last night, Ronnie could rightly wield some celebrity power of her own here, so she had every intention of simply preparing a period-appropriate meal in as period-appropriate a manner as possible and leaving the consequences to the investigators. She refused to lose sight of her own loyal viewers. Plus, the idea of clashing with Peyton Stanford amused her.

She checked her reflection in the mirror, the new collar-length haircut, her trademark "outdoorsy" look, no jewelry or makeup. No custom-designed wardrobe, just dress shirt, jeans, and sneakers, appropriate for this late spring day.

"Whatever," she said on a sigh, and stepped out. "Oh, how sweet. Someone's waiting at the door." *Remember: You're completely on your own here, but it's only a guest appearance. Then you can just drive home.*

A bubbly young producer named Jamie ushered her inside and Ronnie stepped carefully around the stacks of *Paranormal Pursuit* gear she'd seen on TV. The house, with its low, beamed ceilings and dark woodwork, offered a muted, claustrophobic atmosphere but antiques everywhere stole her admiration for it all.

"How old is this place?" she asked, and Jamie flashed a smile.

"Seventeen fifty."

"Built before the war. It's in amazing condition, like a museum."

"The owners, Tom and Patty Wilder, are only the seventh different family in its history," Jamie said, leading her toward a brightly lit room, "and they've put a fortune into restoration."

"I can see that." Ronnie stopped, in awe of the mammoth fireplace in the compact, cozy parlor.

"But they never planned on sharing the house with spirits," Jamie added, gesturing to the room ahead. "Over here, this originally was a bedroom, but the Wilders are considering it as their future dining room. Come in and meet everyone. They'll fill you in."

A wrought iron candlestick chandelier, restored and electrified, hung from one of many beams over a long oak table and made the dining room with its plaster walls the brightest place in the house. Conversation ceased and all faces—and an active camera—turned to Ronnie as she entered, an awkward moment that left her a bit speechless. *Do they film every little thing?*

"Okay, everybody," Jamie announced. "The gang's all here now." She offered Ronnie a seat at the table, then joined the cameraman in the corner.

Peyton stood immediately, sharp in jeans and gray suit jacket over a white blouse. A stunning woman in full command of the room. Unfortunately, she'd corralled her dramatic curls at the back of her neck, and the severe look did little to warm her smile.

Game on.

"Good to see you again, Peyton."

"Hi, Ronnie." They shook hands over the table. "And hello from the *Paranormal Pursuit* audience to you and all *Casual Cook* viewers." Peyton took a deep breath. "Okay. Let's do introductions. Ronnie, this is Eric, our main camera operator. Caroline is our researcher and Brian is our tech wizard." Ronnie exchanged smiles and handshakes and sat when Peyton did. "Everyone does a bit of everything, actually, and doubles as an investigator, too. And, in the corner, the tall silent guy with a thousand pounds on his shoulder is Sam, the scene cameraman and the viewing audience's all-seeing eye."

Eric shifted to face Ronnie. His thick red hair bobbed with the motion, and his bright expression glowed with energy. "So how do you really feel about this?"

Ronnie liked him instantly. "Honestly?" She looked directly into Sam's camera. "I think the network's lost its freakin' mind." Everyone laughed, and she relaxed, glad to sense agreement. "Well, really. How desperate will we appear, doing this?" She intended to be herself as much as possible, to keep things as honest as she could. That's who she was and who her viewers loved. If certain words or actions rubbed Peyton or the network the wrong way, too bad. They could edit them out. She leveled a look into Peyton's scrutiny across the table. "We play it by ear, and, with a little luck, everything should click."

Maybe it was for the benefit of the camera, but Peyton offered a complicit smile. "We're counting on it."

Ronnie leaned forward, arms folded on the table. "I've seen shows you've done in restaurants, taverns, and inns, so I'm here to bring a little 'spiritual life' to those kitchens and dining rooms."

Peyton volleyed back. "For the benefit of our combined audience, Ronnie, why don't you explain what *Casual Cook* brings to the *Paranormal Pursuit* table."

"Well, I'm not sure how familiar you all are with *my* show," Ronnie began, "but I specialize in fundamental cooking techniques and basic, simple recipes. I've often found that the old-fashioned ones, outdated or nostalgic recipes, are incredibly popular, and might suit your needs perfectly. In a place like this, I'll use period methods as much as possible to create period dishes, in an effort to support your investigation."

Peyton elaborated for the audience. "I'm excited to have you with us. Adding your approach to ours will give us another critical tool." Ronnie stifled a grin. *She's so full of it.* "It happens quite a bit," Peyton went on, "where we pick up on scents of the past, the smell of cigars, perfume, the aroma of different foods." She glanced at each team member. "They often trigger surprising results."

"That's happened many times." Caroline sounded like a peppy college cheerleader.

Brian, the crewmember Ronnie thought looked like a linebacker, reset his ballcap and propped his chin on his palm.

"Can you cook in one of these big old fireplaces?"

"Over an open fire? Yes."

"In the dark?"

"Without electricity? Yes."

Peyton collected her papers. "We're about to do our walk-through and collect some baseline readings, so I think you'd find it helpful to join us."

"Before the tour," Ronnie stopped her, "how about a little rundown on this case?"

Peyton plucked a page from her pile and slid it over to Ronnie. "We found this copy of a 1780 map of the area, and you can see how undeveloped it was, how few roads or farms." With a long, slender finger, she traced their road to an irregular tract of land. "We're here. The house had become the Barrow Tavern in 1777 and had a rebellious reputation during the war. Supporters of the king weren't welcome, often turned away violently."

"One was killed here," Eric added. "A hazy image of a man resembling him, dressed in that period, has been seen in the tavern room several times."

"When they bought the place, the Wilders were told about the occasional footsteps and shadow figures, and they grew accustomed to them, at least for the first ten years," Peyton continued. "Then, more recently, they undertook a large-scale restoration, beginning with things like the roof and chimneys, and that's when activity grew problematic."

"What constitutes problematic?"

"Being pushed, being grabbed and scratched. The shadow figures grew bigger, artwork and lights fell from the walls. They've had shelves collapse, personal items moved."

"A couple of times, fireplace fires reignited on their own," Caroline said.

Peyton's tone was decidedly more academic. "Spirits often resent owners and want them gone. It's particularly evident where modern changes are involved, when restoration or renovation alters what spirits are used to."

Ronnie had to give them credit for their intensity. "And here that means a *Colonial* haunting."

"Apparently so. But there's also an incident around the turn of the twentieth century." Peyton handed Ronnie a photocopy of a news article from that period. "The house was a private home at the time. A local farmer, Nathan Fuller, was accused of assaulting the owner's daughter, and not long after, they found he'd been murdered. His body was discovered out back and some people believe his spirit lingers."

"So, there could be *two* ghosts?"

"Essentially, yes. It's quite often the case with places this old. Each of them had attachments here."

"I haven't uncovered any more possibilities yet," Caroline added, "but I'm sure others died here, maybe during childbirth, the war, who knows." She touched Ronnie's arm. "With what you can add, this will be *so* exciting."

Her exuberance made Ronnie smile. Caroline seemed older on TV, when, in reality she couldn't have been more than twenty-two. "I'm looking forward to it," Ronnie said, knowing Peyton had followed their exchange. *Yes, a white lie. Just don't expect me to buy into all this, hook, line, and sinker.*

"Time to get this show on the road," Peyton declared.

Brian began loading batteries into handheld meters and passing them out. "It's getting late, and we still have more cameras to set up."

"We'll start in the kitchen," Caroline told Ronnie. "Follow me."

Ronnie made way for Sam to precede them as they passed back through the parlor, to film the group's entrance into the kitchen. She noticed the half-step down just in time to avoid stumbling, then had her attention swept away by the hand-hewn counter and cupboards. Brian and Caroline roamed the room, holding their meters aloft and calling out electromagnetic readings Ronnie didn't really grasp. Eric, meanwhile, moved among them with his close-up camera focused on Peyton.

"No unusual readings," she said, interpreting the team's information for the audience, "and that's not too surprising because there are no utilities in here. The very old stuff usually generates over-the-top energy. We could pick up some from a water source, especially when primitive plumbing like this has such a short run to a well, but so far…" Caroline shook her head to confirm their meters registered nothing abnormal.

Ronnie ran a palm along the pump handle, tempted to flex it to see if water flowed into the adjacent oak bucket. "The owners restored this?" With a grin toward Sam's camera, she sent an aside to her own viewers. "We have our work cut out for us, don't we?"

"Restored?" Peyton repeated. "Yes. Well, so far, just the pump, chimneys, roof, and windows."

Ronnie watched, intrigued, as Peyton passed a meter across the face of the cavernous stone fireplace, as wide, deep, and tall as its match in the parlor. "Will that magic wand of yours speak if it finds something?"

Peyton raised an eyebrow. "Of course. When it finds the joker in the room."

She continued her scan and Ronnie joined in the detailed inspection. So much for Peyton's sense of humor.

A worn iron pot hung inside the fireplace, suspended by an iron swing crane over dusty old coals, and Ronnie instinctively thought of food, of concoctions she could produce. Stepping over the hearth, she ducked inside and swung the pot out and in. The very idea of bringing such antiques to life, of using a fireplace built before the Revolution, made her blood hum. *This really is very cool.*

"Still think you can handle this?" Peyton asked.

Ronnie actually liked her coy smile. "I'm getting into the swing of it."

❖

Peyton leaned on a chairback and peered at the two monitors set up on the dining room table, studying the feeds from cameras positioned throughout the house. Taking a turn at the keyboards, Eric fine-tuned the images. Then Sam passed by, nearly tripped over the river of wiring, and shook everything on the table.

"Sam, please be careful," Peyton said on a sigh. "I know you have to shoot us doing this, but…"

"I will. Sorry. I'm leaving you to it for now," he said, and carefully maneuvered toward the kitchen with Jamie in tow. "We need to shoot some of Ronnie."

"Yeah," she mumbled at the monitors. "True."

She couldn't begrudge *Casual Cook*'s airtime; a contract was a contract, but she did worry about it shifting viewers' attention away from *Paranormal Pursuit*. Hadn't Ronnie already shifted her attention a little? That unassuming persona worked wonders on audiences, but her jaunty, brassy side took Peyton back a bit, put her on alert. While she conceded respect for all those attributes, it was unsettling to realize that, in Ronnie, she also found them intriguing, maybe even a bit provocative. Having the *Casual Cook* on her mind this much was bound to lead to distractions she couldn't afford.

Eric snickered as he typed. "Peyton, relax. This really could work out well. We just have to settle into our routine."

Peyton tried to bury her doubts. Maybe it was simply having a co-star on-scene that gave everything a shaky, first-time feeling.

Already, the stealthy Sam seemed off his game. But then, maybe sharing the limelight would bring out the best she had to offer.

Eyes glued to the feed from the central staircase, she spoke into a walkie-talkie. "Caroline?"

"Yes, Peyton."

"Please give that camera a quarter-turn toward the wall." She waited as Caroline made the adjustment. "Excellent. Brian, you're good. Both of you come back and lights off as you go. We're ready."

Eric pushed his chair back and stood. "I'll give Ronnie the extra walkie, just in case, and let her know we're about to go dark."

Brian strode into the room and chose his favorite night-vision camera from the selection on the table, then went to the wall light switch. "Want me to work my way up to the master bedroom?"

Peyton waited as Eric returned and adjusted his camera, then she gave Brian the okay to turn off the chandelier.

"Caroline," she said, "how about you watch the monitors for now? Eric and I will be in the tavern room." Guided by her own night-vision camera, she left with Eric filming her from behind.

Converted generations ago from smaller rooms, the long tavern comprised the entire far end of the house, and they stopped upon entering to scan the surroundings. A sizeable oak bar lined one wall and several small sets of primitive tables and chairs filled the space, a rustic rec room by today's standards. A chill and the earthy scent of old wood permeated the room.

"The family says this is the most active room, unexplained sounds and shadows," Peyton narrated, walking to a corner table by way of her camera's green-lit screen. "This is the area where a Tory named Henry Smythe was shot during the Revolution. They often find this braided rug pushed aside." With her foot, she flipped the rug in half and aimed her camera at the vacated patch of plank floor. "They claim this dark area of the wood is blood stain."

"Faded a few hundred years."

She looked at Eric's lens and the audience. "If it is Smythe, maybe moving the rug is his way of making his presence known, of making sure no one forgets him."

"Or he's out to trip someone."

A crisp knock sounded from the bar. Peyton turned toward it sharply. "What was that?" Eric dutifully kept his camera trained on her no matter what. She'd grown used to that, being the center of attention, sharing with millions of viewers every personal delight and breath-catching fear, portrayed in god-awful green or unflattering infra-red light.

"Henry Smythe?" she called. "Please knock again to let us know you're here." They waited in silence. "Make any noise you wish. We're here to tell your story. I'm Peyton and this is Eric." She rapped her knuckles on the bar top. "Can you knock for us, please?"

Hearing nothing, they moved cautiously around the room. A door at the opposite end drifted open with a creak.

"There," Eric said, pointing beyond her. "It wasn't open a second ago."

Peyton closed it, set the hammered iron latch in place, then tugged. "No way this opened on its own, unless it hadn't been closed originally." She opened the door, and they scanned the small room beyond. "Pantry."

"Is there another door in there? Kitchen access? Something smells really good."

She peered in. "There is." And yes, she could smell meat roasting. "There's light coming from the other side."

A knock from deeper within the pantry gripped them.

Peyton knocked twice in response and panned the shelves with her camera. A surprising drop in air temperature made her shiver.

"Got really cold in here all of sudden." A ball of dim light appeared on her screen, floated from the ceiling to the kitchen door before disappearing. She took a breath and looked into the darkness beyond the screen. "Did you catch that orb?"

From her pocket, she pulled a tiny recorder that captured electronic voice phenomena. "I didn't think we got high enough EMF readings to generate energy for an anomaly." She switched on the recorder and began a slow-paced inquiry, giving any spirit enough time between questions to answer in whatever way or at whichever inaudible level it chose.

"Please tell us your name. Are you unhappy here? Do you like the owners, the Wilders?" She stared at the device, hoping it was picking up electronic voice responses at some irregular frequency. "Is it your shadow the Wilders see? Have you been touching them?" She flashed a hapless look into Eric's lens.

"Ask about Fuller."

"Are you Nathan? Were you murdered on this property?" Waiting in silence like this, not knowing if responses were being recorded always tested her patience. "Or are you Henry Smythe? Are you loyal to the king? Why are you here?" She brought her recorder closer to the kitchen door. "Can you give us a sign that you're here? Open this door? Make a noise for us, please."

More silence. Then a faint whistle.

Peyton turned to the camera and Eric whispered, "I heard it, too."

She held the recorder at arm's length and spoke louder. "Did you whistle? Please open this door."

The latch lifted and the door inched open. Peyton held her breath.

Ronnie poked her head into the opening. "Hi. You two coming through here?"

"For God's sake!" Peyton lowered her recorder in disgust. "No! We're—no!" She shoved the door closed and stormed past Eric into the tavern. "Let's listen to the playback. Maybe we got *something* before Julia Child interrupted us."

At a table in the dark, aided only by their instruments' tinted light, Peyton fumed as they listened to her recorded questions go unanswered. After only a minute, she stopped it to speak. "Can you believe she…Of all moments to—"

"Peyton. It's an innocent mistake. I'm sure she's kicking herself."

"We were right there with it, that orb. All that energy passed within a foot of us. We could have—"

Eric held up a palm. "Play back some more. Maybe we got a response after all."

She swore under her breath as he raised his camera and focused on her. Playback included her earlier questions—and then a guttural sound.

"Could you make out what it said?" Peyton straightened in her seat and backed up the recording to repeat it.

"Or are you Henry Smythe?" was her question.

"Yes."

"'Yes,'" she quoted, amazed. "I'm sure that's what it said."

"Me too. Keep going."

"Are you loyal to the king?"

Peyton seized the recorder in both hands, wishing she could squeeze clarity from it. "What does he say there? 'You be'? I can't…"

"Maybe it's 'truly,' as in truly loyal to the king."

She let the recording continue. *"Why are you here?"*

"Home."

"Whoa."

"Damn," Eric said on a breath. "Clear as could be."

"He definitely said 'Home.' He thinks this is his home?"

"I'd say."

"I wonder if we have anything on Smythe's history. Maybe his ancestors had ties here."

Caroline's clipped voice crackled out of the walkie-talkie, and they promptly returned to the dining room. They found her tracing a line across a screen.

"What's going on there?" Peyton asked, staring at the monitor as they pulled up chairs. "Is Brian asleep on that bed?"

"No. I told him to lie there and not move an inch. See this little hunk of iron thingie here? Well, it was over here by the door." She leaned back so Peyton and Eric could lean in. "I saw it move."

"You what? If that's what I think it is," Peyton said, "it doesn't skate across a wood floor. It weighs a ton."

"Sure does," Ronnie interjected, surprising them with her arrival. She looked beyond them to the monitor and Eric spun his camera up at her. "You heat it by the fire, and it warms your bed," she continued, "or use it to press things. It's solid iron, can't mov—"

Caroline sighed. "Well, sorry, but it did. All by itself."

"Impossible," Ronnie said.

"No, really. Watch." She folded her arms. "See? Then the door closes." Eric dropped back to film Ronnie and Peyton staring at Caroline. "We might need to pry Brian off that bed. He was going to bolt but then the door closed by itself and now he's glued to the bed."

"Take my camera and go get him," Peyton told her, "and have Sam film—" She looked to the opposite side of their room. "Sam, have you been in the kitchen all this time?"

"Just some," he said, his voice floating from the dark corner. "Did some snooping, then we were upstairs, but I got you guys doing playback."

Jamie appeared at Eric's side. "I wanted enough background on hand, so we checked out the little bedrooms."

"Well, please go back up there with Caroline and film Brian in that bedroom." Shaking her head as they left, Peyton slowly turned in her seat and looked up at Ronnie. "Do *you* have any adventures to report, that is, aside from interrupting our biggest moment of the day?"

"Christ, I'm sorry about that, really. I was right outside the door when I heard you ask, and I didn't think. I hope I didn't screw things up."

"We had a terrific opportunity there."

"Did you see something?"

"Did *you*?"

Ronnie shrugged. "No. Like what?"

"Like…" Peyton sighed in frustration. "Like an anomaly. A floating ball of light? It went right through the door."

Eric leaned between them. "We did get some great EVPs…er, voice responses," he added for clarification. He looked to Peyton as he continued. "Time to go after more, right?"

Peyton took a subtle breath, acknowledging his effort to quell her temper. "Yes." She had to be more patient. Ronnie was new at this. "I also want Caroline to get more details from the Wilders, maybe check town records and the historical commission. The EVPs we got certainly sounded as if Smythe has some deep connection here."

"EVPs? As in voices?" Ronnie asked and Peyton nodded. "You got voices from a Tory."

"Yes." Peyton bit back her annoyance.

"So…a Tory from seventeen-something literally *spoke* to you? Seriously?"

"Henry Smythe, yes. The recordings are hard to deny." Peyton wondered how long her patience would last. Ronnie questioning the veracity of their work while on camera made Peyton cringe. "EVP responses are electronic voice phenomena," she explained steadily, opting to educate Ronnie *and* her *Casual Cook* viewers. "They can be happening at any time all around us, but at frequencies we can't hear without specialized equipment. We're certain Henry called this place his home."

Ronnie straightened. "That's wild, isn't it? Could I hear them?"

"First," Eric interrupted, "is there any chance we could eat?"

"Oh, yeah," Ronnie said with a laugh. "I forgot. Of course. How about I set everyone up in the tavern?"

Not a bad suggestion, considering the source, Peyton thought, and went to survey the room again by flashlight.

"If this was Smythe's home," she pondered aloud from the doorway, "hopefully he'll be drawn to a family meal." She turned to Eric's lens. "We'll set up a laser grid running from our table to the pantry at the end of the room. If that was his energy upstairs, strong enough to move one of those iron bed warmers, he should stomp a noticeable path across the grid."

"I'll get you some light," Ronnie said and hurried away to the kitchen.

Peyton sighed as she and Eric opened another equipment bin. Now, mouth-watering aromas reached her in the tavern, exactly as planned. She couldn't avoid acknowledging Ronnie's work, but… "Doesn't she know we have better success in the dark?"

"Here," Eric said, "take this laser and I'll get the REM-pods." He set a hand on her shoulder. "Don't get all worked up about her. Ronnie's just new at this, that's all. Things will level off."

His words echoing in her head, Peyton crouched and positioned the puck-shaped laser beacon on the tavern floor. Ronnie's interruption really hadn't been disastrous. And, yes, Ronnie was in her head. Because she could hinder the investigation? Because that smile and homey charisma could detract from *Paranormal Pursuit*'s drama? Because she had tons of audience appeal? Because she was appealing, *period*?

None of that mattered. Peyton knew that doing her job, here and now, did. She had her own role to play. Clutching a penlight between her teeth, she tweaked the laser settings for distance.

Mellow light flooding the room drew her attention, and rising, Peyton spotted the pair of flickering candlesticks on the table. Although her first impulse was to object, she had to admit that Ronnie's choice of lighting was perfect.

Chapter Four

With three candlesticks of her own in the kitchen, Ronnie had plenty of light to work. Lord knows, she had fumbled around enough late-night campfires in her day, and this was a lot more convenient.

Meanwhile, Sam, who evidently had been assigned as her cinematic shadow, lurked in the darkest corner, filming everything in natural light or no light at all. She did take some comfort in the knowledge that his camera could flood a room with light, if needed.

"I think it's time to check our work," Ronnie said to viewers in Sam's lens. "Smells good enough to eat, so let's do that." Using a fire poker, Ronnie swung the stew pot toward her, out of the fireplace, and gripped it with a swatch of thick leather hide hanging nearby. "Want to get your exercise without thinking?" she asked the camera.

Once the pot was on a piece of slate on the table, she put the lid back on the hearth and shoveled the waning coals into a recessed corner to die. Next, in the fireplace's opposite corner, where a built-in oven contained her favorite quick-rising bread, she leaned in with the poker, lifted the little iron door aside, and slid the loaf onto a cutting board.

"I confess to a little online research," she said, displaying the bread to Sam, "but this is what bread in 1776 looked like. I think we done good."

Grinning, she stepped back from the table and set her hands on her hips, pleased with her efforts, despite the sweat that dampened her upper body. She sent a sideways look to Sam and the audience. "Can you imagine toiling over a fire like that all day every day?" She shook her head. "Boy, we have it easy today, don't we? But you know? This is damn hot work, but honestly, a Revolutionary War fireplace? Are you kidding me? It doesn't get any more satisfying than this."

Not bad for a gig I didn't want.

She inhaled deeply as she stirred and groaned with pleasure. "Oh, we have done well today, boys and girls. How I wish you all could smell this." She fanned the air above the pot toward Sam. "Where's 'Smell-A-Vision' when you need it, right?" The stew steamed, the aroma of bread filled the kitchen, and she dared any of Peyton Stanford's crazy ghosts to resist such temptation. "The plan is for the *spirits* to smell it."

She grinned inwardly as an old cartoon image of Casper the ghost came to mind, floating around her, drooling over her food. "Come out. Come out wherever you are," she said on a light laugh. "Come and get it."

She ladled her popular beef stew into crocks, grateful she'd loaded her van with all the necessities. The stew was heavy with locally grown vegetables and the beef had rendered to a tender chew, all in a rich, lightly seasoned broth. *Perfection.*

At the sound of footsteps behind her, Ronnie hurried to set silverware, napkins, and the bread and butter on a large wooden tray. "Thanks for the help," she said, waiting for whoever it was to appear. "I'll be right out behind you with the stew."

She turned to either side, turned completely around, but saw no one. "Okay, so that was weird." With a look to Sam, she asked him as much as the viewers, "You heard that, too, didn't you? Are we hearing things?" Shrugging it off, she added the first four crocks of stew to the tray and headed for the pantry, a shortcut to the tavern. "Let's bring this load in now." The door was ajar so she toed it farther open, but before she could move, it swung shut in her face.

"Hey. Look, Casper, my hands are full. I'm what, *not* supposed to cut through here?" She gave the door a little kick. "Fine. Have it your way."

Great. Now I'm talking to freaking ghosts. That didn't take long.

She chose the alternate route through the dining room but then changed her mind about delivery until she'd filled all the crocks.

Back at the table, she discovered she'd miscounted and sent Sam a puzzled look. "I'm missing one." She needed a seventh crock for herself and left him to shoot elsewhere while she dashed out to her van. "Maybe I am a bit out of my element after all," she grumbled. "Could've sworn I counted right the first time."

Sam and his ever-present camera fell in behind her when she returned and they found Peyton in the kitchen, checking out the stew. She greeted them with a glint of surprise.

"So, there you are."

"Must be the heat. I came up one short," Ronnie said, showing the crock she'd retrieved. "Did you think you'd catch me slacking off?"

"At least you hadn't fallen into the fire."

"Depends on what's cooking." Enjoying the exchange, Ronnie tipped her head toward the hearth. "Careful *you* don't trip and fall in."

"I don't fall that easily."

"Neither do I."

"Because you're always so serious, all business, I suppose," Peyton said.

"There's a time and place for everything, but sometimes you have to make your own."

"Agreed, when practical."

"Ah, practical. And if a spirit overtakes you?"

Peyton folded her arms. "Well, it *is* all about the spirits, isn't it?"

"And how hungry you really are."

Pausing an extra beat, Peyton seemed reluctant to break eye contact. Ronnie could feel those surreal blue eyes probing, searching for something. Amazing, she mused, how much can be conveyed in a silent moment.

Finally, Peyton spoke. "Speaking of hungry, they sent me to find you."

Ronnie deliberately waited an extra beat before pointing to the pot on the table. "Have you tried it yet?"

"No, but I did peek. It looks like stew."

"Thanks for the rave review." She removed the lid and immediately dropped it onto the pot. "Shit! I-I mean…Damn!"

"Are you burned?"

No, I always do this dance in the kitchen.

"I'll live." *Man, that hurts.* She stepped to the oak bucket and plunged her fingers into cold water.

Peyton used the leather swatch to move the lid to the fireplace. "It's safer over there, you know."

"Funny," Ronnie said, drying her hand, "I thought that was where I'd left it."

"Uh-huh, right," Peyton said. "No. It was covering the pot when I got here. Now, let's get going."

I know what I did. Sam and his camera weren't here to prove it, but that little camera on the tripod over there must have. They'll see.

Ronnie frowned as she filled her crock. "There must be a ghost in the house, huh?"

"An astute assessment. For a rookie."

The pantry latch clicked, and they pivoted to see the door float open several inches.

"Hey!" Peyton darted toward it. She yanked the door open and stared into the empty pantry for a moment.

"What are you expecting to see?"

"Anything. Who knows? Would've been nice to catch a shadow figure or some anomaly on camera."

"And here you are, whipping open a door, unarmed."

"True, dammit. We should never be without some instrument because we know something's in this house."

"Well, seeing something in there sure would've shocked the hell out of me."

"Just wait. Your time will come." Peyton picked up the bread tray and waited for Ronnie to take the crocks. "We need to put our dinner plan into motion right now. If that was our friend Henry Smythe, he's either hungry or irritated with us."

Ronnie almost shook her head at Peyton's fixation but thought better of it. She followed her through the dining room, more than a bit confounded by her own situation. *Yes, ladies and gentlemen, it's yours truly, the* Casual Cook, *bringing you a family meal in a Revolutionary War homestead. Remember to share with the ghosts.* She did shake her head this time. *God help me, I'm getting into this.*

Peyton stopped short before entering the tavern. "Is there any butter for the bread?"

Ronnie looked at Peyton's tray, ready to point it out, but there wasn't any. "I *know* I put it on that tray."

"Do you see it here?"

Irritation mounted, with Peyton as much as with herself or what, if anything, had been playing games in the kitchen. Ronnie flashed her a quick, stern look, and went back for the butter.

By the time she joined the others, the tavern had taken on an eerie feel, shadowy and softly lit, and staged with enough surveillance gear to make the CIA jealous. Little motion detectors the team called REM-pods sat in every strategic spot, their minimal green lights poised for interruption. Static cameras on tripods triangulated the room toward the open pantry door at the far end, and a web of laser-induced pink light dots covered the floor like a celestial runway. Everyone sat armed with some meter or device at the ready. Apparently, no spirit would go undetected.

"Ronnie, hats off to you." Brian raised a slice of bread in her direction. "After getting creeped out upstairs, this is settling my nerves in a big way. Dee-licious."

Eric nodded as he chewed. "If Colonials ate this well back then, it's no wonder they won the war."

"Y'can say that again," Caroline said. "We've never eaten on location before, and this is fantastic. Thanks."

"You're all welcome. I'm glad it turned out as I hoped. Cooking over an open fire is always a fun challenge, but it's tricky to produce something period-appropriate *and* appealing."

Peyton held up a spoonful. "Here's hoping Henry finds it appealing."

Ronnie sampled the stew and smiled. "What happened upstairs, Brian?"

"Aw geez. You know, when that damn door slammed, my whole body went cold. Like *freezing* cold. Shit. I could even see my breath. And I couldn't move off the bed. Then something grabbed my arm *hard*, and I felt it scraping, pulling. That's when I screwed outa there."

"Sam caught it on tape, too," Caroline added.

Brian showed off his forearm. "Check this out."

Ronnie had seen such telltale marks on the episodes she'd watched with Cheryl but here they were in the flesh, literally. Brian had a trio of five-inch welts trailing along his forearm to his wrist.

"Wow!" She looked up at him, genuinely shocked. "That's for real! I mean, sometimes what you see on TV is…well, those marks are real."

"Of course, they're real. He didn't scratch himself," Peyton declared. "Nothing we air is fabricated."

Ronnie caught herself before she snapped. "I wasn't insinuating otherwise. It's just an entirely different sight in person." She would much rather have told Peyton to chill. If that attitude surfaced again, Ronnie vowed to throw it back, on camera or not. She shook her head at Brian's arm. "That's wild."

"We were checking Sam's playback just a few minutes ago," Eric told her, "and he caught this anomaly floating over the bed just before Brian got grabbed."

"It's safe to assume Henry Smythe doesn't want us here," Peyton said, "us or the Wilders, for that matter, especially after their restorations disrupted *his* place."

"Henry Smythe!" Brian yelled, brave now among many at the table. "Time for supper. Come join us."

"Fine victuals here, Henry!" Caroline called out, joining in the taunt. "We're enjoying a hot meal in your house. Want some? Smells great, doesn't it?" She turned to Ronnie beside her. "We're doing a conference call later with a woman from the historical commission. We'll find out about Henry's background."

Okay. Granted, I'm a little curious, but I don't really care all that much.

The device on the pantry floor beeped and flashed, and every head turned in its direction. Ronnie felt Caroline lean closer.

"I suppose you already know, but REM-pods detect motion within a pre-set distance," she whispered. "We got a nibble."

Sam spun from his chair, grabbed his camera, and positioned himself at the opposite end of the room.

Eric dropped his spoon and picked up a device next to his crock of stew. "This senses structured light," he said, and Ronnie figured the explanation was for her and her viewers. She'd seen this used on TV and found it the most fascinating of all their instruments. The "SLS camera" gathered concentrations of light or energy invisible to the naked eye, and, supposedly, when those concentrations were substantial enough, they condensed into disjointed stick figures. It all seemed ridiculously far-fetched, but she couldn't explain away the images either. *Look at me, daring something to form on his screen.*

Peyton activated a meter Ronnie knew was called a "spirit box," and its obnoxious white noise shattered the hushed intensity in the room. From watching past episodes, she had learned that the meter scanned radio frequencies, searched through static for any voice or abnormal sound. Everyone listened keenly for any interruption of the raucous noise.

Two REM-pods just *outside* the pantry door went off.

"Brian," Peyton said in a steady voice. "Get the Ovilus. We need to make contact now."

He pushed his food aside and drew the handheld device closer. This supposedly detected inflections of energy, inaudible to people but strong enough to form sounds, and if any matched those in a pre-programmed dictionary, it would speak and display them on the little screen.

Caroline pointed past Ronnie's face. "There," she said on a short breath. "Did you see the farthest lights on the laser grid go dark? Something's stepped through the beams. He's coming this way."

Peyton, Eric, and Brian were all standing now, staring back and forth from the laser grid to their instruments. Ronnie finally managed to swallow a mouthful of bread and almost forgot to breathe. *Damn, if all this doesn't have me on edge. They're ready to catch sights and sounds, and even I'm glued to whatever this is, but...seriously?*

"Henry Smythe. Is this your home?" Peyton asked.

The static of the spirit box continued unbroken, but Brian's Ovilus spoke in its computer-generated monotone.

"*Father.*"

Peyton turned to him. "Did it just say…"

"It did," he said, and held up the device for her to read. "Father."

"Did your father own this land, Henry?" She checked with Eric but he looked back at his screen and shook his head.

White noise cut to silence and in that instant, Peyton's spirit box broadcast a three-syllable word.

"Sounded like 'Bethany' or…or 'can it be,'" she wondered aloud. "Damn. I can't tell."

Taken by the tension in the room, Ronnie watched them all consider the utterance. "I thought it said 'enemy,'" she offered.

The Ovilus spoke again, and Brian popped onto his toes. "That's it." He pointed at his screen. "Enemy."

Ronnie felt goose bumps rise along her arms.

"Henry," Peyton tried, "did enemies come here, to your father's house?"

"Did they eat here?" Caroline asked. "Did they take your family's food?"

Peyton reached out with the spirit box, held it closer to the grid. "Are you upset that we're here?"

From the Ovilus: "*Go.*"

Brian raised his screen for Peyton to read. "'Go.'"

A fourth REM-pod beeped and flashed from the perimeter. Waiting for the corresponding grid lights to go dark, Peyton turned her attention back to the floor and so did Ronnie. When several pink dots went out, closer still, Ronnie stiffened in her chair.

"We are not the enemy, Henry," Peyton said, moving toward the grid. "You want us to go?"

Ronnie wondered if it was wise to approach whatever was disrupting the laser lights, and her own fascination surprised her. "There's really something coming?" she asked, and immediately wished she'd kept her musing to herself. Peyton flashed her the evil eye.

His focus never leaving his screen, Eric moved up behind Peyton. "I still have nothing."

"He *has* to be right here," she said under her breath, and indicated a spot not ten feet in front of her. "Henry, this is not your home. Not anymore. There are no more enemies. It's long past time for you to go."

Suddenly, the white noise from Peyton's spirit box stopped again. "It's dead," she said, shaking the device. "Batteries were fully charged a half hour ago."

"The Ovilus is dying, too," Brian said, "and these are fresh batteries."

Peyton mumbled a curse. "It's drawing from our energy sources."

Eric stepped forward, SLS camera extended in both hands. "I hope this thing hangs on." He slowly panned the grid but sighed at seeing nothing.

More grid lights went out, only five feet from where he stood, and Ronnie was shocked to hear her heart pounding in her ears. Caroline elbowed her and smothered a gasp with her fingertips.

"Henry," Peyton tried again, "we're simply conveying a message. The Wilders own the house now, this tavern, and you need to leave. Forever."

Eric inhaled sharply. "There!" Brian and Peyton surged toward his camera. Caroline moved in as well, and Ronnie went with her. She saw Sam step up to film them all.

She gaped at the tall formation of connected lines on the screen, a stick figure whose left arm extended over his box-shaped head. The line that was his lower leg swung forward from a junction at the knee and the entire image came closer. She looked beyond the camera to the grid and saw another cluster of lights go dark.

"Jesus!" she said on a breath. "This is crazy. Is this really…?" A stream of frozen air wafted over her, and she rubbed her arms briskly. "Peyton, you can almost touch—"

"Shh!" Peyton said and inched to the front row of grid lights. She reached out and Ronnie watched her image appear in the foreground of Eric's screen. Peyton's hand was inches from the stick arm.

"We are pleased to meet you, Henry," she said in a conciliatory voice. "Will you shake my hand, please?"

Ronnie thought she'd faint if Peyton felt any connection. *Shit, it's freezing in here.* She shivered but couldn't look away.

"There's that damn cold again," Brian said softly. "He's close, all right."

Eric whispered. "Peyton. Less than a foot now."

Ronnie alternated looking from the screen to Peyton and saw her reach into the void.

"Inches now," Eric reported.

Peyton leaned forward, hand extended. "I'm Peyton. This is the Wilder house."

"Contact," Eric announced.

Staring at the screen, Ronnie saw Peyton's hand pass right through Henry's stick arm. *What the...*

"Tingling to my shoulder," Peyton said slowly, sounding dazed. "Frigid."

The exchange made Ronnie blink. *Holy shit.*

Eric looked up. "He's gone."

Peyton lowered her hand as the grid lights returned and the REM-pods went quiet. But she stood unmoving, probably hoping Henry would reconfigure. Ronnie took note of her stillness. She'd said her arm tingled, but from what? The energy they all talked about? Meaning...his touch? *My freaking heart's hammering. This is nuts.*

Then both candles on the table went out.

Chapter Five

"We're wrapping this up for now, Ronnie, and Jamie said you can call it a night."

Peyton stood just inside the kitchen as Ronnie buzzed around, tidying the room. Having her here all afternoon and evening had not been as disruptive as anticipated. Neither had her energetic work ethic nor her capable, dark-eyed presence. But, really, had she even been necessary? *Yes, she made a difference.*

Ronnie stacked crocks on the table. "Thanks, but I want to clean up." She turned, and spotting Sam with his camera in the corner, added, "I need to get the fire going to—" she stopped. "To heat some water."

Seeing Ronnie's face contort, Peyton looked, too. "What is it? The fire?"

"Well, yeah," Ronnie said, and reached for the poker. "I put it out before we ate but it's going pretty good."

"So…you mustn't have."

"I know what I did, Peyton."

"Like with the pot lid earlier? And the miscounted bowls? The butter for the bread?" Peyton immediately regretted listing things on camera.

"Please, ump," Ronnie sent her a pleading look, "can I have one more strike?"

"Well, I just meant…"

"Those things are my fault, huh? Shouldn't you be naming a ghost as the culprit?"

Peyton had no idea how efficient Ronnie was as the Casual Cook, but here in this role, she did appear to be lacking, and Sam was recording every ounce of proof. "Normally, I'd be the first to agree," she said, "but you aren't on your own set here and, really, it's understandable if all this has you a bit shaken."

A flaming ember popped onto the hearth, and Ronnie shoved it back with a serious thrust of the poker. Clearly, pointing out Ronnie's miscues, even rationalizing them, might not have been helpful, especially on camera.

"Look, Ronnie. It's okay, though. Everything went well, regardless, and the meal—"

"Save it." Her demeanor brisk now, Ronnie pointed to the fire. "Fires don't reignite on their own. Not my fires."

"Look, it's all right. You *were* a little…eh…off in here earlier, and probably just thought the fire was—"

"No. I don't make mistakes with fire. Ever."

"Okay. Okay. So—"

"I'm surprised you're not giving your pal *Henry* the benefit of the doubt."

"Well, he's not *mine*," she said with a short laugh. "Considering what we *all* experienced in the tavern, I'm surprised *you're* not giving him the benefit of the doubt."

Ignoring her, Ronnie used the little fireplace shovel to scrape the flaming coals forward beneath the crane, then gathered kindling and a thin log to build up the fire. She worked methodically, practiced and confident, shirt sleeves cuffed to the elbows. The Casual Cook certainly added a little melodrama, a different kind of entertainment to their case, and Peyton thought she might have to admit that these skirmishes were worth it.

Ronnie groused as she hung a pot of water over the fire. "Should've had water heating while we ate. My mistake."

"Since you brought him up," Peyton offered, "it *is* quite possible that Henry kept the fire alive for you for that reason."

Looking surprised by the comment, Ronnie stopped half-way across the kitchen. "Why? To get us out of his kitchen faster?" Her grin dared Peyton to take her seriously.

"Quite possibly, yes." Sensing Ronnie's irritation had abated somewhat, Peyton pulled out a chair at the table and sat. Besides, she was tired. "I wasn't surprised to learn his family owned the land prior to the war."

"I did think your conference call was interesting. There are a ton of Colonial-era homes here on the Cape and every one's bound to have an elaborate history. Guess you picked a winner." She stepped closer, tall and formidable at the table, hands in her back pockets. Her curious expression was compelling. "You're thinking Henry got your message and, what, left in a huff? I mean, he did go off-grid, right? Pun intended. Then, those candles… Do you think he blew them out?"

"Do you?"

Ronnie crossed her arms and glanced at Sam in the corner. Peyton watched her jaw flex, as if she chewed on difficult words, and wondered what answer she'd give to their collective audience.

"Okay, so I thought it was all, well, pretty wild, and the candle thing was cool, but who am I to say? *You* believe he blew them out, don't you?"

"Yes. That's exactly what we're hoping, that he made a parting statement."

She thought Ronnie still had a ways to go, but her skepticism could be weakening. Right now, she didn't have the energy—nor much of a desire—to test it further. Thankfully, today's extremely productive shoot was over, and Ronnie had fulfilled her obligation.

"Well, you're all set now," she said, hoping Ronnie would catch the dismissal. "The Wilders are due back in two days, so we'll run a few more experiments tomorrow, spend the day checking the readings, playing back footage from all the cameras, and make sure there's still no sign of him. I doubt there will be. Thank you for your efforts. I think *Casual Cook* made a difference today."

"You're welcome. And good luck tomorrow."

"I don't know too much about our next case yet, but I'm sure you'll be notified when we have one where it's appropriate for you to step in again."

Ronnie nodded agreeably, an unexpected reaction to a brush-off that sounded more glacial than necessary. *Either she really doesn't give a damn about any of this or she's too easy-going for my own good.*

"Whenever you guys are ready, I'll be there." She gathered items to wash in the oak bucket. "I'm shooting two more *Casual Cook* episodes this weekend, and the timing works out perfectly for me, actually." She strode back to the fireplace, sure-footed on the stone floor and capable, maneuvering the heavy iron pot and its boiling contents. Peyton grew a bit more exhausted just watching.

"I'm thinking of cheating," Ronnie went on, whispering as she poured so Sam's camera wouldn't pick up her words. "Y'know, of just repeating this beef stew recipe for my show. It's quick and so simple. The fire is the trickiest part." She smirked at Peyton over her shoulder. "That is, when you don't have a ghost assistant."

"Be honest," Peyton said, rising and stretching. "You know you'll miss Henry."

"Yeah, tell me another one." Ronnie shook her head as she piled each washed crock beside the bucket. "I'm not even going to *attempt* to rationalize what went on out there or in this kitchen. I'm leaving that to you."

"You know, I could blame Henry for all your…for all that went on in here, seeing as how you won't own up to any of it."

"All right. You tell me." Ronnie spun around, grinning. A dripping crock in one hand, she pointed to the others. "Count them, Ms. Stanford. Those are our seven. I *did* count correctly the first time. But this one," she held it higher, "guess where I found it? On the pantry floor."

"Come on." With a tilt of her head, Peyton slammed her hands to her hips. "You had to have dropped—"

"I never went into the pantry with these. And you've never dropped crockery, have you?" She chortled. "I'd have a handful of pieces if I did. But there isn't even a chip missing. Freakin' weird, that's what it is." She added a knowing smile. "Sounds like your Henry's doing, wouldn't you say?"

Damn, this woman's taunting was maddening.

"For God's sake. He's not mine, you know."

"Uh-huh." Ronnie raised her eyes to the ceiling. "You get the last laugh, Henry."

❖

"In a couple of hours," Ronnie said into the phone and draped a leg over the couch arm. "I just wrapped my second shoot and then, at two o'clock, Jamie's Zooming in for the *Paranormal Pursuit* edits. So, get over here."

"I'm just ten minutes away," Cheryl answered. "I want all the details."

"Bring Greek salads from Artimo's."

"Of course. You're a chef and I'm bringing you food."

"I did my beef stew at eight o'clock this morning and just roasted a pork loin in back-to-back shoots. Neither of which I want for lunch. And I don't feel like cooking."

"Yes, dear. So, you're going to review the *Paranormal* shoot and they'll accept your input?"

"That's the plan as I understand it."

"Did they record much of you working or did Miss Hollywood hog the camera?"

"Did you just insult your paranormal paramour?"

"I did, didn't I? Well, she doesn't need to be so haughty about everything. After what you described on the phone the other night, I think she could have been nicer to you."

"Bah. I didn't mean to make her sound like a monster. She's just trying to keep things the way she always has them: her way. I just shrugged off the attitude and did my thing. Hey, I get a front-row seat you'd love."

"Figures. Now, tell me they got a lot of you in the kitchen."

"In the kitchen, the dining room, the tavern. They got quite a bit. Sam spent a lot of time with me, and we had fun, actually. At times, it just felt like we were doing YouTube videos. Piece of cake. But I'm not sure Peyton liked being without her studio guy following them everywhere."

"Bet she cuts it down."

"Yeah, she might. And she's allowed to."

"Oh, no. Stop right there. You're the guest star, Ron. I know your contract inside and out, and she can only go so far. I can't wait to see this. I'll be the judge of how much camera time you get."

Ronnie's heart warmed whenever Cheryl got defensive. They had explored the gamut of careers, locales, and romances since their college days and finally, thankfully, settled just a half-hour apart. Cheryl adeptly wore the many hats of agent, sister, best friend, and sensible adult in the room whenever Ronnie needed one.

Like now. Ronnie prided herself in having a long fuse when it came to patience, but this instance could require a shorter burn time. Cheryl was right: There could be no settling for "cameo" bits on *Paranormal Pursuit*. Her *Casual Cook* devotees deserved better than to witness a damn ghost chaser treat their star like a private caterer. Even after two successful seasons, Ronnie still saw *Casual Cook* as the coolest pastime in the world, and her popularity a baffling bonus, but both were as fleeting as they were priceless. To defend them, she would take any step necessary in a heartbeat.

Right about now, though, sensitive input from an intimate partner would be nice. Too bad being single and scarcely dating preempted that. But no, a business eye was required, and Cheryl knew exactly what was at stake and how the game was played.

Ronnie synchronized her camera and huge flat screen in preparation for Jamie's Zoom meeting and settled onto the couch just as Cheryl marched into the living room.

"Food's here." She dropped her iPad on the coffee table and waltzed into the kitchen with Ronnie on her heels. She took two Styrofoam containers from the paper bag and tossed her jacket over a stool. "Just get forks. We'll eat out of these. It's almost show time." She headed back to the living room.

Shaking her head at Cheryl's loyal dedication, Ronnie grabbed forks, napkins, wine glasses, and a pinot grigio from the wine fridge and hurried after her.

"Sit on the floor," she said, squeezing down between the coffee table and the couch. "I've set the camera this way."

Cheryl joined her on the floor, and they opened their salads. "I just realized she'll see us eating."

Ronnie dropped her chin and plucked at her faded Janis Joplin T-shirt. "Thank God I dressed for the occasion."

Cheryl rolled her eyes at it, a forkful of salad poised at her mouth. "So, tell me. Are you still a skeptic?"

"Hey, I didn't embarrass myself—*or you.* Got through the whole shoot without laughing or kicking or screaming."

"But are you ready to admit there's more to paranormal investigating than you thought?"

Ronnie hiked a shoulder as she chewed. "Some things did get bizarre, and, God knows, they have all the toys. They're so serious about everything."

"And that surprised you? We watched how many damn episodes? You admitted Peyton's all business, not just some pretty face the network flaunts on TV."

"Oh, she is a pretty face, no argument there, but being on location with them is entirely different than watching them on screen. I did all right, though, kept my thoughts to myself, and played along. I certainly didn't want to insult them." She poked at her salad. "Actually, I was a lot more surprised by stuff than I expected to be. I mean, I still think this whole concept is weird and what they do is *out there*, for sure, but they're a good group. I like them."

"And you like Peyton? How was she to work with?"

"She's okay. Maybe a little uptight, but I can live with that."

Cheryl stopped eating. "Did you put her on the defensive?"

"I don't think so. Eh, well, maybe. We did go back and forth a couple of times, but I think we're good." She jabbed her with an elbow. "You know, she's even hotter when she's agitated. It's a little distracting."

"You're not supposed to agitate her, Ron. God. How are you supposed to warm up to each other?"

Ronnie fluffed her salad with her fork. "'Warm up'? We're co-workers, remember." She stabbed a tomato and shook it at her. "I know what you're getting at."

"It would be nice if you became friends."

"Does she have any?"

"Oh, stop. Peyton's no cold-hearted bitch. You don't really think that, do you? I mean, she's..."

"All business, directorial, and consumed by her work. Yes."

"And a team player, considerate, and smart."

"And hot. Yes, I get your drift."

"Shit. If you don't find all that appealing..."

"It's not that I don't. I *do*. Jesus, I'm human, remember. In fact, I get almost too hyper-aware when she's around. Do you know her eyes almost aren't even blue? Sometimes I think they're white, they're so light. They go right through me like an X-ray. And watching her mind work, the expressions change on her face, it's like...like watching clouds pass in a sunny sky." Cheryl's eyebrows shot up. "Okay, so I'm not a metaphor person, but she's... mesmerizing."

Cheryl lent her a perfunctory nod. "So, you're not dead."

Ronnie snickered. "Heh. But she's too...unsettling, and I can't afford to see her that way." She returned to poking at her salad, and mumbled, "Beguiling."

"I see." Cheryl bumped her shoulder. "Here's Jamie."

After fifteen minutes of viewing, Ronnie still hadn't said much to Jamie, hadn't seen much worth an objection or change. In fact, she felt rather pleased by what had been produced.

She pointed at the scene of herself just inside the old fireplace. "Thank God the fire caught like that, so quickly. Looks like I know what I'm doing in there."

The camera captured Ronnie explaining her challenges in the rustic room, chopping meat and vegetables, stirring the stew over the flames, raving about the smells, and emphasizing the significance of it all. "This scene works really well," Jamie said. "We did shorten a long shot Sam took into the pot. I think he was hungry."

"He stole half my carrots."

"Personally," Cheryl said, "I like the banter with the camera, the audience, and that you explain your process and how yummy the food smells, why that's important. Viewers are involved, especially when you take them around the kitchen and talk about the meals people ate back then."

"We liked it all, too," Jamie answered. "A perfect fit for us. You're a natural on camera, Ronnie. If you weren't such a pro, this would never have worked."

"Just a casual cook, remember."

Cheryl jabbed a finger toward the screen. "What's that? Beyond you at the table, in the corner."

"Excellent observation," Jamie said. "A light anomaly. Good catch." She replayed the prior few seconds. "Over your shoulder, Ronnie. See the orb crossing the pantry door?" Ronnie leaned forward. "See how it floats into the room, reaches the fireplace, and disappears?"

"It's not…dust or…"

"No. Trajectory says differently, as you'll see."

"I never noticed it."

"I know, but Peyton spotted it immediately during analysis. I have more tape of that session. She was psyched to see that the static camera got it because Sam just caught a glimpse of it. She cursed him for being too preoccupied with food and said we shouldn't leave him alone with you for so long."

Ronnie laughed.

Cheryl almost bounced with delight. "So, there was 'activity' in the kitchen right off the bat."

"Looks that way."

"Wait." Ronnie held up her fork, recalling Peyton's stubborn insistence about Ronnie's issues. "Are you saying I had my very own ghost? That light thing had been toying with me the whole time I was in there?" *Must I buy into this whole scene to feel vindicated?*

"Peyton thinks so."

"Oh, sure. *Now* she thinks that."

"After spotting the anomaly."

Ronnie hmphed. "She preferred blaming me," she said to Cheryl. "*I* was the one blaming Henry. Well, I was teasing, but still… She got on my nerves for a bit."

Jamie explained, "Peyton told the crew and the Wilders about the missing crock and the other things, the fire starting back up, but when everyone saw that orb, they knew something else had been going on all along."

"There it is again," Cheryl said, and they watched the orb drift over Ronnie's shoulder as she kneaded bread dough, then dissolve into the pantry door. "It came so close to you. Did you feel anything?"

Ronnie had to think back. "Cold. I *do* remember feeling cold."

"This scene follows immediately," Jamie added. "The anomaly went into the pantry, where Peyton and Eric picked it up. We're keeping all this, especially with you two in there."

Ronnie chuckled as they watched an aggravated Peyton shut the door in her face.

"Shit, Ron." Cheryl nudged her. "I can't believe you opened the pantry and interrupted their session."

"Well, I wouldn't have if I'd seen that orb thing go over there, but I didn't. I just heard Peyton and thought she was talking to me."

"An innocent mistake," Jamie said. "At first, Peyton wanted it cut, but it adds too much to leave it out. Any first-timer might have done what you did, Ronnie. It's innocent, relatable."

"I guess it *is* kind of endearing," Cheryl muttered.

Ronnie groaned. "I'm a cook, not a drama queen. Endearing is a word—"

"Quit it," Cheryl went on. "Now, I like this scene, too, delivering supper with Peyton. You two going back and forth is cool. Did you really forget to put the butter on—"

"Don't you start, too. I *did* put it on the tray. And no, I can't explain why it wasn't there when she looked. Bad time for Sam to be elsewhere."

"We couldn't explain your weird happenings either," Jamie told them, "and, unfortunately, we had some inopportune problems with the static camera. Peyton thinks they could have been energy draws, like when the butter moved, or the pot lid ended up back on the pot or the fire reignited. She said it was asking almost too much, but the power required for inanimate objects to move could have come from the camera."

"Gee. Lucky me," Ronnie mumbled. "Too bizarre."

Cheryl just grinned at her. "Both your audiences will get into it."

"Well, Peyton really pushed me to admit I was off-kilter." She shrugged at Cheryl. "I don't really mind looking like a rookie if she doesn't mind coming off like a—"

"Stop."

"Ronnie, FYI," Jamie said. "Peyton didn't like the interaction either. In fact, we all agreed she came on too strong, but it's chock full of storyline and personality. Viewer allegiance will ramp up. And *I* love that neither of you seemed to realize Sam was shooting from the corner."

"He's good." She couldn't believe he'd captured the bantering with Peyton.

"He also did a great job in the tavern, which comes up now. Lighting goes from grainy and dim to rich and warm when you bring in the candles."

Cheryl leaned against Ronnie's shoulder and whispered, "The lighting's very romantic." Ronnie banged a knee against hers under the table.

Jamie continued. "As you all talked, as Brian recounted getting grabbed in the bedroom, the static cameras bring out the atmosphere, the food, and all the expressions around the table, yours and Peyton's in particular."

Cheryl leaned close again. "I love it whenever the two of you go back and forth. Viewers will go crazy on Twitter over it."

They watched carefully as recordings from the tripod cameras showed meal-time conversation halting and instruments going off. Then Sam's work displayed the entire room.

"I like watching the lights on the laser grid. Very sci-fi." Cheryl slid her salad aside and leaned on her elbows, transfixed by the screen. Crewmembers jumping into action with their devices seized her full attention. "A spirit's coming," she surmised, her voice low and preoccupied.

"Yeah. Supposedly it's Henry," Ronnie said. "It got pretty weird."

REM-pods lit and beeped, and Cheryl tossed her a glance. "This is awesome," she whispered. "I can't believe this. Oh, look at that!" She squinted at the shot taken over Eric's shoulder. "I love it when a stick man shows up!"

"That was the wildest part. Everybody was ready to freak."

"Oh my God." Cheryl gasped and sat up straight. "Peyton's trying to touch him!"

Ronnie watched Jamie grin in the corner of the screen. "I think she's hooked," Ronnie told her.

"A great investigation, a great shoot will do that. Audiences will eat it up, the comradery around the table, the stick figure, especially all the interactions between you and Peyton."

Cheryl threw up a hand. "Shut up, both of you. You're ruining the suspense."

Chapter Six

Peyton sighed heavily and stretched out in the recliner. Eric appeared on the wide screen of her home theater, toasting her with a can of beer. She wished she felt as satisfied, as relaxed as he looked. Their most recent investigation in New Hampshire had been a bust, a frustrating exercise with little evidence and no resolution to show for their efforts, but what really plagued her was that damn Barrow Tavern crossover case two weeks ago.

Something about it just nagged, even though the Wilders had been thrilled with the team's findings, especially because unwelcomed spirits hadn't materialized since their visit. Maybe her unrest boiled down to anticipating another shared investigation with Ronnie, and not understanding why bugged her.

"You don't look too enthused about another cooking adventure," Eric said, adjusting his laptop camera.

"I suppose if we knew how the crossover format will be received, I wouldn't worry so much. I've never liked stockpiling a season's worth of shows in the can, anyway, not getting viewer feedback until after the fact. And, God, with *this* format? Our fans tune in for the paranormal. What if they don't want cooking thrown into the mix? Who knows what they'll think? We could be killing ourselves doing crossovers."

"We've hashed this out before, Peyton."

She rolled her eyes. "This is June, and the show won't air until September."

"The advance screenings will tell us a lot. Until then, we can only go by what the network honchos are saying, and they loved it. Barrow Tavern was our most successful investigation in ages, and Ronnie was a terrific addition. She didn't do anything to diminish our case. Quite the opposite."

"I guess not, although she came close."

"Come on, Peyton. It's not like some Muppet came in and stole the show. We should appreciate Ronnie a lot. She brings a celebrity's huge following."

"I know. I know." *That neighborly style of hers is undeniably appealing, but it has to appeal to our following, too.*

"The network's really psyched about this next case with her. Everyone thought you two were getting along fine by the time we wrapped."

"I can't explain it. Ronnie on location again…It just turns my stomach into knots."

"What bothers you about her? Is she too laid back? She came across like anyone would who was new to this, actually better, even more enthused as things went along."

"Having a spirit playing tricks on you in the kitchen… She tried to avoid being taken by that but couldn't. I could tell it got to her a little. So…I'll grant you, her skepticism did seem to turn a little."

"So, what is it? Don't tell me you're jealous."

"What?"

"You're sharing top billing with someone who's as self-confident and knowledgeable as you are. She's adored for what she does, just like you. You're each comfortable with your image. You sure you're not even a tad jealous?"

"Be serious."

"Well, if you're not jealous, you better figure out what it is before it affects your work. Are you attracted to her? Is that it? She's family, you know."

"So what? That's been common knowledge since her show debuted."

"Well, so are you but there's never been more than the occasional murmur of it."

"Oh, so I should bring in my lesbian ex because she's a chemist and Jamie could work her in—"

"Now, *you* be serious. You guys broke up a year ago. Besides, Abbey's crazy as a loon and would probably blow up our vehicles or something."

Again, Peyton sighed as she mixed herself a cocktail. "Look, Ronnie's orientation is totally irrelevant. I don't care about her wardrobe, either, or her folksy informality or—"

"That she's an amazing cook or that she's wildly successful."

"Right. Or those."

"Or her killer smile." Drink in hand, Peyton stopped and glared at him before sitting again. He pointed at her, grinning. "Gotcha."

"You don't 'got' anything." She shook her head as she settled back into the recliner, sensing where he was going.

"You're taken by her, aren't you? That devilishly handsome look?"

"Knock it off. Stop trying to cause trouble."

"She's thrown you off your stride. Admit it."

"Eric."

He shot up in his seat and beer dribbled to his chin. "That's it, isn't it? You know, it's okay if she turns your head, has you looking twice. You're allowed."

"No, I'm not."

"Yes, you are." He sat back, confident. "You need someone like her in your life. Ask her out."

"Are you kidding? This conversation is over."

"Don't cut this off. You really should ask her out."

"I will not. We have responsibilities to think about."

"God. You can be such a fart." He leaned forward with another thought and Peyton almost winced. "Know what Mason said when we watched the edits?"

"I don't want to know. Your husband is biased. He doesn't count."

"Yes, he is, and he does. He thought you two are hot together."

"Stop, for Christ's sake. Mason's perpetually horny, that's all."

"Well, good point, but he could be on to something. You guys *do* look good together on camera."

"God. Give it a rest, will you? You know damn well we have absolutely nothing in common. All that overblown charm? And that...that athletic physicality or whatever it's called? It's just too much. I don't even want to imagine what you're suggesting."

The concept threw Peyton for a loop. The idea that others could be reading something into professional interactions with Ronnie made her heart race. Ronnie had derailed Peyton's concentration more than once during their investigation, had her laboring to stay on course several times, but Peyton thought she had handled herself well.

"I'm not suggesting a thing," Eric went on, "except that if Mason sensed something, maybe viewers will. Maybe the network execs will."

Peyton downed half her drink. "Don't you dare tell me the network is scheming such a thing. I'll have my lawyer break their kneecaps."

Eric laughed. "Oh, don't get all defensive. Ronnie's cool. I like what she added to the dynamics at Barrow Tavern." He finished his beer. "So. Are you going to ask her out?"

"Drop it right now." She had to get her mind off Ronnie Sharp. His points were jumbling her thought process. "We need to talk about the next case, because that old mill last week was a real dud."

"Especially following Barrow."

"Enough about Barrow. Next week we're going to Glastonbury, Connecticut."

"Right."

"Harris and Deirdre McFadden have a Greek Revival built around eighteen fifty. I guess its last update was in the nineteen twenties, and since then, has mostly been kept period-appropriate."

"You're kidding. For a hundred years?"

Peyton chuckled at his incredulity. "We've lived too close to New York City for too long."

"But a house stuck in the Roaring Twenties?" He snorted. "Wonder how Ronnie will like that."

Back to her again.

"We'll see soon enough," she stated, irritated now. "Either she makes something out of it, or she goes back to her campfire and waits for the next full moon." She dropped her head back and closed her eyes. *Where the hell did that come from?*

"Ouch. That was cold."

"Yeah," she muttered, too ashamed to look up at him. "That was rude."

"Stop. Being. A. Bitch. You don't mean that crap for one second. You're just doing a piss-poor job of convincing me you're not interested."

Peyton took a moment to see his point and wasn't proud. No, she hadn't given "interest" in Ronnie much thought, although that had required some effort. Maybe too much effort. Ronnie was approachable, genuine, and, yes, very attractive, and under different circumstances, she probably would have sought out more private conversation, maybe even suggested getting together. But these circumstances were not ordinary; they were professional.

"Ah, so, anyway, the McFaddens…" She peeked at the screen and saw him shaking his head at her redirection. "They told Jamie that paranormal activity has increased since they bought the place over a year ago, and they're worried they are among foes, not friends. Family seldom visits and no one stays the night. Even the McFaddens don't like sleeping there."

"Sounds like a fun place."

"They bought it with total renovation in mind, had plans drawn, but after fourteen months, they're going to sell unless we can get some answers or do something to help them."

"Gee. No pressure." He reached for the keyboard on his laptop, prepared to sign off. "Okay, boss. We'll hit the road Monday morning. See you then." He glanced up at the camera one last time and sighed. "Ease up on yourself, okay?"

Peyton stared at the expansive black screen and tried to make sense of what she now considered a predicament. Eric read her too well. If he envisioned her with Ronnie, and Mason already was conjuring it, who else had? Viewers? She probably could let her guard down a little, but God help her if everyone witnessed her straying from her mission. *That* could not happen.

This upcoming case looked to be challenge enough, stepping into the 1920s *and* dealing with spirits who could be far older than that.

Resorting to her phone, she located the email Jamie had sent about their next case. She had to plan the team's approach and needed more details about the house and its history. She also needed to ensure Ronnie Sharp came adequately prepared.

Eric's words signaled for attention, and she snickered.

"Why did the network have to choose her instead of another paranormal team?" She began to pace. "Eh. Because another paranormal team would've boosted its ratings against ours, that's why, stupid." She scrolled through the emails, found Jamie's, and brought up a handful of pictures, but her mind didn't really see them. "Ronnie Sharp," she whispered warily, "you're a suave one, you are, but you've still got a lot to learn." She exhaled hard. "I think I do, too."

Finally, the pictures on her cell registered. The bedraggled two-story home boasted a covered front porch that probably had stories of its own to tell, and an interior that was clean and serviceable, but certainly aging and inconvenient. The kitchen cabinets appeared to be metal, the sink a worn porcelain, and the stove a classic wood or coal burner of cast iron.

"After a year in the place, the McFaddens must have a *real* stove somewhere." Unhappy with the paltry amount of info from Jamie, she dialed Caroline. "Fill me in, please," she asked after Caroline's chipper greeting. "I only received a couple of sentences and a half-dozen pix and that's it."

"The McFaddens already have a real estate agent lined up, ready to go public, so I can send you the company's private link. There are about sixty photos and a ton of details, but the history is another matter."

"What's really been going on?"

"I have a lot of notes from my call with them last week. Want me to send it all?"

"Yes, please, but give me a summary now. Is this situation really worth bringing Ronnie Sharp back again?"

"Well, this was a boarding house back in the day and the kitchen played a big role, so I think Ronnie could take it from there."

Peyton lay back in the recliner and stared at the ceiling. She figured Jamie sent the same info to Ronnie and couldn't help but wonder how the Casual Cook would meet this challenge. "We'll see." *Have to get her out of my head.*

"Are you doubting her? Didn't she do great at the tavern?"

"Oh, no. I mean, yes, she did fine, all things considered."

"I thought we all agreed she was a huge help, a catalyst, even. Do you think this McFadden job will be too much for her?"

"I can't be sure, so we'll see. Bring me up to speed on what we're dealing with."

"Well, when the original owner died, his wife inherited his lumber fortune, and they say loneliness led her to turn the place into a boarding house around eighteen fifty-eight. Not long after, boarders started disappearing."

"Really? How many?"

"According to newspapers of the day, six."

Peyton almost gagged on her drink. "Six?"

"Yeah. Three bodies were never found but three were discovered in the cellar. And, by the way, in eighteen sixty-four, when the law closed in on her, the widow hung herself in the attic."

"Damn. Do they think she's been patrolling the place ever since?"

"Yup. Sounds like she's unhappy to have 'intruders.' I found other accounts of trouble in the years that followed, physical injuries, a fire, even a shooting. The place stayed in the family until eighteen seventy, when a Civil War veteran bought it, but two years later, fire nearly destroyed it. *And*—he was killed in the fire."

"Jesus. How many spirits are we dealing with?"

"Eight at least."

"Man, that's a lot."

"The widow could be the dominant one."

"If she had the strength to murder so many people, she would be."

"There were a couple more owners until 1926, when a wealthy family moved in and rehabbed the place. That's the look it has today, preserved by a couple generations of family but now sadly fading."

"But it's livable? The McFaddens have been living in that era for a year or so?"

"Oh, there's a decent little suite in the rear of the house, straight out of the nineteen eighties. That's been their home base for reno jobs they tried tackling themselves. Apparently, contractors don't stick around long. Masons did some of the chimneys but quit and refused to come back. The place is a mammoth project, too big for amateurs and too stressful when things are constantly going wrong."

"Such as?"

"Well, there are the usual: tapping, footsteps, large shadows, you know. Then, last spring, Harris was pushed off a ladder and broke two ribs. Deirdre felt someone sit on her bed several times, even stroke her hair. They've had food catch fire, rooms fill with haze, often find everything open in the kitchen, and even occasionally hear the gongs from a grandfather clock."

"And, of course, they don't have one."

"Right. But we know the Civil War soldier had one. There's a picture of him standing in front of it."

Peyton's list of issues lengthened as she left for her office down the hall. She needed to keep track of all this. "How often do they run into these things?"

"Every day it's something inexplicable, a curious little thing, or an unnerving big thing, or a scary huge thing. Their two adult kids and the grandkids all have had experiences and they can't stand the place."

"And the McFaddens, what's their story?"

"They're retirees in their late sixties, both from Vermont. He was a bank CEO and likes to tinker. Deirdre sold her party planner business to enjoy her hobby—which is, you ready? Cooking. They planned a state-of-the-art chef's kitchen, so she's super bummed now."

Peyton stopped typing notes and stared at her cell. "Cooking? Really?" She heard Caroline chuckle.

"Jamie was pumped, telling me. She can't wait to get you and Ronnie on this case."

"Cripes. Cooking? The widow couldn't collect freaking stamps or something?" She rubbed her eyes.

"Are you calling Ronnie? Um…to let her know about the kitchen, I mean?"

"There probably isn't much I can tell her that Jamie hasn't already, I'm sure."

"Oh. Okay." She sounded disappointed and Peyton didn't want to guess why.

"Can you get your info to me tonight?"

"I'll do it now, all the stuff I put together. Do we leave on Monday?"

"You're as eager as Eric. And no doubt Jamie's already put Ronnie on notice." Feeling a bit surrounded by the Casual Cook, she sighed. "Yes, Monday. Enjoy the weekend."

Chapter Seven

His bulky camera aligned on his shoulder and producer Jamie stuck to his hip, Sam hovered just off to Ronnie's right and recorded her approach to the black cast iron hulk in the corner.

Ronnie wanted him to capture her respect for the 1903 Glenwood range and trusted that all viewers would appreciate her putting it to use for the first time in…well, she still didn't know. Neither Caroline nor Jamie knew exactly, except that, about ten months ago, the McFaddens had foolishly fired it up after a decade of non-use—before calling the fire department, a chimney sweep, and then a mason. Inspectors eventually gave the go-ahead for the chimney and the antique range, which, to Ronnie's endless joy, needed only cosmetic upgrades.

She ran her fingers reverently along the once-shiny bumper in front, its nickel plate pitted with age, and sent a smile to the camera. "This is a true gem. It's seen better days, for sure, but re-plating these bumpers would be *so* worth it." She turned the damper open on the rear stovepipe and opened the side-mounted firebox, then inserted crumpled newspaper and kindling. "Now." She flicked a stick match to life and gave Sam and his camera a promising look. "Let's cross our fingers."

She set the newsprint afire, closed the box, gave the Glenwood an affectionate pat, and stepped back. Sam edged back as well but she knew he still had her on camera as they watched the stove. Out of the corner of her eye she caught him pointing at it.

"I see it," she said quietly, and her nerves tightened. Wisps of smoke trickled from the four round burner plates on top. The last thing she wanted right now was a backdraft or clogged chimney to fill the kitchen with smoke. She silently urged the fire to grow, for heat to rise and push the cold air and smoke up the pipe.

But it continued to weasel its way out around the burners. She held strong to her faith in her kindling strips of kiln-dried maple, knowing she didn't have much of a choice but to hope. Unable to re-open the firebox and tend the fire without unleashing a cloud, she held up crossed fingers to the viewers.

Smoke still trickled from the plates and now the kitchen grew hazy.

"Probably time to open a window," she said, and hustled to one of the three in the kitchen but it wouldn't budge. She shrugged at the camera. "Just our luck, huh?" In the background, Jamie sent her a frantic look. Ronnie tried another and managed to raise it six inches. "Ah! The back door will help." She propped it open.

She glanced sheepishly at the camera before turning back to the stove. Much to her relief, the wisps of smoke had stopped. *Thank you!*

"Hey, you guys in the kitchen?" Peyton strode into the room on a mission. "Whoa! We *did* smell smoke!"

Ronnie gazed right past Peyton's surprise and consternation, straight to the lusciously form-fitting black jeans and red polo shirt. Half a beat later, she noticed the narrowed eyes requesting some response.

"Ah…smoke," Ronnie fumbled, "yeah, see, the—"

"The what?" Peyton asked, waving both hands across her face.

"Now, now, Ms. Stanford," Ronnie said. "Down, girl. We're under control." She gave a nod to the audience. "Aren't we?" She gathered a few beefier pieces of firewood from the crate she'd brought and opened the firebox, confident now in the draft. "Give credit where it's due, Peyton," she said, adding the wood to the young fire. "Ol' faithful here just forgot what to do, been asleep too long, that's all. It's back on track now."

"Well…" Waving away the dissipating smoke, Peyton eyed Sam. She obviously knew she was on camera and reined in her ire. "Well, that's…that's good."

Relishing the view, Ronnie couldn't resist the temptation. She crossed the room and took Peyton by the hand, letting surprise boost her confidence. "C'mere." She held Peyton's hand over the stovetop. "Feel that? Warmth's coming." Peyton's slender hand was cold, and Ronnie liked seeing her rub both in the growing heat.

"I-I'm relieved it's working," Peyton offered, and stuffed her hands into her pockets.

"Ye need be of greater faith."

"Oh, I have faith in many things."

"The Glenwood?" Ronnie posed, unpacking her necessities on the table.

"That might be pushing it."

Ronnie shivered at an unexpected chill but attributed it to having left the stove. Unfortunately, the June warmth outside was no match for the wintry feel in this spacious empty house. Brian and Caroline joined them next, and Caroline immediately hugged herself.

"Man, this is the coldest room in the place," Brian said. "You got that going just in time."

"None too soon, I know. The stove was a little reluctant at first, but the kitchen should feel normal soon."

Brian produced a thermal camera and panned the room. "Plenty of heat showing by the stove and the front of you, Peyton, and everywhere else it's decent." He pivoted to the doorway, where Peyton had originally stood. "Except by the door. Very cold. We walked through that, so…"

Peyton studied his screen and pulled a voice recorder from her pocket. "Let's try an EVP session right here on the chance something is already with us."

"I'll go grab an EMF detector because we need new readings," Caroline said, still talking as she rushed past Peyton. "I'll see if Eric has all our systems up yet."

Brian removed his ballcap and scratched his head. "Y'know, we sure didn't have this cold patch in here earlier. Our baselines were normal on the initial walk-through. Something's changed in just this first hour."

Ronnie couldn't dispute that. The mighty Glenwood should be tempering the feel of this room, but, then again, it most likely needed more time to reinvigorate a place left closed and idle so long. If crew members wanted to attribute the cold to a spirit, good luck to them. She decided to stick with what she knew best.

She adjusted the stovepipe damper, closing it half-way to moderate the fire and accommodate her old-fashioned percolator. "There'll be coffee pretty soon." She turned to Sam's camera. "And we're going to put together ham-and-cheese biscuits for a late lunch, once the oven heats up."

Brian grunted with approval and Jamie offered a thumbs-up, but Ronnie wasn't sure the preoccupied Peyton heard a word she'd said. Or maybe Peyton didn't approve of lunch after just a few hours on the job. Or maybe a working kitchen made investigating more complicated than a dormant one. *But wasn't that the point of my being here?*

"I won't be messing with your readings, will I?" she asked. "I mean, heating up the stove and the oven will—"

"We'll compensate for it," Peyton said in a monotone, turning away to speak to no one in particular. "Is anyone here with us? Are you here, Georgina Wallace, wife of Roger Wallace? Tell us your name, please. Did you live here? Was this your boarding house?"

She stopped her methodical, intermittent questioning. Brian and Caroline lowered their instruments, and everyone listened intently, while Sam silently recorded in the corner.

Peyton pressed the playback button, and the tinny speaker aired her questions and lots of static. Surprisingly, Ronnie found herself interested in any response.

"Are you Georgina Wallace, wife of Roger Wallace?" Peyton's recording asked.

The playback netted a brief, unexpected garble and earned everyone's attention.

"Didn't it sound like George?" Brian asked. "Not her full name but some of it?"

Peyton replayed it several times and her crew agreed. She surveyed the room, intense, seeking, and clicked the playback button again.

"Was this your boarding house?"

More dead air. They all held their collective breath. Ronnie stopped kneading her biscuit dough. *Here I am, all caught up. Again. Wouldn't Cheryl love to trade places?* She watched Peyton wander as if entranced, past the table to the chilly doorway.

"Still getting an ice-cold reading right where you're standing," Brian reported.

Peyton confirmed his reading with a nod and slipped her free, undoubtedly cold hand into a pocket. "We are here to meet with you," she continued to whomever or whatever might be listening. "Is that okay? Will you speak to us? Or do you want us to go? You can communicate in any way you wish."

She stopped again. "Caroline. The SLS camera." She withheld another playback until Caroline returned and aimed the structured light sensor at the doorway.

"Nothing," Caroline said, eyes on the screen, and rotated in place to check the whole kitchen.

Peyton pressed the recorder and they listened to more of her questions go unanswered.

Ronnie shivered and realized her hands, arms, and shoulders were remarkably cold. "Feeling kinda blue over here, Brian," she whispered, referencing the colors on his screen.

With a grin, he turned his thermal camera on her. "I can see that. Your image definitely should be more in the pink."

Steam suddenly hissed off the stovetop and everyone spun to the sound. Coffee bubbled from the percolator and splashed onto the searing hot cast iron.

"Crap!" Ronnie grabbed a potholder and snatched the percolator off the surface. "This shouldn't have…" She ran her eyes up the stovepipe to the damper. "Dammit." She quickly spun it back from full-open to half-way—where she knew she'd positioned it earlier. "Stove was wide open," she said, looking back at the others, incredulous. "That's definitely *not* how I set it. That's way too much air, too hot."

"Is it loose enough to have just rolled back open from its own weight?"

Pleased Peyton understood the principle, let alone asked in a reasonable manner, Ronnie shook her head. "No. In fact, it's stubborn and needs a firm hand."

"No more cold spots now. Everything's looking normal again." Brian lowered his instrument and flexed his shoulders. "Hey, maybe Georgina communicated 'any way she wished' and said hello."

"Or," Peyton added, "she doesn't want us here and tried to smoke us out."

Ronnie didn't really care. She was aggravated. Obviously, now, the Glenwood couldn't be trusted and required her strict supervision. No way this damper turned by itself, but she had no realistic explanation, either. Crew members were ready to fault a force they couldn't see—not even with their precious instruments—but Ronnie hated playing that game. Without a legitimate problem to address, using the Glenwood would be a risky challenge.

"I guess the damper *had* to have rolled back by itself," she said, hands on her hips, "but if you really believe Georgina's ghost used this to send a message, please tell it…*her*…to use words or knocks or nudges or whatever. Tell her there's NO messing with fire." She glared at the venerable antique and caught herself wondering about the ghost of a deranged widow.

"I think we need to regroup," Peyton said. "We really need to determine if we're dealing with Georgina. I hope Eric heard that name on the monitors."

"Well, aside from those couple of syllables," Brian said, "we've gone dry on your EVP responses, we have no SLS imaging, and nothing on my thermal."

Ronnie grew impatient with all this. Or maybe it was curiosity getting the better of her. She wasn't so sure of a lot of things anymore. Frustrated, she stabbed her biscuit cutter in flour and popped out dough rounds with unusual vigor. Hell, even *she* felt energized about this case. Enough to voice her thoughts.

"Um, forgive my ignorance here, and I know this is an unsolicited opinion, but doesn't this classify as a good start to your investigation? I mean, damn. Even *I'll* admit that stove thing was fu—um…really odd."

Caroline's face brightened. "Yeah. I bet we'll have even better luck after dark."

Ronnie returned to her biscuits, holding up a few to the camera to keep her cooking fans involved. She knew Peyton still looked her way and probably wanted to tell her to mind her own business. But this *was* her business; they *both* were on camera here for a reason. *Can't tell if she's ticked off at me or…or what she's thinking.* Then, Peyton surprised her.

"You know, Ronnie's exactly right." Peyton gestured to the doorway and then the Glenwood. "We didn't even plan to start in this room, so we may have gotten ahead of ourselves."

Ronnie watched her address the others and, finally, turn to her. The look this time was tempered, almost concessionary, and definitely welcome.

❖

Peyton's intensity grew in direct relation to the list of "hot spots" in the house, especially by late afternoon, after a more detailed tour by the McFaddens. Already, having documented minor encounters in the parlor, second-floor rooms and, obviously, the kitchen, Peyton had high hopes for the McFaddens' future family room.

With a battery-powered lantern at her feet, she spoke to the crew and cameras around her. "I do want us back in the kitchen, but there could be more in here than we originally thought."

"They said they're in no hurry to finish this renovation." Gliding a palm over the wallboard, Eric kept his camera trained on Peyton. "Just piles of books and some seating, and lots of work to do."

"This once was a birthing room. Then, a bedroom," Caroline said, "changed by the soldier who bought the house years later." She turned to Eric's camera. "This is where they found his remains after the fire."

He observed, "So, it would make sense that the McFaddens often smell smoke in here."

"And why the shadow of a man always runs them out," Peyton added. "Trying to save them from the fire?"

"He *was* a brave guy." Caroline read from notes on her phone. "Lt. Col. William Wooster, 20th Connecticut Infantry, fought at Gettysburg and even survived Andersonville prison."

"Andersonville?" Eric asked. "That could explain him using this as a bedroom, if he came out of there debilitated."

"But to buy a place as big as this, with four bedrooms upstairs, he must have had a large family." Peyton clicked on the digital recorder. "Colonel Wooster? Are you with us?" She moved to the doorway and Sam, ever silent and filming from the corner, stepped aside.

"We are friends," she called out. "Can you speak with us in some way? Would you rather we leave? Do you not want the McFaddens in this house?" She held the recorder out a little farther. "Colonel Wooster, are you here? Is this room not safe? Is that why you urge them out of here?"

Caroline came to her side. "Are you the shadow the McFaddens see? The one in the upstairs hall? Can you climb stairs?

"You better check the kitchen," Ronnie grumbled from the doorway.

They turned to find her leaning against the frame, hair disheveled, a dishtowel draped over her shoulder. Her trademark easygoing demeanor seemed seriously depleted.

"The kitchen?" Peyton asked, alarmed by her haggard appearance.

Ronnie nodded and ran her fingers through her hair. "Yeah. Shocked the bejeezus out of me. I was sorting firewood and, I know lighting in there isn't great, but everything went really dim." She wiped perspiration from her forehead with a quick backhand and pointed to the door in the corner.

Reflexively, Peyton gave it a glance and wished Ronnie would just blurt out whatever else she saw. "And?" Her walkie-talkie crackled with Brian's voice, and she grabbed it off her hip while pressing Ronnie to continue. "So, in the kitchen? There's—"

"Well, right now, I don't know, but at first, it reminded me of a brown out. It wasn't smoke from the stove. When I turned around, there was this dark fog above me. I was speechless. I couldn't move."

Peyton took a step closer. "So..." She brought the walkie to her mouth, about to speak. *Jesus, this is like pulling teeth.* "Then what?"

"It retreated, seemed to shrink, as if it was being sucked into the back corner."

"Was it shapeless," Peyton persisted, "not like a person?"

"Shapeless, yes." Ronnie waved a hand across the ceiling. "Big."

Peyton turned to the tripod camera in the corner and was about to speak into the walkie when Brian's voice came out of it. She jumped.

"Yes to what Ronnie said, Peyton. We got it on Camera Three."

"Seriously?" she asked him. "A dark cloud?"

"No joke. Happened so fast...Come in here and watch the playback."

"Not yet." She studied the door to the kitchen.

"The cloud," Brian added, "it's—"

Peyton pointed to the door. "Go ahead, Caroline. Open it."

"Nuh-uh. *You* open it."

Brian said, "Peyton—"

"*I'll* do it." Ronnie hustled across the room. "It seemed to pass right through, so it might be gone by now." Before Peyton could say anything, Ronnie swung the door open.

Everyone took a step back.

A stormy cloud hovered across the ceiling, and the tangy aroma of charred wood wafted out.

"Look at that!" Caroline exclaimed.

"Well, now," Ronnie said, looking more puzzled than shaken. "There has to be an explanation, right?"

She stepped toward the threshold, but Peyton grabbed her arm and tugged her back.

"No, Ronnie. A little caution with the unknown."

Eric edged closer to the opening, eyes on his screen. "The camera sees right through it."

Peyton moved alongside him, her recorder extended. "Ronnie," she whispered, "you're sure about that damn stove?"

"Hell, yes. It's running really low, and it's all been inspected, remember, so it's good."

Peyton leaned against Eric's side, eyeing his screen. "Who are you?" she called out. "Please tell us your name." Tension tightened her shoulders and arms, and she squinted into the room. "What's the meaning of this?" she demanded. "Tell us your name, now!"

The ensuing silence bothered her more than usual. So did the presence in front of them and the strength of its scent. All of it, more pronounced and prolonged than she had ever encountered before. She seriously hoped her recorder picked up answers, some semblance of EVP but, as much as she wanted to play back the intake, she didn't dare. Not at this moment.

"It's moving," Ronnie said, her voice soft just behind Peyton's ear. She pointed to the ceiling light. "See it drifting toward that other corner."

Peripherally, Peyton saw Eric's camera rise to capture the haze floating across the light. "Damn, if it doesn't look like smoke," she mumbled.

The room cleared gradually and when Peyton crossed the threshold, the others followed.

"I don't smell it anymore," Ronnie said, gazing around until she faced Peyton. "Do you?"

Peyton appreciated the camaraderie in Ronnie's tone but thought the bewilderment in her eyes spoke volumes. Here was a confident woman, a self-made success story, knowingly out of her comfort zone and hip-deep in someone else's for all the world to watch. It took courage just to be a beginner in this field, Peyton knew, and suddenly she doubted she would have consented to such a role if she'd been in Ronnie's shoes.

"No, I don't smell it," she finally answered. "You're right."

She's into this so much more than she expected.

"I'm glad it's gone," Caroline said. "This was way too creepy."

Peyton had to agree, and she wanted answers. "Let's get back to the monitors and see what Brian caught, check for responses." She waited for Ronnie to look her way, to realize the invitation included her.

Chapter Eight

Ronnie accepted Eric's invitation and took a seat with the crew at the dining room table, which was somewhere beneath cameras, water bottles, meters, lanterns, notes, monitoring equipment, and an overflowing platter of her sugar cookies.

Feeling a bit less of an "outsider" now, she found these analysis sessions intriguing, even fun. Delving into the mystery of the case was novel entertainment and roused her curiosity, but she wasn't quite ready to abandon her skepticism. And as she applied her own common sense to their evidence, she kept those opinions to herself—often unsuccessfully.

"Practically every room has a bazillion doors," she observed, "but that one in the corner…"

"We'll get to it soon," Peyton said, not looking away from the monitors.

Ronnie moved to stand behind Peyton's chair for a better view of them. "I peeked behind that door earlier and there's a staircase landing."

That made Peyton turn and look up at her and Ronnie noted the hint of admonition. She stifled a grin. *Wait until you see. Freaking spooky.*

"Typical design," Caroline said matter-of-factly, "back stairs from the kitchen. Up *and* down, right?"

Ronnie nodded. Thank God for Caroline's enthusiasm, lightening the heavy mood Peyton created. She wondered what Peyton did to relax, how she spent her free time, if she had a soul sister like her own Cheryl. Maybe her intense personality explained her being single, or at least, that's what the celebrity gossip said.

"You like opening doors?" Peyton asked. "And did you check out those stairs, too?"

"Hell no. It was dark in there. I shut the door right away."

"*That* unknown gave you pause?"

"Well…yeah, it did."

"I see. Yet you would walk into some inexplicable haze."

"For that, I had safety in numbers, you know? I was with the experts, and you held me back."

"Spared you from yourself," Peyton said, shaking her head, and turned to the others.

She emphasized the importance of their standard "due process," and directed attention back to Colonel Wooster in the family room. She'd deliberately set aside the creepy kitchen incident, at least temporarily, and Ronnie swallowed a snide remark that bubbled up. That cloud thing was a real mystery, had to be a big deal, and not jumping right on it simply looked to Ronnie like Peyton asserting her authority. *Putting me in my place. She can't possibly run with that attitude twenty-four seven.*

With a click from the recorder, Ronnie's attention returned to the staticky voice that filled the room.

"Colonel Wooster? Are you with us?"

As usual, everyone waited for some response. Ronnie almost chuckled at how all eyes implored the device.

"Can you speak with us in some way?"

Bits of garble followed, three of them, abrupt and rapid. Everyone leaned closer as Peyton replayed the sounds. Doubting the noise amounted to much, Ronnie listened harder anyway.

"Barks?" Caroline asked. "Like a dog?"

"Grunting," Eric said.

"Or coughing," Peyton offered.

Thinking it was a stretch, Ronnie considered the sounds as coughing. She thought they would fit, if fire had taken Wooster's life. Then she chided herself for having become so enthralled by it all.

"Colonel Wooster, are you here?"

"Yes."

Everyone, including Ronnie, jerked in surprise.

No. Freaking. Way.

"Holy shit!" Brian's face lit up.

Peyton bit her lip and played more. *"Is this room not safe?"*

The crew's yearning for some form of confirmation was palpable. Holding her breath for whatever came next, Ronnie realized she was just as anxious.

"Georgie."

"Georgie!" Caroline's arm shot out, pointing at the recorder. "As in Georgina."

Peyton's tentative grin revealed her pleasure. "He could be telling us Georgina's the reason the room isn't safe, maybe even that she caused the fire." The rest of the playback held no further reward, however, and she shut off the device. With a sideways look at Ronnie, she observed, "Our session ended there—when you came in."

"Sorry." Ronnie shrugged. "But I just thought you might care that an honest-to-God cloud was filling the kitchen."

"Of course, we care," Peyton said stiffly, tinkering with the recorder to reach the next batch of questions. "The timing was just…off a bit."

"But look what we got," Eric said. "Now we have both Georgina *and* Wooster on our hands."

"Any chance they are connected?" Ronnie wondered aloud.

"Unlikely," Peyton answered.

"Well, when did Georgina do her dirty deeds?" Ronnie suddenly wanted to know, surprised by her own interest.

They both turned to Caroline.

"Had to be sometime between eighteen fifty-eight and sixty-four."

"Were Georgina and her husband from here?" Peyton asked.

"Nope and he may have struggled because of that. Roger moved his lumber business and even some of his workers to Glastonbury around eighteen fifty."

"From?" Ronnie knew her curiosity was gaining control.

Caroline's gaze rose to hers, then Peyton's. "From Atlanta."

Ronnie folded her arms. "*That* would have been awkward in the eighteen fifties, don't you think? A family from the deep south here in Yankee country?" She could be overstepping here, because investigating wasn't in her job description, but this mystery was becoming as intriguing as any she'd read, streamed, or seen on TV. She couldn't help pushing further. "What if the workers he brought were slaves?"

Thankfully, Peyton hadn't cut her off yet. In fact, Peyton actually seemed to be pondering the hypothetical.

"We know Wooster bought the place in eighteen seventy," Peyton said for confirmation. "I assume from the Wallace family?"

"He did. From their only child." Caroline scanned her notes. "A daughter who had married at fifteen—*fifteen*—in eighteen fifty-eight and moved away."

Ronnie laughed. "I'd scoot too if I had Georgina for a mom."

"Me, too," Caroline said, and bumped her shoulder to Ronnie's. "Anyway, so, yes. Georgina dies in sixty-four and the house is empty for six years when Wooster buys it."

Peyton absently tapped her pen on her recorder. "That's not much of a connection."

Ronnie risked another question. "What about the people Georgina supposedly murdered here?"

Caroline slid her phone onto the table. "I didn't go into that much detail, at least not yet." She turned to Peyton. "I could dig deeper."

Peyton arched an eyebrow at Ronnie. "Is the Casual Cook concocting something out of all this?"

Ronnie smiled broadly, happy to be asked. "Well, yeah. I mean, maybe all these historic pieces don't gel into one incredibly ironic tale, but what if they do? It sure would make one hell of a movie."

She ignored Peyton's pointed stare and reached past her to write on a clipboard. Inches separated them now, and although Ronnie hoped to draw Peyton's attention to notes she scribbled, Peyton seemed in no hurry to look away from her.

The up-close and personal examination made her senses hum, but she did want Peyton to take her seriously. After all, as the Casual Cook, she was legally bound to this paranormal gig and determined to play a meaningful role in this episode, no matter how awkward or weird everything became. *Besides, I'm getting into this.*

"So, look at the years," she offered. "The Wallaces were here in the eighteen fifties. Southerners, successful big business owners—most likely slaveholders, which was illegal in Connecticut at the time, if I remember my history correctly. They wouldn't have been the life of anybody's party, not around here, and that could have led to his business problems. What if the occasional boarder was an abolitionist or…or a Union soldier? How would Georgina have reacted to them?"

She leaned back slightly and queried Peyton's eyes at dangerously close range. She labored not to sway beneath Peyton's breath on her lips. Labored not to sway closer. Their mouths were tenuously aligned.

She turned crisply back to her notes, internally shaken and perspiring, relieved to have snapped out of that moment before her disorientation became noticeable. She frantically collected her thoughts.

"How…" she cleared her throat. "How do you think a high-bred lady of the South, desperately out of her comfort zone, would have greeted an abolitionist or soldier? With Yankee pot roast?" She snickered. "More likely a rebel welcome. What if Georgina was 'doing her part' here, fighting for the South? Remember, if it's all true, she killed northerners during the Civil War."

"Yeah," Caroline said. "So, keep going."

Ronnie forced herself to look at others around the table. "And then," she scribbled another date, "in eighteen seventy, holy crap, a Union officer, *of all people*, moves into her home, and ol' Georgina freaks. Her fighting spirit comes out of the woodwork—literally—and she does her part to get rid of another Yankee. She sets the place on fire."

"And maybe she's *still* fighting," Brian suggested, excited by the theory.

Nodding at him, Ronnie straightened and raised her palms haplessly. "See what you've done to my mind?" It was a kick to think she could have connected the dots and solved the mystery, despite the fact that this whole ghost premise seemed like a game.

Peyton eyed the wild script on the clipboard. "The timeline obviously works, Ronnie, and the scenario is interesting, but that's about as big a stretch as I've ever heard."

A bit more frazzled than when she'd started presenting her case, Ronnie sagged onto a hip. This wasn't her investigation, she wasn't a professional in this field, and, therefore, probably should have kept her nose out of it. But surely, her scenario made sense. Okay, so maybe, she'd gushed about it a little.

"I think that whole idea is pretty cool," Brian said.

"It does add up," Eric admitted, looking at Peyton, and she returned a half-hearted nod.

Ronnie almost snorted. *Sure, she'll concede to him.*

Peyton stared at the image Brian had paused on the closest monitor, a shot of Ronnie cleaning a cast iron pot, and drummed her nails on the table. She appeared to be considering the scenario, not the image of the Casual Cook doing her thing in the kitchen. Now, Ronnie itched to learn if the recorder had captured any ghost voices to back up her theory. *Damn. How did I get so hyped up about this? Cheryl should see me now.*

"You ready to run the kitchen scene?" Brian asked.

"What we really need," Eric added, gesturing to Peyton's device, "is more EVP answers like those we just got. If you don't have anything on that recorder, we'll need to crank things up."

❖

Peyton couldn't afford to lend much credence to Ronnie's far-fetched theory, especially when delivered with that glib grin. Their investigations required evidence that couldn't be debunked, not simply posited, so she watched the entire kitchen cloud scene on the monitor without speaking.

As the others mumbled observations, Peyton searched all the monitors but saw no activity elsewhere in the house. Something had chosen that room, filled, and possessed it until the human presence there fled.

Peyton pressed the playback button on her recorder.

"Who are you? Please tell us your name."

"Come on, dammit," Brian said on a sigh. "Give us something."

"What's the meaning of this?" Peyton's recorded voice commanded. *"Tell us your name, now!"*

A deep rumble broke through the static.

They looked at each other. Peyton saw Ronnie straighten in her seat.

Eric whispered, "That was a long growl if I ever heard one."

Caroline cleared her throat. "Thank God we didn't hear that while we were in there. I would've been gone."

Another bit of garble interrupted the soft hiss.

Caroline lurched over the table. "What was that?"

Peyton replayed it. "Did it say, 'How'?"

"House?" Ronnie suggested, and Eric said he thought so, too.

Again, Peyton replayed it, and they heard nothing further.

"Damn, I wish we got more." She dropped back in her chair. "We need to try again. Let's start with the colonel, see if we can pick up where we left off." Everyone collected a device and headed to the family room.

"I'm going back to the kitchen to start supper," Ronnie told her as the others filed out. "Who knows?" she added, and elbowed Peyton's arm. "Maybe the cloud will come back."

Peyton bit back a retort at the levity.

"Could you handle it if it did? You ran last time."

"Well, it gave me the creeps, but yeah. I think I could this time."

"I see." Peyton set a hand on her hip. "So, if spiritual energy never really manifests into something visual or measurable, a silly dark mass is no big deal, right?"

"But there has to be a legit reason for it, right? Like *some* answer."

"Why do you think we're here? For kicks?"

Ronnie ran a hand back through her hair, a nervous habit Peyton had detected several times. She thought it far more telling than Ronnie realized. *More concerned than she wants to be. She's caught up in all this and now can't explain her way out. And she's cute when she's flustered.*

"Don't get me wrong," Peyton went on. "I *do* understand any hesitance you might have. Coping with contradictions of logic, lending credence to things we've grown up dismissing or disbelieving, that takes a few years in this field."

"I'd guess quite a few." Seeming a bit disconcerted, Ronnie sighed. "Maybe I fried too many brain cells in my youth to be open to this stuff."

Peyton smiled. "I fried my share, too, which probably is why my brain *is* open to it. I will admit, though, you're holding up fairly well for someone not programmed for all this—yet."

"Yet."

"That's right. You're getting into this, aren't you?"

Ronnie grinned at her sheepishly. "On that note, I should just get back to work." She turned away, then hesitated. "Will you guys be coming in soon? To check out that corner door?"

It sounded like more of a plea than a simple inquiry and Peyton was moved by Ronnie's uncertainty. It was wise to respect the unknown. Maybe Ronnie didn't even realize she was learning to do just that.

"We will, definitely. We'll go directly in from the family room."

Ronnie's angular jaw flinched as she nodded, perhaps a sign of relief or maybe resignation. But she pursed her lips and met Peyton's eyes with a spark of determination.

"I'd be lying if I said I wanted to meet that fog again," Ronnie said, "but the Casual Cook is no wimp."

"Good. I'm glad."

Ronnie backed away. "I'll be firing up the stove, just so you know, and I won't let it smoke us out. I'll try not to get in the way."

Not for the first time, Peyton wondered about the impression she was making on her. The hard-nosed professional or the self-centered bitch? She hoped it was more the former than the latter, for

Ronnie's sake and that of fans of both their shows—fans who never missed a trick. Ronnie *was* trying to fit in and doing a good job, overall, mastering conditions in that kitchen, dealing with a world she really knew nothing about. Maybe her light-hearted approach was a coping mechanism.

A little more empathy on my part wouldn't hurt.

Back in the family room, an hour of scans and readings, even a prolonged EVP session of questions netted nothing. Peyton played back her recordings on the spot to no avail and grew restless to move on to the kitchen. Whether it was the previous cloud encounter or Ronnie's plea that drove her, she wasn't sure.

But she nearly forgot her mission when she led the group into the stifling kitchen. Ronnie worked with her back to them, stripped down to a sleeveless black T-shirt, and flashing a chef's knife with authority as she turned two raw chickens into parts. With crewmembers fanning out around her, Peyton stood and watched Ronnie drizzle oil, sprinkle seasonings, and talk to the audience the entire time. She gathered chicken parts and spun to the two large cast iron skillets on the stove.

Caught watching, Peyton felt her cheeks redden and suddenly wished she was as invisible as the spirits they were chasing.

"Wicked hot in here, I know," Ronnie offered. "Sorry." She looked back briefly to Sam's camera. "This hellish heat is why folks used summer kitchens years ago." Sizzling intensified with each chicken part she laid in the pan. "Wait till you smell this, though." She waved Sam closer. "Come on over here. You guys need to see this. It's going to be great."

Peyton flicked her gaze away from Ronnie's ministrations, from the lean arms and broad hands and purposeful strides as they shifted from stove to table and back. She found herself in the background of Sam's shot, in perfect range of the tripod camera in the far corner of the room, and, as always, the subject of Eric's dutiful handheld. So many eyes caught her gawking.

Idiot. Let everyone see you check her out. I have to worry about stuff like this now? Thank God for edits.

She exhaled toward her forehead.

Ronnie hovered over the skillets, situating hunks of potato among pieces of the searing meat. "I'm gambling Mrs. Georgina Wallace of Atlanta will be tempted by this Yankee's oven-baked version of fried chicken." She adjusted the contents of each pan and asked Peyton, "How about some corn bread with this?"

She opened the oven and, without pause or grunt, hefted a loaded heavy skillet into each hand and slid them inside. The corded muscles along her arms relaxed as she shut the oven door and looked to Peyton, still awaiting an answer. Glistening with a sheen of perspiration, half her hair stuck upright, Ronnie cocked an eyebrow and waited.

Guess I know why so many women are addicted to her show.

This time, Peyton caught herself ogling.

Jesus.

She swallowed hard and tried to remember Ronnie's question. How had she *not* been so taken by this woman's presence before? Too wrapped up in the case? Too responsible for the show? Too consumed by ego? Maybe that empathy she'd talked herself into earlier had opened more than her eyes. Whatever the reason, she couldn't deny the primal jolt that had nailed her feet to the floor and her mouth shut.

God damn. What did she ask?

Ronnie scooped a cannister of flour off the table. "Easy enough to throw on some biscuits, if you'd rather I ditch the cornbread."

Cornbread. That was it!

"Oh, no. Do your cornbread. I-I just…ah…I just spaced out there for a minute."

"No problem. The heat will do that. It's already melted half my brain." She quickly set to work at the table. "Cornbread it is."

Peyton released an inward sigh of relief, grateful Ronnie had let the gawking slide without comment. But she had definitely been caught—by Ronnie and the whole viewing world—and now there was this *thing* between them. An entirely different kind of spirit to worry about.

"You want to tackle that corner door now?" Brian asked, his hands full of equipment.

Peyton forced herself back on track. Thankfully, Sam's studio camera angled away from her to Brian. "What's the thermal read in that area?" she asked him.

"As we'd guess, it's cooler. The *only* spot in here that is, actually. I have the DVR, if you want it."

"Good idea. We'll set it up on the landing Ronnie saw."

"And Caroline has the SLS. She's getting a few REM-pods, too," Eric added.

Peyton took the Ovilus Brian offered, hoping any energy they encountered would be recognized and voiced. Words would be a huge plus. In fact, *any* sound would be welcome as long as it drowned out the rumblings coming from her conscience.

"We need confirmation," she said as Caroline rejoined them. "Let's do this." She took a breath to reset her concentration and gather her nerve, and, as Eric stepped back to film their advance, she left Ronnie to her business in the kitchen.

Chapter Nine

Antique hinges complained when Peyton opened the old plank door. Stale air and cobwebs greeted her and the indirect light from the kitchen led her onto the landing. She switched on a night-vision camera with its green-lit screen and scanned the narrow musty staircases that led in opposite directions. A second later, Sam and his bulky studio camera arrived at their rear.

"Let's put the full-spectrum camera here, between floors," she said, and Brian knelt and positioned the DVR. "A REM-pod, too," she continued. As Caroline adjusted settings on the little device, Peyton turned to the flight down. "We'll go this way and put another at the bottom."

"Why didn't we set up a tripod in the basement before this?" Eric muttered as they worked their way down single file.

"I was going to," Brian said, "but…Guess I got distracted going for batteries."

Peyton shook her head at the critical mistake. Until now, she hadn't realized the error either and thought she must have been distracted as well. *Better get a grip.*

She edged out onto the hard-packed dirt floor and the others joined her, instruments pointing in every direction. Stone walls delineated the room which expanded beneath only half the house, and Peyton was glad they didn't have a myriad of small chambers to investigate. Most of the space was empty, except for nearby piles of McFadden possessions and new fixtures awaiting installation. An aging water heater somehow still survived in a front corner.

"EMF readings are steady," Caroline reported, wandering along the perimeter. "Oh. Here, they're not. The meter's climbing. Way up now." She retreated several steps when Peyton arrived to look and the readings returned to normal, but they spiked when Caroline again stepped closer.

Peyton pointed to an old pipe that ran from the ceiling and disappeared into the floor. They all looked down at the area.

"Dark blue," Brian reported. "Colder than anywhere else."

"Could there have been a well here that someone filled in?" She half-turned to Eric's camera and slipped information to viewers. "Water sources can promote energy, magnify it, which could explain these high readings here."

"An old well," Caroline repeated, nodding. "Used to be. An article I read said police found one of Georgina's victims in a basement well."

Peyton scanned the floor with her camera. "There were other victims down here, too, right?"

"Two. All her victims were men, by the way." Caroline went back to the staircase and set up a REM-pod on the floor. "The... ah...the three down here? Death certificates all cited poison."

Brian snickered. "She must have been some cook."

Peyton drifted to each corner of the room, camera in one hand, recorder extended in the other. "Is anyone here with us? Were you hurt in this house?"

Brian lowered his thermal camera to switch on the Ovilus.

Instantly, the computerized voice spoke. *"Sick."*

Every head snapped toward the device.

"Did Georgina's food make you sick?" Peyton asked the room, feeling her heart rate increase. "Did she poison you?"

"Us."

They looked to each other, all eyes energized as they contemplated the significance.

"How many of you?" Peyton yearned for the Ovilus to respond. "She made you sick? Were you all here together?"

"Muster."

Caroline leaned closer to read the word on Brian's screen. "Muster?"

Eric filmed directly over Brian's shoulder to capture the printed response. "Muster," he repeated. "As in muster the troops?"

Peyton's mind spun back to Ronnie's far-fetched scenario. "As in, maybe, they were reporting for duty?"

"Are there Yankees down here?" Brian asked.

Peyton raised the recorder again and turned in place. "Are you a soldier? Did Georgina poison you because you are a Yankee?"

"Cider."

Brian's mouth twisted as he stared at the word. "Cider?"

"Did Georgina poison you with cider?" Peyton asked. "It's okay to tell us. You are safe."

Caroline tried, "Help us tell your story."

Brian's Ovilus remained silent.

"The war is over," he said, "and we're at peace."

"We're *all* at peace now," Peyton added. "You can rest in peace also."

That damn deafening silence ate at her nerves. Yes, they'd received some choice words, but were they enough to confirm their suspicions about what plagued this house? She believed Ronnie had theorized correctly. The spirits of soldiers could be present, as could Colonel Wooster's. And Georgina Wallace's could connect everyone. And then there was cooking and poisoning, most likely multiple poisonings, and that consuming dark cloud in the kitchen.

The kitchen.

Brian shook his head at his blank screen and Caroline cursed the quiet under her breath.

Everyone jumped when the REM-pod at the staircase began beeping. The tiny light flashed vigorously, indicating some form of energy had passed within range. Then the REM-pod up on the landing sounded.

Eric panned up the staircase. "Going to the bedrooms or the kitchen."

"My guess is the latter," Peyton said, and immediately envisioned a resurgence of that dark mass surrounding Ronnie. She hustled to the steps, and they followed her up.

❖

Stirring the boiling pot of cranberries, Ronnie strained to multitask. It was frustrating as hell to talk to a cooking audience while eavesdropping on what was happening downstairs.

"Don't get distracted," she advised viewers, "not while berries are boiling. Keep the lid on as much as possible or you'll be chasing them around the room. Think grasshoppers in a jar."

She intercepted bits of the distant conversation, realized she hung on each question Peyton posed, and really wished she could make out what that computerized voice said.

"Sounds like the team's getting something down there," she told the camera, and figured Peyton must be pleased to elicit any responses. "Good for you." Even a modicum of success counted when you were as dedicated as Peyton, and, on Peyton, success was extremely becoming. Those eyes spoke so eloquently, and Ronnie wondered how deep a look they would permit. *Isn't there something about "a portal to the soul"?*

"Dangerous eyes," she murmured, careful to keep certain comments from being recorded. Some things even editors needn't hear.

She scooped out berry pulp and added ingredients to the crimson liquid, talking as she worked. "Once your sugar dissolves, add the cache of mulling spices. Go easy with the sugar, by the way. I know this is the pure stuff, only cranberries, and it's tart with a capitol T, but you're in charge of the sweetness." Her mind drifted to Peyton's sweet curves and sharp mind, the enchanting smile that wasn't seen enough on TV.

The term took her back. "Enchanting" perfectly described the feeling that consumed her here in the kitchen earlier, when she'd been the object of Peyton's prolonged gaze. Inappropriate timing for such thoughts to surface. They were especially hard to dismiss, though, knowing Peyton had appeared just as riveted by the sight of her. *What was on your mind, Ms. Stanford?*

Agitated beeping sounded from the basement.

"Uh-oh." She spared the doorway a glance as she stirred, then spoke toward the camera. "I think this place could be getting creepier by the minute. Maybe a thirsty spirit smells cranberries cooking?"

When the piercing beeps started on the landing, she whirled around. Her heart pounded a little harder at the idea of another bizarre entity joining her in the kitchen. And then she heard footsteps on the stairs.

"Hey, that *is* you, isn't it, guys?" She dashed to the table and grabbed a bottle by its neck, hardly convinced it would serve her well against anything paranormal. "Shit," she grumbled. "Look at me." *Some non-believer I am.* A wave of cold air rippled up her arms and across her neck, making her shiver in the sweltering kitchen.

The REM-pod fell silent as the crew paraded in. Caroline promptly hit the wall switch and dropped the room into blackness. The little lights from Peyton's and Eric's handheld cameras, Brian's thermal, and Caroline's EMF meter became dots in the dark. Then Sam added his to the mix, with Jamie close behind. Ronnie could do without all that eeriness in their half-lit faces.

"What's happening up here?" Peyton asked without looking at her.

"Well, just some beeps, except once you guys arrived, this big-time chill set in. No offense."

"I can see that," Brian said, staring at his thermal camera.

"Am I blue again?"

"Sure are. You still feel it?"

"Yup." Ronnie waved the bottle she held at the camera. "We need to add more of *our* spirits to this." She emptied the contents into the pot and stuck out her free arm. "Look at these goose bumps. Why am I cold?"

"Who just came upstairs?" Peyton asked the room. "Give us a sign please. Tell us your name."

Eric moved closer to record a close-up of Ronnie's entire arm. "Smells good over here. A witch's brew?"

"Not exactly. I just added more hard stuff to some homemade cranberry juice. The bottle I added earlier wasn't enough to make this a truly old-time libation."

Brian looked up from his screen. "Libations get my vote. What's in it?"

"Hard cider."

All cameras and instruments dipped as heads turned her way.

"What?" she asked the stunned expressions. "You'll like it. Honest."

"It's not that," Peyton explained, stepping up to peer into the pot. "From the responses we got in the basement, we're thinking Georgina did her deeds with poisoned cider."

Ronnie looked at the pot, too. "No way." She hadn't given it a second thought, choosing a hard cranberry cider to complement their meal, but now she actually wondered if the idea had originated with *her* after all. *How nuts is that?*

"When did you add the first bottle?"

"Not long after you all went downstairs."

"Why hard cider?"

"Why?"

"Yes, why did you choose that?"

"Well, what the hell would *you* choose? Milk? Cider's what you're supposed to use."

Peyton looked at Caroline, Brian, and Ronnie, and then into Eric's camera. "Our soldier may have reacted to it, come up here seeking a way out."

"A soldier?" Ronnie asked. "You've come around to the soldier theory?"

Peyton exhaled hard and shoved the recorder into her pocket. "Yes," she stated, her jaw stiffening.

Ronnie couldn't let it go. "Like one of those Civil War guys you claimed was 'a real stretch' to connect to this place?"

Peyton leaned in closer, her eyes simmering. "Yes. Okay? Please chill." She issued a flash of white-blue fire and turned away, holding up the Ovilus. "Soldier. If you're still with us, please let us know. Tap, knock, make some noise. Speak, please."

They waited but heard nothing.

Caroline whispered, "But could it have been Georgina on the stairs?"

"Georgina," Peyton called, "if you are here, signal us somehow."

Listening with the others, Ronnie peered around the room, trying to see things as everyone else saw them. She rubbed her arms and realized the chill had left.

But, at the doorway to the parlor, a REM-pod went off.

Caroline switched on the SLS camera and Ronnie strained to peek at her screen. Nothing showed other than colored outlines of the room's features. Suddenly, the white lines of a disjointed stick figure popped onto the screen, presenting in the doorway, and Ronnie took a breath, stunned.

"Fuck!" She slapped a hand over her mouth.

Caroline's body jerked. "There it is!"

Mesmerized, Ronnie watched the figure's arms rise in staccato movements. "It's little," she managed, curiosity overtaking her surprise. "Maybe five feet tall?"

Peyton hurried to see, leaning against Ronnie's arm. "Can't tell gender, though."

"You can't?" Ronnie whispered. "Maybe look for boobs."

Peyton slapped her shoulder. "Can you behave yourself?"

Ronnie fought back a laugh. "Sorry. Nervous release, I guess."

"What if it *is* Georgina?" Caroline asked.

"It could be." Peyton looked out over the device. "If you are a soldier, could you salute us?"

The figure's arms lowered but its legs flexed at the knees and shifted forward.

"Cold," Brian reported, "and coming this way."

Staring at the vacant doorway, Ronnie discovered her palms had grown damp. She rubbed them on her jeans. *What's harder to fathom, me here in this unreal situation or that inexplicable image on the screen?*

"Mrs. Wallace?" Peyton pressed, holding the Ovilus toward the doorway. "Georgina? Is that you? Wave to us please."

Silently, they watched and waited. A stick arm rose to shoulder height, and the body shifted toward them with a craggy step.

"Mine."

Everyone jumped at the unexpected voice from the Ovilus.

"She said, 'Mine'?" Caroline asked.

Peyton said, "Nothing here belongs to you, Georgina. Not anymore."

Eric turned to her. "What does she think is hers?"

They all hovered around Caroline's SLS screen. Peyton swiped hair from her face, determination hardening her soft features. She appeared ready to lunge forward, and Ronnie was captivated by the intensity in her posture.

The SLS showed the figure's arm bend at the elbow in the direction of the stove. Ronnie looked that way as well and found smoke billowing from around the burner plates.

"Smoke!" She hurried to disperse it with her hands. "There was some earlier, but I thought it was just from a nasty gust of wind outside."

"Georgina," Peyton said in a firm voice Ronnie thought impressive, "stay away from the stove. It is not yours. This is no longer your home." Ronnie stared, awestruck as the smoke petered out. For the benefit of the audience, she gave the camera a wide-eyed look and pointed to the stove. Peyton's tone hardened. "Georgina, you have no rights here. You must leave this place forever. Now!"

"Yeah," Brian added. "Your work here is done. Go!"

Her eyes never leaving her screen, Caroline stepped back. "She's coming toward us." Ronnie retreated out of her path. "She's—" Caroline looked up abruptly. "She's gone." She panned the SLS around the room, nodding. "Gone." She lowered the device and exhaled hard.

The REM-pod in the parlor went off next. Peyton dashed through the doorway.

"Damn," Eric said on a breath, and hustled after her.

Brian followed with his thermal camera back in action and Caroline on his heels. Ronnie shook her head as she turned to the stove. *Damn, this is some crazy stuff.* She gave her concoction a quick stir, waved for Sam, the camera, and viewers to follow, and hurried after them.

The REM-pod fell silent once everyone reached the front door, and Ronnie amusedly thought Georgina may have seen herself out. She watched as crew members checked their instruments, listening for any possible sound.

Peyton hung the Ovilus around her neck and focused on the green screen of her camera. Frown lines creased her forehead as she slowly pivoted in the entryway and came to a stop with Ronnie in her sights.

Ronnie saluted into her lens just to lighten the mood. "Anyone for cider?"

Chapter Ten

Ronnie actually had reservations about everyone eating supper in the kitchen, and having Peyton designate the room as a "hot spot" didn't help. She'd never had paranormal worries before but could feel today's unexplained creepiness gnawing away at her logic. In contrast, the team seemed to take the day in stride, caring more about warmth and table space, so she forced her focus back to food and prepared for everyone's arrival.

Sam and his camera crept closer as she piled roasted vegetables into a huge bowl.

"I never was a parsnip fan," she told him and the viewers, "until I discovered this old farmhouse recipe."

"I'll take the carrots," he said. "The other things, eh…not so much." Behind him, Jamie nodded in agreement.

"Our ancestors would be so disappointed." Ronnie waved her serving spoon at the camera. "All of you, give these a try. You'll be surprised what the sweetness of carrots can do for parsnips." She placed the bowl on the table beside a heaping basket of cornbread squares and continued addressing her viewers. "You saw how easy all this was to prepare. Some chopping, a little seasoning, some mixing, and toss everything in the oven for a while." She paused to point at the stove. "We've seen how much of a pain a wood-fired oven can be, but it really adds a special flavor. So, go ahead and try this outside, too."

"Like on a backyard fire pit?" Sam asked.

"Or a grill. And cover it, simulate your oven."

"No more talking." Brian strode in with purpose, rubbing his hands together. "God, I could eat the air in here, it smells that good." He lit two more candlesticks on the table.

Holding a skillet of golden chicken parts, Ronnie interrupted Peyton's walk to the table and fanned the aroma up into her face. "Yes? No?"

"Definitely, yes." Peyton inhaled appreciatively. "But I'm still annoyed with you."

"And your judgment is flawless."

"You had to be a smartass at exactly the wrong moment."

"I'm famous for my impeccable timing." Ronnie winked and Peyton sat down, shaking her head.

Sam stepped closer, focused on the skillet.

"Check out these beauties," Ronnie said. "Just enough time, don't spare the heat, use a trusty old cast iron, and voila!" She piled pieces on a platter with artistic flair and methodical patience, giving Sam time to capture her work.

Caroline lingered over the platter. "Wow, look at this. You just put these in the oven?"

"Yup." Ronnie passed out mugs of hard cider. "Really just skin-side down in a screaming hot pan." In an aside to viewers, she leaned toward Sam. "I used a little lard to stay true to the period."

"Lard?" Peyton looked horrified.

"Don't worry. A little won't kill you or your figure." She sat between her and Caroline. "I'm counting on this recipe being a hit with all of you—*everyone*," she said toward the ceiling. "It's just some basic seasoning, nothing fancy, because the typical household back then didn't have much beyond salt and pepper. Besides, most other spices would burn. Season later." She glanced at the camera. "And don't forget to flip the chicken about half-way through."

"Okay, *Casual Cook* people," Eric announced, tucking himself into the table. "Less talking, more eating."

Sam left his camera running, positioned perfectly on the counter, and followed Jamie to the table.

"Listen. I, ah…Taking a moment here." Peyton cleared her throat and looked at Ronnie. "As much as I wanted to strangle you earlier, and, well, maybe at other times, too, but… Considering all that went on here today, you have pulled off a miracle and I want you to know we appreciate it. Thank you."

The compliment took Ronnie aback. It was nice to know Peyton's manners could get her past their jousting. The temptation to call her on it, though, to see her eyes flare, her lips draw taught, that was hard to resist.

"You're saying that, unlike the last time, I wasn't my own worst enemy in the kitchen?"

Peyton's look advised her not to start trouble. "Apparently, so."

"Even though you sent Georgina up from the cellar to give me grief."

"Can't you accept a compliment without being an ass?"

Ronnie grinned. "Sure. I was just curious about where such a humble concession was coming from."

"It wasn't a humble concession."

"Oh, okay. I *did* think it sounded a little out of character for you."

"It was a compliment. Do you know what a compliment is? Must be a rarity for you because you obviously don't know how to accept one graciously."

"I guess the source is what threw me."

"Hey," Eric said, waving his fork from Ronnie to Peyton and back. "Not that either of you seems to give a damn, but if you don't quit it, we'll stick you in the corner."

Caroline bumped Ronnie's elbow. "This meal is terrific. You know, if Georgina or the colonel appeared right now, I'd ignore them."

"Uh-uh," Jamie said. "Can't do that. The whole purpose of cooking here is to pump up the action."

"And it worked—again." Brian grinned at Peyton across the table. "There's no question what roused today's activity."

"Hear, hear," Eric said, raising his mug of cider.

"Cheers to the Casual Cook," Sam added, and everyone drank.

Peyton turned to Ronnie, mug in hand. "No mystery ingredients, I take it?"

"No milk, either."

"No poison?"

"If your head hits the table, I promise to pick it up."

"Thanks a lot." Peyton shook her head while the others laughed.

"You know," Jamie said, pausing to drink, "I honestly never thought chicken could taste this good."

Too busy stuffing his face to speak, Brian nodded enthusiastically.

Peyton examined the cornbread in her hand. "At the risk of tossing you something you can't catch, I have to admit this is the best cornbread I've ever had."

Ronnie graciously accepted the many compliments, but Peyton's struck a chord. Maybe they could advance beyond the stilted, awkward maneuvering of strangers thrown into a single project, and shift toward mutual appreciation. She figured they already shared some degree of mutual respect, albeit muddled by exasperating head butting, but *appreciation* was different.

She gave that concept more thought as conversation dwindled and they devoured everything she'd prepared. She was pondering the significance of *attraction* when a heavy thump sounded in the parlor. Both the table and the wide plank floorboards beneath her feet vibrated as if someone had dropped a hundred-pound sack in the next room. Everyone stopped eating, even mid-chew. Then came a succession of faint knocks.

Peyton stared at the doorway, transfixed as if expecting something to materialize.

With a reluctant sigh, Brian shoved his chair back. "I'll go." He snatched a camera and recorder off the counter and hurried out. Eric left with camera in hand as well. Sam and Jamie jumped up and captured reaction at the table before chasing after the others.

"Poor timing," Ronnie whispered, thinking she should keep her voice down in case more knocks floated into the room. "But that *is* what this is all about."

"Oh, I *so* want to pass on this one," Caroline said on a sigh.

"You know? I think I might, at that." Peyton sounded frustrated, tired.

Ronnie looked from Caroline on her right to Peyton on her left. "I thought we had finished with the mysteries."

"It's hard to ever be sure. Have you had your fill for the day?"

"Mm-hm," Ronnie answered. "Need to give it all a rest for a while."

Peyton helped herself to more cornbread. "If I didn't know better," she began through a smug little grin, "I'd say we won you over today. Finally." Ronnie tried to dismiss the assessment with a shrug but that only made Peyton continue. "That haze in here earlier rattled the Casual Cook, and she knows it. And the stove—"

"And those EVP responses," Caroline added as she cleared the table.

"Okay," Ronnie said, and sat back. "Yes, it bugged me, not being able to explain them."

"Uh-huh." Peyton sat back, too, looking quite satisfied.

"You're pretty pleased with yourself, aren't you?"

Peyton wiped her amused smile with a napkin. "About as pleased as you are with this meal."

"Well, you two can toss all this around, if you want," Caroline said, "but I'm going to run some playback on the monitors. *I'm* supposed to be working."

Elbows on the table, Peyton rubbed her eyes and Ronnie wondered how long a day or night Peyton was willing to put in. She didn't budge when everyone left, and, for someone constantly charging forward, she appeared to have run out of gas.

I should have packed a couple bottles of wine.

"It's been quite a day," Ronnie said, rising to start on the dishes. "I know it certainly has for me, and, I'd guess, you guys, too. Do you still think Georgina's really gone?"

"I did until those knocks sounded. One or two can mean anything or nothing, but that was four in a row, so I'm not convinced. It's not that far-fetched to think that, after what, a hundred fifty or so years, a crazy woman like Georgina has figured out how to stick around."

Unsure what to think, Ronnie looked over her shoulder as she scrubbed, and watched Peyton stand and stretch her arms above her head. Her clingy polo shirt detailed every refined inch of Peyton's stomach and breasts, and Ronnie turned away from the titillating view.

Go there at your own peril.

"Now that I've eaten, I'm dragging," Peyton said. She pushed up her sleeves, warily eyeing Ronnie's pile of dishes. "Move over. I'll help. It's only fair."

"No, no. You're not helping, but thanks. This won't take long. Your ship needs its captain, doesn't it?"

"They're not adrift at sea," Peyton assured her, and yawned behind her hand. "Trying to get rid of me?"

Ronnie sent her a sideways look. "Not when you're preferring my company."

"Ha. I'm *preferring* a little escape from the chaos."

"Then, I'm just trying to keep your ship from running aground."

"Of course, you are." Peyton pinched the bridge of her nose. "I'll be joining them in a few. Right now, though, I really just want to leave things to the editing process, let those guys run with whatever that was."

"Hope no one squeals to the network."

"They wouldn't dare. Even you wouldn't." Peyton frowned at the tripod camera in the corner. "Besides, I'll swear you all to secrecy."

Ronnie understood Peyton's need for these few minutes away from it all. She hardly seemed ready for paranormal combat.

"The hotshots will think their crossover scheme backfired," Ronnie teased her. "They'll be crushed to learn that when we cranked up the paranormal activity, their star went AWOL."

Peyton dismissed that scenario with a flip of her hand. "The crossover didn't backfire. I'm sure the team is making contact out there as we speak, doing just fine without me."

"That's dereliction of duty, you know," Ronnie countered, grinning. "The network will take the star off your door."

"Will you quit with the star thing?" She set her hands on her hips. "Tell me you don't seriously think I have a freaking star. Jesus, Ronnie. Do *real* stars even have stars on their doors anymore? I don't even have a door." She laughed when Ronnie did, and Ronnie was glad to hear it.

"I think we're both pretty tired."

"Yeah. God, it's going to be a long night."

"Are you guys camping out here?" Ronnie shuddered at that thought. She'd survived horrendous thunder and lightning storms camped in a tent, but this place was just too...*active* to imagine it in the dead and dark of a calm night. Unlike the crew, she could leave at any time, now with dinner behind them, and her home and bed appealed in a very big way.

"Yes," Peyton said, "well, you aren't expected to, but we'll set up cots and spend the night."

"Hm. So now *you're* the Girl Scout."

Peyton leaned against the counter and grinned, reminded of the wisecrack she had delivered months ago. "Point for you, yes. We need a few hours' sleep before tackling the three o'clock hour."

"Three o'clock? Why three?" Ronnie doubted any of them would be sharp at that hour.

"It's a favorite time of night for paranormal activity."

"Isn't midnight when bad stuff happens? You know, all the witches come out?" She held up dripping hands and wiggled her fingers, mocked casting a spell.

"Midnight's for Cinderella or whipping up a snack. Not for agitated spirits."

"Well, that's one of many things I've learned from *Paranormal Pursuit*," Ronnie said, rinsing the last of the dishes. "I'll be counting them tonight instead of sheep."

"You do that." Peyton offered a weary smile as she headed for the door. "I'll quiz you sometime."

Chapter Eleven

By nine thirty that night, Peyton was ready to sleep for a month. Shuffling Ronnie's coolers and crates out and their own overnight gear in had eaten the last of everyone's energy. Adding to that, she was perplexed to feel more emotionally drained than usual. Ronnie was to blame. Their refreshingly civil one-on-one in the kitchen was a distraction she had to park somewhere before it gained any traction.

The house seemed almost *too* still since Ronnie's departure. Even the crew's spirit felt a bit depleted. *Has she only been gone an hour?*

"I've got fresh batteries for all our instruments," Brian announced as they watched camera footage and sorted through gear on the dining room table. "We can run all the cameras—including the one we now have in the cellar—we can run them straight through the night." He pulled up a chair next to Caroline at the monitors. "I'm actually looking forward to sacking out in the family room. I don't think the colonel will show, so I bet it'll be quiet."

Caroline gestured over her shoulder. "Well, that cot back there has my name on it and I'm very happy to be staying right here."

Eric nodded. "I'm banking on quiet in the cellar. Cold, but my sleeping bag can handle it. Just don't forget to wake me up if I sleep through my alarm." With a glance at Peyton, he added, "It may not be quiet for you in the kitchen, though."

Peyton considered that. By far, the kitchen had been the most active room in the house, and that fact she readily attributed to

Ronnie's efforts, but she had lived through creepier investigations. Here, however, the team hadn't been able to debunk that kitchen cloud incident, or the mystery of the smoking stove, or the stick figure that appeared to cause it.

Each occurrence could revisit her tonight, and Peyton found herself wishing she'd questioned Ronnie further about the cloud, its density, smell, speed, its weight upon her. And what if she needed expertise with the Glenwood? She actually wished Ronnie hadn't left.

"Let's set our phones for three o'clock."

Brian quickly established his alarm. "Ronnie left us the cookies, you know."

Eric took off for the kitchen. "Hey, there's a note on this cooler. She left us bottled water and leftover chicken," he yelled back.

Peyton wondered how Ronnie would react to sleeping on a cot in the kitchen. Probably wouldn't faze the Girl Scout, but a solo paranormal encounter could deflate that effervescent spirit of hers in an instant.

Eric came back and passed out cookies. "We're lucky Sam didn't eat them all before he left. These could be the highlight of our whole damn night." He held one up to the camera in the corner. "We're finishing them, buddy."

"Sam will curse you when he sees that on tape," Caroline said.

"Hey," Brian countered, "he and Jamie took off to find an ice cream shop. They get to lounge in the RV." He sneered at the camera. "No sympathy from us."

"I'm with you," Eric said, nodding at Brian. "They've got ice cream and we've got bottled water and cookies?"

"Don't forget the chicken. We'll devour that at three o'clock," Caroline said. "Thank God, Ronnie's such a good cook."

Brian slouched in the chair. "I kinda miss her, buzzing around, full of energy and ideas."

Peyton had to agree. Ronnie changed their routine, added a wide-eyed reality so often dismissed in their line of work, and Peyton could see the audience appeal she'd initially doubted. She had been so caught up in *Paranormal Pursuit*'s dominance, she hadn't seen any need for proactive adjustments to their process. Now, however, she couldn't ignore how Ronnie had grounded the show, humanized it in ways viewers were bound to appreciate.

Why, instead of behaving like a two-year-old, didn't I think this through in the beginning? Because she presses all the God damn annoying buttons even more than I thought she would. Because she can be a pain in my ass, especially on camera. Because the littlest exchanges turn into ridiculous snark contests. Because I wasn't expecting a woman to settle into my head.

Eric leaned toward her in his chair. "I'm surprised by how much she's added to our cases, stirred up activity. You are too, considering how you felt at the outset."

Peyton chose not to meet any particular pair of eyes. She'd mostly gained insight into herself and discovered she could be doing better. Evidently, Ronnie had tweaked her thinking.

"I am surprised, yes." *As much by myself as by her.* Peyton straightened in her seat and summoned her professionalism to the forefront. "I'm just really pleased we've learned to better appreciate kitchens."

Eric arched an eyebrow. That was pathetic and they both knew it.

"Yeah," Brian said, "especially when kitchens turn out as productive as this one. Good luck to you, sleeping in there."

They laughed as they separated for the night, and Peyton was pleased to see their spirits lift.

Alone now in the kitchen, she set the Ovilus, a lantern, and a walkie-talkie on the table, and changed into sweats. The lantern intensified the shadows in the large room, as if the memory of that dark cloud wasn't enough to rattle her. To keep her nerves in check, she stretched out on her cot and summoned the scene of their dinner gathering, of Ronnie confidently scurrying about, prepping and serving and chatting as much with the audience on camera as with them. Their individual approaches differed so dramatically, yet somehow seemed complementary, and she conceded that their fan bases just might agree.

After one last look around, she shut off the lantern and the world went black. All she could see were the two tiny "active" lights from equipment stationed across the room: the green one from the REM-pod on the floor between the basement and family room doors, and the red one from the static night-vision camera in the corner. At least they provided a bit of company in the darkness. She closed her eyes, wondering if her team had dozed off already. She, too, hoped to be consumed by sleep—and nothing else—for the next few hours.

But just prior to their alarms sounding at three, a lengthy high-pitched creak came from the family room door. Peyton bolted upright, instantly awake. The REM-pod began flashing, its piercing beeps loud enough to rouse the silent house. She fumbled for the Ovilus on the table and heard Brian's heavy footsteps approaching in the family room.

Caroline's voice came through the walkie. "Peyton? I've got you on camera."

Peyton finally found the Ovilus in the dark and switched it on. The computerized monotone spoke immediately.

"GO." The bright white capital letters made her blink.

Peyton shivered. "Georgina?" she asked the darkness. "Are you here?"

Brian appeared in the family room doorway, only his haggard face illuminated by the colored lights of an SLS screen. His haunted look gave Peyton another chill.

"I got this blast of cold air," he said quietly. "Shivered so friggin' hard, I woke up. Then that pod started."

The basement door latch clicked. Erik eased into the kitchen with his night-vision camera focused on her, his face bathed in devilish green light.

The REM-pod continued to strobe off both men as they advanced into the room.

Peyton stood and faced them, concluding that the three of them now surrounded whatever was tripping the device. She was tempted to light the lantern but didn't want to scare off this entity and lose the opportunity to interact.

"*We* are here now," Peyton declared over the REM-pod's beeping. "This home is for the living, not you." For a moment, she worried about agitating this energy to the poltergeist level, where projectiles could actually become a danger.

Brian switched off the REM-pod, repositioned it beside the stove, and activated only its light. No sooner had he stepped back than it began blinking furiously.

Something iron clinked and the stove's firebox door swung open. Nearby, the poker leaning against the wall clattered to the floor. Snatching it up, ensuring that no spirit would, Peyton glanced at each man and figured she looked just as shaken.

"You will *not* start a fire in that stove!" she shouted, raising the poker like a scepter. She surveyed the room for an orb of energy, a light anomaly, something.

The REM-pod went dark.

"Where'd she go?" Eric asked.

Brian panned the room with the SLS. "Nothin'." He swore under his breath. "Don't even try playing with us!"

From the Ovilus: "*Ron.*"

Peyton stared at the device. It vibrated as her hand shook.

"Shit," Brian murmured.

Eric leaned around his camera, his eyes wide.

Peyton swallowed hard, then took a deep breath.

"Ronnie is not here. She's not starting a fire, and neither are you!" She shook the poker vehemently. "*No one* is starting a fire in that damn stove! Do you hear me?" She turned in a circle as she spoke. "Georgina? We're assuming it's you. Give us a sign." The Ovilus, the entire room remained silent, and Peyton nodded. "I still swear it's her."

Nothing from the Ovilus.

"Dammit."

Eric whispered from behind his camera, "Anyone else freezing besides me?"

"Yeah, me," Brian said.

"And me." Peyton glared into the space before her. "Oh, she's with us for sure. Somewhere."

The frayed remnants of her patience dissolved. She had faced ornery spirits before, young and old, assorted forms of persistent energy that battled for dominance, but never had an elderly female *murderer* posed such a challenge. Aggravated now, and angry, she set the poker atop the stove, let it rattle loudly on the cast iron, and swore as she flung mussed hair off her face.

"God dammit, Georgina Wallace. You are leaving this place tonight. Now. This isn't your damn stove. This isn't your damn house."

They all turned when two distinct knocks sounded at the table.

"You listen to me," Peyton declared in that direction. "I'm talking to you, woman to woman. You can take any form you like but we won't be intimidated. Do you understand that? We're staying and you are going. Now, get the hell out!"

They stood motionless, waiting, listening, peering into the darkness.

Eric slowly released a breath. "I don't feel that chill anymore."

Caroline's voice from the walkie startled them. "Hey? Eh… Serious breeze coming into the dining room here. The front doo—"

The REM-pod at the front door interrupted her and they hurried toward it. Caroline met them there just as the device shut off.

"We've been here before," she said. "*Now* is she gone for good?"

They just stared at the door as the heavy brass latch jiggled.

Chapter Twelve

Ribs should be ready in an hour," Jeff said, dragging a lounge chair under the umbrella. "My wife says they're as fantastic as yours." He looked up at Cheryl for confirmation as she joined them by the pool.

Eyes closing, Ronnie smiled as she basked in the sun and inhaled the smell of barbecued ribs in the smoker. Lazy afternoons like this were what summer was all about.

"They're out of this world," Cheryl stated as she opened a bag of chips. She plopped into a lounge and reclined at Ronnie's side. "This will be the third time he's followed your recipe. God, they turn out *so* good. You'll see."

"Can't wait. I'm starving." Ronnie rolled her head to see Jeff. "I hear that smoker is your new best friend."

"Oh, you heard right. She's hot stuff."

"If you give it some woman's name, I'll never return your leaf blower."

He sipped his beer and shook his head. "Nah. No name yet. But what's up with *your* new friend? How's that going?"

Ronnie caught the conspiratorial glance he sent Cheryl. *Here we go.* She closed her eyes again and turned her face back to the sun.

"Peyton's stopping by next weekend, probably Saturday afternoon."

"Really?" Cheryl immediately set the chips aside. "Are you cooking dinner for her? Will she stay on the Cape long? Does this have anything to do with the advance screenings?"

Ronnie rolled her head toward Cheryl this time and squinted at her. "Damn, girl. Are you done?"

"Well, does it?" She drew her chair back upright. "Those test audiences loved both crossovers. Network's been patting itself on the back for a couple weeks now, for God's sake, so are they rushing to set up the finale? Is that why she's coming? What did she say? And why haven't I been notified?"

Jeff snickered. "I bet she's staying at your place."

Cheryl's animated look became impish. "She *is*, isn't she? Oh, yes!"

"No, she isn't." Ronnie sighed and sat up, righting her own chairback. "Jesus Christ. You guys are bad."

Jeff laughed as he went to check the ribs and Cheryl sat sideways in her chair to lean closer to Ronnie.

"You're doing the Cheshire cat thing, dammit. Come on, Ronnie, spill."

"Apparently, the network execs considered how the screenings went and don't want to wait too long before setting up the last crossover."

"The two-hour live one." Cheryl looked off to the fence, dreamy-eyed.

"I guess they see it as a ratings slam dunk, but the location has to be spot on, with all the accommodations for a live shoot. Peyton doesn't want to leave it up to them. She always selects their locations, but the network wanted to get involved for this one, and she told them no. So, she *has* to produce a winner. She called because she's having trouble with that."

"So, she needs you, huh?"

"She has a few promising sites but called to see if I had any ideas. We thought it best to get together so I can show her some locations."

"A perfect opportunity. She's coming alone, I hope. How long will she be here?"

"She's coming with Jamie and Caroline. They're flying in on Tuesday and leaving sometime Monday—and they've already booked a B&B in Chatham."

"Too bad at least she couldn't stay with you," Cheryl said as Jeff rejoined them.

"Hey," he offered, and tapped Ronnie's shoulder. "Make her change plans."

She chuckled at his encouragement. "Stop reading into all this. They have a busy schedule, seeing places with real estate agents, owners, and even some little ghost hunting group from this area. Plus, they'll be doing legwork on any potential locations. I told her to call when she's ready to check out some of my suggestions, so most likely Saturday afternoon."

"See?" Cheryl tried. "She should be staying with you."

"Things are fine just as they are."

"Ronnie."

"Look. Left to ourselves with no producer or crew around, we would probably frustrate the hell out of each other. How could we work together if things degenerated into arguing or slamming doors or…or throwing dishes? What then?"

Cheryl grinned as she sat back in her chair. "Sure. Ah-huh. Or cocktails and laughing and teasing and getting buzzed and spending—"

"This is about work, and our styles clash as it is."

"Please. You're overthinking this. It's only one show."

"Regardless. You know, I don't think we have one thing in common."

Cheryl raised both palms. "You're both gay."

"Oh, for Christ's sake."

Jeff snorted. "You're chicken, that's what you are."

"Ronnie," Cheryl tried, "you don't know what you don't know."

"I know our conversations always end up like challenges. Not that she's…combative, really. I mean, she certainly has a nice side, too, but usually we square off."

"And you can't handle that? *You*?"

"Definitely chicken," Jeff muttered.

"It's not about that. And I am not chicken."

"You are," he said, grinning, "and she sounds defensive, so she is, too."

Cheryl nodded at him and sent Ronnie a knowing look.

"Since when is the Ronnie Sharp I've known for twenty-odd years *not* attracted to such a dynamic woman?"

Jeff cleared his throat. "Don't forget the steaming-hot sexy part."

Ronnie rolled her eyes. The two of them were relentless. She reached for her margarita, which had become as watered down in the sun as her argument. "I'm not blind, but I have to be prac—"

Cheryl thrust herself closer. "That's a load of crap and you know it." She sat back, looking quite satisfied with herself. "Get in that pool right now. You're losing your mind in this heat."

Thinking it best to just keep her mouth shut, Ronnie hauled herself out of the lounge chair and dove in.

She shivered as she touched bottom and shot upward to daylight, and the bracing cold made her thoughts race. Such good friends with such good intentions, she mused. But she was right to exercise caution with Peyton, to keep a tight rein on emotions that hadn't seen active duty in some time. How could they work together if something developed between them? True, there would only be one more show to worry about, but they just basically tolerated each other *now*.

She climbed out of the water and toweled off, shaking her head at herself and the entire matter. All this concern was ridiculously overblown. No big deal.

❖

Ronnie trotted down the porch steps, a bit more amped up than she thought she would be to see Peyton. Being contractually bound to a project with a stranger had become so much more so quickly. They shared a professional—manufactured—relationship, but, after several months, they still set each other off in a heartbeat. Ronnie figured that was the spark she felt so often lately, the spark that had her smiling at Peyton's arrival.

But she couldn't help shaking her head at the rented white BMW convertible.

With all her wild curls somehow corralled into a ponytail and dressed casually in blouse and shorts, Peyton swung long, toned legs out of the car and set her sunglasses atop her head. Ronnie actually wished she had a camera. *If she wasn't already a network star, she should be.*

"Hey, ghost hunter," she said, knowing she'd once perturbed Peyton with the tag. "Too bad you ended up with a junk box rental."

Peyton held her hands out from her sides. "When you're worth millions, why not?" She offered a handshake and Ronnie accepted, then converted it to a quick, platonic hug.

"Come on in. GPS get you here okay, or did you have to flash those sweet legs for directions?" She heard Peyton chuckle as she led her up the steps.

"Took you all of ten seconds to jump back in the saddle."

"Just don't ever go investigating dressed like that." She held open the screen door. "You'll have spirits all over you."

"Thanks, I think."

"Let me get us drinks," she offered as they moved inside. "Something to kick off the afternoon. Fresh lemonade, maybe?"

"Anything cold would be great, thank you." Peyton entered the living room and Ronnie wondered how the beachy décor compared to a high-end urban condo. "This is adorable," Peyton said, turning in place, eyeing everything. "Did you have this done? Or did you design it all yourself?" She raised a hand quickly. "Silly question, right? You did all this."

"I did." Ronnie gestured around the room. "Make yourself at home."

"It's beautiful, really. It's certainly not the classic Cape Cod cottage," she continued, following Ronnie to the kitchen, "so much more spacious, airy inside than I imagined."

She sounded surprised, and Ronnie wondered if Peyton hadn't believed a homeowner, Ronnie in particular, could have created such a space.

"I can be dangerous with a hammer."

"Not a doubt in my mind."

"It was the first time I could afford to design an old farmhouse the way I wanted," Ronnie said, handing her the lemonade. "This kitchen was my priority." She watched Peyton survey her pride and joy. She doubted that someone who never cooked could appreciate all the quartz counter space or the professional appliances. The antique-brick wall oven, the custom cabinetry, and the meticulous country detail were probably lost on Peyton.

"You know I hardly spend any time in a kitchen, but there's no question that this is special, Ronnie. It's so breezy, so sunny."

"Thank you. It keeps me smiling."

"I love all this natural light. You shoot your show in here, don't you?"

"You've actually seen it?"

Peyton scowled at her. "*Yes, I have.* Well, a few. And I think I've seen bits of this kitchen before."

"We do most of our shooting here, yeah. Thank God it's big enough. It keeps the budget—and my stress level down." She waved her toward the rear door. "Behind you there are bedrooms down that far hall, and downstairs, I have an office and a couple other miscellaneous rooms, but out here," she led them onto a screened-in patio, "is where I usually hang out."

Peyton gaped at the expanse of grassland far beyond the stone patio. "I never expected to see that on Cape Cod."

Ronnie pulled out chairs for each of them and sat at the table. "Having a horse farm for a neighbor isn't as rare on the Cape as you'd think. There are twenty-two acres of serenity out there."

"I'd find sanctuary in it, too. I don't blame you." She sat as if dazed.

Ronnie pointed to a corner of her property. "And that is my forest refuge."

"I never would have guessed you had all this back here. How much land do you have?"

"Almost five acres, a couple of them woods for serious quiet time. I *do* contemplate nature, now and then."

"Seems a little out of character, but okay. You cook in those woods, too?"

"On a fire pit, whenever I can."

Peyton sat back and sipped her lemonade. "Year-round, I bet."

"Doesn't everyone?"

"I'm not sure I could handle the cold, cooking in a coat."

Ronnie had to smile at the image of Peyton bent over a cookfire in boots and mittens. "Nothing beats the smell of bacon on crisp morning air." She raised her glass and winked. "You might be surprised how much you like it."

Peyton laughed lightly. "Now you're pushing it."

"I just count my blessings." She wouldn't trade this precious location for anything. "With all the traveling you do for the show, is New Jersey 'it' for you?"

"Oh, God," Peyton said with a sigh, and brushed a loose strand of hair from her cheek. "I suppose I should know by now, but there's never time to focus on me, really." She shook her head. "Planning the show, covering every base, managing every detail every week, sometimes these past six years feel like forever. *Paranormal Pursuit* has been a catch-22: success provides the means but only if I stay on top of it."

Ronnie wanted to suggest she reprioritize things but thought better of it. And offering some jocular remark would be cruelly insensitive. "A wicked juggling act."

"Exactly. We rode atop the ratings for several years but lately competition has come at us from so many directions, diluted the viewership to where we're just holding our own." She leaned on the table and studied the glass in her hand. "The network wanted me bouncing all over the country, not focusing on New England this season, but I insisted. This region offers better, older locations, easier pickings, as they say."

"And they've seen you were right."

"Yes. Most of the shoots have been productive, especially our crossovers, although it kills me to give the network any credit for that concept. The historic themes should have nationwide appeal." She cast Ronnie a skeptical look. "Next season, though, God knows where they'll want us."

The impulse to sympathize rose in Ronnie's throat. *Thankfully I don't have such worries.*

"Well, if Jersey isn't 'the' place, you're bound to find it in your travels. I hope you can take advantage of all that traipsing around, make it worth your while…for you personally."

"Thanks. One day at a time." A pensive little smile reached her eyes and nearly took Ronnie's breath away. Suddenly, Peyton patted the table with emphasis. "It better be easier to find than the spot I desperately need for our shoot."

"No prospects yet?"

"Eh, nothing that's really struck me. So, I'm anxious about what you've got up your sleeve." She glanced at Ronnie's tank top with its Red Sox logo. "Well, if you had sleeves."

Both the tease and the quick inspection resonated. Knowing so little about this celebrity on her patio was torture. Having Peyton here, relaxed and unreserved, felt unexpectedly easy. The uplift in her own spirit was a noteworthy surprise. Even the tendency to joke and tease seemed muted.

Chapter Thirteen

Conversation covered everything from antique shops to clam shacks once they hit the road in the topless BMW. The wind in their faces was heated, the sun even hotter, but the drive was postcard beautiful. Even though anyone else doing it would have irritated the hell out of her, Peyton actually enjoyed Ronnie playing tour guide, her insights and enthusiasm as well as her humor.

She'd obviously been outside a lot in the weeks since their Connecticut investigation. Ronnie's lean athleticism was as evident as ever, but the bronzing around her tank top and shorts had been pleasantly disarming when Peyton pulled into the driveway earlier. Now, it glowed in the August sun, along with hints of red in her hair. The coloring deepened those lively dark eyes and made her trademark smile all the more magnetic.

Infectious, that's what it is. And, honestly, it's not just physical, is it? Funny, how I'm okay with all of it now.

But she had to face the risk of a growing distraction. The term bounced around in her head until she realized that *at*traction was more accurate. She considered trying not to look so keenly at Ronnie in conversation. That notion promptly flew off on the wind.

Ronnie directed her along the shore, where houses became fewer and farther between, and Peyton marveled at the glimpses of ocean around each curve.

"Take your next right," Ronnie said. "We're going up there."

Peyton slowed, turned onto old, broken pavement, and looked over the windshield to the hill ahead. "We're driving up there?"

"*You* are taking this immaculate, absurdly expensive sports car up there."

"Jesus."

"Unless you'd rather we get out and jog. It's a quarter mile or so."

Peyton's sunglasses thwarted her hard look, so she pursed her lips firmly. "Not today, thank you." She came to a sudden stop. "But I can let you out, if you feel the urge." Ronnie looked up to the challenge, sinewy muscles from shoulders to calves. *Probably runs the damn Boston Marathon every year.*

"I'll pass. I want to see your face when we get there."

Peyton cautiously picked up speed. "I just thought Cape Cod was flat."

"Where do you think bluffs come from?" Ronnie asked with that smirk Peyton had initially found impertinent. She didn't mind it as much now, had learned to let it slide. That sassy curl of her lips revealed more about Ronnie's character than even Ronnie probably realized, the confidence in her identity, her skills, and her positive approach to life. *And, damn, it's flirty.*

Ronnie sat up straighter, tugged at her seat belt, and Peyton stifled a grin at her apparent irritation with the restraint. As Ronnie absently tapped her long fingers on the doorframe, Peyton again saw the eagerness she infused into everything she did.

"Ready for my number one suggestion?" Ronnie said, pointing ahead.

"Your top choice, huh?" She slowed to dodge sizeable potholes. "No one's cared for this road in forever, it looks like."

"True. And yes, my top choice. I'm predicting it's the site of *Paranormal Pursuit*'s grand finale. Once upon a time—"

"When, exactly?"

"Well, I don't know *exactly* when it was built, but I've always heard it was sometime before nineteen hundred. It's called Miramar, originally somebody's mansion. Then, it was sold and converted to a grand hotel after the turn of the century."

"Prior to Prohibition."

"Yeah. It operated as a hotel for ages, but in its prime, it was *the* hot spot for well-to-do vacationers. You'll see the appeal once we get to the top."

"When was it last occupied?"

"I talked to a real estate agent in town last week and she thought it had been the family home until the nineties."

"And since then, what?"

"Over the years, developers have tried to buy it, but the great-grandson of the original owner is being a stickler. Apparently, he's asking an astronomical price and has stipulations about preserving it, and no builder has been willing to bend that far."

"So, it's been empty for thirty-odd years?"

"For the most part, I guess, yeah. According to the agent, the owner lives in Louisiana, Baton Rouge, I think, and he comes for a week or so every year just to wallow in the nostalgia. He's quite the character, it seems, around ninety years old, and still keeps a couple of rooms on the ground floor livable with portable gear."

"At ninety?"

"Yeah. Crazy, huh?"

"I'll say. Do you know if he's using a local property agency? Is it even on the market now?"

"I'm told it is. The legal firm he uses is in Boston, but his attorney lives on the Cape so he's reachable if you want."

"I'll call him as soon as we see—holy shit!" Peyton stomped on the brake and stared, some hundred yards from the crest of the hill. "My God. Look at this. It's…perfect."

Alone in an empty field, Miramar stood three stories tall. Multiple sharp rooflines included a lighthouse-like tower, all of which loomed large against the azure sky—and would be classically ominous in the dark. Traces of several paint colors were barely visible after years of seaside abuse, and what had been superbly crafted scalloped shingles now showed signs of rot. Elaborate details still clung beneath the eaves, to window and doorframes, and along the wrap-around porch.

Peyton turned to Ronnie in amazement. "Wow."

Ronnie beamed back at her. "Yeah, wow." She urged her to continue up the driveway. "From what everyone's told me, it's right up your alley. Haunted as hell."

Parking abreast of the broad staircase, Peyton looked up, trying to take it all in.

Without question, this aging Victorian could be one of the most classic, dramatic settings she had ever explored, and she couldn't fathom the extent of its paranormal potential. But would they get permission? The network itched to start the production clock. Their season-opening crossover would air and stream in two weeks and the network wanted to have details for this finale firmly established by then. They would have to move quickly to get through all the red tape.

"We've tackled forts, homesteads, asylums," she said with awe, unable to take her eyes off the building, "but this…"

"The setting's straight out of a horror movie, don't you think?" Ronnie asked, getting out and walking around to Peyton's door. "It's menacing, painfully beautiful." She stood with hands jammed into her back pockets, grinning behind black Ray-Bans like a kid with all the answers. "Well?" Impatient, she sank onto a hip. "Get out, for Christ's sake. Let's go."

She hustled away, her lengthy strides taking her around the corner of the building.

"Ronnie! Wait, dammit!" Hoping her sandals held up, Peyton broke into a trot to catch her. "Up here, being so isolated," she yelled, running, "it's so lonesome, it—"

She rounded the corner and slammed into the view. She felt her jaw drop. With a palm extended beyond her, Ronnie presented an uninterrupted one-hundred-eighty-degree vista of the Atlantic Ocean.

"Beat *this*, Ms. Stanford."

"Holy…I don't even know. Jesus, this is magnificent."

They strolled across the expanse of field, what most likely had been lawn in a previous life, and Peyton wandered toward the edge of the bluff. Ronnie slid fingers around her arm and drew her back several steps.

"Careful, Peyton." She pointed to the turf ahead. "Bluffs are unpredictable so keep your distance. It's a long drop to the water."

"Will do." A palm shading her sunglasses, Peyton surveyed the open ocean and endless horizon. "No wonder the family wants this preserved. God, I can't imagine what this is worth."

"Here on the Cape? Priceless." She tapped Peyton's shoulder. "*This* is where some Hollywood star should spend her millions."

Peyton chuckled. "Don't look at me, but if I did have that bank account…boy." She looked back at the building, just as majestic from the rear. "Sad that it's reduced to this today. Think of all the wild times that went on in such a grand spot."

"There once was a pool somewhere around here, too, I'm told, and a car barn coming up the drive. They say it was one hopping place during Prohibition."

Peyton stopped, her thoughts spinning. "If we ever got the okay to shoot here, I'd want a lot more detail about *those* days."

"Prohibition?" Peyton nodded and Ronnie gestured to the ocean. "Well, Cape Cod was rife with rumrunners back then. Bootleggers brought goods ashore undetected for a long time and used secret accesses to these beaches, like trails and tunnels, so…It wouldn't surprise me if they even came in right here and supplied Miramar."

Peyton felt her heart skip with anticipation. "Seriously? This beach? This hotel?"

"I don't see why not. Those days were 'anything goes,' so who knows what went on. You'd need to do some serious research."

Peyton's imagination ran wild as they walked back to the front. Bootlegging? High-rollers? Expansive parties? Gangsters, maybe? Even killings? The possibilities for residual energy here were endless. But time for all that research was in short supply. *We haven't even met the owner's attorney yet.*

Ronnie cautiously ascended the front staircase and bounced a little on the porch decking.

"Seems safe enough."

Peyton joined her and they peered through the etched antique glass of the main doors.

"Look at this entryway," she whispered reverently. "It's amazing."

"I know," Ronnie whispered back. "You could park five cars in there."

"Oh, I've got a really good feeling about this," Peyton mused aloud, her voice still hushed. "Such a grand old place."

"Is that a *Gone with the Wind* staircase or what?" Ronnie asked, equally quiet.

"Yes, absolutely."

"Why are we whispering?"

Peyton chortled as she straightened and tried the door. "Damn. I can't wait to get inside."

"Let's try to find another way in." Ronnie was down the steps before Peyton could stop her.

"Ronnie, stop! We can't just—We have to make arrangements!" Ronnie ignored her and disappeared around the side. "Jesus, woman. You're crazier than I thought." Peyton hurried down the stairs and followed. "Hey! Let's not get arrested today!"

❖

Peyton came in from the living room, chuckling as she slipped her cell into her hip pocket. "Now, they're going bar hopping in Provincetown. First time there for both of them."

"Let's just hope they can find their way back to your B&B. Hey, um…Are they 'family'?"

"Why? Are you interested?"

"What if I was?"

"I'd wish you luck."

"I didn't mean to be nosy, just curious."

"Jamie's straight and Caroline's still figuring things out."

"I see. So that just leaves…you."

"Like I said, good luck with that, sister."

Ronnie laughed as she collected plates and napkins from a cabinet, but she could feel that thought digging itself into long-term residence at the back of her mind.

She grabbed the pizza box off the island, the pitcher out of the fridge, and headed for the back door. This wasn't the fine dining

Peyton probably was used to, but this was *Casual Cook* territory. "All the more pizza for us," she said. "Could you bring the glasses chilling in the freezer?"

She arranged things on the patio table and lit several candles, shooting for relaxation, not intimacy in the setting.

No question, she was glad Jamie and Caroline had their own plans for the evening, because this day with Peyton had been too good to share with anyone else. They hadn't really squared off once. Maybe finding the location of her dreams contributed to Peyton's mood, because the weight Ronnie had seen in her eyes earlier seemed long gone. Or maybe it was the company. Regardless of the reason, Ronnie didn't want this day or their time together to end.

But was this setting too much? She wasn't sure how much Peyton would read into it—or how much she wanted her to.

Peyton stepped down onto the patio and paused. "Oh, this is *very* nice."

Ronnie watched her take in the porch and the distant pastures, muted now in the twilight. She looked good standing there as if she did it regularly, poised like the celebrity she was, her posture runway straight as always, but her demeanor decidedly at ease. Ronnie thought she could gaze upon her for hours—but not without longing. *Do I need to reel this in?*

Peyton inhaled and exhaled deeply, deliberately, her eyes closing for a moment. The day's sunshine had blushed her skin, her nose and high cheekbones, even the cleavage descending into her white blouse.

Ronnie felt that warmth stir her chest and wasn't sure it was appropriate right now. After all, they were co-workers here. She had no intention of taking this…this feeling any further, but, damn, she was only human.

Peyton set the frosted glasses on the table. "Margaritas? I'll pour. Are you a salted-rim girl?"

Opening the huge pizza box, Ronnie looked up again and tried not to fall into Peyton's eyes, so bright they glowed in the seductive candlelight. "A what—oh, um…No." She ran a hand back through her hair. "Not me, thanks."

"Me neither." Peyton poured for each of them. "Can't be bothered."

Ronnie had to laugh. *Somehow, she should have known.*

Peyton eyed the pizza and waited to hand her the cocktail. "God, that looks good. But I'm surprised you didn't want to make your own."

Ronnie straightened, prepared—and willing—to meet those eyes again, and exchanged a plateful for a drink. "Can't be bothered," she quipped as they sat. "Well, no, that's not really true. I *do* make them, but I'm being lazy tonight." She sent her a sideways look. "Besides, my dough balls are frozen."

Peyton's laugh was genuine, spontaneous, and unrestrained, and Ronnie added the moment to today's list of little victories, instances where Peyton relaxed that professional veneer she wore so well and shared her real self. The possibility that Peyton could be enjoying a freedom she rarely had made Ronnie both sad for her and pleased with herself, and she wanted to know more, do more. *Because I like her. A lot.*

Still smiling, Peyton raised her glass. "Well, here's to dough balls."

"And to my favorite pizza joint on the Cape."

Peyton took a healthy sip and her long eyelashes fluttered. "Well now." She ran the tip of her tongue across her lips. "I know my way around margaritas, and this is fabulous. You mix a mean drink."

"Glad you like it. But I'm a little heavy-handed with alcohol, so watch yourself. We've got a whole pitcher ahead of us." Poised to bite into a slice, she added, "Now try this. The shop owner, Dawn, makes everything herself, including the sausage."

Peyton moaned with approval as she ate, and Ronnie liked the sound of it. They shared grunts and nods of agreement as they munched their way through their first slices.

"These onions," Peyton said, tipping closer to examine the pizza in the box. "They're incredibly sweet, especially if *I* notice. Does she make them, too?"

"Yup. Dawn grows her own." Ronnie gestured to her substantial garden in the side yard. "I grow them, too." Peyton raised her eyebrows as she chewed. "Fresh produce, you know."

"I have to say the classic New York pie doesn't come close to this."

"Pizza is *so* underrated." Ronnie couldn't resist a little cheekiness. It simply slipped out whenever she felt this wired. "Sometimes I don't know where we'd be without it." She set a second slice on Peyton's plate and took one for herself. "How could we chill like this, with friends, watch movies without pizza? God forbid a New Englander watches a Super Bowl without it." She shook her head, pushing the point to amuse her. "I mean, who knows what momentous historical decisions were made over pizza? It may have saved the world, for all we know."

Much to Ronnie's delight, Peyton played along, her golden eyebrows inching closer together. "Oh, there's no doubt that pizza helped secure the Camp David Accord." She bit back a grin and her eyes sparkled. "Maybe even the Paris peace talks."

"Exactly." Ronnie leaned closer, confidentially. "But do the French make decent pizza?"

Peyton dropped back, laughing. "Honestly, Ronnie. I want one of *yours* someday."

"It'd be my pleasure," she said, wondering if the occasion would ever arise.

Chapter Fourteen

Peyton frowned at what remained of her second slice of pizza. "Jesus. What a…I never stuff my face like this."

Ronnie chuckled and set her piece aside to refill their glasses. "You're on the Cape, remember. Salt air makes you ravenous. It's some freaky science phenomena."

"Phenomena, huh? Well, you'll get no argument from me. It's all delicious food for thought."

Peyton sat back with drink in hand, content to simply enjoy the moment, but found herself contemplating far more than that. She'd dealt with phenomena for years but never like this. *This* outdistanced her comfort zone, her practiced readiness for whatever life presented, for whatever showbusiness or some inexplicable sound or shape asked of her.

No, *this* was a restful, easy, sheltering phenomenon, and it sent her back to before professional dictates reconfigured her life. With a jolt she barely concealed, she acknowledged that the revelation came from her soul. Someone she hadn't even wanted to meet last spring supplied this undemanding moment, someone kindhearted and yes, sometimes maddeningly annoying, but undeniably charming. Their connection felt curiously profound.

And now there were jitters in her stomach. *How much have I had to drink? Don't blame the pizza.*

Night had fallen and the enclosed porch had coalesced into their private sanctuary, romantic in candlelight. Peyton surreptitiously observed Ronnie, leaning back in her chair, staring off at the fireflies beyond the screen. Legs extended, ankles crossed, Ronnie ran a hand through her hair, possibly feeling a little ponderous in this tranquil silence.

Peyton traced a finger through the condensation on her glass. "Thank you for this tonight, for this afternoon. I really appreciate all of it, your hospitality, your help with the location."

"You're so welcome. We didn't argue much either, did we?"

"Not much." But the look Ronnie sent as she drank was mischievous.

"That could change, you know."

Peyton raised her glass. "Promises, promises. I don't scare easily."

"So I've seen, and that's a good thing."

Peyton shifted in the spacious wicker chair and crossed her legs, still replaying memories of the relaxing afternoon. The tingle rising along her calf said Ronnie appreciated what she saw.

Okay, yeah, so I asked for it.

She tried not to smile when Ronnie finally caught herself and averted her eyes. Nothing wrong with a little innocent flirting, she mused, and watched Ronnie busy herself with closing the pizza box.

Just what are we getting ourselves into?

Ronnie settled back in her seat, drink in hand. "We were so lucky to see Miramar on a perfect day. I'm glad you had the chance to get the full effect."

"And I can't thank you enough. That memory's never going to fade, Ronnie. It was perfect all around." She took a drink as she pulled out her phone and stared with wonder at an overall shot of the building. "The team will go nuts when I send them these pictures." Abruptly, she flopped the cell onto the table. "I'm pretty sure I can convince the attorney, but that owner. He could be the stumbling block to all this."

"At least you reached the lawyer tonight. You said he sounded intrigued, flattered, even. It's not every day that the star of a number-one TV show gets you on the phone. So, that's a positive sign."

Ronnie's team spirit gave Peyton hope. "If we get the okay, the network will push us right into production. We'll really have to crank up the research process." She took another sip. "So will you."

"Oh, crap. That's right. Roaring Twenties food." Ronnie scrunched her lips and looked adorably perplexed. "But we could end up with more time than we think, if the attorney drags his feet getting the owner's okay. Won't that piss off the network?"

"They'll be all over me about that, so it can't take too long." She shook her head as she topped off both their drinks. "Never could understand why they insist on having so much in the can before a season launch, especially these days when things are done so much faster, digitally." Ronnie agreed before taking a drink. "Totally unnecessary stress, if you ask me," Peyton added.

"For now, all we can do is root for the attorney—and whatever Miramar has to offer. Supposedly, that's a lot."

"Tell me what you've heard. Who, what's in there?"

"Oh, wow. Miramar's legendary. The locals, kids, real estate people, they all have tales to tell, so who knows what's legit." She paused to sip her drink and Peyton noticed the quizzical look she lent the glass, maybe surprised to see it almost half empty already. Or maybe she was pondering that legitimacy.

"What do *you* think?" she asked. "I mean, now that you're an *experienced paranormal investigator*."

"Hell, I'm not that, that's for sure." Ronnie sat back looking thoughtful, hands cradling her glass. "But I'll be realistic. Miramar's been sitting up there, naked, succumbing to Mother Nature's every whim for ages, over a hundred years of blizzards, hurricanes, salty wind, and scorching sun. A wooden structure can only take such a beating for so long before things start to crumble and snap, to creak and sway. Severe drafts, the clouds of dust and sand, they're all reasonable to expect so I don't know how much credence to give—"

"But you've faced the hard-to-believe, heard actual responses out of thin air. You've seen firsthand that the unexplained really exists."

"I'll grant you, I'm curious, yes."

Peyton frowned, disappointed that Ronnie wasn't more on board. "I guess I'll take that."

"Hey, I'm excited to explore the place." Ronnie quickly gave Peyton's hand a reassuring squeeze. "Don't get me wrong. Apparently, plenty of intriguing things happen at Miramar. I was told that more than one potential buyer has lost interest after touring the place because too many weird things happened. Even the lights turn on by themselves occasionally."

"Really? And can you explain that?" She really wanted to heighten Ronnie's interest. And it was fun trying.

"Well, I-I can't. Um…Maybe static electricity?"

"Residual energy? That's what EMF readings are all about."

"That's your domain. I don't know anything about that stuff. But there's plenty for you guys to sink your teeth into…like the ghost."

"Oh, so now you believe there's a ghost."

Ronnie's jaw flexed. "It's what people have said. *I've* never seen him."

"Therefore, the ghost probably doesn't exist?"

"Do you want to hear about Miramar or just needle me?"

"'Needle'? Now, there's an idea." She'd never been the teasing type but couldn't resist ruffling Ronnie's feathers. She crossed her arms, grinning. "Please go on. Tell me about your ghost."

"Listen, I've never…It's not *my*—" Ronnie recognized the taunt and cut herself short. "They say a man wearing formal clothes from the twenties haunts the place. I don't know who he is, though, or how or if he's even connected to the building."

"Probably is. I want to check it out."

"Well, he's dark and blurry, I guess, a big guy, like tall and well over three hundred pounds, and a dapper dresser. People have seen him a lot, full-length, fedora to spats, on the stairs, the dance floor, in the kitchen and dining area."

Can't wait to get in there, Peyton thought as her attention drifted into the Roaring Twenties. She pictured a bull of a man overseeing rollicking crowds dancing the Charleston to lively bands, prohibited alcohol flowing like water…

"And supposedly this dapper ghost smokes cigars," Ronnie added, bringing Peyton back to the present. "Folks say they often smell it whenever he appears."

That's not surprising, Peyton knew, and a promising sign. Smells were so critically important, such as with Ronnie's cooking. Then, in a panic, she shot up a hand.

"Wait. Stop. Shit, dammit. How did I not think of this until now?" *Because I'm frigging buzzed.* "Do you know whether the kitchen is functional?" She hurriedly uncrossed her legs and shifted to the edge of her seat. "If it's not, we're screwed. No Miramar. You realize that, right? Why didn't we peek in the kitchen? Or did we?" She pinched the bridge of her nose. "Jesus, I can't remember. I don't think we did. Did we?"

"We did," Ronnie said softly.

"Because it's impor—We did?"

Ronnie laughed.

Peyton rolled her eyes at herself, silently cursed her foggy brain as she sagged back into her chair. "Sorry for the freak-out. I completely forgot."

"Check your pictures. You took a couple, fought through the reflection off that window. Remember seeing the little propane stove on the counter?"

"Yes!" Peyton lurched upright and keyed her cell. She swayed in her seat. *Oh, I'm in great shape.* "I remember now. A camping stove, you said." She struggled to fine-tune her memory as she flipped through her photos. "Here it is, with the little propane bottles on the floor." She swiped to the next image. "These shots were so tough to get through the…the…" words trickled out as she grew distracted, "through the glass. Look at this." She handed her the phone. "The row of propane bottles under the table."

"Yeah, so?"

"Flip back one picture. There are four of them." She watched Ronnie examine the image. "Now go forward again. In that shot, there are only three."

Ronnie looked up, bewildered. "There were only a few seconds between these pictures."

"And no one was around."

Ronnie studied the photos again. Her interest in something Peyton took so seriously was gratifying. Apparently, Peyton did stand a chance of persuading her to buy into the case one hundred percent. Having Ronnie closely aligned with their effort, aligned with *her,* hadn't mattered much before, but it did now.

❖

But all Peyton's pondering really wasn't addressing the immediate issue. She labored to clear her head. Miramar was a challenge she couldn't afford to lose, not if that bottle incident was an indication of activity inside.

She took another look at the photos. "So, this shabby little room was an addition off the back, wasn't it?"

Ronnie nodded. "Right, obviously not the actual kitchen. This room has to be what the owner used in a pinch, probably because the real kitchen is a lost cause."

Peyton resorted to another long sip as her mind raced and her hope teetered. She wanted Miramar for their finale in the worst way, but without a kitchen, there could be no *Casual Cook*, no crossover.

"Shit."

"Hey," Ronnie said through another laugh, "Don't worry. I'll finagle something."

"Oh, right. We're going *live* for this finale, don't forget. This room is a wreck."

"Well, it can be cleaned, at least. I have one of those stoves and a couple of better models, too. I can get by in a crisis. Hell, Peyton, I've cooked on the ground." That self-confidence bolstered Peyton's faith. She wanted to believe Ronnie could save the day, and, watching her rise effortlessly, not showing the slightest margarita influence, Peyton believed she could.

"But I might not be able to use a 'period-appropriate' method," Ronnie said.

Peyton didn't look up at her, didn't want to see doubt in her eyes. She nodded vaguely toward the table, then twitched in surprise when a fingertip lifted her chin.

"Don't look so glum," Ronnie said. "We got this."

The gentle touch vibrated through Peyton like approaching thunder. The reassurance heightened its impact, left her overwhelmed, and she desperately wished she was a bit more clear-headed.

"Yeah, well…Right now, *you've* got this. *I've* got a little less."

"You focus on getting permission. I'll take care of the *Casual Cook*."

"Miramar's classic, Ronnie. It can't slip away." She heard the plea in her own voice, knew her practicality was succumbing to alcohol. She stood, too unsteady for her liking until Ronnie slid an arm around her waist. Now, she had to tamp down sensation as well. "Thanks. Looks like I was a little too thirsty for my own good."

"Oh right. You're such a lush."

"Not true. Lush is a pretty old-fashioned word for you."

"How old do you think I am?"

"Loaded question."

"No guesses?"

Peyton narrowed her eyes to assess her. "Hm. Thirty-five."

"Wow, you're good." Ronnie started to steer them toward the kitchen but stopped. "How old are you?"

"Old enough to know lush is an old word." When Ronnie grinned and moved them on, Peyton added, "And young enough to admit I'm thirty-eight. Why?"

"Huh?"

"Do you have a problem with that?"

"With what? Of course not." Ronni stopped again and looked directly at her. "What if I did?"

"Do you?" Peyton searched her eyes, those rich, warm pools of dark chocolate calling her name. *Pressing your buttons for a change is delicious fun.*

"Do I have a problem with what?" Ronnie asked. "Your age? No. Why?"

"Well, *you* brought up the age thing. I'm wondering what you think about it."

"About you being thirty-eight? Hell, I don't know. Nothing. I don't think anything about it, one way or the other. I don't really care."

"Then, why did you ask?"

They'd been stopped at the steps to the kitchen for a while. Ronnie released her and raised her arms in futility. "I just wondered, you know? You're making something out of nothing here, Peyton. We're practically the same age. That's all. I…"

"You what?" Peyton swayed.

"I…I don't know what." Ronnie shrugged. "I-I guess I like it, that we have that in common." She ran her fingers back through her hair and sighed. "Okay? Can we go in now so I can show off my coffee skills?"

"You're a barista, too?" Peyton asked and turned to climb the three steps. She wobbled going up and hated having to grab the doorframe for balance. Across the threshold, she turned back for a response and enjoyed the height advantage that drew Ronnie's attention up to hers. "You're going to conjure up espresso?"

"Honey, you wait and see what I conjure."

Having spent years dealing with surprises, Peyton stood confidently blocking the doorway, effectively daring Ronnie to climb the steps toward her. She didn't think twice about the suggestive stance, didn't stop to attribute it to her fuzzy brain or liquored self-control. For whatever reason *she didn't care to consider*, it was a dare she was willing to lose.

Ronnie came to a stop in Peyton's personal space, tantalizingly close. Peyton hadn't expected her heart rate to rise or her breath to catch in her throat. That only happened during investigations when she was excited or nervous.

A knowing smile rose at a corner of Ronnie's mouth, and she cupped the edge of Peyton's shoulder. "Espressos coming up."

"Was I swaying?"

Ronnie grinned. "A little. Like talking to a moving target."

"God." Peyton blinked. "Amazing, all the melodrama alcohol can produce."

"I bet neither of us puts down a pitcher of margaritas very often."

"You'd win that bet."

Ronnie nodded toward a stool at the kitchen island. "Have a seat."

Peyton watched her steady gaze soften and found it impossible to look away. "You mean before something dangerous happens." *Did I just say that?*

"What's your definition of dangerous?" Ronnie asked gently. "Or should I ask how much leeway we should grant tequila?"

"Be careful granting leeway to spirits."

"Says the superstar spirit chaser."

"I'll make a believer out of you yet."

Ronnie laughed lightly. "Keep trying."

Suddenly, Peyton thought that if Ronnie didn't kiss her right now, she'd kiss Ronnie. Peyton's diluted self-control wavered, and a sigh escaped. She knew she should care what it said, care about propriety, but right now she couldn't even spell the word. She had initiated this doorway meeting, so what did that say? Could the booze have driven her this far off kilter?

"Some working relationship we have here, isn't it?" *God. That's all I've got?*

"Yeah. And we thought tequila was dangerous. Time for espresso." Ronnie tipped her head toward the machine on the counter and went to work.

With her feelings now a jumbled mess, Peyton acknowledged that the urges roiling through her most private places were leveling off. The deafening heartbeats softened, and now she could actually hear her conscience well enough to listen to it.

The cushy living room furniture appealed as a safer, smarter alternative to the kitchen stool, so she relaxed into one of the large, upholstered armchairs. At least her self-control hadn't dissolved into a total loss. It could be rebounding.

"This room is so tranquil," she said, loud enough for Ronnie to hear. "I need a place like this to unwind." The sky-blue walls and vanilla trim were a soothing combination. The driftwood accents, the fieldstone fireplace, and the rich greenery of the houseplants all contributed to a calm she appreciated. A modest-sized room, uncluttered and welcoming, a lot like its owner.

"That's my everyday room," Ronnie answered from the kitchen. "You'd laugh if you saw my place to unwind. It's downstairs. I'll show you sometime."

"Tease. A room for Ouija boards and séances?"

"Yeah, right." Her head popped into view, and she eyed Peyton slyly. "Try mirrors and leather." She disappeared back into the kitchen.

Whoa. How to stay so toned and fit... No.

"Get back in here! Talk to me, Sharp!"

"Ah, the gentle sounds of a commanding ghost hunter!" Ronnie yelled back and entered the room with espressos. "Just kidding about the room. It's my time machine back to the seventies. Turntable for vinyl, state-of-the-art sound, black lights, the original 'escape room.'"

Peyton sipped her coffee and nestled deeper into the chair, picturing Ronnie's creation and her in it. "I think 'groovy' is the word for that. A far cry from mirrors and leather."

"Well, it *is* soundproof, so…"

"The option is there to convert at any time?"

Ronnie snapped her fingers. "At the crack of a whip."

"Good one," Peyton said on a laugh, and almost spilled her coffee. She dabbed a napkin to her mouth, grinning at a memory. "I once dated a woman who was into whips and leather, back in college in LA. We went out for three months before she shared that side of herself."

"I can't see you being into that."

"Definitely not my thing." She almost shivered as the past came back clearly. The fog in her head was lifting and she was relieved. "Like I said, three months." She sipped again. "I wasn't into her BDSM and she wasn't into my paranormal. Today, she's a producer on Nickelodeon."

"Really? And you've gone on to fame and fortune chasing spirits."

"Shaking in my boots for everyone's entertainment. I've adapted, though, and learned to handle the fright as well as the pressure, but it's all still pretty stressful." She set her empty cup and saucer on the coffee table. The espresso was working, thank God, buzzing through her system and kicking the alcohol into submission.

"A lot of stress, I'm sure," Ronnie said. "Please know you're welcome to visit my time machine anytime you feel the need."

"I appreciate that, thanks. I might take you up on it." She leaned forward on her thighs, gauging her stability. Reluctant or not, she did have to bring this evening to an end and she had doubts about driving.

"Hey, I don't offer my *groovy* hideout to just anybody, you know," Ronnie added. "It's private and refreshments are free. The home-grown ones are particularly relaxing."

Damn, if this woman doesn't make me smile.

"Sounds dangerously intriguing." Peyton reached for her cell and punched in a number. "Excuse me for a second, but…speaking of being 'particularly relaxed,' I'm playing it safe and calling for a ride. I think my BMW would rather spend the night in your driveway than submit to my sloshy command right now."

Ronnie laughed. "I could have given you—"

"As if you're in much better shape."

"There's a guest room right down that hall and you are more than wel—"

"You're sweet to offer but we have an outrageously early appointment in the morning." She mouthed a "thank you" before speaking into the phone. "They're only a few minutes away," she said, standing when the call ended, "but…back to this hideout of yours. You make it hard to resist."

"Good." Ronnie stood and set her hands on her hips. "Listen. After we wrap this crossover, come and spend a few days. It'll be after Halloween, but the weather will still be decent enough for relaxing walks on the beach. We can chill out downstairs and eat like pigs. I hear the cook is pretty good."

"She's *very* good. And very generous."

"Shutting off the world for a while would do us both good. Please consider it at least?"

"I promise. Thank you."

Ronnie walked her to the door and handed Peyton the BMW keys. "I'll open the garage. Tuck your mean machine away for the night and you can pick it up whenever your schedule allows. Just punch in the words 'car code' on the keypad if I'm not here."

"Thanks, Ronnie." Peyton moved the car inside and Ronnie closed the door. "Tomorrow looks to be a crazy day, but we'll do our best to get it out of your way."

"No worries."

Peyton sighed hard as the Uber swung into the driveway. "Unfortunately, I have to climb a mountain tomorrow. I think securing Miramar is going to be a challenge."

"Wish I had more inside information on the owner for you."

"You've given me so much already." She opened the car door and placed a hand on Ronnie's upper arm, an affectionate gesture she hadn't expected to make. "You've been a huge help. And today has been a joy."

"You know, I wasn't sure how we'd get along, left to our own devices, and all. I guess that was silly."

"I confess to that, too. You'll be my first call tomorrow, after I meet with the attorney." The promise jumped freely off her lips.

"You don't have to do that, but thanks. I'll be waiting." Ronnie surprised her by drawing her into a hug. Flustered by the gesture, unsure she could keep her own feelings in check, Peyton guardedly set her hands on Ronnie's sides. "Good luck, Peyton. You'll convince the guy. He won't be able to resist you."

Snug in Ronnie's arms, against her chest, Peyton tried not to lose herself in the solid feel of Ronnie's torso. Self-control was slipping away.

"I want our show at this location," she admitted softly, "and I want you there."

Her knees weakened when Ronnie slid both palms to her shoulders and held her at arm's length.

"Me, too." Ronnie tipped her head slightly and lowered that easy smile.

Peyton knew what was about to happen and she could hardly wait. Impressed Ronnie would take such a step, Peyton welcomed it, even wished she herself had taken the initiative. Something inside her dissolved with that slow, gentle kiss.

Ronnie flexed her fingers into Peyton's shoulders as she drew back, but Peyton wanted more and that stunned her. There was no escaping the tenderness or the honesty Ronnie offered. Heat chased that sizzling kiss right down to Peyton's feet and she knew her entire world felt it.

Taking both Peyton's hands in hers, Ronnie gazed down at them and shook her head slightly. Peyton wondered if she regretted the kiss. Locks of hair slipped forward and shadowed her face, and Peyton was tempted to comb them back with her fingers.

"So…" Ronnie began on a breath and met Peyton's eyes. "Some working relationship we have here."

"Y'think?"

Ronnie cocked an eyebrow and grinned. "Will you hate me in the morning?"

The look of playful challenge grew more alluring each time Peyton saw it, and she couldn't resist responding in kind. "In the morning? I hate you now."

"I'm flattered."

Peyton tapped Ronnie's lips with a fingertip. "Me, too."

Chapter Fifteen

Ronnie clapped excess flour off her hands and darted for the phone on the table. She'd tried to avoid clock watching all morning and now it was after one. *Finally.* Peyton's meeting with the attorney had been at eleven and certainly was crucial, but that kiss last night had planted itself at the front of Ronnie's brain from the moment she opened her eyes this morning.

She stayed in bed an extra hour, wondering if she'd overstepped, if her raging libido had spoiled everything or flung her into something life-changing. How did Peyton feel about it in the light of day?

Not knowing was a killer. A blazing shower hadn't helped settle the mental wrestling. Neither had baking a Boston cream pie or enough cheddar cheese biscuits for half of Cape Cod. Jamie and Caroline had flashed in and out for the BMW without any indication of Peyton's state of mind. And Cheryl's call at noon only made things worse. Her arrival—and inquisition—were imminent.

Taking a breath to steady herself, Ronnie read the phone number she had been waiting to see.

"Hi. I really haven't been doing laps around the phone or anything."

Peyton's light laugh meant so much. She didn't sound like her world was a mess, that the attorney had crushed the Miramar plan or that she'd stayed up all night wishing she'd slapped the whack-job who kissed her.

"Hi," Peyton answered. "If I could get EMF readings over the phone, yours would send the needle flying. I wish I had your energy."

"Well, you sound energized. How are you?"

"This morning I was energized. Not so much now. We're in waiting mode. I didn't really expect to finalize an agreement with one meeting, but I was hopeful. To be left hanging was rough."

"What did he say? Was he receptive, at least?"

"Yes, and he was very polite and formal. We laid everything out for him, gave him the package, literally, fact sheets, clips of both shows, all the financial and liability details. Initially, we thought Jamie had him wrapped around her finger." Ronnie heard snickering in the background. "You don't know a Roland Meyers, do you? He lives in Brewster."

"Sorry. Doesn't ring any bells."

"Damn. Well, I think our most persuasive avenue was with the publicity this could mean for selling the place. That really appealed to him."

"Hell, a two-hour commercial for Miramar, nationwide? Oh yeah. I'm sure he saw dollar signs everywhere."

"Absolutely, but the problem is reaching the owner, Sebastian Baker. He sounds a little eccentric. Apparently, he's been 'incommunicado' for weeks and will be for several more. Meyers has authority to engage with a sale, but our proposal is beyond his purview. He's going to try to reach him."

"Where the hell is he, the moon?"

"Meyers wouldn't elaborate. We really pushed the money factor, though, and I *am* confident we'll get the green light once Baker is made aware, but the network has to be patient, and that's a problem."

Peyton's frustration grew painful to hear. In the background, Jamie and Caroline discussed their upcoming flight home, and Ronnie suddenly felt constricted by time. She had hoped for a few private minutes with Peyton today, but in an hour, all three of them would be gone.

Considering how last night ended, Ronnie wanted to help more than ever, to see Peyton face-to-face and discuss *everything*. She'd love to segue from this high-priority business conversation to a personal one but would never insult the gravity of Peyton's situation. Besides, what if Peyton didn't want co-workers overhearing private details or knowing that something special happened? What if Peyton didn't want to bring up last night at all?

Ronnie sat at the table, frustrated, wondering if she should even be hoping for exclusive time together again. At least she could offer support. That was safe.

"Go make your case to the network, Peyton, and don't let them bully you. This is *the* location and it's worth waiting for. Bring Max and have her throw your star power at them."

Peyton sighed and Ronnie could feel her weariness.

"Thanks. I appreciate that," Peyton said, her voice hushed. "You're sweet, you know?" Ronnie let that blossom in her chest before Peyton continued in her usual voice. "But the network's so anal about having things locked up in advance. Not only could it take weeks to get an answer, but that answer could be a 'no.' The network won't risk waiting if it could come away empty-handed *and* behind schedule."

"This blows, you know." Ronnie paced into the living room and back. "Look, I'll help you find another place, if you want, an alternative in case—"

"I think you know I'd enjoy that, but if the network finds out 'plan B' is immediately available, that's where we'll end up. I want Miramar, Ronnie. I do. Shit. Now, I'm whining."

"You're entitled to whine. Listen, I'd love to poke around more spooky houses with you, too, but if we don't, how much waiting time can you weasel out of the network?"

"I might be able to get two weeks. It'll be a fight, but…maybe."

"Our opening crossover drops in two weeks."

"Arggh! I know!"

Ronnie pictured the wrinkles above Peyton's nose, the look of heavy consternation across her face. Peyton could use some of last night's leisure now. This dilemma would consume her all the way back to her New Jersey condo and beyond.

Peyton spoke away from the phone, something about a suitcase, and came directly back firmly in debate mode. "You know, there isn't one decent reason why we can't shoot *during* the season. No argument for it holds water. We can shoot as soon as the ink is dry, whenever that is."

"How late in the season are you willing to wait?"

"Well…" She hesitated, caught by a black-and-white deadline. "As late as possible, I suppose."

"I hate to bring up the…the ghost at the back of the room, but… advance work, time, they're so key to going live, even more so if we have to dig up another location."

"Tell me about it. Going live is exciting, but God, I hate it."

"Fans love it, though. I've done it twice and nearly lost my mind, but those episodes blew the roof off my numbers."

"Viewers have no idea what we go through or what we risk. We never know what we'll encounter or how any of us will react. Locations can get tricky, too, physically dangerous. We often need those multiple takes and really rely on edits."

"We didn't need a single second-take in our crossovers," Ronnie reminded her with a touch of pride. "Even that time Brian thought he'd peed himself or when Caroline's bra strap caught in the stairway."

Peyton laughed softly. "You're right, but we had edits. Going live is such a huge gamble."

"It'll be a *grand* finale, for sure. In the meantime, think positively. I bet—what's his name, Meyers—he'll come through in time. If not, you—"

"I will fight for Miramar."

"I'm glad. Good luck, Peyton, and call if I can help. Let me know if the Casual Cook's two cents or…or a pizza will resolve things. Remember the Paris peace talks."

"Ah, yes. The Camp David Accord." The softness in Peyton's voice made Ronnie smile. The fondness was evident.

"Don't forget. Please keep me in the loop?"

There was nothing else to say. She was more than willing to help find a "plan B" location even though Peyton didn't want to consider it right now. It was the smart thing to do, though, *and* would provide some much-needed time together to see where they were headed. But, for now, Peyton was going to stand her ground and Ronnie could only wait.

❖

"How long did she stay last night?" Cheryl leaned in the living room doorway, arms crossed, ready to pry details.

Ronnie returned to her floury mess on the counter and began cleaning up. "How long have you been standing there?"

"Since 'I'd love to poke around spooky houses with you, too.' Are you changing the subject because she spent the night?"

"She didn't, as if it's any of your business."

"It *is* my business. Why didn't she stay? Don't tell me you two ended up at odds. That's unacceptable."

"Matchmaking is not your business. We had a great time and hit the jackpot with Miramar, then chilled out here for the evening with pizza and drinks. We talked shop."

"Like the Paris peace talks?"

"Jesus. I kissed her, all right? Satisfied?"

Cheryl jerked upright. "Really? On the lips?"

"No, her knee."

"A real kiss? Like—"

"I didn't shove my tongue down her throat, if that's where you're going. But yes, a *real* kiss."

"Yes!" Cheryl punched the air. "I've got to hear how this happened."

"Well…we *might* have had a little too much to drink."

"Ronnie. She can hold her liquor. I've seen her do it, so…You didn't whip up your nuclear margaritas, did you?"

"Hey, my espressos were perfect."

"God." Cheryl dropped onto a stool at the island and watched Ronnie put ingredients away. "You're making this difficult. Where do things stand?"

"They couldn't get a definitive answer this morning. The attorney has to contact the owner, but the network wants a location immediately. Peyton's worried. She wants Miramar badly and will have to lobby for time."

"Do you even know if the kitchen in that place is usable?"

"No, but a room out back could be."

"Okay, so she'll call you?"

"Yes."

"There's no backup plan? You're *not* going 'spooky house hunting' again?"

"No."

"Well, that sucks. I just got your revised contract for the finale, and I was going to ask about all the blanks still in it, but now I understand." She filled a glass of water for herself and sat back down. "So, get to the good stuff."

"I told you everything."

"You kissed her and that's it?" Ronnie nodded and Cheryl swore under her breath. "She just turned and walked away, drove off. Did she kiss you back?"

"Aren't you getting a little personal?"

"Of course, I am. I need to know these things. Did she?"

"Yes, and it was mind-blowing." She joined her at the table, knowing the grin she couldn't hide gave her away. "Brief but mind-blowing."

"I love it. Did she say anything?"

"She said she hates me now."

Cheryl laughed. "I love it. Do you think she told Jamie and Caroline?"

"No, and she may not." Ronnie frowned at her phone. "I think privacy means a lot to her." She flashed Cheryl a hard look. "Unlike *some* people I know."

"Did you take her downstairs?"

"Back to the seventies? No," Ronnie chuckled, "but I told her about it, and she didn't run screaming into the night. We had a good laugh about it. It wasn't just the margaritas talking, either. They hit us both, Peyton more than me, and she called for an Uber. I wouldn't have let her leave otherwise."

"You were hoping for it, weren't you?"

"Actually, I was rooting for the sharp and steady Peyton Stanford, because when she's at her level-headed best, she's..." Ronnie almost sighed. "It was a great day, a fun evening that went a little further than I expected. She...she got to me."

"Sounds like you got to each other."

Ronnie tipped her head, trying to find anything wrong with that statement. "Yeah, maybe."

"It's about damn time, you know," Cheryl said gently, and set her hand atop Ronnie's. "If she doesn't see your strength of character, that warmth in your soul, she's no spirit chaser. She's a fraud." She patted her hand and sat back. "I'd probably have to stop watching her show."

"*Probably*, huh? A true friend."

Ronnie's cell rang and before Cheryl could peek at the incoming number, Ronnie swiped the phone off the island and stepped out to the patio.

"Tell me you have good news already," she said, unable to contain a smile.

"Just that our Cape Air flight is only ten minutes behind schedule," Peyton said. "Listen, Ronnie, I never got around to saying...to telling you how much our day *and* evening meant to me. I really enjoyed our time together."

"I'm glad. So did I. Very much."

Knowing that the feeling was mutual shook Ronnie's already fragile propriety to its core. Just as Peyton returning her kiss had rocked her last night. Hard to believe that she, the cavalier, "take life as it comes" Casual Cook, might have had her world rattled.

Was something really brewing here? Would it be a problem if their "connection" showed on camera? Ronnie didn't want to worry about it influencing their professional rapport, but a flicker of doubt *did* cross her mind. Audiences at the advance screenings had raved about the on-screen chemistry between them, had seen their often-stilted cooperation and tolerance of each other as entertaining. How viewers would react to *attraction* was another matter...especially if last night led to something greater. Regardless of how difficult it might be, professionalism had to be her top priority.

Ronnie sat in the chair Peyton had used. She could envision everything about her, sitting here aglow in candlelight, the two of them connecting over beaches, dapper ghosts, and frozen dough balls. *Freaking pizza.* Memories were tactile. Her senses reeled and words seemed unattainable, distant.

She heard herself say, "So, you've no idea when you will be back."

"I don't. Ideally, next week. At least before Labor Day. Miramar will require a lot of advance work, but everything depends on how it goes with Meyers and the network. I've asked for a meeting tomorrow in Manhattan to plead my case, so we'll see."

"I'll keep my fingers crossed."

"Please do," she said, her voice softening. "I'm looking forward to coming back."

Chapter Sixteen

Max adjusted her sunglasses and gazed over the balcony railing at the park across the street. She swirled her glass lazily to clink the ice cubes, a tell that indicated her mind churned just as deliberately, and Peyton sensed this much-anticipated, restful afternoon at home was about to fade.

Labor Day Weekend had provided a sorely needed respite, despite the fact that Max showed up a half hour early. The day had been gloriously sunny and warm, the perfect setting for casting aside job tension, Miramar worries, and personal uncertainties. Worn to the bone, Peyton unwound in the good news from Max: Even after two weeks, *Paranormal Pursuit*'s crossover with the *Casual Cook* still trended big. Even after the other night, when Peyton and her team aired a standard week-two episode.

Viewership had been high for each show and that had Peyton smiling. Of course, she wanted her standard format to sustain the program, and she firmly believed it would. At the moment, viewers were simply caught up in the novelty of the crossover, of the entertaining addition of Ronnie Sharp, and that was fine. In a few weeks, their second crossover would drop, perfectly timed to send *Paranormal Pursuit* cruising toward the finale atop the ratings.

For now, however, she had lent that crossover finale enough consternation. Permission for Miramar still hung in the wind and the network still hung over her like a guillotine. Somehow, she had won that grace period to secure the place, and then, influenced by the debut crossover's success, the network had miraculously extended it. But there *was* a drop-dead end ahead. Her confidence that Meyers would come through remained high, although now, after several weeks, she'd begun giving more thought to Ronnie's offer about a "plan B." And that meant heading back to the Cape.

Which, in turn, brought Peyton around to smiling as she closed her eyes in the sun.

"Whatever's on your mind, Max, out with it."

"Well…Has she called you lately?"

"Who?"

"Oh, please."

"We spoke a couple of days ago."

"In other words, you called her?"

"I did."

"I bet she was surprised by the network's deadline concession. What did she say about the crossover ratings?"

"We had talked about those already and couldn't be happier."

"Uh-huh. Just so you know, I spoke with Jamie."

Peyton squinted at her. "What about?" When Max shrugged and didn't turn to her, Peyton sighed heavily. "Max. Who I call, what I do on my own time is my business. You're my agent and Jamie is my producer."

"Correct. We're family with a vested interest in your professional success."

"I thought you came over here to relax on a holiday weekend. Stop hounding me. Please say you and Jamie weren't gossiping."

"No, we weren't gossiping. I wanted reactions to the show's smooth sailing."

"Right."

"The crossover's ratings ran higher than expected, Peyton. The trade outlets were aflutter for days after it aired. Internet chatter spiked across all formats."

"I know, Max, and the chatter is still out there."

"Ed Rankin and his programming people are ecstatic, and the network is eating up every percentage point. It's no wonder they gave you another two weeks to get this Miramar place. I called

Jamie because I was curious about what she had heard, how they all saw it."

"Saw what?"

Max set her drink and sunglasses on the bistro table and folded her hands in her lap. "The chatter has been…interesting, don't you think? Viewers thinking you two are 'cute together,' are 'perfect for each other,' was something I hadn't really anticipated."

Peyton tossed her a dismissive wave. "Yeah, so there were a few of those. You know *Paranormal Pursuit* generates feedback from all parts of the universe. And I do mean *all.* Tweets come in all shapes and sizes."

"Jamie also senses a special chemistry. Luckily, Rankin's in Lala Land right now and just laughed at the idea."

"Is there an issue here?"

"You're not fooling me, Peyton, and I know you're not fooling yourself. You're too heavy a thinker to overlook what's happening."

"I'm not overlooking anything."

"You couldn't have overlooked a few of those Tweets and Facebook comments." Max cursed her cell phone, and finally fished it out of her tote bag. "Listen, Peyton. Fans don't miss a thing. These are just a few I saved."

"Really? You're going there? I'll refresh your drink. You're getting too worked up."

"Don't you leave that seat." Max poked the screen a few times and began reading aloud. "'Aren't Peyton and Ronnie fun together?' 'Love how they put up with each other.' 'Are they teasing or flirting? All tingly when they went face-to-face in the kitchen.'" Max paused to flash Peyton a serious look. "'I think they're cute,'" she read on. "'No question they're flirting. I hope there's more of this.'"

"Oh, Max. I saw those, but so what? Let the crew be curious and Rankin amused and fans titillated. Ronnie takes her job just as seriously as I do. Bottom line. End of story."

"Fine."

Max stood and collected her purse and sunglasses. Peyton walked her to the door, knowing Max hadn't finished.

"I *do* like her, Peyton. Really. Regardless of whether you want to admit it to me or yourself, Ronnie's winning some of that interest you devote to the dead. She has an indefatigable spirit, if I dare refer to such things, and you have a genuine affinity for them." She turned to Peyton in the doorway. "I am on your side."

"Well, thank you for that."

"By the same token, however, it's my job to stay on the ball, to stay one step ahead, so I'm advising you to keep your wits about you. So far, it seems viewers like what they're seeing. We want that to continue. Audience perception means every—"

"Max. I get it."

"Sorry to tell you what you already know, but…"

"But you're still going to."

"Well, sometimes it's not enough to simply consider audience perception. We often have to guard against it as well. Your fan base watches the show for paranormal adventure and, at times, for the *Casual Cook*'s contributions. Are they watching for romance as well, now?"

Peyton laughed. "Whoa. You know you really are reaching, Max."

"Am I? You're going back to Cape Cod next week, aren't you?"

"With Jamie and Caroline, yes, to get a jump on the Miramar research. My precious extra time will disappear in a hurry, so I'm playing a hunch that we'll get the okay by then." She hiked a shoulder. "If not, and I've played my cards wrong, we'll need help generating a 'plan B' fast."

"Ronnie's help."

"Yes. She's local, a terrific resource."

Max's soft gray eyes analyzed Peyton's motivation. Without question, Max's concerns had merit. They weren't new, however. Already, Peyton had lost sleep because of them. Show stability, audience reception, sponsor support, network reaction, crew performance, even personal desire…so many unknowns. But she specialized in confronting unknowns.

"I'm eager to go back."

"I know." Max patted her cheek and strolled off to the elevator.

Peyton closed the door after her and thumped her forehead against it.

"God. Really?"

She returned to the balcony, running both hands through her hair. "What are you doing, Stanford, asking for trouble?" She slumped back into her seat to think and narrowed her eyes against the setting sun.

If their crossover's reception was any indication, she had successfully achieved the ratings-boost objective and now had to advance purposefully from there. Certainly, without the *Casual Cook*, it was conceivable that *Paranormal Pursuit* could drop from front-runner status back into mediocrity. After all, they had followed the crossover debut with a damn good investigation of their own, but social media still reverberated about the Barrow Tavern episode. She had to keep *Paranormal Pursuit*'s head above water. A few fans reading something into interactions with Ronnie wasn't the real issue here.

She cautioned herself against losing focus. Crossovers aside, she had a full slate of independent *Paranormal Pursuit* episodes ready to go, solid investigations that would serve the program well.

That had to remain her paramount concern, despite the insistent background noise of private temptation. How much more complicated would life become if there was "something" with Ronnie? Potentially, a lot. But what if it only amounted to a fling, an affair? Did it even have to be a "thing"? What happened to casual? And what if it grew into something deeper? An inner source she hadn't heard in ages told her to clear her head. Jesus, it *was* only a kiss. Granted, she'd been swept off her feet, but…

Getting way too carried away.

And then the nightmare chore of keeping things professional, private, evoked images of dissatisfied viewers, a ratings crash, sponsor losses, even cancellation. She grew tense, trying to envision every interaction during the second crossover, which had yet to air.

For God's sake, get a grip.

No Tweet or Facebook comment had been negative. Plus, only their live crossover finale remained on the schedule. They would only interact on camera one more time.

She had to stop blowing this out of proportion. *Paranormal Pursuit* was strong. The fan base was loyal, the show ran like a finely tuned machine, and, honestly, both could withstand a tremor in the status quo. Those were critical pluses, considering this little urge to test the waters with Ronnie wouldn't subside. That kiss had sealed the deal. Heaven and Earth didn't move very often, but they had then. She'd felt them move, her heart skip, and her mouth melt into the tenderness of Ronnie's lips.

A kiss hadn't shaken her like that since things were new with Abbey four years ago. And then, they were fleeting. Abbey thrived on Peyton's success, the notoriety, and bustle of production schedules that sent them all over the country, living the high life, and that was the extent of the relationship. Peyton still believed the emotional strain sucked vitality out of her show and blamed it for *Paranormal Pursuit*'s current struggles. She mustn't let emotion take charge again.

But that anxiety didn't exist when she considered Ronnie's impact on her or the show. They respected each other as professionals and their careers were similar enough to share and appreciate common ground. They worked *together* and, even though Ronnie still wasn't all-in with the paranormal, she was a team player—and a good one, supportive and enthusiastic. Peyton wondered if that dynamic personality ever dragged because there was such an infectious, upbeat energy in her, even in her smile. No wonder she was such a terrific kisser.

❖

"I want to pay," Peyton announced.

"No." Searching for her wallet in her backpack, Ronnie edged ahead to the restaurant's pickup window. "This was my idea, so—" She grinned when Peyton elbowed her out of the way.

That captivating white-blue fire sizzled into Ronnie's brain and down her spine. She thought Peyton's determined, no-nonsense look even more enchanting here, on the Provincetown sidewalk.

"No," Peyton insisted, handing cash to the young blonde behind the counter. "You've taken your whole day to cart me around."

"Hey, I'm thrilled about it, glad I got the chance." Ronnie wished Jamie and Caroline weren't arriving this evening and renting transportation for the three of them. At least she had been able to pick Peyton up at the airport and spend the day with her.

Peyton adjusted her sunglasses atop her head before passing Ronnie their sodas. "I got this." She picked up their flimsy cardboard box of food and they started to turn away.

"Wait, please!" The teenager hurried back to the window. "Are you…Sorry, but you remind me of someone on TV." She held out Peyton's change and Peyton shook her head.

"Thank you, but you keep it."

"It's that ghost show! Am I right? It's…um…*Paranormal Something*?"

"*Paranormal Pursuit*, yeah," Ronnie injected.

Eyes widening, the girl pointed at Peyton. "That's it! You're Peyton. We watch you all the time." She flicked her gaze to Ronnie and her eyebrows rose. "Y-you were on it a few weeks back, right? You're the Casual Cook, aren't you?" She almost hopped in place. "Oh, this is awesome, seeing both of you. I can't wait to tell—" An older man arrived at her side, his stern look ordering her to move things along. "Gary, these women are on TV, on *Paranormal Pursuit* and the *Casual Cook*. Sweet that they're eating here, huh?"

He made a quick study of Ronnie and Peyton. "Sorry, ladies, I don't watch much TV, but thank you for your patronage." He turned back and mumbled to the teenager before walking off.

Ronnie leaned toward the window. "What's your name?"

"Celia Tomasi. Thanks for asking." She turned her starstruck smile to Peyton. "And thanks for the tip."

A customer behind them in line tapped Peyton's shoulder. "Excuse me. You're Peyton Stanford from *Paranormal Pursuit*?" Already prepared, the woman held up a notepad and pen. "Could I have your autograph, please?" Peyton set the box of food back down at Celia's window to oblige her.

"Yours is the best of all the paranormal shows, you know," the woman said. "My daughter and I watch regularly, usually her friends come over, too. Funny, huh, bonding with teenagers over ghosts."

"That's great. I love hearing that," Peyton said. "Thank you very much."

"And Ronnie Sharp. Please, make my day."

Now, Ronnie had to unload the sodas to sign. She grinned at the woman and flicked a look at the crowd that was forming. "We should step aside," she whispered, backing away. "Your name, please?"

"Meg Perkins," the woman said as she leaned closer. "I've done so many of your recipes." She looked back and forth between them. "Having you two on the same show is such a treat!"

"Well, thank you. Glad you like the concept. We're having fun doing it." She handed paper and pen back and reached for the sodas at the window.

Celia stood beaming from the other side. Ronnie plucked a napkin from the nearby dispenser and stole the pen from Celia's hand. She stooped to write on the counter and peered up at the teenager. "C-e-l-i-a. Correct?"

Celia giggled. "Wow, yeah. Thanks."

Ronnie wrote her name and handed the pen to Peyton. Celia looked ready to drool on her newly endorsed napkin.

"We're leaving now," Ronnie whispered to her as they retrieved their drinks and food. "We've caused enough commotion. Thanks for being a fan, Celia."

"S-sure. You bet." She waved. "See you guys on TV."

"Well, that was sweet," Peyton said as Ronnie led them around the corner.

"It never dawned on me that we'd be recognized. I mean, it does happen to me once in a while, but I forgot I'm with a star."

"Yeah, right. My limo and bodyguards are off today."

"Therefore, I get to escort you to our fine dining experience. Lobster rolls taste better when you're on the beach." She brought Peyton beyond the parking lot and down onto the Provincetown Harbor shoreline, pleased to spread out a blanket some fifty feet from the water. Peyton seemed to forget the food for the scenery.

"It's been years since I've been here," she said, sighing at the view. "I forgot how good it feels, how much I love it. Thank you."

"You're welcome. There's truly no better place to unwind after hours of traveling." She examined her lobster roll, wondering how it would settle amidst the butterflies in her stomach. "I thought you could use the downtime before jumping into work." She bit into the roll and hoped Peyton reveled in the taste as well.

"I may not have much downtime, you're right about that." Peyton took a bite and nodded vigorously. "*This* is pure decadence, Ronnie." She took another bite.

"It is, isn't it?" Ronnie thrust her chin toward the docks as she chewed. "We can take a walk out there, if you want. McMillian Wharf is different these days, lots of artisans."

"I'd like that." Peyton wiped her mouth, scanning the pier. "I feel like a first-timer, so anywhere you suggest."

"You know, I…I'm happy you're back. It's really good seeing you again."

"I feel the same way." A smile began across her lips, and she looked back vacantly to her food. "It felt like a long month."

"Very."

Ronnie exhaled to calm her nerves. She brushed sand off her calf before biting into her roll again. Every motion seemed calculated, awkward. She didn't know where this conversation was going but tried not to dwell on it. Chances were that, once Jamie and Caroline arrived and they all were settled in their B&B, time alone with Peyton would be rare. The three of them had practically a whole century of records and history to review, resources to interview, and, with any luck, meetings with Meyers.

The prospect of opportunity lost did nothing to soothe Ronnie's nerves, but it helped to see Peyton appearing a bit unsettled, too.

"I decided to redesign my condo," Peyton said suddenly. "Quite the can of worms I opened, but it got me through the month."

Ronnie chose not to list the projects and chores that had helped her pass the time.

"Sounds like big changes. A whole new theme? Colors and furniture, too?"

Peyton finished her last bite. "Mm-hm." She drew the napkin across her slim, naturally rosy lips, and then tended to her delicate fingertips. "Probably lots of carpentry, too. I'm ditching modern for...don't laugh. I'm going for beachy."

"An oasis in urban New Jersey," she managed. "I like it."

"I was taken by the airiness of your place, the refreshing feel. It was numbing enough to get back to a hectic, congested city, but when I walked into my place, I immediately wanted out. It reflected my life too well, compartmentalized and formal. I knew it didn't have to be that way."

"Well, what are we waiting for?" Ronnie scrambled to her feet. "We have to go buy stuff for your oasis." She slipped into her backpack and collected their trash.

Peyton shook out the blanket. "Hold on a second." She stepped behind Ronnie and stuffed it into the backpack. "I'm really glad to be back," she whispered at her ear.

Ronnie turned. "You know this could put us on the cover of every gossip rag in the country."

"That might be inevitable."

Chapter Seventeen

The living room of their B&B offered plenty of quaint, Cape Cod charm, and the longer Peyton stayed in the wingback chair, the deeper she sank into it. Exhausted by multiple errands, frustrated by canceled appointments, and listless from a hearty steakhouse dinner, she saw the same emotions on the faces of her coworkers. Out of nowhere, she wondered what Ronnie was doing.

Yesterday went by in a blur, the fun and freedom, the headiness.

"Waiting another two days to see Meyers sucks," Jamie whined from the sofa. She released her ponytail and shook out her hair. "He's stalling. We set up that damn appointment so long ago. I don't have a good feeling about it."

"Yeah," Caroline grumbled, "like he may not have any news for us." Her focus rose over her magazine. "He's had over a month, for God's sake. Hope the owner didn't die or something."

"Let's not go there," Peyton said. "We have to stay positive this week."

Jamie stretched out on the sofa. "With just the info we got today, Miramar gets better by the minute. It meets all our needs. We really have to land it and soon."

"It was exciting to learn that the original owner, Jonathan Baker, actually died there," Caroline said. "That gives us a candidate for who's haunting the place. The historical people were a wealth of knowledge."

"We'll probably be visiting the society for more." Peyton sat forward and thumbed through the notes on her tablet. "But I have doubts it's Jonathan. In pictures of him, his fashion style matches what people have seen, but…See this?" She turned her tablet around on the table and Jamie and Caroline peered down at the scratched black-and-white image. "Look at Jonathan in the middle," Peyton said, pointing. "He's so slight, and what, maybe five-foot-five? Supposedly the spirit image is dramatically taller, and burly."

Jamie settled onto her side, her head on the armrest. "We haven't come across any big guy yet."

Caroline reached for her own tablet on the floor and began perusing notes from the day. "Way too many people visited Miramar back then. He could be anyone, I suppose."

"To haunt the place all these years," Peyton said, "he had a solid attachment, maybe he died there, too. Tomorrow when we hit the library and town records, I want more details about the Prohibition era. Who managed the place through that craziness? It's unlikely that Jonathan did. People that affluent delegated."

"I made an appointment to go back to the police department," Caroline said. "The patrol officer had a detailed description. And the sergeant thought their old records went back to those days."

Peyton opened a folder of papers. "We need to go through all of these guest registers. Maybe we'll find some 'regulars' or those who stayed for long periods." She shook her head at the various handwriting styles, some too elaborate to decipher. "God bless the historical society, but I wish all this was downloaded."

"Mrs. Haggarty," Caroline recalled. "Forty-three years with the society? And her grandmother before her? Small-town America rocks."

"People just need their memories tickled," Jamie said with a grin. "They've forgotten what they know. But can we reach them all?"

Caroline nodded. "Some, at least. Like Wendall Johnson, the hardware store manager's father. He didn't just see that ghostly image, it pushed him."

"I wanted to adopt that man," Jamie said. "A sweet great-grandfather. I'm psyched he agreed to talk on camera. His makes four testimonials already. Putting a couple of them on, right before we cut live to Miramar, will make a knockout cold open."

"His incident happened ages ago," Peyton said. "The Haggarty family experiences are more recent, and the police have current ones, so activity has been constant." She restacked her papers and rubbed her eyes. "Hopefully, the police will agree to describe their encounters on camera. That'll be gold, coming from them."

"I think we'll get even more, Peyton." Caroline tossed her tablet aside and slouched in the chair. "Tomorrow, after the library, we have appointments at the senior citizen complex and the assisted living facility in town."

"Excellent."

Jamie reached for the television remote control and glanced at Peyton. "Are you seeing Ronnie tomorrow?"

"I am. She's taking me to meet with the real estate agent she spoke to a while ago, then to Meyers's office. Hopefully, he or someone will agree to show us around. I want to get inside sooner rather than later."

Jamie sat up and muted the sound on the television. "Not to be a third wheel, or anything, but I'd like to go along for that."

"Me, too," Caroline added. "My appointments are later in the afternoon, so…Too bad the guys aren't with us. They can't wait to see it up close."

"You all have to see it, yes. I'd thought we'd do it later in the week, once we *hopefully* get Meyers's okay, but sure. Tomorrow's fine. We'll coordinate once we're finished with the real estate agent, so get what you can in the morning. Hopefully, tomorrow will go as scheduled."

"Do you two have plans for dinner tomorrow night?" Caroline asked, and Jamie looked for an answer as well.

"No. This is becoming too busy a week. We have to cover every inch of groundwork possible in advance." She knew they had to be curious. The questions were bound to come.

"Ronnie's very understanding," Caroline said.

Jamie sat up and crossed her stockinged feet on the coffee table. She looked evenly at Peyton. "Keeping things professional won't be easy."

Peyton almost grinned. "Just what do you two think has been going on?" She watched them exchange glances. "Yes, things have changed with Ronnie, we've grown closer, but that's really all there is to it."

"You know how much one camera can see, Peyton," Jamie said carefully, "and we use how many?"

Peyton offered them a pouty face. "So, you're saying no sex on the SLS camera?"

Caroline laughed.

Even Jamie's guarded expression slackened. "I was just saying, that's all."

Caroline leaned forward. "But audiences might not mind."

Both Peyton and Jamie turned to her in surprise.

"Mind what?" Peyton asked. "Sex on the SLS?"

"Hey, sure!" Jamie said, flailing a hand through the air. "Let's watch stick figures fuck!"

"Shut up! No!" Caroline was indignant. "Of course not. I-I just meant that social media seems to like you two together. There were lots of positive observations after the first crossover. I bet people might like that…twist."

Jamie shook her head. "Eh…Twists can be trouble." She looked from Caroline to Peyton. "This is your producer speaking. We only have to get through one more crossover. Then you're free to—"

Peyton held up a palm. "Do *not* go there." She puffed a breath up to her forehead.

God. Can this get any more complicated?

❖

Turn a New York City driver loose on Cape Cod's curvy narrow roads and the captive passenger in you immediately welcomed distraction, such as a tour of an abandoned historic hotel…or the proximity to a beautiful woman. From the back seat, Ronnie indulged herself with Peyton's profile up front while Jamie zoomed them all toward Miramar in the rented SUV.

Unfortunately, Ronnie sat directly behind her, privy to the close calls and the speedometer. Beside her, Caroline seemed oblivious to Jamie's death-wish approach, alternately checking the scenery and jotting thoughts on her tablet. Ronnie couldn't help but be impressed by Peyton, similarly unfazed, half-turned in her seat summarizing the data gleaned from their various sources.

The three of them obviously had tapped many in the past few days, at least part of one Ronnie had hoped to spend with Peyton. Eager to reconnect, she had been disappointed when the group's two days of work had stretched to three. Thankfully, Peyton's phone call promised better luck today.

Yesterday, plans blew up when the real estate agent canceled, and Meyers' office mysteriously never opened and didn't return calls. As a result, Peyton teamed with Caroline and Jamie at the town library, a stint she carried on singularly once they left for afternoon interviews, and stretched until nine o'clock when the facility closed. The ten hours of engrossing but tedious research showed in the creases at Peyton's eyes, her occasional yawn. And yet, her voice somehow still carried that remarkable lilt of excitement.

"I couldn't believe it when Meyers called last night." Peyton caught and held Ronnie's attention with a look that promised a myriad of things. Ronnie had already lost count of how many times she wished they were doing this alone. She had a lot on her mind, too, but not the opportunity. She resigned herself to simply appreciating that glamorous face, and worked to concentrate on every word from, every motion of Peyton's lips.

"Inviting us to meet him at Miramar was the last thing I expected him to say."

"It's a good sign, offering us a tour," Ronnie said. "He's heard from Sebastian, evidently."

"I'm hoping." Some of that trademark energy returned to Peyton's expression. "You'd be surprised by how much ground we covered yesterday. God knows, it's just a start, but we've learned a lot already."

"Surprised? No. Impressed, yes."

"Thank you."

Peyton winked before looking down at her tablet. A private acknowledgement had never felt so seductive. Ronnie's insides clenched and she bit back a grin. Glancing up, Jamie averted her eyes in the rearview mirror, and Ronnie wondered if she'd caught that exchange. Whatever Peyton's co-workers gathered about them wasn't going to diminish this feeling.

"Sebastian is the last of the Baker line," Peyton began. "His older brother died in the early Vietnam years and his sister drowned."

"At Miramar," Caroline inserted.

"Right. Including Jonathan, that makes two confirmed deaths in the place, but we still need those certificates to learn the causes. Anyway, that's how Miramar went to Sebastian, and he lived there from the seventies to the nineties."

"A big place to live in alone," Ronnie said.

"He moved to Louisiana in 'ninety-seven, and, according to Meyers, didn't start really entertaining purchase offers until about ten years ago. He liked dropping in out of the blue for a few days and having the place to himself, but the last time was two years ago. *The man's going to be ninety in July.*"

"Amazing."

"I know. The Baton Rouge society columns are full of his escapades, the wealthy, rather eccentric, *very* senior citizen. He obviously enjoys *meaningful* time away."

"Ah. The 'incommunicado' thing," Ronnie said. "You still don't know where he went?"

Peyton's gaze lingered an extra beat, long enough for Ronnie's thoughts to begin drifting in it. But then Peyton shook her head and looked back to her tablet. Ronnie sighed inwardly.

"I interviewed a woman who knew him years ago," Caroline said, "and she remembers him vacationing in Paris back in the eighties, so he might still have connections there."

"How sweet is that?" Ronnie mused aloud. "Maybe there once was someone *meaningful* in Paris...and there still is."

Jamie smirked at her in the mirror. "Look at you, *Paranormal Pursuit*'s guest investigator."

Caroline held up her tablet. "The globe-trotting bug could have started with great-grandfather Jonathan. He did his share before and after he opened the hotel *and*, interestingly, he preferred the company of highly successful men. So much so, we're thinking he could have been gay."

"We were told he had married and had a son," Peyton explained, "but when he opened Miramar as a hotel in nineteen fifteen, he did it alone. There's no evidence of family being around then, but we have yet to tackle the town records. We're surmising they divorced, she got custody, and then disappeared, maybe died or moved away. Jonathan never remarried."

"Census records will tell us more, like when the son, Andrew, took up residence," Caroline added. "Evidently, the place passed to him when Jonathan died in 'thirty-four."

"And that's a key death certificate," Peyton interjected, arching an eyebrow at Ronnie. "Jonathan died at Miramar, but we're banking on a police report to tell us how. We've heard a slew of possibilities: he either fell or was pushed down the stairs, he OD'd on pills and alcohol, he was shot, he drowned in the bathtub…" She shrugged.

"As for father and son," Caroline said, "it doesn't appear they were close. Going all-in on a glitzy hotel might have been Jonathan compensating for losing wife and son."

"If you ask me," Jamie observed, "I'd say Jonathan's interests strayed from family to fun long before that, if you catch my drift. Once he got rid of family responsibilities, he cranked up the high life in his Prohibition paradise."

"Well, gay or not, *something* led to the divorce," Peyton added, "and it's just one of the million factors in our investigation. I hate that our clock's ticking." She looked back at Ronnie. "Us running around, making assumptions and deductions is so risky, but, until now, not having Meyers or, ideally, Sebastian Baker himself, we haven't had much choice. Our legwork isn't usually this difficult, and Meyers may not have all the answers, but he could move this process to the next level."

"Offering a personal tour today *has* to mean we're getting the green light," Ronnie offered. "Meyers wouldn't go to all this trouble, just to say, 'Good-bye, thanks for asking.'" She reached forward and gave Peyton's shoulder a squeeze. "It's going to work out."

"Thank you for being so patient."

"Thanks for including me today. This is exciting."

Jamie almost missed a turn and swore as she braked hard, rocking everyone in their seats.

Peyton wiped her hair off her face. "Jesus, Jamie. Relax, girl." She reset herself, better able to see Ronnie in the back seat. "Why didn't we have you drive? You know the area."

"Look," Jamie said, "time is of the essence."

Peyton rolled her eyes at Ronnie. "Actually, it is. Just getting a grip on the history is dragging us down. Plowing through turn-of-the-century records will be a test of patience, and the Prohibition Era, even worse. And, God, Miramar's stuff from that period is a rush-hour jumble of visitors, guests, vendors, contractors, employees... So far, the only curious thing I've come across is a predominance of Irish names."

"I betcha," Jamie began in a pitiful brogue, "ol' Jonnie had himself a fine, handsome lad, a sailor who prob'ly kept Miramar a-flowin' in the Jamison's, dontcha know?" They chuckled at that, and looking a little sheepish, Jamie whispered, "My apologies to the Irish."

Ronnie tipped her head to Jamie. "Cute, but actually something to keep in mind," she advised Peyton. "Rumrunners' best booze came from Ireland. Miramar had to go through tons of it, which means big money and dependable connections. If Jonathan really lived the glitzy gay life, it's easy to imagine he had a plentiful supply of 'interests.'"

"Irish connections."

"Possibly. And very special friends locally."

"A woman at the assisted living place showed us this photo of her grandparents." Caroline handed Ronnie her tablet. "I took a picture of it." The photo showed a well-dressed couple laughing amidst a crowd of dancers in an elegant ballroom. "She said, growing up, she heard lots of stories about Miramar galas, all the drinking, dancing, and dining."

"What a place," Ronnie said. "Could it still look anything like this?"

"Another man remembered that his grandfather was a houseboy there," Jamie told Ronnie in the mirror, "one in an army of them. He said they had quite the operation."

"Mostly a male one. Housemaids were in the minority," Caroline continued, back scrolling through notes. "Their boss acted like he owned the place, a real taskmaster they all hated, but jobs were hard to come by in the twenties, so…"

Ronnie stared at the passing scenery and contemplated the many stories and descriptions, the scenarios they created, the mystery that was Miramar, a place she thought she had known for years. She figured Peyton had to be processing stuff constantly because just this nasty boss had Ronnie's imagination working overtime.

Mindlessly returning to a forward view, she found Peyton watching her, a satisfied grin on those delectable lips.

"The taskmaster," Ronnie said in an intentionally ponderous tone.

Peyton simply nodded. They were on the same wavelength.

Chapter Eighteen

Too busy ogling the building, Jamie stopped their SUV in the nick of time, a foot from the rear of Meyers's Mercedes. Peyton hardly noticed, none of them did, preoccupied with staring out the windows and wriggling into suit jackets.

"Damn. What a place," Jamie said. "This will be a challenge."

Caroline whispered, "I'm a little creeped out already."

"It looks a little sadder under this overcast sky," Peyton said. Slipping her phone into her jacket pocket, she sent a fond look back at Ronnie. "In the summer sun, it's grand."

Finally, everyone exited the car and Meyers appeared, assuming a position at the top of the stairs and standing as tall as his diminutive size would permit. He smoothed a palm down the front of his suit and clasped his hands at his midsection with the cool, guarded air of an undertaker.

Peyton slowed just enough for Ronnie to arrive at her side. For some reason, she felt more secure, having her close by as they approached.

Caroline moved up behind them. "I want a job with a car like his."

Ronnie half-turned in her direction. "A Mercedes that color is shameful."

From Ronnie's other side, Jamie mumbled, "Kalahari Gold. Our executive producer owns one. This guy does all right."

Peyton smiled up at Meyers in his forest green suit and matching tie, still expressionless and solemn. She thought he suited the place perfectly.

"Attorney Meyers." She extended a handshake. "We're very happy to see you again." His small hand was just as damp as the first time they'd met, and she fought back a grimace before introducing Ronnie. "Thank you for inviting us here."

"Good morning, ladies. I thought it the practical option, to discuss your offer while showing you around." He nodded slowly, almost deferentially at the doorway. Peyton itched to step into that grand entryway, but politely waited as he continued. "The property is in just as much need of rehabilitation as this wonderful structure, but there is no denying the potential for a triumphant return to glory."

We want to borrow it, not buy it.

"Without a doubt," Jamie said. "Miramar has our utmost respect and, as we've said before, that will show in our work."

"Hopefully, we've conveyed those assurances sufficiently," Peyton added, "to you and, through you, to Mr. Baker."

Peyton wished he would nod or offer a semblance of a smile, something to confirm they had succeeded, but he remained silent and scanned the stark front grounds, the acres of treeless lawn turned to weeds. Apparently, he was lost in the view or its memories. Then, abruptly, he shuffled his feet and cleared his throat.

"Ah, yes. Yes, you have," he said, and glanced back at the open door. "Your proposal was quite thorough." He fidgeted with his tie. "Yes, that…that was most appreciated."

Peyton exchanged a quick look with Ronnie and was relieved to see that Meyers's behavior seemed a little "off" to her, too. Something nagged at him. He appeared unsettled, veiled in what felt like artificial confidence, and far too nervous for a top-flight attorney. She wondered if having visitors here unnerved him.

"Recently, I had a lengthy conversation with Mr. Baker and passed along your assurances," he said, "along with details of the proposal. As I have previously made you aware, Ms. Stanford, he is keen to consummate a *sale*, not the rental or leasing of his former home. However, he fully appreciates how your proposal could assist in that regard."

Hope rose in Peyton's throat, and she hung on his every word.

"Consequently," Meyers continued, adjusting his tie again, "Mr. Baker has authorized me to consent to your request. I am available to meet with your legal staff at your convenience."

Peyton fought to contain a swell of relief and happiness. Around her, she noted the joyful glances, and felt Ronnie pat her back.

"That's wonderful," she responded, knowing she couldn't stop smiling. "Thank you for this. It's not often we're afforded an opportunity to showcase such an incredible place, so please accept our sincere appreciation. You'll convey our thanks to Mr. Baker, I hope?"

Meyers nodded regally. "As soon as we conclude our tour."

"And I'll be in touch with our legal team as soon as we're finished," Jamie said. "You'll have all the necessary documentation as soon as possible. I'll make sure legal reaches out to you directly."

"Very good." He gestured to the doorway. "Shall we?"

Grinning, almost giddy, they followed Meyers into Miramar's grand foyer. Peyton immediately felt enveloped by the musty air, the soaring ceilings, the rich mahogany woodwork. That *Gone with the Wind* staircase splayed out at their feet, albeit some twenty feet ahead, and drew all eyes to the second-floor balcony, which led left and right.

"It's magnificent," Peyton said on a breath, and spotted Ronnie staring straight up. "Can you even imagine living here?"

"I can't believe I'm *here*, period. Between my neck creaking and my jaw dropping, I'll be a complete mess in an hour." She dipped her head closer and lowered her voice. "Congratulations on a major victory. I'm happy for you."

"For us."

"I think we're in for quite a trip, Peyton. I never dreamed Miramar would be *this* cool."

Peyton assumed they all felt like tourists right now, lucky ones with a personal guide through the museum. So much history, so many lives affected here. So many traversed that staircase—and apparently some still did. Could these walls talk? Would they?

She realized a tightness had settled in her chest but, instead of spoiling this tour, it heightened that familiar pre-investigation anxiety.

Caroline wandered closer and spoke while continuing to look around. "Whenever we do our preliminary visits, the daytime ones before investigations, I always get this weird feeling."

"Like how?"

"Like I'm being watched, like something's waiting for us, waiting to happen. It's like a heavy anticipation weighing you down. Hard to explain."

"I know exactly what you mean."

Caroline turned to her. "You're feeling it right now, too?" Peyton nodded and Caroline pursed her lips. "What are we in for here?"

"Allow me to offer a summary floorplan." Meyers stood in the middle of the cavernous space, arms raised at his sides.

Jamie snickered softly behind Peyton. "Is he our ringmaster now?"

Peyton hissed over her shoulder. "Stop."

"We'll start on your right," Meyers began. "You will see that the dining room, with stage and dance floor on the near end, extends all the way back to the kitchen, which encompasses the rear of the house, full width. And to your left, we first have the library. It adjoins the parlor, which, like the dining room, extends almost back to the kitchen. The second floor," and he pointed up, "has the family suite on the right, and the remainder is composed of guest accommodations. The third floor was primarily for staff quarters. It also features access to the tower sunroom, which originally served as a vantage point to view ships at sea. Andrew Baker ordered the conversion following World War II."

"Is there an attic?" Caroline asked.

"Prior to the hotel, there was. It became the third-floor staff quarters when Jonathan Baker saw the need, I believe in nineteen twenty. The extensive cellar *does* remain, however."

"How extensive?" Ronnie asked, and Peyton eagerly awaited that answer. She vividly remembered Ronnie mentioning rumrunners and their secret means of reaching the beach.

"I'll show you," Meyers said. "We'll work our way around this floor first, then go up, and then we can go downstairs."

Conveying tidbits of history along the way, Meyers led them from one first-floor room to the next. Scatterings of abandoned furniture did little to occupy each space or absorb the echoes of voices and footsteps. Nor did the grungy antique floors or the bare walls, some with their once opulent wallpaper now fading and peeling. Windows were plentiful and typically dramatic, but daylight struggled to penetrate the dusty, pitted glass and created an eerie ambiance in the massive rooms. Time seemed to have stopped here decades ago.

Jamie surveyed the parlor fireplace and the corroded brass sconces to either side. "We'll be shooting live, so I have to ask about utilities."

"Electricity is adequate, unchanged since Sebastian's residency, but adequate."

Jamie sent Peyton a cautionary look. Having sketchy electricity for their investigation complicated things, but Peyton wasn't too worried. They had overcome such handicaps before, relied on generators or laid power from their RV when necessary.

"As for natural gas," Meyers continued, "there is none this far off the public way. And water has always come from wells on the property. However, the most recent one hasn't been used or actually serviced at all in decades."

"A prospective buyer would have her hands full," Caroline observed.

"Indeed."

"It's safe to assume," Peyton began, "that this and other fireplaces do not work."

"Correct." Meyers stared at it, and she assumed he remembered when it did.

A firm knock sounded to her left and she turned. Two more sounded, higher pitched than the first. Peyton exchanged glances with the others and looked right at Meyers for a moment before speaking.

"This must have been a popular room. Have there been reports of unusual activity here over the years?"

"Eh, not that I can recall."

"Really? Mr. Baker or townspeople, visitors, workers, no one ever encountered anything in this room?"

Now, Meyers looked around. "Possibly a time or two, a sound or a…a voice. Sebastian has often said he never felt alone here."

"Why is that? Has he ever gone into detail?"

"His recollections often are rather…morose, and yet quite vivid. Sometimes pleasant, sometimes disturbing. I have attributed that to the solitary lifestyle of a gentleman of his years, so I cannot speak to their validity."

"Visual or physical encounters? The scents of anything in particular?" Another knock caught her ear and she acknowledged Jamie's glance with a slight nod.

"Well, he has spoken of frequently seeing images from varying periods. I believe this has contributed to his reluctance to stay at Miramar for any length of time, quite probably led to his decision to sell. Now that I recall, he has said his sister, Eleanor, appeared to him more than once in this room." Meyers wandered to the windows and stared at a spot on the floor. "He saw her seated here, he said, and confided that after each sighting, he endured extended bouts of depression."

"Eleanor passed in 'fifty-five," Caroline offered. "Was Sebastian living here then?"

"No, neither Sebastian nor Daniel, their older brother, but they had come home for her upcoming wedding. For the entire previous year, she and her fiancé had prepared to move in, and Sebastian's father, Michael, welcomed the idea, despite being counseled against it. All needless upheaval, I'm afraid, because Eleanor drowned just days before the ceremony."

"Now *that's* a tragedy," Caroline said.

"Who counseled against her moving in?" Ronnie asked. "Sebastian or the brother?"

"Hardly. As I understand it, Michael's house manager and long-time family friend, Patrick Doonan, was of the position that only men of the bloodline had the privilege of living here. He was a close companion of Jonathan Baker's, the first hire for the hotel, and sincerely felt duty-bound to uphold the Baker family honor.'"

"Sounds like Doonan thought he was living in medieval England."

Meyers barely nodded at Jamie and gestured to the far end of the room. "Moving on."

"I'm very curious about the kitchen," Ronnie said, advancing to the door in the corner. "Is it this way?"

"Yes," Meyers said, opening it and leading them along a short hallway. "A utility room there…and the kitchen." He swung open another door and stepped aside.

Peyton trailed behind and watched for Ronnie's reaction. A little wide-eyed, she scanned the room, her dark brows hiked in surprise.

Peyton stopped at her side. "Like something out of Hollywood."

"I-I don't know what to look at first," Ronnie managed, her voice full of amazement. "It goes practically all the way across the building, for God's sake. And these," she eyed the pressed-copper ceiling panels, "these are spectacular—and fourteen feet high."

"Commendable observation, Ms. Sharp," Meyers said, stepping closer. "That they are. In need of a vigorous cleaning, but perfectly intact since nineteen fifteen. Original to the hotel."

"Wow." Ronnie wandered along the huge oak prep table that occupied the center of the room. "How big was the hotel staff?"

"Let's see…" Meyers frowned as he thought. "In its busiest years, I…" A narrow door behind him wafted open several inches. He gave it a cursory glance and promptly moved away. "Ah…Yes, the staff. I-I would estimate a dozen or so."

Peyton knew the door had distracted him. She looked back at it just as it drifted closed, and she spun to see if anyone else noticed. No one had.

My kingdom for the SLS right now.

"Considerable updates were made after Sebastian assumed ownership in the latter nineteen seventies," Meyers went on, "and then, in the early nineties, he again addressed the countertops, the light fixtures, appliances."

Peyton followed Ronnie to the stove along the wall and stared down at a forlorn stainless-steel beast, scratched and dented, and lacking in luster, knobs, and pride. "It's some thirty years old." She could almost feel Ronnie's disappointment.

"Yeah, and electric. It probably was state-of-the-art in its day. The ghost of this thing probably haunts the house, too."

Peyton immediately put cooking at the top of her list of concerns.

Ronnie leaned against her shoulder. "But we're not defeated," she amended, and Peyton appreciated that glint in her eye. To Meyers, Ronnie stated, "Is there any power for this?"

"Service has been disconnected. The wiring remains intact, however."

"I'm surprised he didn't go with propane."

"A common arrangement, yes, Ms. Sharp, particularly in a seaside region, and prior to this conversion to electricity, that was used."

"So, propane storage must have been just outside here." She went to a rear window and rubbed some grit off the glass to check. "Maybe under this overhang?"

"Yes. Next to that small addition, the kitchen extension."

Peyton hovered over Ronnie's shoulder. "Sorry, Ms. Casual Cook," she whispered, "but don't even think about bringing in propane."

"Shit. I don't like electric stoves," Ronnie said on a sigh.

❖

Peyton steadied herself with a hand on Ronnie's back as they looked through the cleared spot on the window. The contact made Ronnie turn her head and their cheeks nearly touched, but Peyton didn't mind the intimate proximity a bit. Ronnie apparently didn't object either, lingering before she withdrew to let Peyton access the view.

"In the more recent years," Meyers continued, "Sebastian adopted that paltry addition you see extending out there as his… what you might call a 'refuge.'"

The run-down addition Peyton and Ronnie had seen in August jutted out from the house, just to the right. "The extension really doesn't look all that sturdy," Peyton said, straightening. "When was the room last used?" She caught Ronnie's eye, confident she remembered the little camping stove and propane bottles.

"Two summers ago, I believe, during Sebastian's last trip east." Meyers nearly smiled. "Sebastian made his own way, cooking and sleeping as close as he could to 'his ocean,' as he called it. For reasons I could never comprehend, that little place became a bit of a sanctuary for him. Make no mistake, however, he revered the house as fervently as his ancestors, and insisted all his employees do the same."

Meyers opened the door to the extension and let them step inside. Roughly the size of a modest bedroom, the addition was filled with cobwebs, wooden crates, sagging boxes, miscellaneous hand tools, and sand. Everything was covered in beach sand that had blown in through gaps in the windows and simple framing.

Peyton joined Ronnie at the makeshift table, and they examined the rusty camp stove. "Everything's just as we saw it," she said quietly, "even the portable propane bottles on the floor. They haven't moved since I took those pictures."

"I noticed," Ronnie said, and shook her head. "This will be a project-and-a-half."

Observing from the doorway, Meyers offered, "I imagine Sebastian anticipated returning, but it's possible that the years have finally caught up to him."

"Would you object to us cleaning this room?" Ronnie asked. "Making some space to cook?"

"Cook? In there? When there is a grand kitchen at your disposal right here in the house?" He looked back at it, as if to make sure, and Peyton struggled not to laugh. "But, why would you consider such a thing, Ms. Sharp?"

Peyton waited eagerly for Ronnie to explain. For someone hardly a believer in the paranormal, Ronnie had talked herself into advancing the *Paranormal Pursuit* cause, and Peyton loved it.

Go ahead. Tell him about the propane bottles moving. Admit that this is one spot where you suspect paranormal activity. Explain residual energy.

"For one thing," Ronnie said, "that grand kitchen isn't much more serviceable than this little space out here. Look, maybe we will end up in there, maybe it's a crazy idea, but there's just something about *this* room. It owned Sebastian's heart and soul, you said, so there is that."

"Are you suggesting the room has some…some spiritual connection?"

"Are you aware of any?"

Oh, very smooth, Ronnie.

Peyton forced a look of genuine interest to avoid grinning.

"Am *I* aware?" Meyers looked taken aback, as if cornered. "Uh, well, I…not *really*, but…I mean, I have heard stories over the years, certainly."

"About this room, Sebastian's private nest?"

Meyers clasped his hands at his midsection again and began rubbing them. "I'm afraid stories have originated from all parts of the property over the years."

"'Over the years,'" Peyton repeated, unable to resist jumping into this. "Could you estimate how many? Since Miramar was built? Since it opened as a hotel?"

"Since…uh…Oh, I can't really say."

"How long have you worked for Sebastian, Attorney Meyers?"

"I've been retained by the Baker estate since nineteen eighty-five."

"So, in thirty-seven years you really haven't experienced anything personally. You've just heard stories. In almost forty years."

"Well, I have had my fill of the odd noises and such but hardly more than that." He straightened his shoulders, his eyes flitting about the room. Peyton thought he braced himself for something. She was tempted to look around the room with him.

"Regarding your question, Ms. Sharp," he said suddenly, "cleaning to cook out there *is* a peculiar request, you must admit."

Ronnie responded with a bright smile. "A paranormal TV show asking for *all* of Miramar is peculiar, Attorney Meyers."

"Point taken. Well, it is quite…shabby, but I-I suppose I have no objection to you using it, if you are up to the task. A new owner is bound to rid himself of the room quite promptly anyway. Now, if you're both ready, we'll move on."

They followed Meyers back into the kitchen, and Peyton took her time so Ronnie could gain on her, then whispered over her shoulder. "I'm hiring you full-time."

"I work for food."

Distracted again by how much she enjoyed Ronnie's company, Peyton chided herself back to the task at hand. "He had no intention of stepping into that space, did he?"

"No," Ronnie whispered back. "Awfully edgy."

They passed through the swinging door of the butler's pantry and the dining room stretched out before them. Caroline and Jamie greeted them from the opposite end, silhouetted against the front windows.

"We're in another zip code," Caroline said, her voice echoing off the high ceiling.

Peyton stopped and set a hand on one of the three little tables in the room. "I can only imagine this place full of tables covered in white linen, crystal, fine China. All the well-to-do in their finery."

"I can't imagine *feeding* them," Ronnie observed.

"Many an exquisite meal was served here," Meyers said. "The chandeliers are long gone but the room glittered on many an evening." His heels clacked against the hardwood as he led the way down the middle of the room. "During his residency, as late as 'ninety-five, Sebastian entertained regularly with minimal help, a far cry from the sizeable young staff that labored here in the early years."

"Running this place must have been an organizational feat, way back then," Peyton said as they trailed him back to the foyer. "That job belonged to Patrick Doonan? The loyal house manager?"

"The life-long 'companion'?" Ronnie added.

Caroline nodded encouragement to Peyton from Meyers's opposite side. More details about this man, the taskmaster who oversaw the operation, were critical.

Halfway up the grand staircase, Meyers gripped the banister and came to a stop. They all stopped with him and watched as he surveyed the walls like a tourist.

"Yes, Mr. Doonan." Meyers fussed with his tie. "As children, Sebastian and his siblings summered here, you see, including through the war years, visiting Andrew, their grandfather. They grew up quite familiar with hotel life and Mr. Doonan and his rules."

"What was he like?" Caroline asked. "Was he strict?"

Meyers had only taken two more steps before he stopped again. The subject gave him pause, and Peyton knew it was evident to all of them.

"Quite strict," he said, steadying himself at the banister. "He was protective of the hotel and took his responsibilities extremely seriously. Of course, it was his home as well."

"Possessive, then," Jamie concluded.

He sighed. Selecting his words so carefully seemed to exhaust him.

"You could say that, to a degree."

"To a fault?" Caroline pressed.

"Well, I suppose there may have been occasions where Mr. Doonan overstepped his authority."

"Just to clarify the chronology," Peyton said, "Doonan's employment at Miramar ran from Jonathan's days into Andrew's?"

"Correct. Mr. Doonan worked here from nineteen fifteen until he passed in 'fifty-three of an accident in the cellar."

"He died here?" Jamie nudged Peyton.

"One of the young kitchen boys found him. He'd fallen and hit his head, they think two days prior."

"Two days?" Jamie repeated. "Is the cellar *that* big?"

"It is large and rather convoluted, as I'll show you, but no. Staff simply hadn't had a reason to visit that part of the cellar, until his absence grew curiously prolonged."

"No one *wanted* to find him, I bet."

He turned away from Jamie, unresponsive, and Peyton found that odd. Questioning her with raised brows, Ronnie discreetly held up three fingers. Peyton nodded. *Yes, we're up to three deaths in the house.*

"If you'll follow me," Meyers said, continuing up the stairs, "we'll visit the ballroom and the family quarter—" A violent coughing fit caught his voice. Bent forward, choking and tugging at his tie, he suddenly pitched backward into Ronnie, and they tumbled halfway down to the foyer.

"Jesus!" Peyton exclaimed, rushing down to Ronnie. "God, you went down hard." She set a hand on her shoulder. "Did you hit your head? Are you all right?"

"Yeah, I think. To both questions." Ronnie righted herself on a step and exhaled. "There might be a headache in my future, though. What the hell happened?"

Caroline knelt beside Meyers. "You okay, sir?"

"I-I am," he said, sitting up with Caroline's help. "Thank you, miss. Unfortunately for her, Ms. Sharp helped break my fall." He began brushing off his sleeves and pants. "I'm unspeakably sorry, Ms. Sharp. I do hope you haven't been injured." He stopped his ministrations long enough to look at her, several steps below.

"I'm good." Ronnie stood cautiously and tested her right arm and elbow several times. "I have to say, though, Meyers, neither of us is young enough for acrobatics like that."

"You are quite right." With a firm hold on the banister, Meyers hauled himself to his feet.

"What was that all about?" Jamie asked, sounding more irritated than concerned.

"Just a…a slip on my part. I apologize. I must have been off-balance from the coughing."

"Looked more like you were gagging."

Peyton climbed back to his step. She had plenty of personal experience with spirits on staircases, none of it good, all of it indisputable. Everyone—including Meyers—knew he had been shoved by something. "You've been physically disturbed by things in this house before, haven't you? I'd guess many times."

"Well…as I've said, on occasion—"

"More than occasionally, I'd say, and far more tangibly than the odd noises you mentioned earlier. Sharing those experiences would help us a great deal."

Meyers smoothed the front of his suit jacket and answered her inquiry with a foreboding look. "I freely share what I can, Ms. Stanford."

What you feel safe sharing.

He checked his watch and pointed up the stairs. "Shall we?" He started up without them.

Jamie shook her head and whispered to Peyton. "That might be the end of sharing."

Peyton sent a glance to each of them. "Do you get the impression that Doonan may not like sharing either?"

Chapter Nineteen

How close she'd come to stealing a kiss. Ronnie would have made the most of that one-minute escape with Peyton if she'd had the nerve—and if Miramar's tower hadn't shuddered in the wind. Meyers had waited for them at the bottom of the ladder for a reason. Now settled in the corner of a local bar, they were free of his jittery presence to rehash the tour, and she smiled inwardly at that temptation.

"When other aspects of the building just totally blow you away, blow away a ballroom that big, you are in dreamland," Caroline said, shaking her head. "My mind keeps jumping from one stunning place to the next. The staircase, the ballroom, the tower, that creepy maze of a cellar. Damn."

Peyton flipped curls back over her shoulder and finished typing on her tablet. "And I'm trying to keep track of things like Eleanor sitting in the parlor, a little kitchen door that spooked Meyers, the noises in the tower, and yes, *everything* about that creepy cellar." She took a long sip of beer. "And, of course, Meyers being thrown down the stairs into you." She sent Ronnie a curious look. "How's your head?"

"Still attached, I think."

"We've got our work cut out for us," Caroline stated, "and covering that place—*live*—is going to be wild."

Jamie sat forward, concentrating, both hands around her beer glass. "It's going to stretch us pretty thin. We'll need more cameras and cables than ever, but we can do it."

"The motor home has to be brought up from Jersey," Peyton reminded her. "Every power source has to be on standby. And we'll need extra time to test it all."

"More pre-production work for everyone," Jamie said.

Ronnie began calculating the time and help she'd need to prep Miramar's kitchen addition. It didn't look like a fun project, but the alternative didn't either.

"I can bring in some of my production people to help get that addition in shape."

"Ronnie, I hope you don't mind, but I think it's best if we use the main kitchen," Peyton said, touching a finger to the back of Ronnie's hand. "We'll have electricians check out that stove."

Ronnie had her doubts. She steadfastly preferred real fire to electricity when it came to cooking and had a lot more confidence in her own skills in that ramshackle addition than that decrepit kitchen. Peyton's simple touch represented an olive branch, of sorts, and Ronnie appreciated it, but still disagreed.

"I really do think I can make that little room work for us."

"And I don't doubt for a minute that you could perform miracles in there. I know you don't like electric stoves, and I'm sorry, but that big kitchen has a lot to offer. It's a real eye-catcher and there's more room for you to work, for us to maneuver."

"From a production standpoint," Jamie added, "it really is an ideal set."

"Okay, if that's what you want." Disappointed but resigned, Ronnie tried to be practical. "We probably would end up in the kitchen eventually, anyway."

"It's the perfect spot for our 'family meal,'" Caroline said, ever excited.

"I had visions of using the dining room. You only get one chance in a lifetime at something like that." She refused to sulk. "Just be prepared to replace that stove. How fast can you get electricians in there?"

"Access is our overriding issue," Peyton said with a groan. She sat back and absently gathered her wild curls behind her head. "You could get a bill through Congress before you'd get our legal people to hurry about anything."

Jamie snickered. "Yeah. For something like this? When they have to fine-tune customized liability coverage to suit Miramar," she paused and snickered, "they'll probably re-write the whole damn book." She leaned forward, low over the table. "They'll shit their pants."

"Well, the whole kitchen issue is bound to take time," Ronnie said. She still believed she could clean the little addition and have an array of camp stoves running like clockwork within two days if they wanted. *Maybe I should have all that prepped as backup.*

"We'll need two weeks, minimum," Jamie said. "Electricity is a major issue, and I agree that we should rely on the RV. Power from that Class-A is reliable, proven."

"The kitchen can be isolated, can't it?" Ronnie asked. "Use a separate line?"

Peyton nodded. "We've done that before."

"We'll isolate it, yes," Jamie said. "I'd feel safer if we ran cable wherever we are going to need power, circumvent all the old existing wiring. The electricians might say it's still viable, but our needs could be a strain and I'm not taking any chances." Pausing before taking another drink, she cocked an eyebrow at Peyton. "Sorry, Sebastian Baker, but *Paranormal Pursuit* is not rewiring your massive century-old Victorian. Nuh-uh. We're not doing you that favor."

"No," Peyton said. "Blowing our budget and timetable isn't part of the deal."

Jamie lowered her glass and looked to each of them. "So, set-up and testing obviously will be a lot more involved for this shoot, *even more so* because we have live feeds and social media links to worry about."

"To be safe, two weeks, you said?" Caroline groaned when Jamie agreed.

"We're not quite into October yet, so let's try to keep the stress level down." Peyton drummed the table, and Ronnie figured she was trying to convince herself. "Granted, there's no time to waste, but with the finale scheduled for Halloween, we actually are doing okay."

Now, Caroline chortled. "You *know* network won't see it that way, Peyton. They're going to come down on us now like the plague."

"Then, we'll tell them to light a fire under legal." Peyton sipped her wine and angled her head toward Ronnie. "They had hoped we'd be shooting today."

"I thought I saw an email alluding to that," Ronnie said. "I ignored it."

"So did I."

"It killed them to double our grace period for Miramar," Caroline continued. "You'd think the finale was dropping tomorrow, for God's sake."

"The debut crossover's great numbers bought us the time," Peyton said. "The second airs next week, so I'm betting that reception will keep them out of our hair."

"It better be just as big a smash." Jamie downed the rest of her beer and pushed her chair back. "Look, sorry to wrap this up, kids, but I need to start pumping out emails and phone calls."

"You and me both," Peyton muttered, and they finished their drinks.

"We have to pack, too, don't forget," Caroline said on a sigh as they left the table. "Early flight tomorrow." She surprised Ronnie with a quick hug. "We'll see you soon, I hope."

"For sure," she said, and waved as Caroline left with Jamie.

Peyton stepped around her, heading for the bar. "I'm paying the tab. Don't argue."

Ronnie fell in behind her and watched as she spoke to the bartender. So many words came to mind, too many to articulate. She was too swept away by the vision of Peyton simply reading the receipt, the good fortune of just the two of them in this moment, and hardly noticed the customers nearby. Peyton's crazy golden mane rimmed her shoulders and partially obscured her face as she flashed her credit card, and Ronnie cleared that view with a finger, drawing the soft, unruly curls back.

"Stay. At least one more day."

The bill paid, Peyton took Ronnie by the sleeve, and led her from the bar and out to the parking lot without saying a word.

Maybe Peyton hadn't heard her. Had she spoken too quietly? But then, maybe with strangers around…

They reached the rear of their cars, including the SUV with Caroline and Jamie inside, and Peyton spun to face her. They stood excruciatingly close, and Ronnie's entire body hummed with an electricity that had to come from her. Curiously, the concept of a spirit's energy flickered in her mind. When Peyton smiled, those penetrating eyes transmitted magic.

"Did you say one more day?" She cupped Ronnie's cheek. "I don't think that would cut it, do you?"

"Let's find out."

"Ronnie, I can't," she whispered. "There's no way, not right now."

"Soon, then."

"Soon, definitely."

The current between them flared when Peyton's fingers slid into Ronnie's hair. Seized by anticipation, Ronnie reeled at the pressure of Peyton's hand drawing them together, and then she dissolved into lips so plush, so soft. Arms encircled her neck and Ronnie gathered Peyton to her, deepening their kiss, encouraged by Peyton's luxurious response.

She leaned against the car for support, to feel the full length of Peyton's frame pressed to hers. The tailored business suit wrapped Peyton's figure just as intimately as Ronnie did, and the rich fabric seemed to melt beneath her fingers.

Peyton kissed her long and hard before slowly pulling back, and Ronnie struggled to open her eyes. Her strength had drained. She didn't want this reality to change.

Peyton pecked her lips lightly. "I've wanted to do that all day."

"And now you're leaving. Thanks a lot."

Peyton smiled, that irrepressible light in her eyes softening, tugging. The magic was powerful. "I owed you one from that wonderful evening at your house."

Ronnie exhaled carefully for composure. "When you come back, look for a puddle right here on the pavement. That'll be me."

A not-so-distant voice sounded from the far side of the SUV. "Are you two done?"

Chapter Twenty

Ronnie dodged the fire pit's rising smoke as she rotated bratwurst and ears of corn on the grate. Having Cheryl join her for supper capped off a fine day. The early-October chill was invigorating. It re-energized her after harvesting the season's last produce from her garden and pondering two weeks' worth of long-distance conversations with Peyton.

She was grateful for Facetime. They learned so much about each other, grew significantly closer. They discussed the upcoming investigation, vented about the infuriating wait for Miramar, and resorted to sappy topics like teenagers, lost for hours. But the additional flirtations and very adult innuendos left Ronnie—and, she believed Peyton, as well—even more frustrated by their separation.

Thankfully, the Miramar okay was due at any moment. Everyone stood ready to hit the ground running. Peyton would finish her ridiculously long list of commitments and return.

Ronnie drizzled butter over the corn and plucked potatoes from the coals. She added them to plates of sausages for Cheryl and herself and joined her next to the fire.

"How you can just whip this up so effortlessly still fascinates me," Cheryl said, drawing a bottle of sparkling wine from the cooler at her side.

"Practice, my dear girl. Are you warm enough?"

"Ha. I've already taken off my jacket." She poured wine into cups for each of them and passed one to Ronnie. "Don't add any more wood to that fire just yet."

"Do you think Peyton would get into something like this with me?"

"Are you serious? Of course, she would."

"Well, you used to think she and I were from different planets."

Cheryl hiked a shoulder. "And you are. But does it look like it matters?"

"I can't tell if she would sit out here in the woods—"

"She would. She's not some diva." Cheryl gestured to Ronnie's vest. "Although…she might think twice about you in that disgusting old thing, with paint and pine tar all over it." She leaned closer to inspect a particular spot. "What did you paint such a bright yellow?"

"Hey." Ronnie tugged the zipper up, defiantly. "It's mustard."

"Such a Casanova. It might take some doing to get Peyton Stanford to cozy up to that."

"Cut it out. You know I hate risking *real* clothes near fire."

Cheryl held up her cup and smirked. "I'm so freaking happy for you, I can't stand it."

"Is that what this bubbly is for?"

"Yes. Plus, we have to celebrate the second crossover. Ronnie, the numbers coming in are still insane. *Still.* Congratulations all around."

They toasted and dove into the food. Everything tasted fine, another routine outdoor success, but now Ronnie's appetite waned, her concentration diffused over several subjects.

The network's message after the show aired had been beyond flattering, thanks to an explosion of viewer ratings and fan reaction. Less than an hour after receiving it, Cheryl had called to discuss renegotiating Ronnie's *Casual Cook* contract for huge money.

Email, snail mail, and social media excitement had been running high for days now, and not just about her fabulous oven-baked fried chicken or the mysterious cloud in that Connecticut kitchen or the ghost of Georgina Wallace.

The additional hot topic had become "the odd couple," and Ronnie knew she shouldn't be surprised. Combining "star power" had been the key to the crossovers all along, but it was the connotation of "couple" that lingered with her. Sure, she'd pondered the concept several times, wondered if they came across to fans as allies or adversaries or something else entirely. She really hadn't worried about that *something else*, confident the crossover would never morph into some soap opera.

But she now had a different perspective through which to view the show. She had more input than she'd ever expected, and there was no doubt that fans saw *a lot*. She tried to imagine how Peyton was reacting to all the fan feedback.

"Basically, you keep playing things just like you have been," Cheryl advised, analyzing how to attack her ear of corn.

"You reading my mind is scary."

"Part of the job." She munched half-way along and stopped. "Your personalities, those reflex actions and responses that make each of you who you are, they are hard to control. They could make things tricky for you now."

"I guess. And cripes, we're going to be live for *two hours* on *Halloween*. Is that pushing our luck or what?"

"Hey, suck it up, buttercup." She resumed eating.

"Awkward, yeah. We need some private time to…to, you know, to—"

Cheryl pointed the ear of corn at her. "No sex." Ronnie's jaw dropped, but Cheryl glared and put down the corn. "No screwing around until after the shoot. Don't tell me you weren't going there."

"I was going to say, to get a grip on things between us, to stabilize—"

"Stabilize," Cheryl mumbled around a forkful of potato. "Don't make me laugh with food in my mouth." She swallowed hard. "Getting a grip is more like it. I know it's been a while, but—"

"Yeah, yeah. Okay. I hear you. Cripes, don't start on my love life."

"What you guys have been doing on-air has been golden, pretty much. One more crossover and you two can take the romance up as many notches as you want. Just keep being yourselves."

Ronnie poked at her food. "Network won't step in, will it?

"God, no. There's really nothing to step into—at the moment. Besides, they're obsessed with the Miramar deal and the crossover numbers are keeping them pacified."

"But they're reading the same stuff."

Cheryl nodded as she finished chewing. "Exactly, I know. Some of those tweets while the show was airing? They were hard to ignore. Like when you were cooking the chicken and Peyton came in and drooled over you for a whole ten minutes?"

"She did not," Ronnie said, grinning as she sliced more sausage. "It was only a few seconds."

"I have some favorite tweets from that scene. 'Peyton's hungry for more than chicken.' 'Ronnie's ready for hot action, down to the sleeveless.'"

"I saw them, too, Cheryl. Enough."

"And *you*! When you guys were throwing around theories at the dining room table and you leaned in to write the chronology? That stunt drew a few good ones, too. What were you thinking, or weren't you?"

"I just had an idea and wanted them to get into it. I wanted them to visualize."

"You just *had* to squeeze in beside her? God, Ronnie. At one point there, even I wanted you two to kiss." Cheryl set down her plate to post air quotes. "'Look how Peyton checks her out!' 'If they were any closer…' 'Flirt much, Ronnie?' 'It's obvious they both want it.' I think that one said it all."

Ronnie chucked her paper plate and what was left of her meal into the fire. "I give up. If I was so bad, then Peyton was too."

Cheryl laughed roundly. "To be honest, I do hope you two 'stabilize' things before the Miramar shoot. Try to be a little more cognizant of…of glances, words, inflection—definitely inflection—and personal space. No crowding."

"For God's sake." Ronnie stalked to the woodpile. "People are going to see what they want to see."

"There's a difference here, though, Ronnie." Cheryl sipped her wine. "Your viewers are *wanting what they see*. Inadvertently or not, it's happening. Both your individual shows have seen dramatic upticks in numbers, but the chatter…Increasingly, it's about the crossovers. The Ronnie Sharp-Peyton Stanford thing is becoming a popular storyline."

"The crossovers are *supposed* to bolster each of our shows. Interactions between us just happen. They really are nothing. If they've become something unique unto themselves, there's nothing I can do about it."

"You don't have to and probably shouldn't, but I'm just saying we can't be surprised if the network tries to exploit it."

"You can't be serious. Exploit what, really?" She shook her head. "Please."

"Exploit you two, *this*, the *thing* with ratings that makes them salivate. As long as your numbers are up, network won't care what you two have going on, but it knows viewers care, and that's all the impetus network needs. Hell, if you two really *didn't* have anything going on, the network would insist, because viewers want it." Cheryl pivoted in her seat to face her.

"This is insane."

"Viewer anticipation is everything, Ron, and that's what you guys have created. Fans now feel a common bond, like strangers aboard the same ship. Throw in hints of attraction between our heroines, and ohhh yeah. That's just plain yummy. Frankly, I don't think it will be long before the network's unable to resist capitalizing on it."

"We've given them what they wanted and then some. They should leave us alone now."

"Are you seriously expecting common decency from the network?" Cheryl watched her poke logs in the fire. "What if they proposed a new show for the two of you?"

Ronnie stopped and stared at her. "What have you heard?"

"Relax. Nothing, but the topic came up the other day when Max and I were talking. She's been at this way longer than I have, Ronnie, and knows things, knows more movers-and-shakers than I do."

Ronnie sat down hard, feeling far from grounded.

"Well, have *they* heard something?"

Cheryl shook her head. "Just amused observations about 'Stanford and Sharp.' But, as Max pointed out, amused observations have been known to take root." Grinning, she gave Ronnie a little sock in the arm. "Hey. You really should be flattered, not looking like you've been run over by a truck. This is all just talk, but I thought you'd like to know."

Staring vacantly at the fire, Ronnie listened to the echoes of "Stanford and Sharp."

"I don't even know how to feel about it."

"I know, hon, and I really did hesitate to bring it up. I'm not sure if Max will discuss it with Peyton, either, but like me, she might feel compelled to. And fairly soon."

"Jesus. Everything's hanging on the Miramar finale, isn't it?"

Chapter Twenty-one

When the Depression hit, Jonathan planned to bring in a close friend as a business partner to keep Miramar's head above water. The talk is there was a lot more between them than a business relationship and Doonan had to be furious about that."

Caroline's narration amounted to background entertainment as Ronnie and two of her production assistants hustled to convert Miramar's filthy, voluminous kitchen into something usable. Legalities formalized last night finally set wheels in motion, which brought people, vehicles, and a semi-controlled chaos to the once-solitary place.

Tucked into a corner of the kitchen, safely away from electricians milling around the stove and Ronnie's hyper-cleaning efforts, Caroline continued to summarize from notes on her tablet. "Anyway, Jonathan died before he sealed the deal with *his other man*. It sounds like he had had pneumonia, so they attributed his death to 'consumption,' even though people say he'd been recovering. Police found him in bed."

"Alone?" Ronnie asked and grabbed another roll of paper towels to dry the newly washed counters.

"Apparently alone, yes, but back then, certain 'untoward' things weren't disclosed."

"Are you thinking murder?" Ronnie surveyed the old granite, scarred and dull but sanitary. She considered herself lucky to be making headway because this information was getting harder to ignore. "You know, murder? As in, maybe Doonan was jealous of the business partner or wanted to quash the plan and took it out on Jonathan? Smothered him, possibly?"

"It's all possible. Doonan opposed adding anyone to the household, even Eleanor. A man in the senior citizen complex told me Doonan was vehemently against her moving in, that they argued, sometimes violently, from the moment the family announced her engagement."

"So, you think Doonan also had something to do with Eleanor drowning?" Ronnie backhanded sweat off her forehead. "No. Wait." She frowned and waved off the notion. This was getting to be too much work. *Freaking soap opera.* "Doonan died before her, didn't he?"

"That's the thing," Caroline said. "He was gone a year by then."

Ronnie sighed as she inspected cabinets and shelves, needing to select strategic spots for necessities. "Therefore, Doonan couldn't…" Using a small tape measure, she noted dimensions for a water dispenser she would need on the counter. "Doonan couldn't have had anything to do with Eleanor's death because he was already dead."

Caroline waited until Ronnie turned. "Why not?"

Suddenly reminded of their real purpose here, Ronnie spared Doonan's ghost a thought.

A brief thought, because Peyton strode into the busy kitchen. Her designer jeans, NYU sweatshirt, and denim Reeboks were smudged and dusty, as disheveled as her failing ponytail. Ronnie leaned against the counter to enjoy the view.

Peyton winked and went to the huddle of activity behind the stove. "Alex." She handed the technician a box of parts. "Your guy at the truck said you're waiting for this." She looked at the wiring coming from the wall. "How's it going?"

"Believe it or not, the stove actually works fine, oven, too. It needs a helluva clean-up, though." He rummaged through the box. "We have some miscellaneous knobs that might fit." He wiggled one into position. "The power is okay, but my gut says not to trust it.

I'd feel better if we brought you a separate line right to…here." He pointed to a junction with his screwdriver.

With a sizzling pop, a long spark arced to the tip of the tool and threw him back against the table and onto his butt. Everyone yelled something and lurched toward him.

Dazed, he sat up and examined his hand. "Whoa, that was lucky."

"That shouldn't have happened!" one of his men said. "Everything's off-line. You saw me do it."

Alex stared at the offending junction as his two electricians helped him up. "Yeah, I know you did. It's not your fault." He ran his hands down his thighs, massaging the muscles, then straightened with effort. "When dispatch gave me this address," he told Peyton, "I knew something weird would happen, but I figured we'd be okay with you paranormal people here."

"I'm sorry that didn't make a difference," she said as Caroline handed him a bottle of water. "You're really okay?"

"Oh, yeah. I've been tossed around plenty in my day, just not after doing everything right." He looked back at the wiring. "No explanation for that. And now we're *definitely* running our own line."

Jamie hurried into the room, followed by Eric, Brian, and another electrician. "What happened?"

Peyton held up a palm. "Everything's fine."

"Alex may have a little more gray hair, though," Ronnie said, and Jamie blanched.

With a chuckle, Alex swiped off his cap and smoothed a hand over his bald head. "Ordinarily, I'd take what I could get, but…"

"You get shocked?" Brian asked.

Alex jutted his chin toward the scene of the crime. "Shouldn't have, with all circuits broken and checked, but yeah, you could say I got zapped."

Ronnie shook her head at the incident. She really wasn't looking forward to working on that thing. She mumbled under her breath to Peyton, "God damn electric stoves."

"We can't be too careful," Brian said. "This is some place you picked out, boss."

Ronnie knew Miramar had stunned both Brian and Eric this morning, their first visit here. They had stood out front for ten minutes, little boys gawking at Santa. She almost patted herself on the back. The perfect choice, as long as no one got hurt. She knew Peyton shared the sentiment.

"Miramar has a reputation," Peyton admitted to Alex.

He and his crew chortled. "You could say. After a few calls out here, we learned to at least try to decline. Too many creepy shadows and noises, even for grown adults."

"We have to bring extra batteries when we come here," one electrician offered. "They go dead wicked fast. *Weird* fast."

"I thought I saw a ghost once," another said, sounding eager to join the club. "A grayish-white thing by the parlor windows. It was gone in a flash, though, as soon as I saw it."

Caroline stopped typing notes and leaned toward him over her tablet. "You didn't get a description?"

"Not really, but I had the feeling it was a woman. It sorta flowed onto the floor, like a gown would."

The electrician beside Eric leaned against the wall and Ronnie noticed the small door at his side drift open. With a subtle nod, she called Peyton's attention to it. Peyton then did the same to Eric.

"Excuse me," he said, stepping in front of the electrician and seizing the door. Brandishing a penlight from his pocket, he stooped and leaned in. "Nothing. Maybe a storage space, unless there's some secret panel." He pocketed the light and shut the door. "We'll take a longer look at that."

"I've had doors close in my face," Alex said, "and some open after I close them."

Curious about the door to the kitchen extension, Ronnie opened it after a struggle. "This one won't be opening by itself. I don't remember it being so stubborn when Meyers showed us around, though."

She stepped into the messy room and shivered violently. Enveloped by arctic air, she quickly wrapped her arms around herself. Chilly October felt like frigid January. "Boy, this is bad." She turned at Peyton's arrival in the doorway. "Guess it wouldn't be fun using this space as a backup."

Peyton surveyed the walls, windows, and ceiling. "Unless there are holes in the floor, I don't see why the temperature should be so severe."

"Nothing in here is airtight." She rubbed her arms briskly, wishing she had a coat over her sweatshirt. "I can understand it being chillier than other rooms, but damn. The temperature outside has to be thirty degrees warmer than this."

Peyton waved her back into the kitchen. "So, come out of there." She swung the door closed and forced it shut. "There's another possible explanation," she said confidentially, and put a hand to Ronnie's bicep, "but I don't have an Ovilus at the moment."

Ronnie stared back at her. She hadn't thought of that.

"Y'know, that door," Alex said, shaking a finger at where they stood, "that thing locked me out twice in one day." He shook his head. "This house has never liked change."

❖

Peyton ordered a dessert of tiramisu to share, and Ronnie watched her eye their server as the young woman left.

"She got your autograph, go get her number."

Peyton sipped her coffee and purposely glanced in the server's direction again. "Oh, she'll be back." Teasing steered their dinner conversation away from tomorrow night's live shoot and she happily took advantage of it. "*You* should ask for her number. She checked you out thoroughly while you signed."

"Sure, she did."

"As if you didn't notice. When you handed the paper back, you just *had* to give her that Ronnie Sharp 'come into my tent, baby' smile—"

Ronnie cocked an eyebrow at her. "You think I have a 'come into my tent, baby' smile?"

"Oh, please. It practically knocked the poor woman's knees right out from under her."

"Ah. You like it, don't you?"

"She had to bite her lip. Did you see that, or did her co-ed hotness strike you blind?"

"No, I didn't see it." Chuckling, Ronnie reached for her coffee. "Is this what eating shrimp scampi does to you?"

"When a woman bites her lip like that…You know what it means. I've seen you do it."

Ronnie put down her cup and folded her arms on the table. "And I love it every time you do it. Tell me what it means."

"If I have to tell you, we have a serious issue at this table."

"There are no issues at this table. Solid oak is very sturdy."

"God." Peripherally, Peyton spotted their server returning. "She's coming back. Don't start trouble." She leaned back in her seat and exclaimed to the server, "You're bringing us the largest dessert in the world?"

"Tiramisu especially for Stanford and Sharp," she announced, setting the oversized confection between them. "It's on the house. We're happy to have you both here." She tipped forward slightly. "I apologize in advance for the intrusion, but would either of you mind if I got a picture?"

Peyton and Ronnie leaned toward each other over the table and raised their cups. The server snapped the photo, then a selfie, and thanked them profusely as she backed away.

"Gee," Peyton said toward the tiramisu. She sank her fork in and watched Ronnie do the same. "I wonder what she'll be doing at eight o'clock tomorrow night."

"You'll have to flirt with her on camera." Ronnie took a sizeable bite and groaned with pleasure.

"It's not flirting with *her* that worries me." Peyton sent her a wary look before diving back into the dessert.

"Do we really flirt on camera like Twitter says?" Ronnie asked. "I mean, yeah, we tease a lot, so is that what flirting is today? I guess I'm really out of touch."

"Hell, Ronnie. I thought we were too busy pissing each other off to flirt." She shrugged. "Who knows how people out there think anymore? All I *do* know is that tomorrow, viewers will have to be a secondary concern because that energy in residence may not be welcoming. How we interact, you and I…We'll just have to trust our instincts."

"I know. You probably got the 'keep it in your pants' lecture like I did."

Peyton nodded as she finished another bite. "We don't have anything to worry about, really. Do we?" She did believe viewers exaggerated what they saw in the crossovers. She and Ronnie didn't deserve all that suggestive chatter.

"We'll be fine unless you bite your lip at my 'come into my tent, baby' smile."

"You wish," Peyton said on a laugh, and dueled with Ronnie's fork as they both went back for more. "I'll fight the urge."

"It's going to be a long two hours." Ronnie sighed and set her fork down.

"You can say that again."

Peyton sat back with her coffee and watched Ronnie aimlessly rotate her delicate cup in its saucer. Short incremental movements, the ginger touch of a strong but gentle hand. Her thoughts seemed miles away and Peyton wondered about them, where they had gone.

Her pondering ended with Ronnie's cautionary quip. "You've got to acknowledge our server, though. She might be someone you shouldn't let get away."

She can't really be hiding behind comedy, can she?

Ronnie's bulky fisherman's knit sweater looked irresistibly warm and snuggly, and she looked dangerously irresistible in it. The charcoal color sharpened her brilliant smile and, somehow, added even more depth to her dark eyes. Better not let any of that steal her concentration tomorrow.

She refocused and stirred her coffee again. "Hm. I think she's a little young for me."

"Very pretty, though. The femininity is nice."

"You like that, do you?" Ronnie just grinned. "Did you like those hoop earrings?"

"I prefer clip-ons."

Peyton almost spit out her coffee. "Oh, now, that's a visual I can do without. I meant *on her*."

"They're nice, but a little sparkle is seductive."

Peyton knew her diamond studs had plenty of that, even in this restaurant's subdued light. "What else does Ronnie Sharp find seductive?"

"A stunning blonde asking about seduction." She reached across the table and ran a finger over the back of Peyton's hand. "A woman who knows her own mind and goes after what she wants. A woman who sees beyond the physical and isn't afraid to touch it."

Peyton looked down to hook Ronnie's finger with her own. "How do I respond to that?"

"You just did."

Peyton couldn't keep dismissing this feeling. Acknowledging and rationalizing had kept it under her radar, but this…this *feeling* had a name that deserved to be spoken. Desire. Tomorrow, she simply had to be cognizant of it, not let it get the better of her, and maintain the professionalism that had made *Paranormal Pursuit* such a success. That's all. *As the paranormal world descends on me…and millions of viewers scrutinize my every move.*

"I'm done sharing you with the public, at least for tonight," Ronnie said, signaling for the check. "We're going for a ride."

"We are?"

"I know it's a little late, but so what." She paid the bill and they had almost reached the door when a couple at the last table stood.

"*Paranormal Pursuit*," the redhead said to stop them from passing.

"Thank you," Peyton said. "Are you ladies fans?"

"Oh, *are* we! Of both of you." She touched her companion fondly. "Carla and I have two date nights every week, one for each of your shows."

"I couldn't believe it when the crossover was announced," Carla said. "It was just too good to be true, kind of a crazy idea."

"We thought so too," Ronnie admitted, "in the beginning, anyway."

"So…" The redhead hesitated, then looked from Peyton to Ronnie and back. "We thought you two were, you know, a couple, because of what we picked up watching, or maybe it was just gaydar or whatever, but…it's really true?"

"Well, we're…" Peyton turned to Ronnie. "What are we?"

Ronnie faced her squarely and grinned. "A work in progress?"

Peyton looked back at the couple and rolled her eyes. "As seen on TV."

Both women gave a little cheer.

"We thought so!" Carla said, trying to keep from shouting.

"We absolutely *love* it!" the redhead added. "And tomorrow's your live finale, right? From here on the Cape? *So* perfect, your special show on Halloween night. We can't wait!"

Carla shook her head. "We can't believe we've met you. Thanks for stopping."

"Thanks for watching," Peyton said as she stepped to the door.

Ronnie tipped back and winked. "Wish us luck."

❖

"Where are we going?"

Ronnie loved that curious expression on Peyton's face. She opened her Wrangler's passenger door and Peyton gathered her coat and settled in. "Maybe to hell if we screw up tomorrow."

"Ain't that the truth."

Ronnie hopped behind the wheel and found Peyton was struggling with the seat belt.

"Sorry," she said, closing in to help. "My last passenger was a Patriots running back so this needs to be adjusted."

"The football Patriots?"

Ronnie chuckled as she pulled out of the parking lot. "Yeah, those. Xavier came over to pick up stuff I made. He's hosting a bachelor party for his older brother, who's an old friend of mine."

"Do you get invited to games?"

"Yup. Even a Super Bowl once. You're a Jersey girl, so Giants or Jets?"

"Eagles, if I have to choose."

"Ah. That says you follow football. I can't believe I never asked before."

"Does it mean we are going steady now?"

Ronnie flashed her the goofiest grin she could muster. "You wanna?"

"Hmm. I just might, if you'll tell me where we're going."

"What if I won't?" she asked, choosing a dark side road and cruising onward.

"So, this is a surprise?"

"Premeditated, I confess."

"Are we going off the Cape?"

"God no. Too far."

"Sightseeing at night. This is a tough one."

"Well, where would you like to go?"

"Right now, anywhere but on television." Ronnie downshifted as she prepared to turn again, and Peyton recognized the road. "Miramar?"

"I want us to see it in the dark."

Peyton pivoted as far as her seat belt would allow. "Are you crazy?" She flopped back. "Maybe I'm crazy."

Maneuvering up the rough road, Ronnie started having second thoughts. Peyton hadn't said another word. Had she misread Peyton's fascination with the place? Maybe she wasn't keen on seeing any more of it than necessary. But under an almost full moon on a crystal-clear night, this would be as equally memorable a sight as their first, on that gorgeous August afternoon. She decided to keep their visit brief.

Finally, the woodsy environs shrank back, and the property was revealed. Headlights skimmed the front field and illuminated the empty Victorian far ahead.

"It looks so isolated and forgotten," Peyton said as they drove closer.

"Like it's at the edge of the world, all alone."

Peyton flashed her a look. "We know it's not alone."

Ronnie stopped before reaching the front steps, and they sat in silence, staring. Ronnie switched off the headlights.

"Whoa," she whispered.

The moon bathed the building in silver light, lengthened shadows into black voids. A stiff ocean breeze crested the bluff and whirled against the Wrangler's windows in a steady low moan of welcome.

"Yeah, whoa," Peyton whispered back. "Now, it looks even scarier."

"Yeah, um…Come on," Ronnie said, trying to instill courage in both of them. "Let's get out."

"And do what?"

Ronnie was out of the car and headed to Peyton's door. She opened it but Peyton still sat buckled in. "Ronnie, do you really—"

"Relax, will you?" Ronnie draped herself over Peyton's lap and unbuckled her seat belt. "That was fun," she said grinning, and surprised her with a quick kiss. "Come with me." She held out her hand.

"I'd ask if you're always this impossible, but why bother." Peyton took her hand and stepped out.

Ronnie led them to the front steps and felt Peyton adjusting her hand, tightening her grip.

"Very Hitchcock, isn't it?" Ronnie said as she gazed up the face of the building.

"Oh, yeah, sure, full of romance and roses. And we just started going steady. What was I thinking?"

"Aw, but it's just a sad old building. And it *is* romantic in the classic sense."

"You picked a great spot to turn into a softy, Romeo." She swung their joined hands toward the steps. "Listen. Just because I have a key now, do *not*—I repeat—do *not* even think about going inside."

"No?"

"Hell, no."

Ronnie laughed roundly. "God, such a sexy command voice. Don't worry. We're staying the hell out of there. Tomorrow will be soon enough."

"Exactly. The lovely Mr. Doonan can have it for one more night."

The breeze stiffened and ruffled their coats, slapping a loose downspout against the porch.

They both jumped.

"Shit," Peyton said. "He heard me."

Ronnie hustled them around the side of the house.

When they turned the corner, the breeze became wind, a blustery precursor of an angry sea somewhere off the bluff. Reflexively, they dipped their heads to it as Ronnie walked them toward the edge.

"At least it's not a bitter wind," she offered.

Entranced, Ronnie watched as Peyton scanned the black ocean, blond curls white in the moonlight soaring behind her in the wind. Her navy blue coat flared and she gathered it around her, standing with arms crossed, looking every inch the goddess of the sea.

Ronnie swallowed hard.

"The moon is so bright," Peyton said, turning her face up to it, "like daylight."

"My father used to claim the moon was full if you could read a newspaper outside at midnight."

"I think he's right. I can see whitecaps out there."

"That usually means a storm is brewing, but this moon is too special. I wanted you to experience this, how the New England Atlantic never sleeps."

"It's beautiful," Peyton said on a sigh, and leaned against her.

Ronnie slipped both arms around her and drew her in. "Happy Halloween."

Peyton chuckled into Ronnie's coat and settled her head on her shoulder. "Same to you."

Rebellious curls danced at Ronnie's cheek, tickled. She turned into them and closed her eyes. "Cold?"

"No. This feels good." She uncrossed her arms and locked them around Ronnie's waist. "*You* feel good."

Heart racing, Ronnie squeezed her closer. "I brought you here to kiss you, because…you know…ocean and moonlight and everything."

Peyton looked up at her and grinned. "And such a romantic haunted house."

"Shh."

Chapter Twenty-two

When Miramar came into view on Halloween night, the first thing Peyton did was pound the dashboard. "What's with the light show? This isn't some national landmark." Windshield wipers swished valiantly against the downpour, but she felt as much as saw the indignity being forced upon the place.

"Yeah," Brian chortled from the back seat. "Bet you could see it from space."

Eric sighed as he brought the SUV to a stop on the driveway. "Hey, did you notice it's coming down in sheets? Be thankful Jamie's throwing everything she brought into a torture test. She knows what she's doing."

Brian and Caroline poked their heads between the front seats for a better look.

"Storm is supposed to come in waves," Brian reported. "Fade and come back."

Peyton massaged her temple. "Yeah, I read that, too."

"I remember trick-or-treating in the rain," Caroline said, still staring through the windshield. "All our cool costumes wasted, covered by raincoats. It sucked."

"And it sucks now," Peyton stated, studying the many powerful lights. Enough to land a plane. They pierced the rain and over-exposed Miramar to the world. Such Hollywood treatment seemed shameful, embarrassing. "We're not shooting a movie. We only need this for the wide shot when we open and maybe when Jamie brings us back from commercials."

"I know," Eric said. "I agree. Stop worrying. Look, she already put blackouts on those front windows. None of us carrying a camera would want that light blaring in. This isn't Jamie's first rodeo."

As he parked just off the driveway, Peyton eyed their forty-foot Class-A in the side yard. She hoped everyone was up for a mad dash. "We're going to get drenched, but I am glad Jamie stationed the motor home so close to the building. Look at all the cables. Damn. It *would* be pouring."

Thick black power cables draped off a side panel of the motor home and fanned out in different directions. Several traveled onto the front porch and disappeared into a barely opened window. Someone had affixed black cloth across the remaining opening to keep out the rain and light, and it rippled against the wind. That was the library, chosen for their base of operations because power could easily be extended throughout the house.

A cable also ran to the lights out front, and one snaked around to the back, no doubt for the kitchen and maybe the cellar, Peyton thought.

She tried to see outside the SUV for Ronnie's van, but a U-Haul box truck and a Suburban blocked her view to the side and the rain took care of the rest. Ronnie would need help bringing in her gear and could get soaked in the process.

"At least it's easing up outside," Caroline said, and Eric switched off the wipers.

"*Rain* isn't so bad," Brian mumbled. "I'll take it over that monsoon."

Peyton turned in her seat. "Okay. Pass up my bag, please. It's time for us to rock 'n' roll." They stuffed items into carryalls and wrestled into rain slickers, as Peyton repeatedly glanced out the window. *Where is she?*

"Good-bye, coffee." Eric took a parting sip and left it in the console. "Ready?"

"Go!" Brian said, and they charged across the field to the Class-A.

Jamie had the door open for them. "Good thing I saw you coming. Brian looked ready to plow his way in." She gestured to the bathroom. "Shoes off and slickers in the tub. No messing up the place."

"Giving orders already?" Eric asked, pulling off his sneakers.

"He's only staying for a moment," Peyton stated.

He raised his hand as he dropped his slicker into the little bathtub. "Network background, that's me." He pointed at the table and the two large monitors, laptop, and pile of connections.

"Better you than us," Caroline said, rubbing her hands together. "We want to get in the house."

"Speak for yourself." Brian snorted. "Besides, we have time. It's not even five."

Jamie turned to Peyton. "Sam's already inside, getting his settings. He's also adjusting a second camera just like his. You guys will take turns shooting with it because this place is too big to have just one scene camera. You're breaking into two teams, right?"

Peyton said, "Now and then, I'm sure. We'll need a second one available to keep live action constant."

"Any sign of Ronnie?" Jamie sat at the table to help Eric. "She told me she wanted to get started now."

"Now?" Caroline asked. "We're not opening the investigation till seven."

Brian sent Peyton a perfunctory look. "As far as I'm concerned, the sooner Ronnie starts, the sooner we eat. I starved myself all day for her meal. Like Thanksgiving, you make sure you have room."

"I get it." Peyton had to smile. "I think she's going to try something special for us and whoever is floating around, a little simulation of the 'Grand Miramar Hotel' in the dining room."

Eric shook his head as he and Jamie unraveled wiring and plugged things in. "She is amazing, you know. One of a kind." He glanced up and winked at Peyton. "I wish Mason had come with me. He loves that stuff."

"Well, she really seemed so disappointed we weren't using the room, but when I told her our timetable, she reconsidered. We're beginning at seven, to be acclimated and hopefully shake things up for when we go live at eight. After I do the 'greet the viewers' thing, we'll go through an experiment, and—I hate to break it to you, Brian—but then, we'll eat."

Brian zipped his slicker again and stared at her. "No food till after eight?"

Everyone dismissed his complaint. Jamie tossed him a bag of chips off the shelf behind her.

Peyton shrugged. "Yeah, dinner will probably happen somewhere around eight thirty."

"Because of our start time," Jamie reminded him. "Actually, it's very cosmopolitan."

Brian grumbled as he went to the door. "It's cruel."

Peyton elbowed him. "She might have appetizers up her sleeve."

His eyes brightened and he hurried off to the house as the others laughed.

"So," Jamie said, "where is she?" The Class-A's doorbell startled them all, and Jamie chuckled. "Boy, are we jumpy."

Peyton pressed the button and the door swung open. Dressed in black topcoat and bowler, Ronnie doffed her hat and bowed.

"Good evening, Ms. Stanford."

Ronnie ascended the stairs as Caroline, Jamie, and Eric applauded.

Peyton's breath caught and she smiled. "I never know what to expect."

"Behold," Ronnie said to Peyton's gaze, "the finest vision any of us should see in that house tonight." She kissed the back of Peyton's hand.

Eric hooted. "Nice!"

"*Very*," Peyton whispered. *Fight the temptation.*

Ronnie reset her bowler and leaned toward the others, quickly looking around with a conspiratorial eye. "Nice digs."

"Nice duds," Eric responded.

Peyton grazed a palm along Ronnie's back. "Glad you're here."

"Me, too."

Peyton drifted in the moment until Jamie blurted out, "Well, hurry up and kiss, will you?"

"Splendid idea!" Ronnie said, not looking away.

Peyton took her face in her palms. Obviously, she needn't hide it anymore, this thing buzzing between them, not from the team, anyway, and she was damn glad. She fit her lips to Ronnie's perfectly and enjoyed every dazzling second. *While I can.*

"Okay, that's enough." Jamie slid out of the horseshoe booth and Eric followed. "We're done here for now. Everybody out."

Ronnie turned and led the way.

"Where's your gear?" Peyton asked.

"Already inside. A two-wheeler makes things easy."

"We started to get worried. I was ready to help you."

"Thank you, but I couldn't have you out in the rain, melting."

"Hey, this wicked witch doesn't melt."

"That's not what I—" Ronnie stutter-stepped.

Peyton walked ahead to the front stairs. "You have the devil in you, Ronnie Sharp."

"I do not." Ronnie hurried to come abreast of her. "You want to be Glinda, the good witch?"

"Quit while you're ahead, pal."

"Do you like the bowler?" Ronnie pointed to it.

"Changing the subject won't save you, either."

"Well, sure as shit, that other subject went off the rails."

"Yes, the bowler is cute."

"'Cute'? I was shooting for dashing or…or debonair."

"At the moment, you get 'cute.'" Peyton stopped them at the staircase. The others circumvented them, smirking. "Ronnie. The Wicked Witch of the West wouldn't say 'debonair.'"

"Why not? I mean…Shit."

Peyton burst into laughter and pulled Ronnie into a hug.

"You win. Debonaire is exactly right, and I love the bowler and coat."

"And the 'come into my tent, baby' smile."

"I'd come into your tent anytime, baby." She rubbed her nose against Ronnie's. "*After* we take care of business."

"And we should be 'all business,' tonight, I suppose."

"For this investigation?" Peyton almost laughed. "Yes."

❖

Ronnie popped open oysters in the sink like a pro and nestled each one onto a sheet-pan bed of kosher salt. Already, she had two cheeseballs firming in her mini-fridge, eggs boiling for deviled eggs, onions sautéing for the oyster topping, and platters prepared with nuts, gumdrops, and jelly beans. She paused to recount the oysters. Yes, almost two dozen.

Her first self-imposed deadline of the evening dinged on her cell phone, but she worked on steadily as Sam struggled to keep up with her relentless dance around the big kitchen.

It was crucial to have the camera tuned in to her every move because she talked to it habitually. Peyton did, as well. It was a consequence of the trade. One didn't demonstrate appreciation for viewers by failing to look them in the eye. The camera had to be spot-on when needed. *Exorcist* head turning, flitting her eyes everywhere searching for Sam, wouldn't do.

"Good thing you get to practice like this before we go live," she told him. "You'd have viewers bouncing all over the place. They'd get seasick."

"I know. I keep bumping into this damn table. It's too big, but I'll get the hang of it."

Being on the air live at a specific time crimped her process severely, one of the reasons Ronnie hated the format. To make up for being off-camera and her audience missing so much food preparation right now, she planned to take viewers on a tour of the rooms, once things went "hot," explain the appetizers she had put out along the way. She had more than enough time to accomplish that and then detail everything about dinner and dessert before it was time to serve. She shook her head at the memory of a restaurant opportunity many years ago, how she had declined because of the pace and stress. Tonight's came close. Thankfully, these co-workers added something special.

With appetizers now ready, Ronnie tackled the "presentation" part of her job, which, in this case, meant incorporating the *Paranormal Pursuit* effort. She went through Miramar's sad, barren rooms and set out accessories she had borrowed from a caterer friend, hoping for a little of that "period" ambiance.

Here and there, the stools and bistro tables with burgundy runners she set up added a great deal. And chairs and folding tables in the dining room meant even more, especially when she added white floor-length linen tablecloths. She couldn't help smiling once she topped all surfaces with candlesticks and assorted appetizers. *There's just something about Oysters Rockefeller against white linen.* She laughed out loud at herself.

Until she spotted the table in the middle of the foyer. She had set it up only five minutes earlier, complete with deviled eggs and cheese and crackers. Irritated, she promptly moved it away from the staircase and returned it beside the library doorway. Then, she stepped back and shook her finger at it, just as Brian came around the corner.

"*Really* great job again, Ronnie." He leaned closer, oyster in hand. "Just so you know, you're talking to a table."

"Ha. Yeah, I am, aren't I? Damn thing. Looks like we're in for another circus." She continued staring at it. "Help yourself to those goodies before they walk away, too."

Back in the kitchen, she prepped the spiced ham for dinner and set it aside to go into the oven later, then started on the special salad. Peyton arrived, devouring a fistful of peanuts, followed immediately by Caroline, who bounced blindly off the doorframe, eyeing Ronnie through a massive camera lens.

Ronnie stopped rinsing lettuce to wave at the camera. "Ladies, welcome to the bustling kitchen of the Grand Miramar Hotel. Please, please, come right in. Step right this way. My apologies," she presented a little stool by the door, "but seating currently is limited. May I interest you in a cocktail?"

"Cocktail? Have you started without us?" Peyton asked.

"How could I? You wound me, lovely lady."

"Honestly, Ronnie. Is the Casual Cook ever frazzled? You've done so much already, getting all that food together, putting out the furniture, and all." She touched Ronnie's shoulder. "Thank you. It could generate some interesting results. Everyone appreciates it."

"Yeah," Caroline said, "especially Sam and Eric."

"They did a number on the Oysters Rockefeller," Peyton explained. "If you hadn't put some in the parlor, we would have missed out. And they were outstanding."

"Like that apron, Ronnie," Caroline teased her from behind the camera.

Ronnie looked down at herself. The tan suede apron she wore over black shirt and pants hung from shoulder straps to her thighs and tied behind her waist. "Sexy, huh?" With a Vanna White flourish, she gestured to the yellow *Casual Cook* script across her chest. "All the gals love it."

"You are too much," Peyton said as Caroline laughed.

Ronnie pointed at the camera. "Is that Sam's?"

"It's just like his," Caroline answered. "We're going to need more than one, so this thing and I are getting reacquainted. Walking around here, though, you never know what's going to be in your way."

"I'm her guide," Peyton quipped.

"Good," Ronnie said, "because I've already had a table move."

Peyton snapped to attention. "What? Where?"

"In the foyer, so watch your step. That's one troublemakin' table."

"Thanks for the tip." Peyton rubbed the peanut salt off her hands.

"Did I get answers about cocktails? Do you have time?"

"I'd love one," Caroline said. "I need fortification."

"Peyton?" Ronnie went to a crate in the corner and offered bottles of cognac, Cointreau, and triple sec. "Sidecar, circa nineteen twenty-two? You won't convince me Jonathan Baker and Patrick Doonan never indulged."

"Sure, why not. We don't have much time, though. It's going on seven and we'll need to start soon."

Ronnie grabbed a shaker and half-filled it with crushed ice from a cooler. "What room are you going to first?" She composed the concoction and shook it vigorously, pausing to hear Peyton's answer.

"The dining room, then the second-floor bedrooms and the family's suite. Nobody has mentioned experiences in any of those places, so I'd like to either check them off our list or see if we can stir things up."

"For me, that means the ham can go in soon," she said, rimming their glasses with lemon and sugar, "to get that aroma flowing through the house. My humble contribution."

Caroline set the camera on the floor and rubbed her shoulder. "You're making bread again, I hope." She watched Ronnie strain the mixture into the glasses.

"I am, thanks, Caroline. I brought dough from home so it would be ready to go. I just put it in a few minutes ago."

"No frozen dough balls?" Peyton whispered.

Caroline leaned forward. "Did you say 'frozen dough balls'?"

Ronnie grinned as she handed out the coppery-orange drinks. "We were talking pizza a while back. I keep my dough balls frozen."

"Ohh, Okay," Caroline said, obviously missing the joke. "Hey, Brian?" She lifted her glass toward the static camera, knowing he could see but not hear her. "Don't be jealous or anything."

"If that doesn't get him," Peyton said, also raising her glass, "just wait till the smell of bread and ham reaches him. It's going to drive everyone, crazy."

Ronnie tapped her glass to Caroline's and held it against Peyton's. "That's the idea."

"To a safe investigation," Caroline posited.

"I'll drink to that," Ronnie added, "and to Miramar."

"And to us," Peyton said with a nod. "May we *all* get lucky on this one."

They drank in unison and Ronnie waited for reactions. She'd been careful to go easier than usual with the alcohol and was rooting for the citrus flavors to prevail.

"Mm…Yum. Smooth," Caroline said, sipping again.

Peyton liked it too, the approval was in her eyes. "Very nice. Sweet in a gentle way."

"Oh, very perceptive," Ronnie said, warmed by the inference. "I made a smaller amount, too, because time is short. I'm a firm believer that sidecars should be savored like cordials, otherwise you'll wake up on the floor of somebody's car."

"Speaking of floor," Peyton began, "please watch for wiring now. We have static cameras everywhere. We've tried to tuck wiring away or tape it down, but you never know."

"I'll do that."

"Brian put one in the cellar, I'm sure, so watch out for that wire, too."

"Yeah, I see it over there." She went to one of her coolers, came back with several pineapples, and began chopping off tops and bottoms. "Hey, you know, I haven't been able to open that door to the extension. It was really stuck the other day, but I got it. Remember when it was freezing in there?"

"I do." Peyton went to the door and tried it to no avail. "Hm. I remember shutting it, *really* shutting it. I might have jammed it."

Ronnie shrugged. "Who knows? Maybe when the kitchen really heats up, it will open."

Chapter Twenty-three

Peyton examined her cloud of curls in the Class-A's bathroom mirror and decided it was worth enduring a few minutes in the ocean wind to avoid tying it back and narrowing the shape of her face. She leaned in, touched up her waterproof mascara, and added a hint of lipstick. *Nothing stands up in this miserable weather, under those bleaching lights.*

"Ten minutes," Jamie called from the horseshoe booth.

Peyton emerged, checking that she had tucked the white button-down into her jeans and that her modest belt buckle was centered. "Am I good?" she asked, buttoning her denim suit jacket.

Jamie pushed her headphones back from her ears. "You're kidding, right? You, who haven't used a makeup artist in years?"

"I can't stand all that goop, and most cosmetics drive our electromagnetic read—"

"Right. Take this." Jamie held out a cordless microphone, her eyes back on the monitor. "I have network and Brian standing by. It goes network to me, into Brian in the library, out to Eric, and then to you. Easy. No camera goes live without a keystroke from right here. Remember: everywhere there's a static camera, we're watching, not eavesdropping. They all are continuously on screen, but they can't hear. The bigger, scene cameras have excellent two-way mics and give us everything." She hung on the last word and eyed Peyton sideways.

"What? That's good. I want you to get everything."

"I know you know this stuff, generally speaking, but going live means consciously breaking your routine. Sure, we bleep out the curse words and can cut a camera if necessary, but if you guys are in the middle of something good, we can't reasonably just hack a piece out of the action."

"You *could* in an emergency. We could claim a power glitch or someth—"

Jamie's chiding look cut her off. "Fans know *Paranormal Pursuit* doesn't lie to them. Glitches are up to the spirits, not us."

Peyton rubbed her palms down her hips. Nerves were creeping in. *There will be no editing, so no mistakes. Professionalism is what got us all here. No forgetting all those eyes watching.*

Jamie went back to the rundown. "So. From my keyboard, every camera, static or scene, can be cut off, switched, or run simultaneously. Network will link what it gets to all the social media in Lala Land. And, by the way, that's two-way also. We'll see chatter in real time, Peyton, and that's a huge deal to viewers and to us. Hell, you guys can even log in on your cells and watch it."

"As if we'll have time."

"True," Jamie said, "but viewers would like having you guys see their stuff on-air."

"We'll try to work some of that in."

"Okay. Your operations center in the library has all cameras onscreen, and everything there comes to me. You guys monitor your work-in-progress, I monitor what the network receives, network monitors what goes out. Network can only stop the transmission and, therefore, obviously, block links. *I* decide what it gets."

"Excellent. I got it."

"Camera one is sitting out there now with a perfect shot of the facade, and I gotta say, it looks freaking creepy, the flashlight-under-your-chin effect. Could we have asked for more appropriate weather to do a haunted house on Halloween?"

"It still totally sucks."

"The forecast is really nasty in case you haven't heard."

"It can't matter. Not now."

"Good. Oh, we have support gear by the ton here for everything. And walkies." She held up her walkie-talkie. "Old-tech, I know, but that's why I swear by them. Each of you keep one clipped on you somewhere. And your operations center is well stocked with backup instruments and batteries."

"Anything else?"

"Just so you know, your cue comes immediately after the one-minute cold open with the locals' testimonials. We'll fade to black after the last one, then 'bring you into the light.'" She grinned at the phrase. "Are you all set?"

Peyton nodded. She enjoyed openings but despised going live. It gave her teenage jitters. And under these fluid conditions? She could pull it off. She always did.

"Good luck with everything tonight, Peyton, and tell Ronnie I died and went to heaven over the Rockefellers she brought me. You guys be careful…and knock 'em dead."

Peyton laughed lightly at that.

The constant stiff breeze here on this side of the house delivered an unusually pungent dose of salty air and stopped her in the yard. Tonight, she heard the waves so clearly, their relentless, determined smashing against the bluff. A faint, low grumble reached her, and she hoped it wasn't thunder emanating from somewhere out in that blackness where ocean and sky blended. Reconsidering, she hoped it *was* thunder, and not something emanating from the house.

She walked on to Eric who waited in the shadows beside the porch. The scene was surreal, heavy mist falling like snow through all those blazing white lights, tripod studio camera bound in rain cloth perfectly focused and waiting for her to enter the shot. Miramar stood formidably, held in check by a battery of beacons, and she would enter neutral ground, bringing millions with her.

"Brian just told me two minutes." Eric fussed with his headset.

"Test me, please." She spoke into the mic for a sound check.

Eric listened to Brian's report. "Everyone's got you loud and clear." A satisfied smile then overtook his face. "He says social media is blowing up his phone already."

"It's why we're doing this, right?" Peyton sighed. "You think the rain's coming back?"

"Yeah, any minute. We have to get through this bit and get inside."

Peyton didn't want to think about social media, viewers hungry to catch and analyze everything they saw *or thought they saw*. However, she did want to invite viewers along for this ride. That was different. She could only control so much, and she could control viewers' perception no better than she could the weather. She wished for a few more minutes of just mist, although she knew her curls didn't. And wasn't it simply too weird, being eager for the shelter Miramar provided?

"Funny, how ridiculously nerve-wracking this live stuff is for us," Eric said, "considering what we cope with for work." He was delivering the pep talk and she loved him for it. "But we're not rookies, Peyton. Remember: we really do go through this for every show." She raised an eyebrow at him, and he shrugged. "Okay, the audience is a little different. So what? You're refereeing this thing tonight, so let the audience know it. You'll have them right here in a heartbeat." He pointed to the palm of his hand.

Peyton stroked curls off her cheek and cleared her throat as she waited for his cue. "I'll bring everybody inside in a minute or so."

He pressed a hand to his headset and his eyes met hers. Then he waved her away.

Peyton took a breath. She rounded the corner, stepped into the blinding lights, and strolled across the front of the building.

"Good evening and happy Halloween," she crooned deliberately into the mic and moved casually to her designated spot at the steps. "I'm Peyton Stanford and," she blinked up into the mist, "on this *lovely* evening, I welcome you to a very special, two-hour live edition of *Paranormal Pursuit*. For this, our season finale, we're sincerely overjoyed—and lucky—to bring back *Casual Cook* chef Ronnie Sharp to our team. And we look forward to all of you out there partnering with us on what we anticipate being an extremely memorable investigation."

She half-turned, indicated the building at her back, and thunder rumbled offshore.

"Did you catch that? Yes, thunder. Of course, right? Could we have staged this any better? Here in Massachusetts on a Cape Cod bluff overlooking the ocean? Seriously, we didn't script the weather."

The occasional rumbling grew louder, more frequent.

"Before we are inundated out here, let me introduce you to the subject of our attention this evening. The proud Victorian behind me is Miramar." She pivoted slightly to share a quick look with the audience. "Private mansion of the Gilded Age, grand hotel through Prohibition and World War II, and family residence thereafter."

Peyton held out a palm to signal everyone that rain had started. Lightning flickered and bangs of thunder sounded closer than before. She shook her head at the camera.

"Although today, Miramar is retired, we believe you all will soon agree, it is *unquestionably* active. We're here to 'inquire within,' as they say, to connect where possible with whatever is lingering here, whatever has been perpetuating sightings and physical contact—sometimes serious physical contact—for generations." She beckoned the audience with a wave. "Are you ready? Follow me."

She climbed the steps and gripped the door handle, just as lightning crackled across the sky and illuminated everything not already visible beneath the spotlights. Peyton flinched and thunder clapped so hard the porch trembled.

"Time for us to get inside," she told viewers.

She opened the door and smiled into Sam's scene camera. "Here we are. Imagine the lives lived here. It truly is a magnificent building." Sam gave viewers a slow, three-hundred-sixty-degree survey of the foyer. "We've left these little ceiling lights on for now, to show you what served the hotel in the nineteen forties. They are everywhere, dim by today's standards, but, as you can see, they still work. There are quite a few in the dining room," she narrated, and Sam followed her inside, "complete with stage for a touring orchestra or band, and dance floor. Enormous, isn't it? The old lights help with perspective."

Peyton returned to the foyer. "The lights are basically all that's left. We've staged a few little things, because we're always searching for ways to trigger a spirit's interest, right? But although its furniture was removed long ago, Miramar is not *empty.*

"Many people have been hurt here, injured by 'nothing' they could see, as recently as two days ago and, possibly, as far back as one hundred years. The frequency of unexplained incidents is increasing. It's as if Miramar is now fighting to be left alone. And, for an owner, a first responder, someone visiting for any purpose, these attacks must stop."

Sam continued to shoot as Peyton ascended the staircase. "So, what are we up against tonight?" She stopped at the spot where Meyers was pushed and looked back down into Sam's lens. "Shadow figures, dusty cloud-like images, irregular human forms. A large, sharply dressed figure resembling the hotel's long-time manager allegedly has been spotted on this staircase many times, as has the ghost-like image of the current owner's late sister in the parlor. Both died at Miramar. So did the hotel's original owner. We've learned of all sorts of occurrences from a variety of sources, former employees, long-time residents, local police, a personal associate of the fam—"

The little antique ceiling lights flickered, and everything went black.

Thankfully, the beacon from Sam's camera still illuminated Peyton for the audience.

"Hey! Looks like it's time we got to work. Sam? All of you still with me?"

He tapped his headset to confirm his connection to Brian and Jamie. "We're here," he said.

"Excellent. Just so all of you at home know the score, your 'main man' covering entire scenes tonight is Sam Fenner. You'll be riding with him through light and darkness." Sam switched off his camera's built-in spotlight and reverted his imaging to night-vision. "Now," Peyton said and waved grandly around her, "we're on our own."

"It's just the house lights, Peyton," Eric said, emerging from the operations center in the library. "Our power's up." Peyton trotted down to receive the battery-operated lantern he offered.

"Hi, everybody," he said and waved at Sam's camera. "*Something* just took out Miramar's lights, but we've run our own power to keep our static cameras going. Bring up our website, Facebook page, etc., and you'll find them on tripods, lurking in corners all over the place. You can help us keep tabs on those locations throughout the investigation. Be sure to jump on social media and let us know when you spot something we should know about. It's going to be a fun night."

Caroline appeared with two personalized night-vision cameras and handed one to Peyton. "Good thing we're used to working in these conditions."

Peyton glanced up at Sam and the audience as she switched on the camera. "We need to go check on our chef."

"Eric and I will start an EVP session in the parlor," Caroline said.

He agreed. "I'll grab the other scene camera. Here, take my walkie. I think Ronnie already has one. And I'm sure she'll need a lantern."

❖

Peyton walked swiftly down the hall to the kitchen with Sam trailing after her. Bringing along the entire viewing audience didn't sit well, and probably wouldn't with Ronnie, especially if she was stumbling around that gigantic kitchen in the pitch-black.

"Big house," she commented to viewers over her shoulder, and brought the walkie to her mouth. "Hey, Casual Cook," she called ahead. "Hope you're decent. We're *all* coming in." She clipped the walkie to her belt and opened the kitchen door.

Ronnie knelt on the floor, picking up a splattering of banana peels and pineapple remnants by the light of her cell phone. She didn't look up.

"And I thought *my* timing was impeccable," she grumbled.

Sam backed away to the door to include their interaction in his shot while Peyton walked a couple of steps closer.

"What happened?"

"I was about to ask you the same thing." Ronnie sat back on her heels and forced a grin for Sam's camera. "Hello there. I'm Ronnie Sharp and no, I'm really not offering a *Casual Cook* episode from the floor of a haunted house. Pardon my being so indisposed. Makes a lovely first impression, I'm sure."

"What…Did you fall?"

Ronnie shook her head and swiped up a few more pineapple tops. Their leaves flew off out of reach. "You know," she said, sighing toward Sam, "Those of you at home taking notes? Only use the meat of the fruit to make this salad. A table would be a wise choice as well." She threw several banana peels into the trash and dropped back to her hands and knees. "I'm ordering all garbage pails chained to the floor forthwith! So. How goes it with you?"

"Well," Peyton started, trying not to laugh, "we, ah, we're in the dark. Sorry. You know that." Ronnie just grunted. Peyton put the lantern on the floor for her. "House power went out but we're okay. The stove's okay, too, right? The oven?" The red light on the front told her it was, and she turned to Sam. "If you could only smell what we smell. The Casual Cook's spiced ham and homemade bread. I think the oven's okay."

Ronnie tossed the last remnant away and stood, shoving her cell phone into her back pocket. "Thanks for the lantern." She washed her hands quickly in a basin of hot water she had heated on the stove. "I had a bin on the table for scraps as I worked, and I reached behind me for something and heard this crash." She shook her head at Sam. "Absolutely no idea how the thing went from point A to point Disaster."

"Something about you must rub spirits the wrong way."

Ronnie tried to hide her grin, but Peyton spotted it.

"There has been no rubbing," Ronnie declared, striding back to her salad preparations. Displaying a bowl of bright red cherries, she added, "Spirits love my food. It's been proven. Just not trash bins."

That's when Peyton noticed what was under construction at that far end of the table.

"Ah…Chef Ronnie?" She winced at the surprising crack of lightning. Then they all ducked when thunder shook the house.

"No 'chef,' please. Just Ronnie."

"Well, 'just Ronnie.'" Peyton folded her arms and slouched against the wall, "Could you enlighten our audience as to what *exactly* you're making?"

Seven small but erotically suggestive adventures were arrayed in front of Ronnie. Half of a banana stood erect on each plate. That's all Peyton could discern from her distance, but that was enough, and Ronnie's long, knowing look almost made her blush.

"Captured your interest?" Ronnie asked.

"Not just mine, I would guess."

Ronnie waved her, Sam, and viewers to the table.

"I'll finish one now to show you guys. The others I'll do after dinner. See? Simple. A stack of pineapple rings on lettuce, banana standing just so in the center, and then you add…" She dolloped whipped cream onto the tip of the banana, and they watched as it slid down, coating the shaft. "Now, listen, everybody. Before you put your hands over your eyes, I'll have you know that this was an extremely popular dessert salad in the nineteen twenties." She topped it off with a cherry. "It's called 'candle salad.'" She raised her right palm. "I kid you not."

Peyton grinned toward her feet. Brian called her through the walkie-talkie and she snatched the unit off her hip.

"Yes, Brian?"

"I'll give you a dollar if you bring me one."

"Bye, Brian." She clipped the walkie back on her belt. "Well, we know he's paying attention to the monitors." She stared at the dessert. "I bet that was popular here." *In the twenties? With Jonathan Baker and his proclivities?* "I wonder if it was a favorite of Jonathan Baker's." In an aside to viewers, she added, "He established the hotel in nineteen fifteen."

"I bet it was." Ronnie's smirk said she got it.

"You know…It's possible that such a tangible memory drew a response…your trash mishap, I mean." Peyton grabbed the walkie again. "Brian, are you free to run me down an Ovilus?"

"Be right there."

Raising her voice to be heard over the thunder, she informed the camera, "We're going to inquire with the Ovilus. Of course, this way Brian gets the dessert. We'll see how fast he gets here."

"Just an FYI," Ronnie injected, "dinner will be ready whenever you are. There's no rush. Everything will keep just fine."

"Great job, Ronnie." She leaned toward Sam to comment to the audience. "If you've been lucky to catch our earlier crossovers, you've seen that Ronnie's choice of period foods and cooking methods has stimulated energy, residual spirit activity, and led to some remarkable results during our investigations." She glanced back at her. "On top of that, you always manage the very tricky job of accommodating our timetable—which is always unpredictable. You're nailing it again. Thank you." Peyton caught herself appreciating the look in Ronnie's eyes and turned away. Luckily, Brian hustled into the room.

"Here you go," he said, a little winded, and his eyes went straight to the table. "I can't stay, though."

Peyton agreed. "We can't abandon the operation center for any length of time."

"This is yours," Ronnie said, handing him the dish he was ogling.

"Sweet. Thanks, Ronnie."

She gave him a spoon and napkin, and he was gone. "I heard he's starving to death."

"Always." Peyton turned on the Ovilus. "Jonathan Baker?" she called, her voice raised to fill the kitchen. "Mr. Baker, are you with us tonight in your hotel? We are here to talk with you. This is Ronnie, and Sam, and I'm Peyton."

Keeping her pace painfully slow, Peyton made her way around the long room. The Ovilus remained silent.

"We've made a special treat here, I'm sure you remember candle salad. Did you serve them to your guests? Was it a favorite of yours by any chance? Maybe a favorite of Patrick Doonan's, your hotel manager?"

En route to Peyton, Ronnie stepped close to the camera and whispered. "I just heard a major crack from over there. A real snap." She pointed toward the little extension room and moved soundlessly to Peyton's side. "The extension room door. I heard a serious crack of wood. Something snapped. Should we see if it opens now?"

Peyton returned the whisper, turning her head and coming almost too close. "You're sure it wasn't a sizzle of lightning you heard?" Ronnie shook her head. "Okay, then, let's try." Her voice had quivered. *Thank God it was a whisper.* She had to take a breath. She could have kissed her with hardly a move. And squarely on camera. Ronnie appeared to share the anxiety and moved away.

"Jonathan?" Peyton began again, slowly moving toward the extension. Ronnie stayed a step behind, and Sam, several steps behind them both. "Mr. Jonathan Baker? We learned that your son, Andrew, he built this little addition after you passed, didn't he? It wouldn't have met your standards. Did your hotel manager, Patrick Doonan, object to it in your stead?"

The door snapped so loudly, all three of them jumped. Peyton and Ronnie exchanged looks. They both stepped up to inspect the door.

From the Ovilus: *"Wrong."*

Peyton twitched again and Ronnie touched her shoulder, then took a step back.

Peyton frowned at the screen. "'Wrong.' What's wrong?" She implored the old wooden door and the area around it, staying with the methodical, delayed questions, giving the Ovilus time to respond to something. "Did Andrew not build this? Did you not approve of him extending the kitchen this way? Can you answer me?"

Nothing from the Ovilus.

Peyton looked to Ronnie at her side and recognized that bewildered stare. She needed to hear some form of acknowledgement, too. Knowing Sam hovered just behind their shoulders, Peyton spoke for Ronnie's benefit as well as the audience's. "Sometimes, the Ovilus just doesn't pick up on—"

"Protect."

The Ovilus startled them again. Sam backed up a little to include the Ovilus message between them.

"'Protect'?" Ronnie asked Peyton. "Protect what?" She looked the door up and down. "This room?" She turned the doorknob and pulled, but it didn't budge. "Damn. It's just a stuck door."

Peyton watched her try again, the skeptic Casual Cook in determined paranormal investigator mode. She smiled inwardly and turned to the camera.

"Looks like we're off to a good start already."

The door creaked again, as if responding, and Peyton wondered if something was keeping it closed or trying to get out. The latter possibility gave her pause. And just remembering the day the room mysteriously plunged into single digits gave her a chill now. It hadn't wanted to be opened then, either.

"Shame," the computerized voice suddenly droned.

They looked from the printed word to each other, questioning.

Peyton played a hunch. "Your hotel manager, Patrick Doonan, was he your special companion?"

"Stop."

Peyton stiffened. *The hell I will.* "Do you remain in this little room because you are ashamed? For protection? There is no shame in being companions, and you don't need protection. You are free to go, and you *should* go."

They waited but got nothing.

"There's something there, I can feel it." She shook her head, confounded.

"What if this thing *can't* go?" Ronnie asked. "What if it's stuck? The door is stuck. Shouldn't we get it open somehow?"

"And just see what happens?"

Ronnie's concern and her sincerity were written all over her face, in bigger letters than her skepticism, and Peyton struggled to keep those hopes alive as her own heart swelled. Physical contact would demonstrate the empathy she felt for Ronnie's position, and she felt compelled to touch her. She set her hand on Ronnie's arm.

"You felt that cold in there a few days ago and you know what it can mean when something wafts over you. Remember back at the Barrow Tavern, when Brian felt that brutal cold? Ronnie, whatever it was clawed him." She traced a finger down Ronnie's arm, replicating the line of Brian's scratches. "Always consider the consequences before forcing open any door."

Ronnie's intensity receded with the recollection and, as much as Peyton hated seeing that in her face, she didn't regret making her point. Flinging open a door on a restless spirit could be life-changing, in bad ways as well as good, and for a very long time. Ronnie just lacked the experience to know that.

Peyton squeezed her arm and let go. It was then, she remembered Sam, his all-seeing eye, and all the viewers who saw God-knows-what in that exchange.

Ronnie ran a hand through her hair. "So, is there anything to be done?"

I'd like to haul open that damn door.

Peyton placed her palm on it and wished she had the answers. Yet, despite all her trying, she really didn't think she had pushed her luck too far—yet.

"Well, if we could at least establish a name, know who we're dealing with, that might lead to something." She inched them all back a few steps and steadied herself. "Whoever is listening, this little box in my hand hears you. Say your name, please. Jonathan Baker, will you acknowledge us? Or could this, by any chance, be Eleanor Baker?"

Ronnie tipped toward Sam's camera. "Eleanor is the great-granddaughter who died."

"If you'd rather, please knock, open a cabinet, send something to the floor," Peyton continued, and caught Ronnie's eye with a cautionary look. "Are you Patrick Doonan?"

Silent seconds passed. A full minute.

Peyton's frustration and disappointment grew. Ronnie shifted restlessly. Sam reset his camera on his shoulder. This was getting uncomfortable.

Ronnie took a half-step forward and looked to Peyton, as if for permission.

Okay, yes, you can try the door again. Why not? I guess we've bottomed out anyway.

At Peyton's nod, Ronnie flexed her fingers around the doorknob and adjusted her footing, coiling herself for a forceful pull. She checked with Peyton once more, and Peyton realized she must have conveyed doubt or concern because Ronnie's body relaxed and her grip on the knob slackened.

Now, with only a simple, casual hold, Ronnie turned the knob and drew the door wide open.

Peyton hurried to the threshold, and they stared into the room with its gritty windows. All three of them searched through the cobwebs and around the interior framework, from one side of the sandy, dusty mess to the other. Nothing stood out, nothing they hadn't seen before.

Lightning flashed, and night became day, the "black" windows became transparent. The single second of light showed rain still pouring onto the vast, dreary yard, the sea far beyond still imposing its gray background, and, at the edge of the bluff, a dark mass resembling a man.

Peyton grabbed Ronnie's arm. "There!" She pointed to the yard, once again black as night, and Ronnie shook her head. Peyton turned to the camera. "Did any of you see it? The black mass or shadow standing out there?"

"Where?" Ronnie asked. She looked in the right direction, but nothing could be seen beyond the room itself. Windows, backed by the black, rainy night, had reverted to mirrors instead of portals to the outside.

"Overlooking the bluff, when lightning lit up the backyard. It was just a flicker, but I swear I saw something…like a man standing out there. I know the windows are a mess and the rain…We need to see Sam's playback on a decent screen."

Ronnie pointed at the floor beneath the makeshift counter and held up one finger. "I was busy checking that out."

Only one small propane bottle stood, where once there had been four. She crouched and Peyton joined her. Sam loomed over them.

Peyton bent farther down, scrutinizing the area. "There used to be a few here and there's proof, imprinted rings in the dust. It looks like nothing else has moved or even been touched in eons."

Ronnie looked at the floor around her feet. "Could I have stepped on…ruined signs of things, like footprints? Klutzy cook," she added to the camera.

"No, not at all," Peyton assured her as they straightened. "Footprints are rare. All kinds of other things happen, but footprints, not so much. Think: mass of energy. It has no real weight to imprint itself on anything, but it sure as hell can leave a mark."

"Are you going to try that again?" Ronnie indicated the Ovilus.

"Yeah, but I think we may have lost him, whoever he was." She glanced back to the rear windows.

Chapter Twenty-four

"It's right here." Peyton rose from the table and went to the live camera on the counter. "Sam pulled it out of what he shot." She showed the photo on her cell to the audience.

The picture was grainy, overly enlarged, but there was no disputing the fact that the black mass at the edge of the bluff resembled a large person hunched forward.

"And I never saw it," Sam admitted. "My eyes must have been on something else in the frame when that stroke of lightning flashed. I wouldn't have known it was there if she hadn't spotted it."

Peyton passed her cell to Caroline and returned to her seat, eager to resume eating. "This ham," she told Ronnie and indicated her meal with her fork, "is truly amazing. Miramar's spirits are probably salivating all around the house."

Ronnie offered a little salute from her side of the table.

Still staring at Peyton's phone, Caroline's mouth hung open. "This is *so* cool!"

"Let me see it again." Brian leaned against Caroline's shoulder, chewing in her ear. She handed him the phone.

"Such a good catch, Peyton," he said. "Kudos to you for noticing in just the blink of an eye. None of us saw it."

"No," Caroline said, "and we were glued to the screen. Eric and I had thought we'd get something in the parlor but struck out, so we went back to the operations center and got all wrapped up watching you guys at that door."

Acknowledging the audience, Eric nodded toward the camera. "We may not have caught that thing on the bluff, but a few viewers did." Glancing at the lens, he added, "Nice job, out there."

Jamie swallowed hard, eager to speak. She held up her iPad to show tweets scrolling across the screen in real time. "Apparently, we're making viewers hungry with Ronnie's elaborate dinner." She showed the tablet to the audience. "We appreciate you all monitoring the screens for us." She placed the iPad next to her plate to keep tabs on feedback.

"Glad *somebody*'s minding the store," Brian said, and winked at the camera. He indicated the Ovilus on the table. "You guys just say the word."

Jamie said, "It's going to take you guys forever to play back all these nonstop tweets. They're terrific. Some are...*particularly* interesting."

Peyton stopped eating to consider Jamie's observation. The insinuation in "particularly interesting" made her nervous. Ronnie flashed her a curious glance.

"Interesting how?" Peyton asked and turned to the camera. "You guys aren't picking on us for eating, are you?" That would be fine, she thought, preferable to having viewers notice anything between her and Ronnie. "Because this isn't really a dinner break, although in a way, I suppose it is. We've flooded the house with irresistible aromas of specific bygone days," she flashed Ronnie a grin, "hoping to trigger some serious reaction."

"And we're ready for it," Eric chimed in, picking up the SLS beside his dish.

"Hey," Jamie explained, "we have thousands of investigators out there, chatting away. They're calling out shadows, orbs, things moving upstairs, the cellar, the foy—" She stopped to read. "Someone just saw the table move in the foyer."

Brian took off with the Ovilus and an EMF meter.

"Excellent work," Caroline told the audience. "Keep an eye on Brian, see if his instruments get him excited."

Peyton nodded at the camera. "We want to check out all your sightings. Let's just hope we have time." She didn't have a few days, didn't even have all night as in standard investigations. She would have to get selective about where they explored. And not worry about that "interesting" chatter.

"Brian replayed as many of the incidents viewers reported as possible, and pretty much debunked them," Jamie said and lent a thumbs-up to the audience. "But it's smart to always be aware."

"Yeah," Caroline told them. "A few tweets talked about little rocks or something falling from those old stone walls in the cellar."

Brian returned, frowning, and spoke to Ronnie. "The table that moved on you earlier tonight?" He shook his head. "Didn't you have, like, munchies on it?" Ronnie nodded. "Well, they're all gone. Tablecloth was half off, too, but I couldn't pick up a thing."

"At least the eyes on the job outnumber the spirits," Ronnie commented. "Glad we have an army of viewers for such a huge place."

Eric smiled slyly as he sliced the loaf of bread. "They like you two a lot." Everyone reacted in some way, a snort, a grin, all avoided eye contact. Caroline stuck out a hand for bread.

"We can't ask for more than that, can we?" Peyton said, purposely steering that comment toward a less sensitive topic. "Who has better fans? Fans who'll join you in your work?" She raised her glass to the camera. "Thank you all, very much. You're the best."

"Absolutely," Ronnie added, bringing her glass up beside Peyton's. "Fans who like concocting something to eat while watching the finest paranormal show on TV."

Everyone toasted toward the camera.

"And one more thing," Ronnie said. "I never thought I'd find myself cooking for a bunch of spirit hunters, *friends* who live for it, but nothing's ever been this much fun." Now, she raised her glass to the table. "Thanks for making the *Casual Cook* family part of your team for these special episodes. You and your work are astounding."

"Goes both ways," Peyton said. "We love having you." She clinked her glass to Ronnie's, smiled into her eyes, and flicked a look toward the camera. They drank and Ronnie nodded into her napkin.

"So, we're a hit, huh?" she asked generally.

"Oh, yeah," Caroline said and began scrolling backwards on her cell. "Here's one from @cornerstore in Biloxi, Mississippi: 'Ronnie Sharp, come cook for me!'" Everyone chuckled.

"Aw, geeze. Thanks," Ronnie answered. "Unfortunately, I don't like flying and I don't think my car would make it that far, but I'll ship anywhere, and my cookbooks are available."

"Peyton," Caroline said, "this one's for you. At @fortytwowest of Rochester, New York, wants to know: 'What exercise routine do you use to maintain your gorgeous figure?'"

Peyton felt her cheeks flush. "I can't say that's an accurate statement but thank you, at @fortytwowest. Exercise? Well, for at least ten hours every day, Monday through Saturday and most Sundays, going on seven years, I stress. I mean, I work. That'll do it." She hid behind her hand to tell the audience, "I don't recommend it."

"Hey, Sammy," Caroline said. "Here's a Facebook post from Julie Branch in Detroit. 'We want more Sam! He sees everything. Gossip to share about Peyton and Ronnie?'"

"Whoa." Sam blushed. He looked guiltily between them. "Well, first, thanks. I love my job, I love working with each of them, and…and cameramen don't tell tales. That's all I got."

The candlestick in front of Eric fell over onto his plate.

Everyone jumped and he grabbed it quickly, righting it. "Damn." He looked around at the others. "Does that mean it's time to get back on the job?"

"Who are you and what are you telling us?" Caroline asked the room.

Peyton checked to make sure the Ovilus was on as they waited in silence.

"Something wants to make us work for it," Brian grumbled.

"Well," Ronnie said, standing, "let's see if anything happens during dessert." She left for the kitchen.

"We'll help clear this table," Peyton said, and clapped Brian's shoulder. "Won't we?"

Ronnie set about whipping cream for her "candles," and held the bowl high so the static camera could capture her scooping out dollops. The shot wouldn't include any sound so she couldn't talk to her audience, but she was determined to cater to viewers, nonetheless.

Brian put his stack of plates by the sink, playfully complaining about his busboy role, and Ronnie wished viewers could hear him. But, when Peyton came in with leftover ham, passing him on the way out, Ronnie had no regrets about the camera's shortcoming. She wasn't sure she could resist suggestive dialogue and the world didn't need to hear that.

"God," Peyton said with a sigh, "thankfully, the candlestick thing put an end to that chatter before it got too awkward."

"Maybe a ghost didn't want the world to talk about us talking about how the world talks about us. Would have been too complicated."

Peyton stopped at her side. "*We* are complicated."

"Only for another hour or so."

Peyton turned to her, eyeing the apron. "Then, what?"

"Then, you'll take my clothes off?"

Peyton smiled broadly. "So confident we are these days."

Ronnie stepped around her for a cloth to wipe her hands, which forced Peyton to back up against the table. Ronnie knew the camera saw them this way, a little too close, and edged back.

"It's really spacious, isn't it, the table?"

"Ronnie Sharp. Back up."

"Those desserts over there?" She indicated them with a tilt of her head. "With the cream and juicy cherries on top? There's a *very special* way to eat them, you know."

"Jesus. Will you stop?" She bit back a smile.

"And there's plenty of room right here on this table."

"Ronnie." Peyton moved left and sidestepped her. Looking down and away from the camera, she forced back a grin. "Camera. Be good."

"At least they can't hear us."

"They don't have to."

"Think they're good lip readers?"

"We just might find out," Peyton said, stopping abreast of her, ready to exit.

Shoulder to shoulder facing in opposite directions, they eyed each other keenly, and Ronnie couldn't help but grin. She knew Peyton shared this temptation, felt the pressure, the pulse of creating a public spectacle. Viewers were getting an eyeful.

She whispered, unnecessarily. "Bite your lip again and I might lose control."

"You can't," Peyton said on a breath.

Jamie swung open the dining room door in grand fashion. "Hey, I sent Brian back—Um…Hey?"

Ronnie immediately fussed with her towel and Peyton glanced at Jamie, who quickly turned away.

Hands in her pockets, Jamie looked everywhere but at them. "I…ah…I'll…I'll bring out dessert." She took the two closest plates and spun back through the door.

Her back to the static camera, Peyton whispered, "If Jamie saw that, viewers did."

"It wasn't much, just teasing."

"Viewers see everything." Ronnie nodded, apologetic but *so* tempted. Peyton raised an eyebrow, which said she meant business, but it pushed the temptation Ronnie felt toward serious arousal. "Behave, Sharp."

Must be written all over my face.

"I'll do my best."

Peyton's penetrating gaze roamed Ronnie's face, drifted to her mouth, the smirk Ronnie labored to restrain. And Ronnie watched those perfect lips press a matching expression into submission. Their eyes met again.

Peyton offered, "Rain check?"

"By *candle*light?"

"In this black tux shirt?" Peyton flicked her eyes to it. "Minus the apron?"

Gambling the camera wouldn't catch it, Ronnie flashed an appreciative look at her hair. "If you'll be as luxurious, as loose as those blond curls."

"Will you still be a smartass?"

"Any kind of ass you prefer."

"It may take me a while. I'm fussy."

"We've already taken too long."

❖

"And this will carry us into tonight," Ronnie told viewers. Sam followed her around the house as she put out small platters of fudge and thin slices of pineapple upside-down cake. "We have about an hour with you all, and the *Paranormal Pursuit* team is far from done tonight. These goodies should help the team power through." She spotted Sam's cue for a commercial break. "Time to pay some bills, and when you come back, you'll join the others in their experiment-in-progress."

"Jamie says wave," Sam said. Ronnie did, and Sam shut his camera off.

"Thank God," Ronnie said on a sigh, happy to see Sam relax at last. "I *hate* shooting live, don't you?"

"Eh, yes and no. I hate the weight. Peyton's negotiating a splurge for upgraded lightweight units."

"Well, if you're taking a break, I'm mixing lime rickeys," she said as they returned to the kitchen. "I want to snoop around, see how the operations center works."

"The parlor's my next stop, to relieve Eric, who relieved Caroline." He snickered at a thought. "We'll get those lighter units sooner than later." Ronnie knew they would.

Drink in each hand, one of which would ultimately go to Brian, she strolled to the opposite end of the dining room, and up onto the platform stage. She turned in place, envisioning orchestras, galas, and oceans of food. Such was the life then. With clarinet music…

…Just like that.

Ronnie spun around. There was no one there, of course, only cherry-wood walls and echoes of music and dancing through so many years, from Al Jolson and Bessie Smith, through Billie Holiday and Glenn Miller…

…There it was again. A Benny Goodman sound, a clarinetist trilling along the scales.

Ronnie moved off the stage and left. Co-existence with the unknown felt a little shaky these days. That room or something in it sought to carry her away and nearly did. If she was going to be "carried away" at Miramar, there was only one woman she wanted in charge.

She paused in the foyer to appreciate the entry for what it used to be. "Nothing like walking from room to room like you own the place." She chuckled. "Rhett Butler, eat your heart out." Long ago, the carpet up that grand staircase had been a rich burgundy, bound in gold thread. Meyers said so. Ladies descending in all their elegant finery must have been eventful.

She stepped into the library and Brian signaled hello around four large monitors, his face an awful blend of occasionally changing colors. "It ain't NASA, but it's home." He slid half his headset off to hear her and bobbed back in a spring-loaded desk chair.

"So, this is where you've been hiding out." The spacious room was still beautiful, with its mahogany paneling and built-ins, even though it now showed as the team's storehouse/computer lab.

"Missing all the action, yeah." He reached for a folding chair and slid it beside him. "Have a seat and check this out."

"Thanks. This is for you." She handed him the drink and his eyes bulged.

"Whoa, yeah! Thank you."

"Hope you like lime rickeys. Keeping with the theme."

He took a sip and nodded. "Wow. You are something, Casual Cook." He leaned very close. "Peyton better see the forest for the trees."

Ronnie laughed lightly. "I'd be a very lucky woman. But, you know? Only if you feel it's right."

"Amen." He took another sip. "See everybody? On these two screens, we have a quadrant for every room where there's a static camera, and I can click one," and he did, "and it blows up for me. These others are for scene cameras, like when Sam's following you around and taking in the big picture."

"This is very cool. You can watch every room."

"Yup. That is kinda the hard part, trying to keep eyeballs everywhere for any little thing that moves. Now, going live brings in the cavalry. Viewers help us. With all this chatter over here," he pointed to a continuously scrolling stream of tweets, "I can read someone's tip, and can replay that piece of footage and check it out."

"Wow, that's great. Viewers talking to you in real time—on the air—is…well, it's a little intense."

"Yeah, it can be. We still pick and choose what's available for them to see, though, and have the option to keep some things in-house if need be. But we rarely do that because chat lines just blow up at us. So, pretty much everything goes out as-is."

"At least you have that option, to…you know, save our butts if necessary."

Brian sipped his drink and jabbed her with an elbow. "Pulling a room, as I call it, or taking a camera off-line, is easy. In fact, I almost had to do it tonight. And if you don't know what incident I'm referring to, you'll disappoint me."

Ronnie dropped her head back and sighed toward the ceiling. "Yeah, I can guess."

"Whooo-eee. Man, I could've kicked Jamie in the butt for walking in on you two. I thought things were going somewhere good. And I had a front row seat." He snorted, staring at the screen. "You guys were sizzling at each other. I had the finger on the button for that one…but I let it run."

Ronnie scrabbled a hand through her hair and dragged it down her face, mortified.

"See? We're back from commercial." He gestured to one of the large shots on its own monitor. "Sam's got everyone in the parlor and they're working with the spirit of Eleanor Baker."

"They say Sebastian saw her ghost a few times, and one of the electricians said he saw it."

"Well, Caroline thought she did, too, and she's right. I ran back through the previous fifteen minutes before Caroline went in, and there it was."

"No way. Eleanor's ghost?"

"Well, something petite and white covered most of that chair. Didn't move or make a sound. One minute it wasn't there, and the next, there it was, just popped in. Sitting here, even *I* got a little shiver. And then, in walks Caroline and poof!" He nodded at the activity in the parlor. "We're not seeing the spirit's form anymore, but they're having some decent luck so there's obviously energy still in the room."

He increased the volume and Caroline's interrogation and words from the Ovilus came through. Ronnie watched Peyton standing by, adding questions here and there, mostly supervising.

"God, fans must eat this up." She checked the Twitter scroll and shook her head at its continuous flow.

"Fans love it. But when you're lucky to land something as rare as Miramar, a truly dramatic, active place, fans go bat-shit crazy. Because of that, ratings for this episode will break a record. *But then! But then! They add you!*" He sipped and sat back. "Jesus Christ. It'll be off the charts, this one. Numbers for this crossover will be like nothing we've ever imagined. Heh.

"*And*, I have to add, because I can't keep my mouth shut, this *thing* between you and Peyton? Honestly, and I'm telling you straight, it's the funnest damn thing out there."

Ronnie sat, staring at the action onscreen, more than a bit numbed to be involved with this work. "This *thing*? No one planned it."

"Oh, I know. At first, we were expecting all hell to break loose any time either of you blinked." He grinned devilishly. "It's been a blast to watch and we're not the only ones who think so. Check out the chatter."

Ronnie ran the gamut of emotions in just five minutes. She'd be completely exhausted if she read the full two-plus hours of this stuff. She smiled, laughed, winced, grunted, swore, and blushed.

"Ouch. There's one that says Miramar was staged, so that will set Peyton off. But the one that talks about her cleavage—and my ass?" She sighed. "Lovely, huh? We have to expect stuff like that." She asked to see chatter from the beginning of the show, curious if fans' moods had changed as the show progressed.

"Here you go. This chatter ran as Peyton was doing the opening outside."

Ronnie lasted less than three minutes.

"Whoa, baby." She did a double take at a particular tweet and pressed the "hold" button. *A woman actually wrote, "Squirming in my seat! We've just started, Ronnie's there, and Peyton's already wet!"* Ronnie felt her cheeks heat. "This…This is…"

"Oh, yeah," Brian said, seeing what she had read.

"Thank God, there aren't a lot of those. From what I've seen so far, there's some flirty, suggestive talk, but mostly excited, serious, and complimentary."

"For the numbers this will draw?" Brian shook his head, impressed. "Off the charts."

Ronnie perused the monitor images again, looking for Peyton. "You ever feel like Big Brother, spying on everybody?"

"Spirit Brother to you. Nah. This usually is just to collect our evidence. Tonight, going live, I'm glad we could still use our system and feed what we want to the network. Everything's going smoothly."

Ronnie left her public image in Brian's hands and wandered back to the foyer, where a little static camera with a very big eye captured everything in silence. She couldn't allow things beyond her control to weigh her down. It was much less stressful to marvel at the ornate double doors, the hand-crafted trim work, the dining room she was tempted to try again. But she wanted to rejoin Peyton and decided to head for the parlor.

"Hey, I found you," Peyton announced, striding across the Moroccan tiles with that photogenic smile. "At last, I have the chance to say you look *very* fine tonight, Ms. Sharp, tall and dark, in this black tux shirt, drink in hand, roaming these halls by candle- and lantern-light. How do you always look so at ease in any environment?"

Turning slightly away, Ronnie sipped her drink slyly. "It's the vampire in me."

Peyton laughed and poked Ronnie's ribs. "You *are* impossible, you know."

"And your flirtatious side is mercilessly sexy."

"Oh, I like that. I like vampires, too." She squeezed her arm. "I didn't know where you'd be and I was going to raise you on the walkie, but I wanted to search."

"My walkie-talkie is somewhere in the kitchen. I'd rather be searched for."

Peyton grinned. "They are finishing in the parlor, and I think Eleanor got a few things off her chest. It sounds like we all had her pegged wrong. She dreaded getting married."

"That's a significant turn, isn't it?"

"Yeah, but we're not sure if or how it affects Doonan's activity here." She sighed heavily. "God, it feels good to be out of the live shot, even for a couple of minutes."

"It's definitely a relief."

"Just don't forget the static cameras, silent sentinels."

"I won't. I just had an eye-opening visit with Brian in your operations center. Um, you know, in the kitchen, we…we raised his heart rate, apparently. Good thing we kept our clothes on."

"Jamie coming in was a good thing, too."

"So, I guess dancing's out of the question."

"Dancing? Yes, unless you want to give lessons to millions of people."

"Too bad. A while ago, I thought I heard big-band music in the dining room."

"Really?"

"Really. It still might be playing, but if it's only in my head, you'd have to dance very close to me to hear it."

"Did you spike that drink?"

Ronnie grinned as she gazed around the room. "Want to run up and down the staircase?"

"No. Stop," Peyton said, laughing. "We have yet to crack this Doonan mystery and I have one more thing I'd like to try."

"Can I join you?"

"I was hoping you'd ask. We may have to split up, so we'll need Caroline, Eric, and Sam."

"Sounds like a grand finale for the grand finale."

"Come with me to the library, vampire. There's a meeting afoot."

Chapter Twenty-five

Ronnie had hoped for another view from the many windows of Miramar's tower, but on a sunny day, absolutely not on a black, rain-swept Halloween night. She spoke to viewers in the heavy camera on Caroline's shoulder. "Doesn't every cook long to be in a tower during a thunder and lightning storm? Happy Halloween, everybody."

Even though she had two veteran ghost hunters with her, and they all had some form of radio connection to the outside world so far below her, was it really wise to send a casual cook up into this fragile thing without Peyton holding her hand?

"Let me trade this elephant of a camera for Eric's," Caroline said. "I feel confined up here with this cannon."

Lightning flashes lit the ten-by-ten-foot tip of the building and made it feel even smaller, especially when it rocked in the wind.

"It's hard to see out of these windows, with the rain and the blackness out there," Ronnie said. "I can't imagine what you'd get regardless of the camera."

"We should have swapped earlier," Eric said from below them, half-way up the ladder. Caroline readily off-loaded the heavy scene unit for the smaller night-vision camera he offered up to her. "Jamie," he relayed into his headset, "switching out Camera Two for handheld."

As the tower shimmied in the thunder, Ronnie's concentration wavered. She thought of Jamie, controlling things from the RV now, and Brian, drawn into service with Sam and Peyton at the kitchen extension. She wondered how they were doing, flushing anything in there out, making sure it was truly empty and would stay that way. Which also was this team's mission up here. Could both groups actually pinch this thing Peyton insisted was Doonan into a corner between them? Then what? All she knew was that everyone was investing a lot of effort and nerve, and viewers were watching.

Caroline turned on the handheld unit, and Ronnie thought it almost comical, how that small screen's eerie green glow eased her anxiety level a little. She strained to see outside, could make out definitions of the other roof peaks, trees in the distance, the profile of the bluff, and, of course, miles of black ocean.

"Patrick Doonan, are you with us here?" Like the thunder outside, Eric's baritone rumbled around the third floor beneath them and up the ladder. "You cannot hide on these upper floors anymore."

Ronnie stared down at the spirit box she'd been given. The device reminded her of an antique transistor radio in dire need of an antenna. The constant rush of white noise irritated her, and she wished she could "tune in" a radio station, but it was *supposed* to be this constant, scanning all sorts of frequencies for something. At least, that's what Caroline had explained so long ago.

"Don't mean to complain, but this thing is even more obnoxious than on TV."

Caroline nodded. "I know. The Session Master filters out all that garbage, but it's a little bulky, so we don't cart it around much."

"Bummer."

"For sure. Peyton loves it for special sessions, hence the name."

"This third floor is empty," Eric said. "Doonan, you no longer have rights here. Can you hear me? Speak now. The door is closing on you. It's closing on you, permanently, Doonan. Forever. Do you understand?" His voice echoed on the vacant floor and Ronnie listened for a response, through his Ovilus or her spirit box, but heard nothing.

"Hold this up and move around the room," Caroline said, handing Ronnie a little EMF meter. "See if the needle moves."

As directed, Ronnie walked the glass-wall perimeter, eyes on the meter, knowing Caroline conveyed her every move. "It's not even fluttering," she reported over that damn white noise in her other hand. The tower shuddered again, and Ronnie took a quick look outside. *I'd hit that other roof if I fell from here.*

"Now, try lower, knee-level."

Ronnie stooped and repeated her walk. *Look at me, the paranormal investigator. And I worried about oysters and candles?* "Nope. Still hasn't moved."

"This room is closed to you now, Doonan," Caroline stated. "You can't be and you won't be in here anymore."

From the Ovilus: *"Go."*

Ronnie looked at Caroline and they both looked down the ladder at Eric, who was staring at the word on his screen.

"Yeah, that's right!" he yelled. "*You* go!" With a tip of his head, he called them down from the tower.

"We're done here. Hang on to those devices," Caroline said. "I need to climb down first. You be careful in the dark." Ronnie stood by, watching her back down, one hand gripping the ladder, the other still shooting up at her. "Say good-bye, Doonan," she said loudly, almost at the bottom. "This room doesn't exist for you now. We are locking it."

Ronnie backed down the ladder by the scant light of the EMF meter and paused to swing the hatch closed over her head. Padlock in hand, she turned and showed it to Caroline's camera. "With the owner's permission," she said, and clicked the lock in place.

From the Ovilus: *"See!"*

Ronnie froze on the ladder. "As in eyes or ocean?"

"Eyes," Eric said, showing them the screen.

A REM-pod they had positioned in the hallway began beeping.

Caroline urged them onward. "Let's go."

They jumped when a deep, double bang sounded from the stairway.

"What the hell was that?" Caroline asked.

From the Ovilus: *"Future."*

Ronnie puffed a lock of hair off her forehead. "Sure, *now*, he wants to chat."

"'Future' my ass. Come on," Eric said, hurrying down the hall. "It came from the stairs, didn't it?"

The pod had silenced when they reached it, and they started down. Caroline led the way via the night-vision camera with Ronnie close behind. Eric shot everything from the rear, as they carefully examined each step.

"I thought it sounded like something went down a few steps, stumbled," Ronnie offered.

"That was my first thought, too," Caroline agreed. "Something of substance."

Now on the second floor, they walked the hallway of doors.

"Make sure each room is locked," Eric said, and they tried one doorknob after another. "We know everything above us is locked."

From the Ovilus: *"United."*

"'United'?" Ronnie asked. "Who's united? Doonan and Jonathan? Eleanor, who doesn't want to be? Is Doonan missing his tower already?" She raised her palms to the camera. "What do you guys think? This stuff can make your head hurt."

"Maybe, us?" Eric posited. "Maybe he'd rather we were united, doesn't like us working in two places at once?"

"This was his room," Caroline told the audience, and aimed the camera at her own hand wrapping cautiously around the knob. A quick twist proved it was locked.

"These doors." Ronnie pointed as she walked ahead. "The family's suite." They passed the grand staircase to reach the other side of the house, and Ronnie put a hand on each of the double doors' matching knobs.

"Do it," Eric said.

Ronnie tried to crank both open simultaneously, but they were locked.

She turned to them sharply and sniffed. Eric was looking back already.

"Cigar. Do you smell it?"

"Yeah," he answered vacantly. "I sure do."

They backtracked down the hall and Ronnie and Caroline left him to shoot from the rear.

"Ew. I do, too, now," Caroline said.

Another REM-pod went off, and they watched it flash on the first step of the grand staircase.

They came to an abrupt halt at the head of the stairs. Leaning against Caroline to see the image on her screen, Ronnie felt Eric close in behind them. But his lens at her shoulder wasn't what made her breath catch.

"What the hell is that?"

❖

Peyton pivoted in place, determined to keep the stick figure centered on the SLS screen, willing it not to vanish. It seemed equally determined to be out of frame.

"Stand still, dammit." First spotted at the kitchen extension door, the linear white form had made its craggily way into the far corner of the kitchen where the cellar door abutted the butler's pantry, and now, was on its way back. "You want to get into that addition, don't you?" Peyton said to the screen.

"Ready to tackle this door?" Brian asked, poised at the knob.

Peyton hiked a shoulder. "I'd like to see where our friend here will try next, but he could disappear any second, so…yeah, I guess. Go for it."

Brian clamped both hands onto the knob, slammed his shoulder into the door, and yanked backwards. The door flung open and almost sent him to the floor.

Peyton's eyes never left the figure on the screen. It stood motionless some fifteen feet away. "Well?" she asked it. "Are you going in or what?"

The figure turned and shifted toward the door, powered by painstaking flexing motions at every joint, a one-dimensional Tin Man.

"So cool," Sam murmured, shooting the screen over her shoulder.

"He's doing it," Peyton whispered. "Come on. You can make it." How bizarre to be rooting for a human-shaped stick of energy to move on command. Doing so to evict it from this world made her a little sad.

But making contact like this had been a welcomed victory, considering they'd only had prolonged, substantive contact with Eleanor tonight, on a show that had promised so much. They'd chased noises on the stairs, footsteps in the second-floor hallway, a shadow at the tower ladder, and even enjoyed another of Ronnie's fantastic replica dinners, with little results. Kitchen activity *had* spiked, however.

Only that fight with this extension room had amounted to anything, when she and Ronnie had been together. The door had crackled and snapped, and it *had* to have been Doonan, telling them through the Ovilus that they were "wrong" to try opening a sanctuary he relied on to "protect" himself from some "shame." He'd told them to "stop." She still leaned on her theory that Doonan fought to keep his relationship with Jonathan secret, to preserve their reputations as well as Miramar's.

She firmly believed he died trying to prevent anything from changing life here as he knew it. So many things must have pushed Doonan to the limit, whether it was Jonathan introducing a competing lover, Eleanor moving in with her new husband, Sebastian renovating the kitchen, and then, trying to sell Miramar outright. As Alex the electrician could attest, Doonan *still* tried.

She sighed inwardly, thinking it may have simply all come down to heart and home.

"He's gone," Sam whispered, and Peyton realized she had spaced out and stopped seeing the SLS in her hand.

"Dammit."

She walked carefully past Brian in the doorway and into the extension, instantly stricken by intense cold.

"He's still here." She panned the room, shivering, and pointed the SLS toward the window, through which she had seen that form at the bluff earlier. But her screen gave her nothing.

The door snapped and Brian jumped.

"Hey," he told the door, "what's up with you?" He picked up the Ovilus hanging around his neck. "Do you have something to say? Did you split yourself open?" He scanned the old wood. "Nope."

"Patrick Doonan," Peyton called out. "This is your final visit here. Please respond."

"Pair," the computerized voice said.

"Pair of what?" Brian asked the Ovilus.

Peyton sank on a hip, exasperated, and she realized the insane cold had relented. Contact with Patrick probably would end soon, too.

"Who are a pair?" she tried. "Are you and Jonathan a pair?"

"Future."

An immediate response to such a sensitive question came as a surprise. "Whose future?" she continued, excited by this exchange. "Your future? Miramar's future? It's over now, Patrick. There is nothing for you here, not at Miramar, not in this…this little room or that kitchen, that tow—"

"Cook."

"'Cook'?" Peyton frowned.

Brian looked from the Ovilus to Peyton and Sam's lens. "He wants to cook?"

Everyone turned to the swinging door at the dining room. A REM-pod beeped and flashed feverishly. Minus that cold, Peyton had expected their intriguing connection to end, so was Doonan off and running?

She shut the extension room door hard, wedged it as tightly as possible, and led them to the swinging door. Ronnie had packed away the tables and chairs in the dining room so Peyton could set up a laser grid and broadcast it uninterrupted, from one end to the other, ceiling to floor. If that was where Doonan had gone, they could follow him easily.

Peyton swung the door open and the three of them stepped into a cavernous, spell-binding world of pink dots.

"Holy shit, this is a trip," Brian said on a breath.

They searched the rows of dots for a void, where competing energy absorbed and, effectively, blocked a beam of light.

“There,” Peyton pointed, “along the side. See those missing spots…He’s tall, broad.” She raised the SLS. “It’s Doonan. No doubt.”

The void in the grid shifted. The outline formed by missing dots moved farther away along the wall.

“He’s headed for the doorway off the stage,” Brian stated as they started forward.

“Yes, he is.” Peyton looked from the dark profile in the lights to the SLS and back. “I just wish he would manifest—Here he is.”

Brian and Sam leaned closer to see. The figure on her screen had both arms at shoulder height, as if clinging to the paneling. It inched along like a weary traveler, stick legs extending and folding in mechanical repetition.

“Peyton, if he intends to hide upstairs…”

They picked up their pace through the dining room.

“Patrick!” she called, her voice hollow in the huge empty space. “Patrick Doonan! Stop right there!” She studied the screen and stopped them short. “My God, he did.” She looked into the grid.

Brian nodded. “I’ll be dammed.” He checked the SLS, too. “He’s hanging on the doorframe.”

They looked up. The void in the grid edged forward, vanished against the opening, and a sliver of gritty darkness whisked out the door.

❖

Ronnie forgot her nervous state when Peyton’s team appeared one floor below, rushing out of the dining room. Peyton at the bottom of the staircase was a very welcomed sight. Connecting with those eyes, even from this far away, lent Ronnie some needed stability because the thing on the stairs was freaking her out.

Eric descended and Brian ascended, closing on the dark, nearly-translucent mass that appeared to cower at the side of the staircase, halfway down. Ronnie crinkled her nose at the damn cigar smell, thicker now than before. Peyton saw her and nodded.

Leaving Sam behind shooting, Peyton slowly began the trek up. "Patrick. You can see you are outnumbered by the living. Your time is at an end. Speak to us here and now."

As everyone waited for either Brian's or Eric's Ovilus to reveal something, Ronnie felt the thunder vibrate underfoot. The storm still raged outside, inflamed by the howling wind that whipped rain against the windows, repeatedly knocked that loose downspout against the porch. Caroline's nudge made her twitch, and she signaled for them to join the others. Ronnie sent a terrified face into Caroline's lens for the audience.

She gladly gave the entity on the steps a wide berth and edged along the opposite banister, down to Peyton, who touched her hand reassuringly. Ronnie appreciated that and exhaled as subtly as she could. Gradually, all team members had cordoned the weird mass within a semi-circle, but she didn't feel any more secure. *What the hell are they going to do with it now?*

"Do you have anything to say?" Eric asked the entity.

Ronnie almost laughed. *Any last words? Are they going to blindfold and shoot it?*

From each Ovilus: *"Cook."*

Ronnie flinched hard. She didn't appreciate *that* last word.

"No!" she snapped toward the mass and could tell Peyton almost smiled. "What's the significance of 'cook'?" she whispered to her.

"Not sure," Peyton whispered back without turning, "unless he means you."

Ronnie just stared at her.

"God dammit." Brian waved in disgust at the entity. "You're not going back to the kitchen. Your hiding days are over, big guy."

"You won't be terrorizing people at Miramar any longer," Caroline added. "No more pushing people down the stairs. You can see that it never really worked, because here we are."

"And we are staying," Eric stated. "The living prevail."

Peyton checked for a manifestation on her SLS and Ronnie saw the colorful screen go black. Peyton shook it, grumbled a curse, then gave the dead device to Brian.

"Patrick, you no longer have a place here," Peyton said, sounding ridiculously calm and official. "The tower is locked, the kitchen extension is jammed shut, and you have no business left to finish. Patrick Doonan. It's time for you to cross over."

They all stared at the form. Ronnie wondered if sheer will could make it disintegrate.

Then, it started shimmering all over, a barely perceptible quiver. Ronnie shot a glance at Peyton. She wasn't sure if her imagination had finally short-circuited. In a blink, the entity disappeared. Completely.

Everyone looked shocked, baffled.

About to cheer, Ronnie caught herself when the REM-pod sounded on the top step.

Chapter Twenty-six

Son of a…" Brian raced up the stairs. "I'm going after it!"

Eric tossed Peyton his Ovilus, pivoted, grabbed his scene camera, and followed.

Caroline looked to Peyton as she fumbled with her handheld unit.

"We're with you," Peyton told her, starting up, and tugged Ronnie along. "Sam?" she called back.

"Coming!"

Suddenly, Peyton stopped and thrust a palm against Ronnie's chest. "Wait! Listen. Hear that?"

What? The blood pounding in my ears?

"This way!" Peyton turned and ran back down the steps, waving Ronnie and Sam to follow. "It's the REM-pod at the butler's pantry." At the foyer, she yelled for them to wait, and took a sharp right into the operations center. Out in an instant with a replacement SLS and a small pack over her shoulder, Peyton handed Ronnie a lantern and walkie-talkie.

"Thanks, but I've already been deputized, you know."

"You are going to wise-guy me now?"

"No, but we have your walkie. I don't need one."

"You will if we get separated." She backed away.

"Separated?" *That just cannot happen.*

Peyton hustled into the dining room and Ronnie hurried in after her.

"Jesus Christ. Can Doonan or this...*thing* be in two places at once?" Her eyes flew open and she almost stopped in the dining room world of laser dots. "Wow, people would pay to go through this!" She ran to keep up with Peyton.

The REM-pod had gone quiet by the time they burst through the swinging door into the kitchen. While Peyton woke up her SLS, Ronnie roamed the room, searching for any sign of disturbance.

"Patrick Doonan!" Peyton said, angry. "We're not playing games." She turned slowly, almost daring an image to take shape on the screen. "We're not intimidated, Patrick. We're not leaving."

Ronnie approached the little door in the side wall, the one that always seemed to open on its own. It was open now, and she tentatively opened it farther and reached in with the lantern. Eric had thought it was a simple storage place when he looked during "electrician day," but, to Ronnie's eye, one sheet of wood wall appeared oddly older than the rest. She ducked, crab-walked in a few steps and poked it, curious about its condition. The panel fell back into a black hole.

"Um...Peyton?"

"What are you up to in there?"

On her hands and knees, Ronnie withdrew her head and the lantern from the hole and looked back at Peyton and Sam, both squeezed into the doorway. "I just touched it and it fell away into space. I can't see a thing down there, but I think it goes a long way."

Cold air roared out of the hole, forceful enough to make her blink and ruffle her hair. Even Peyton's curls fluttered, and when those mesmerizing eyes hardened, Ronnie knew Peyton's detective skills had shifted to high gear. Peyton beckoned her with a crisp wave and Ronnie scrambled out of the space.

"Damn," she said heavily, brushing dust off her knees. "Did the whole basement just exhale at us or what?"

Peyton shut the little door, but air still vented vigorously from the space and kept it ajar. The chill was tempering the entire kitchen, and Peyton panned the SLS around the room.

"Actually, you might not be far off," she answered. "That door...Every time we've seen it move has been when the subject of a ‘house change’ came up. Think about it. It opened when Meyers took us on that initial tour. Again, when the electricians were here. And now, as we’re closing off Doonan’s hiding places.”

“So…” Ronnie forced her brain to align with Peyton’s thought process. “So, you’re saying something *comes out* of there to object?”

Peyton quizzed her with a steady gaze. “Think it’s a stretch?”

Ronnie certainly thought it was. Peyton must have read that in her eyes because she pressed her point.

“The ‘whole house exhaling at us’ could very well be something objecting. Feel the cold in here now?” Ronnie nodded. “That ‘something’ is in the cellar, probably in that space you so innocently stuck your head into.”

Ronnie looked back at the door, ajar several inches, as if refusing to be denied.

Peyton set a hand on Ronnie’s bicep and flexed her fingers into the muscle. “It’s important that you realize our situation now. I’m thinking whatever is down there is the last concentration of Doonan’s energy—and we may have pushed it too far. It’s possible he’s gone into panic mode, scrambling to hide or to cross over, but…it’s more likely he’s pissed off.”

“Oh. Well, that can’t be good.”

“Not usually. And backing down from him is not an option. That will only empower him, and,” she held up forefinger and thumb a smidgeon apart, “we are this close to success.”

“And,” Ronnie acknowledged the viewers with a nod to Sam, “we don’t have much time left before we lose our support system.”

“True. So…” Peyton looked into the lens. “Everyone ready?” She turned back to Ronnie. “Are *you*?” Ronnie saluted. “Then, let’s go.”

But Ronnie sensed trouble when Peyton snatched up her lantern from earlier to add to their arsenal and walked past the long table, the dining room entrance, and stopped at the cellar door. “Now, we’re going down there?”

Peyton nodded. “Can you handle the Ovilus?”

How does she stay so cool?

“Yes.”

"Here you go. What else do you have on you?"

"About sixty dollars."

"I meant instruments."

"Oh, um…I forgot." She pulled them from her pockets. "One of these and one of these."

"EMF meter…think electric charge in the air beyond what you feel or see. And, ah, yes. A spirit box. Good."

"Freaking noise machine."

"By itself, it is. It's awful." She slipped it back into Ronnie's pocket and winked as she gave it a pat. "Take care of this."

She opened the cellar door, and the old walls closed in as they started down worn wooden steps, lanterns at their sides. Like walking down into a mine. Ronnie was immeasurably thankful that Sam stayed right with them, a lifeline to the outside world, live audience, viewers, fans, voyeurs, be dammed.

The old steps were steep and turned before they reached the stone floor. Huge rocks, probably interlocked by Hercules, Ronnie mused, formed the walls, and nooks and various chambers were everywhere. She lost her sense of space, couldn't conceptualize the overall size.

Construction remnants, discarded antiques, bottles, cartons, crates, leftovers from a hundred years seemed to fill the place, covered in dust and sand. The chilly air smelled a little like the ocean.

Ronnie followed Peyton, who followed the power line for the static camera. It was down here somewhere. Brian had shown some guts just getting it down here.

The black cable ran along a narrow rock corridor, through two rooms, and down another hall where small rocks and chips covered the floor. *Is this debris intended to scare us off?* The cable finally led them out to an enormous boulder, where a tiny red light beamed faithfully atop the isolated tripod. Ronnie couldn't help thinking the camera looked terribly abandoned.

Peyton exhaled hard and Ronnie agreed. Overwhelming, yes. She nodded.

"Sam?" Peyton asked. "Do you have Brian or Jamie? Is everyone back at the operations center?"

One more thing I'm grateful for: Sam's headset.

"They're back. Brian's here." He tapped his ear. "The transmission's a little sketchy, down in all this rock and cement, but decent."

"Hm. We should be okay."

"He wants to know if Eric and Caroline should come down."

"Not really necessary, but eyes on the kitchen would be good." Peyton talked while she meandered around the mammoth rock, surveying the ceiling. "Tell them to keep their ears open for the pods."

Sam conveyed the message softly as Peyton strayed into a little side hallway. "The kitchen…" She looked at the stone wall, up across the ceiling, and down again. "Should be directly above us and…that storage space, that hole you saw going down into nothing? It should come down to…right about here."

Ronnie looked with her as Sam showed the ceiling to the audience. "I don't see any open shaft or anything." But in the wall, there *was* a gap between two boulders, and she peered into it, lantern held high. "Just this. I can fit through here."

She angled sideways, stepped between the rocks, and found the space beyond to be large, flat, and reasonably clear. Imaginative thoughts began intruding, of rumrunners, tunnels, hotel managers, secret trysts…

Peyton followed her in, lantern above her head as she began circling the area. Sam settled halfway into the space, far enough to stay out of their way yet still keep them in his sights.

"Will you look at this?" Peyton said distantly. "Who knows what this space was used for, but I still don't see anything that… Then again," she paused, and Ronnie followed her line of vision, "those rocks up there don't reach the ceiling."

"It *would* make for a serious draft," Ronnie reasoned.

Peyton dropped her eyes to meet Ronnie's and a vicious chill suddenly made them both shiver. "The police report on Doonan's death said he apparently fell, hit his head, and passed on in a 'chamber' off a cellar hallway."

"Like here?"

"We thought it meant back down the hall, by that huge boulder. That's why the static camera is out there." She looked around again. "But now I'm thinking differently."

Thanks a lot. Now, this place is freaking creepy.

"All right," Peyton declared as she performed another SLS scan of the room. Finally, she glanced up at Ronnie. "Ovilus."

Ronnie snatched it out of her pocket and turned it on.

"I'm gambling that *this* is the spot," Peyton told her. "With other places closed off to him, chances are this is where he'll be, and probably where he's been secreting himself away for God-knows how long. It's my last hunch to really get through to him." She spoke sharply as she repeated the scan. "Patrick Doonan." Her voice boomed against the surroundings. "Your final breath was right here, wasn't it? Today, you say good-bye. Patrick. You need to answer us now."

Ronnie stared down at the Ovilus. *If this thing speaks, I'll pass out.* She decided it smarter not to watch it.

"Patrick Doonan. We're going to wait because we *all* know you must come here. You *know* this is the place. Show yourself, Patrick. There's no more hiding."

Silent minutes passed. Ronnie glanced at the Ovilus and flicked her eyes away.

"Enough," Peyton grumbled, and slipped the canvas bag off her shoulder. "Ready for one last experiment?" She knelt and began unloading gear, obviously not needing Ronnie's answer. "Spirit box, please." She held out her hand and Ronnie put the device in it. "We're done with the Ovilus."

"What are we doing now?"

"Have a seat."

Ronnie sat on the dirty stone floor, set the Ovilus beside her, and wrapped her arms around herself against the chill, colder now than just a minute ago. Peyton operated like a pit mechanic on an Indy racecourse: expert, fast, and efficient, but far more attractive. As enraptured as she was fascinated, Ronnie concentrated on observing and forced aside apprehension.

Peyton was too busy connecting things to look up from the small box of wires and dials.

"We nicknamed this the Session Master," Peyton said. "It's basically just a filter. It takes all that noise out of the spirit box and leaves you with just spoken words, utterances we often struggle to understand. This cleans it up." She glanced up, excited. "We ask questions and get responses. If we get lucky, we'll actually have a conversation."

Ronnie watched her attach the handheld device to the box and wire them together. *A conversation? You're kidding.*

"To ensure clear, undisturbed replies, the listener is connected by sound-blocking headphones," she handed a set to Ronnie, "and is blindfolded, for ultimate focus." She handed that to Ronnie, too.

"I'm putting these on?"

And lose sight of you? Down here?

"Yes." She snapped her head to Sam. "I need to trade places with you, Sam. Can you squeeze in here?"

Laboring to keep the live shot steady, he held the camera ahead of him as he worked his way into the space.

Peyton turned back to Ronnie. "I'm going into that gap where he was. Actually, just beyond it, out of your line of vision. I will be posing questions in a gentle, conversational tone. With these things on, there'll be no way for you to see my expressions or know what I've asked, so none of that will influence what you're hearing or your interpretation of it. You won't be able to focus on me or any of this around us."

"Me? Lose focus on you?" Ronnie chortled. "I doubt I could."

Peyton nodded discreetly at Sam's camera, reminding Ronnie of what the audience could hear. "Some other time, Casual Cook," she whispered and snuck Ronnie a wink. "Put those on, please." She retrieved a small notepad from the bag and shoved it into her jacket pocket. "And Sam will be over there, in that far corner, where he can get us both in his shot." She looked up at the camera. "You can still get us if I'm over there, can't you? I'll try to stay visible to you."

"I think so," Sam said, backing as far away as he could. "Yeah. I got the shot, just don't back completely out of that gap."

"We don't have the static camera's watchful eye now," Peyton reminded Ronnie, "so Sam has to get everything."

Ronnie positioned the headset and blindfold on her head, but not quite in place. She wished they could ward off her nervous chill. "And the objective of all this?"

"To really connect with Doonan. If he can get his message across, be *heard*...I'm thinking it might be all he's ever wanted to do. Hopefully, then he'll feel free to depart."

"Cripes. He better." Ronnie blew out a breath. "Well...I guess this should be pretty cool."

Peyton crouched in front of her and covered her knee with a warm hand. She wouldn't have touched her in front of millions of eyes if she hadn't felt the need to reassure her.

"Relax, okay? All you have to do is speak exactly what you hear. I'll talk to Doonan, and you'll repeat what he says. You become an Ovilus, only better. That's all."

Ronnie nodded. *Repeat what I hear. Simple enough. Can you leave your hand there, please?*

Peyton drummed her fingers on Ronnie's knee. *Even though she knows her every move is being caught.* Ronnie thought the risky little gesture said a lot.

Peyton smiled. "The Casual Cook will have to concoct a whopper of a recipe to commemorate this night."

Her look was direct, almost conspiratorial, and deep enough to carry a multitude of messages. Ronnie preferred to dwell on that instead of her own nerves or the cold or whatever was about to broadcast into her head. "Ask Doonan if he wants a doggie bag."

Laughing, Peyton tripped Ronnie's chin and stood. "You bet. Put those things in place now, and I'll come back and get you out of the void when we're done. See you in a few."

Her watchful eyes were the last things Ronnie saw as she lowered her blindfold and snugged the headphones to her ears.

❖

Peyton switched on the Session Master, knowing Ronnie heard only consuming dead silence from it, and sent a hopeful smile to the audience in Sam's camera. She edged almost completely into the space between the boulders, and Sam nodded an "all set."

Alone and almost out of his shot, she looked back to the stone-walled hallway. A shiver shot through her at the sight of three dusty propane bottles in the distant corner, and she inhaled to calm herself. *I knew you would seek refuge down here.*

Turning back again, with only Sam still visible, she composed herself with a breath—and saw it when she exhaled. The underground chill had become far more than that. If contact was coming, literally, this experiment could end up so much bigger than expected.

Please, let this go as planned. To wrap up this night with a home run here would be glorious.

"Patrick Doonan," she began. "Let's talk. Please, acknowledge this connection we have, Patrick." She paused, not hearing a sound from Ronnie. "Let's stop chasing each other around. Neither of us wants to play games, Patrick, and, if you speak what's on your mind, you will be heard."

She glanced at Sam, counting on viewers not losing faith in this bizarre experiment.

"You've told us a few things over the course of tonight, Patrick, and often left us confused. The kitchen extension…Did it provide you protection from shame, two of the words you spoke? Was that becau—"

"See you both." Ronnie's signature energetic voice was flat. Peyton heard her cough lightly and call to her. "Hey, it's me. Letting you know I'm hearing a man's deep voice. That's all. Over and out."

Peyton shook her head and grinned to herself. She held her notebook against the rock and wrote the words on paper: *See you both.* "Patrick? 'See you both?' Who?"

From Ronnie: "Together."

"'Together.' Um…okay. Who's together? Are you with Jonathan? Are you referring to Eleanor and her fian—"

"Stop," Ronnie said. "Finished."

Peyton tensed. She wrote the words and folded her arms across her chest. The added warmth was welcome.

"No, Patrick, we're not finished. We are not stopping. You need this. We're helping you."

She waited. Seconds passed. *Don't you dare take off on me now, Doonan. This is a great start.*

Ronnie droned, "Future."

"You will have a future with Jonathan, once you cross over. He doesn't need you lingering here, protecting Miram—"

"Finished."

Again, with the "finished."

"We *should* talk about your life back then," she said, fighting off a shiver. *It's so cold he has to be right on top of us.* "Patrick, I know it must have been difficult."

"Accept. Together."

"You two *are* accepted now. Together. The nineteen twenties were difficult for relationships like yours, Patrick, and they remained so for decades, but not any longer. There's no need to stop anyone from interfering, no need to hide in the extension, the tower, at Miramar, period. Do not feel ashamed."

The possibility of turning his thinking around, enabling him to free himself had her nerves in knots. If she could avoid frustrating him, this two-way could be the most amazing she'd ever conducted, a personal as well as professional triumph. She cleared her throat and glanced at Sam again before continuing. *Incredible, everyone getting all this.*

From Ronnie: "See you."

Peyton straightened. *Me? No need to bring me into this.*

"Can you manifest yourself, Patrick?" She hoped he would, hoped he wouldn't. A volatile mass of energy was unpredictable. "I want to see you, too. It's okay if we share that."

Ronnie droned, "House home. No people."

Peyton grew a bit frustrated. He *still* opposed people in what he *still* saw as his home.

"Patrick, Miramar was your home for so many years, and you put so much of yourself into it, but it isn't your home anymore. People come here to protect this place, for upkeep, to be sure another family can find happiness in this picturesque spot, just as you did. It's the best you can hope for now. You see that, don't you?"

"Finished."

Peyton swore under her breath as her written list of words grew. She couldn't come up with a reason for his insistence on that word.

"Co-workers," Ronnie droned. Then, for a moment, her voice brightened. "Ah…Hey, Peyton? This is me talking. The voice is louder now."

"'Co-workers'?" Peyton repeated. *He's getting exasperated. Swell.* "Co-workers come here, yes. To help Miramar."

"Ocean."

"'Ocean'? What about the o—"

"Living. Finally."

"Explain that, pleas—"

"Together. You."

Peyton felt her heart jump. Perplexed now, she grew edgy, unsure where he was leading their conversation. Why he kept bringing *her*, personally, back into it baffled her.

"Me, Patrick? I'm only an investigator trying to help you find answers." The silence grew. "I'm trying to restore peace to Miramar. That's what this place should be, right? Peaceful?" She wondered what Ronnie was thinking through all this, what viewer chatter must be like. "What about me, Patrick? This isn't my house, just like it's no longer—"

"Accept."

"Patrick. I can see that—"

"You see."

"I do."

"No."

"I don't?" Now, she was confused. She looked up from her notes and raised her eyebrows at the camera. "What don't I see, Patrick?"

Ronnie remained quiet.

Cold, confused, and tense, Peyton pinched the bridge of her nose. Whatever Doonan was getting at, she had better see soon before he became exasperated and shut this whole thing down.

"Help me see it, Patrick. What is it I don't see?"

More silence.

She drummed her fingers on the notepad, grumbling under her breath. "Just when I thought we were getting somewhere." She scanned her list of the staccato responses, desperate for a connecting thread.

From Ronnie: "Cook."

And then Peyton saw it. Blood pulsed in her ears and her hand trembled. She and *Ronnie* were on his mind?

"What do you mean, 'cook'?" she asked, surprised by the timidity in her tone.

The list before her now screamed for attention and, cold as she was, she broke out in a sweat. Words practically formed sentences. See you both. Together. Future. House. Home. Co-workers. Ocean. You see. Cook. *Did Ronnie hear what she was voicing?*

She looked blankly at the boulder nearby, seeing instead what this lost, frustrated, now seemingly misunderstood spirit apparently had been trying to make her see. He was finished dealing with past relationships in this place. They had come to sad conclusions. And then she and Ronnie arrived. Co-workers. In the moonlight at the ocean, touching in the kitchen, the foyer… Doonan had seen it all, seen her, them, witnessed even more than what viewers witnessed. Was he pushing for a rare happy ending here?

"Patrick? Are you still there? Please explain 'cook.'"

Will this end if I acknowledge Ronnie, feelings for her? Will he be satisfied? Finished?

Breaking her own rule, Peyton slipped back into the room and went to Ronnie, compelled, somehow guided to be in her immediate presence. She crouched before her, not knowing what to do next, uncertain if the time was right to touch her. Peyton *did* know that when she spoke again—from less than two feet away—this remarkably enlightening experiment could come to an abrupt end.

"Fate," Ronnie offered into the silence, still unaware of Peyton's proximity.

Sitting back on her heels, Peyton studied the long line of Ronnie's jaw, how it flinched as if she wanted to speak her own words. *"Fate"? Is it? You and I?*

Peyton watched her cross her arms and briskly rub her biceps in the cold. Ronnie clutched her hands together nervously in her lap, licked her lips, swiped hair from her forehead.

She gets it.

"Surrender," Ronnie droned.

Jesus. "Surrender"?

Ronnie shifted restlessly. "Together."

Now, he's repeating himself. As if I don't hear him.

As if everyone watching doesn't hear him.

There's no way out of this but the obvious way, she thought. Can't pretend he didn't say "surrender…together."

But live on camera?

Peyton glanced at Sam and offered a look she hoped would convey her bewildered anticipation. She believed that, like herself, the audience had to have discerned Doonan's message, and now held its collective breath, waiting for Peyton or Ronnie to act.

Peyton bit her lip. Carefully, she set her hands on Ronnie's knees and Ronnie jerked in surprise and tore the blindfold off. She looked overwhelmed and exhausted.

She sat holding Peyton's gaze, entranced, as if still far away on Doonan's wavelength. With a yank, she removed the headset, an obvious afterthought, and Peyton unplugged it.

"We're…we're done?" Ronnie asked. She pushed the Ovilus away from her side, evidently irritated by the possibility of it contributing to any more spirit talk.

Peyton smiled as if she had rescued something vital, possibly her own heart.

"We are, yes, and we were terrific."

Ronnie suddenly took Peyton's face in her hands and kissed her. Not too long of a kiss, but long enough for everyone to know she meant more than thank you.

Then, she sat back, looking even more overwhelmed than before. "I'd say I got the last word," she said and offered a tired but savvy smile.

Peyton could feel the cold lift in the room. The back of her neck prickled with heat.

From the Ovilus: *"Finally."*

They stared at the discarded device, back at each other, and laughed.

"Patrick Doonan," Peyton called toward the ceiling. "Have you said enough?"

Damn, you, Doonan. Don't even think about coming back with "kiss" or...or "love." It's hard enough for us to handle what just happened. We don't need you throwing more at us or the audience.

They waited, studied the floor, the equipment, their feet. They even sent sheepish looks at Sam and then each other.

"Patrick? Is there anything else you'd like to say? We're still waiting."

Another minute passed. They shared a long, uninterrupted look, a nod, and then stood.

Peyton raised the EMF meter and pivoted in place, scrutinizing the gauge, nodding with satisfaction. At last, she pocketed it and sent Ronnie a smile before turning to the camera.

With a sly, victorious grin, she announced. "I believe he's 'finally' gone."

Ronnie juggled surprise, happiness, and relief. This encounter was over, but something else had begun, even though this wasn't a great time to ponder it. She raised both arms in triumph and clapped for their success.

If Peyton's happy, I'm happy. Hell, after all that, who wouldn't be?

"And, on that note," Peyton told the audience, "I'm sure the powers-that-be have been chomping at the bit to go to commercial, so, we're going to pack up our stuff now, and see you on the other side."

Sam clicked his lens shut and swung the camera off his shoulder with a weary sigh. "Well, *that* was something."

"*That* was freaking awesome," Peyton stated, looking a bit awestruck by the whole thing.

Ronnie laughed, glad—and relieved when Peyton did the same. At least, Peyton didn't despise her for that kiss in front of the free world.

"I think my head's still reeling," Peyton added as she disconnected the Session Master and packed it away.

Ronnie hesitated to ask if Peyton attributed her state of mind to the earth-shattering kiss or the earth-shattering spirit conversation. The shy smile Peyton offered indicated the kiss won.

Ronnie finished wrapping wires and added them to Peyton's bag. She didn't know what to say, and now worried about Peyton expecting an explanation for what had been a completely spontaneous gesture.

"We have to get back upstairs with the living," Sam said, "and pretty quick. Are you two ready for that?"

Peyton stopped and shrugged. "I'm just going to do the closing and it's a wrap. Viewers have the whole off-season to dwell on what they heard—and saw."

Maybe the kiss didn't really bother her too much?

Ronnie retrieved the lantern and fell in behind Peyton, who trailed after Sam, back the way they had come. She grew restless in Peyton's silence.

We can't just let the kiss slide, can we? Kissing a beautiful woman on live television, surprising her like that, surprising the whole world, isn't something that happens every day. God, where did my mind go?

They hadn't reached the half-way point before she decided to get things out in the open. Better to do it now, off-camera, she thought, and touched a finger to Peyton's shoulder as they walked.

"Is it possible Doonan made me kiss you?'

Peyton stopped short and faced her. "Wow, for a skeptic you've come a very long way."

"Well, is it? I mean, it just *happened*."

"You took my breath away and now you're apologizing?"

"I'm not, no."

"Good."

"Good?" Ronnie's pulse throbbed.

She kissed me back, didn't do anything to stop it. Her thinking went out the window, too.

Ronnie couldn't help but grin. Peyton didn't seem the slightest bit worried, and Ronnie felt free to join her.

Chapter Twenty-seven

Peyton squeezed Ronnie's hand and left her sitting on the grand staircase. On Brian's signal, she stepped outside and into a sea of white light.

"So, we've come full circle," she said into the mic, moving closer to the edge of the porch and the blinding spotlights. "Wild storm, wild night, wild ending, wasn't it? Everybody out there survive? We couldn't have asked for better company on this investigation, and every one of us appreciates having you here these past couple of hours."

Team members gathered on the porch behind her, waved, and called out thank-yous to the camera.

"Absolutely not to be forgotten," Peyton continued, "is our producer, the very best, the phantom you viewers never see but without whom you wouldn't see us. In our mobile headquarters around the corner, Jamie Rexford!" Everyone on the porch applauded.

"Oh. Are we missing someone?" she asked, looking around her as the team began chanting Ronnie's name. She couldn't help smiling. *Playing game show host isn't all bad.*

"We're missing a very special someone," she said, turning. "Ronnie Sharp! Get your *Casual Cook* self out here!"

Shaking her head at the team's applause, Ronnie emerged from the foyer and into the lights. She hid the fatigue well, Peyton thought.

Those tiny lines at her eyes so noticeable in the cellar vanished in the brightness.

Ronnie arrived at Peyton's side, waving. "Hey, you guys! Thanks for being with us tonight. What a ride!"

Peyton bumped her shoulder as she continued. "A challenging, enlightening evening, to say the least. I doubt we've ever had more fun on an investigation and you, out there, helped make it so." Everyone on the porch applauded in agreement. "I think we accomplished a lot, and," she exchanged a glance with Ronnie, "I'd say we learned a lot."

"Oh, yeah!" Ronnie added, leaning toward Peyton's mic, "and not just about candle salad!"

They all laughed.

"An amazing ending to the remarkable tale of an incredible place," Peyton said. "We came to know quite a bit about Patrick Doonan, manager of the Grand Miramar Hotel, didn't we? Large, in size and stature, a fast mover." She looked over her shoulder as the others agreed and handed the mic to Caroline.

"Cigar smoker," she said, wrinkling her nose as she passed the mic to Eric.

"Prideful and defiant."

Brian took over next. "Stubborn piece of work." He chuckled and passed the mic to Ronnie.

"A very authoritative voice. Rattled the nerves, unless you were with the *Paranormal Pursuit* team." She winked handing the mic back to Peyton.

"Patrick struggled for decades with his attachment here. He struggled with a lost love, a relationship fearfully hidden from society of that era. From then on, he struggled to preserve Miramar, his lover's pride and joy. He struggled to maintain the family name at Miramar, his only remaining avenue to honor their relationship.

"And, in death, he struggled to stand his ground here." She extended a hand toward the building behind her. "His place, 'their' place, until he finally realized that, at long last, he could tell his story to an ear that would listen." She gestured to Ronnie with a tip of the mic. "We believe he's finally left Miramar, after one hundred and seven years, but he did one last thing before he crossed over. He endorsed a similar connection between women he didn't really know until tonight. To us, that's an expression of his gratitude we humbly accept.

"And it's one hell of a way to end our season," she added and sent Ronnie a grin. "With any luck, we'll drag our intrepid Casual Cook back into the thick of things next season. Judging by the terrific feedback from all of you, we better! So, thanks for being with us, everybody. We hope you've enjoyed this as much as we have. Good night from Miramar!"

The spotlights went black, and the team unleashed a joyful roar.

Peyton laughed as they dashed off to begin tearing down equipment and rolling up cables throughout the house.

"My stuff is ready to go," Ronnie said, "so I'll get my two-wheeler and start."

"I want to help you."

"You've got plenty to do helping your people. It's ok—"

"No, I want to." Peyton touched her cheek. "Get the two-wheeler and I'll meet you in the kitchen." She left Ronnie and hurried into the house.

She heard Jamie in the front yard, congratulating Ronnie, and knew she'd be at her side momentarily.

"Peyton!" Jamie caught up to her in the hallway. "That's the greatest show *Paranormal Pursuit* has ever done, you know. You guys blew the roof off."

"Even with the kiss?" She flashed her a grin as they entered the kitchen's lantern light.

"Shit, yeah. Are you kidding? We couldn't have scripted it any better. What made her do that?"

"Just...being in the moment, I guess. Here, stack these by the door. Ronnie's coming with her two-wheeler." She hauled a cooler to the spot and went back for another. "Maybe Doonan had something to do with it."

"Honestly?" Jamie put one bin atop another at the door. "You think that could really happen?"

"Can anyone definitively say it couldn't?" She passed her another bin. "We get closer to that world than anybody, so if we can't be sure…"

"But *you* are, aren't you. You think Doonan did something."

"He had me in a daze," Ronnie said, rolling the two-wheeler ahead of her. "That's what he did. A blank, one-track-mind daze." She loaded a cooler and stopped to catch Peyton's eye. "There was only one thought, one action available to me. It didn't matter what anyone saw or thought because, in my head, there *still* was no one else around—except you. Our public image was, literally, the furthest thing from my mind."

Peyton stacked a bin atop Ronnie's cooler on the two-wheeler. "In that second as you stared at me, something connected us. When you reached out, I…I don't know what happened. My mind…There was nothing else in that moment for me either."

Hearing Peyton relay a matching sentiment told Ronnie far more than anything some spirit may have conveyed. She doubted Peyton would have been susceptible to such a mental suggestion if she hadn't already been predisposed to it.

She stepped around the two-wheeler and took Peyton's face in her hands, as she had in the cellar. "Any chance I get." She kissed her lightly and lingered, brushing her lips across Peyton's.

Drawing Ronnie closer, Peyton whispered against her mouth. "Doonan's not here anymore."

"That's right," Ronnie answered softly but loud enough for Jamie to hear, "so he gets no credit for this." She kissed Peyton again, tugging playfully on each lip.

Peyton slipped her fingertips beneath the back of Ronnie's waistband and clutched their hips together. The expression of want pushed Ronnie's self-control to the brink and she kissed her harder, kissed across to her cheek, her throat. Jamie moving gear around them could not distract her.

Head tilted back, relaxed, Peyton sighed in her arms. "God, Ron, that's…"

Jamie coughed into her hand. It didn't appear that Jamie could distract Peyton, either.

Breathing harder as Ronnie nuzzled her throat, Peyton managed, "Oh, yes. Imagine all the kisses in this kitchen."

Ronnie kissed up to her chin and held a kiss to her mouth. "Imagine what was done on that table."

"Hey, um…I'll just keep hefting these really heavy bins," Jamie said, passing by with another. "Don't worry about me. I'll just bring them outside. It's only a mile to the front porch. I'm fine." She shuffled out of the kitchen.

"Sorry, Jamie!" Peyton called after her, smiling into Ronnie's eyes.

"Right!" Jamie yelled from the hall. "I know!"

Ronnie maneuvered the two-wheeler around and eyed Peyton's entire form hungrily. "Work's never tasted so good."

Peyton picked up a bin and prepared to follow her out. "I think *we* have exquisite taste."

Ronnie's face hurt from grinning as she led them down the lantern-lit hall.

The dark wood walls didn't faze her anymore, didn't feel as confining, foreboding. Maybe because now the hall was filled with the sounds of busy footsteps, rubberized bins being slapped shut and dragged across wood, sporadic comments and questions yelled between floors. It felt familiar now, and a wave of melancholy struck her at the thought of leaving. So much had happened here.

She stopped their procession in the hall and stood the two-wheeler upright. She turned and lifted the bin from Peyton's arms, then set it aside to clasp her hands.

"Come home with me."

A flirtatious smirk grew at the corner of Peyton's lips. "Are we going to make pizza?"

Ronnie marveled at the foxy expression. "No. Not *pizza*."

"Ah…You're blocking traffic." Caroline's voice.

They turned to see everyone crowded into the hall, apparently enjoying the drama, but lined up to finish emptying the kitchen.

Ronnie spun back around, hoping to hear the right answer.
Peyton didn't make her wait. "Let's get out of here."

❖

Peyton clutched the plush terrycloth bathrobe in both hands and buried her face in it, wanting to bury her entire body in it. She inhaled deeply and could feel the tension in her back and shoulders subsiding. The soothing balsam scent was doing its job already, dissolving knots that had crimped her nerves all night. Eager for complete relief, she slid the glass door aside and stepped into the shower.

Jets of fine, firm spray surrounded her, and she took a moment to simply stand, close her eyes, and surrender to them. From above, the hot steady rain massaged a myriad of images out of her mind. Like documents stashed away in a folder, they could be recalled at will, but she had no intention of reviewing them now. There was no place here for memories of simmering black entities, computer-generated voices, or pink laser-light dots.

Reminded of black lights in Ronnie's nineteen seventies room, a place downstairs she was bound to see eventually, Peyton smiled beneath the steaming flow—and knew the shower door had opened.

Ronnie's broad hand touched her midsection from behind and turned her.

She stood a breath away, holding Peyton's hands and looking like she had a million things to say but wouldn't. Water cascaded over her head, over capable shoulders still showing tan lines, over small breasts with obviously sensitized nipples.

Ronnie's silky, often disarrayed hair flattened as water covered her, deep brown becoming black and bringing even more sincerity to her eyes. They roamed Peyton's face now, alert and wondrous, as if exploring a miraculous place, and Peyton saw reverence, and sweet, soulful desire.

"I couldn't do it," Ronnie said, eyes riveted on her. "I-I couldn't sit out there in the kitchen, picturing you in here…" her eyes trailed down beyond Peyton's chin to her breasts and rose slowly, "picturing you like this. I want you, Peyton."

Layering her arms around Ronnie's neck, Peyton leaned into the kiss and reveled in the skin-to-skin contact. She welcomed the soft, skilled hands and their possessive grip on her hips. They explored her back, grazed upward, felt their way across her shoulders, and down again, and finally rested securely on her ass.

Drawn in against Ronnie's wiry frame, Peyton heard herself moan approval into Ronnie's mouth. Synapses at every point of contact fired and abandoned her legs, left them weak, and she tightened her grip around Ronnie's neck.

Ronnie stepped forward and slid her palms to Peyton's waist as she kissed her to the wall. Smooth, knobby surfaces of river rock pressed into her back, and the startlingly cool sensations clashed with the soaring heat between her legs. Her nipples hardened against Ronnie's chest.

But her concentration blurred at the tentative touch of Ronnie's tongue caressing her own. Peyton encircled it, licked it, drew on it, and wanted Ronnie to reach so, so much deeper. She shoved both hands into Ronnie's hair, unable to get them close enough.

Ronnie pressed her harder against the wall and groaned at the feel of Peyton's breasts in her palms. Sensation made Peyton squirm as they kissed.

Ronnie's thumbs toyed with her nipples, and Peyton surged against her, clutching at her shoulders. She wrapped a leg around Ronnie's hip to urge her inward, and Ronnie lifted it, forced her back to the wall again, and held her there with insistent kisses.

She skimmed a hand along Peyton's stomach, then stopped to massage it deeply while dragging kisses over Peyton's jaw, down her neck. She withdrew slightly to reach Peyton's chest and took a nipple into her mouth.

Peyton writhed, her insides clamored for attention. She held Ronnie's head to her breast, almost delirious with want, and closed her eyes, trembling as Ronnie tormented her nipple, gripped it with her teeth, and slid fingers into her heat.

Peyton squirmed against the wall, reeling everywhere at once, and dug fingers into Ronnie's back to hang on as her body peaked. Fingers played within her, and her nipples tingled. Through half-closed eyes, she saw Ronnie's mouth work at her breast, and her eyes slammed shut when hardened fingers tripped through her sex. Repeatedly.

"R-Ronnie, you're—"

Ronnie raised her head. "Should I stop?"

"Can you?" she asked, cupping Ronnie's cheek.

"No."

"Oh, thank God."

Sliding lower, Ronnie kissed her way along her abdomen. Kneeling, she nursed at the flesh of her hipbone and crossed to the other. Palms ran up Peyton's legs to the apex of her thighs, and Ronnie gripped her ass and held her steady as she nuzzled her way inward.

Peyton seized fistfuls of Ronnie's hair, trying not to squirm at the excruciating rise of every capable nerve she had left.

The first of many strokes made Peyton gasp, and she lost any voice for the rest. She shuddered hard and long against the river rock, water still coming as fast and as hard as she. Finally managing a weary gasp, Peyton wasn't sure her legs were even present, let alone strong enough to support her.

But then, Ronnie's hands were at her waist, holding strong, and Peyton gloried in that strength. She knew the Casual Cook was going to need it.

"One minute, you take my breath away," she said, tracing a line through the water between Ronnie's breasts, "and the next, you destroy my legs…" She dropped her head back and blew out a breath.

Ronnie wanted to eat her alive, jump into vampire mode, and gobble her up. That silken throat begged to be kissed for days.

She sent Peyton an innocent look as she ran her hands up and down her back. "Do you have a preference, breath or legs?"

"Oh, you're a riot, Casual Cook, standing in a downpour." She poked her chest and closed in on her, tweaked both Ronnie's nipples.

"Well, ohh-kay." Ronnie squirmed. "You've got that hot gleam in your eye, Ms. Stanford," she said, backing up at another poke, eager for Peyton to pursue her. "I've seen that hungry ghost hunter look. Think I might be in trou—" She hit the wall and smirked. "God. I can feel that look…so sexy."

She tried to move forward, but Peyton pushed her back with palms over her breasts.

"Flattery," Peyton stated, stepping up against her, pressing her to the wall, "will get you everywhere when I'm done."

Bring it on, gorgeous.

Ronnie knew a smirk pressed Peyton's buttons, and Peyton smothered it in an instant. She kissed her firmly, a languid, penetrating kiss, long and powerful enough for Ronnie to see sunlight in those curls, candlelight on her skin, moonlight in her eyes. Surrendering to the feel of her lips, the taste of her was automatic. Peyton held her face as she kissed her, cherishing her eyelids, her cheekbones, the angle of her jaw.

Ronnie wrapped her arms across Peyton's back and hugged her close, never wanting to let go, and wanting Peyton to know it. She couldn't help but sigh when Peyton licked water from her neck, then slid her parted lips across her shoulder.

"Now," Ronnie said and heard her own voice shake, "now, who's amazing?"

"Shh," Peyton whispered against her breast, and sucked her nipple deep into her mouth.

"God, Peyton."

"Shh, I said."

Peyton inched away to lay a trail of kisses down the center of Ronnie's torso, smiling as she went. Ronnie watched her as if in a dream. *How often, lately, have we done this in my mind?*

Peyton palmed her ass, drew Ronnie's hips against her chest, and kissed her abdomen. It seemed reality was slipping away, and Ronnie wound her fingers into Peyton's curls to cling to her.

Peyton shifted lower and toyed with the tuft of dark hair. She ran her fingers through it and dipped them inside.

Ronnie's knees flexed and she slapped both palms back to the wall for support.

"Yes, oh...Standing is so..."

Ronnie couldn't finish.

Peyton captured her thoughts—and her senses, shouldering her way in, deeper between Ronnie's legs, teasing her mercilessly before driving her up to those incredible peaks. Ronnie vibrated at every stroke. Peyton's magical lips drew Ronnie to the breaking point, held her in place until she collapsed in her arms.

Water still raining, they sat on the floor, entangled, languid, and spent. Ronnie exhaled hard in their embrace.

"Wow, Ms. Stanford." She kissed Peyton's killer smile with all the tenderness she could muster. "My heart's just now returning to normal."

"I can feel it."

Ronnie pressed her ear to Peyton's chest. "I can hear yours, too." She chuckled. "I was just thinking..."

"What, you want to be a cardiologist?"

"No." She wiggled a hand between Peyton's legs and tickled her. "A fantasy I had a while back."

"Oh, really?" Peyton pressed Ronnie's hand deeper. "Share this fantasy, please."

"Doing this under the black lights downstairs."

Peyton laughed as she fondled one of Ronnie's nipples. "I've never had sex under a black light."

Arousal threatening, Ronnie drew back to meet those white-blue eyes. "Well...We wouldn't be *having sex*, you know."

Peyton brought her lips close and whispered. "I know. We'd be making love."

Ronnie closed the distance between them and hummed as she kissed her. "Without question." Inching away, she raised an eyebrow at Peyton's grin.

"Okay, what are *you* thinking?"

Peyton closed her eyes and turned her face up to the falling water. "What would viewers think of us now?"

"Damn." Ronnie laughed. "If we do this again next season, and I bet we will, we'll probably have to practice not touching each other."

Peyton shook her head at that. "Already, I'm against it."

"Me, too. Besides, just the concept is ridiculous, a paranormal investigator and a casual cook on the same show."

"No kidding. Can you imagine? You never know what you'll see on TV."

THE END

About the Author

Having retired from careers in telecommunications and community journalism, CF "Friz" Frizzell devotes her time to creating endearing characters in memorable settings. *As Seen on TV!* is her seventh Bold Strokes Books novel, five of which either have received top honors or been shortlisted by the Golden Crown Literary Society. To date, ventures into historical fiction have garnered the Debut Author Award (*Stick McLaughlin: The Prohibition Years*) and two Best Historical Fiction nominations (*Measure of Devotion* and *Crossing the Line*). In the romance genre, her novel *Night Voice* received a Best Contemporary Romance Award, while *Nantucket Rose* earned a competing nomination.

Friz credits powerhouse authors Lee Lynch, Radclyffe, and the generous BSB family for inspiration. She is into history, New England pro sports, and singing and acoustic guitar, and loves living only an hour from Provincetown with her wife, Kathy, and their chocolate Lab, Chessa.

Books Available from Bold Strokes Books

A Cutting Deceit by Cathy Dunnell. Undercover cop Athena takes a job at Valeria's hair salon to gather evidence to prove her husband's connections to organized crime. What starts as a tentative friendship quickly turns into a dangerous affair. (978-1-63679-208-8)

As Seen on TV! by CF Frizzell. Despite their objections, TV hosts Ronnie Sharp, a laid-back chef; and paranormal investigator Peyton Stanford, have to work together. The public is watching. But joining forces is risky, contemptuous, unnerving, provocative—and ridiculously perfect. (978-1-63679-272-9)

Blood Memory by Sandra Barret. Can vampire Jade Murphy protect her friend from a human stalker and keep her dates with the gorgeous Beth Jenssen without revealing her secrets? (978-1-63679-307-8)

Foolproof by Leigh Hays. For Martine Roberts and Elliot Tillman, friends with benefits isn't a foolproof way to hide from the truth at the heart of an affair. (978-1-63679-184-5)

Glass and Stone by Renee Roman. Jordan must accept that she can't control everything that happens in life, and that includes her wayward heart. (978-1-63679-162-3)

Hard Pressed by Aurora Rey. When rivals Mira Lavigne and Dylan Miller are tapped to co-chair Finger Lakes Cider Week, competition gives way to compromise. But will their sexual chemistry lead to love? (978-1-63679-210-1)

The Laws of Magic by M. Ullrich. Nothing is ever what it seems, especially not in the small town of Bender, Massachusetts, where a witch lives to save lives and avoid love. (978-1-63679-222-4)

The Lonely Hearts Rescue by Morgan Lee Miller, Nell Stark, Missouri Vaun. In this novella collection, a hurricane hits the Gulf Coast, and the animals at the Lonely Hearts Rescue Shelter need love, and so do the humans who adopt them. (978-1-63679-231-6)

The Mage and the Monster by Barbara Ann Wright. Two powerful mages, one committed to magic and one controlled by it, strive to free each other and be together while the countries they serve descend into war. (978-1-63679-190-6)

Truly Wanted by J.J. Hale. Sam must decide if she's willing to risk losing her found family to find her happily ever after. (978-1-63679-333-7)

A Good Chance by Ali Vali. Harry, Desi, and Desi's sister Rachel are so close to getting everything they've ever wanted, but Desi's ex-husband is coming back to get his revenge and rip apart their chance at happiness. (978-1-63679-023-7)

A Perfect Fifth by Jaycie Morrison. Streetwise pianist Zara Keller and Lady Jillian Stansfield couldn't be more different; yet their connection brings a new awareness of who they are and what they truly want in their lives—including each other. (978-1-63679-132-6)

Catching Feelings by Ana Hartnett Reichardt. Andrea Foster expected to catch a lot of pitches from the Alder Lion's star pitcher, Maya, but she didn't expect to catch feelings. (978-1-63679-227-9)

Defiant Hearts by Lee Lynch. In these stories, you'll find your lovers, friends, and lesbians you wish you knew—maybe even yourself. (978-1-63679-237-8)

Love and Duty by Catherine Young. All Princess Roseli wants is to marry her three lovers, but with war looming, she must instead marry Princess Lucia to establish a military alliance between their planets. (978-1-63679-256-9)

Murder at Union Station by David S. Pederson. Private Detective Mason Adler struggles to determine who killed a woman found in a trunk without getting himself killed in the process. (978-1-63679-269-9)

Serendipity by Kris Bryant. Serendipity brings jingle writer Annie Foster and celebrity pop star Bristol Baines together, and their undeniable attraction keeps them close, but will their different paths drive them apart? (978-1-63679-224-8)

The Haunted Heart by Jane Kolven. A ghost, a ring, and a quest to find a missing psychic—it's a spell for love. (978-1-63679-245-3)

The Rules of Forever by Nan Campbell. After reconnecting at their high school reunion, Cara and Lauren agree to embark on a textbook definition friends-with-benefits relationship, but trying to keep it uncomplicated is harder than it seems. (978-1-63679-248-4)

Vision of Virtue by Brey Willows. When virtue and desire come together, be prepared for sparks in this next installment of the Memory's Muses series. (978-1-63679-118-0)

Cherry on Top by Georgia Beers. A chance meeting leaves Cherry and Ellis longing for a different life, but when Ellis's search for truth crashes into Cherry's insta-filter world, do they have any hope at all of a happily ever after? (978-1-63679-158-6)

Love and Other Rare Birds by Angie Williams. Ornithologist Dr. Jamie Martin and park ranger Rowan Fleming are searching the Alaskan wilderness for a bird thought to be extinct and they're about to discover opposites really do attract. (978-1-63679-108-1)

Parallel Paradise by Mayapee Chowdhury. When their love affair is put to the test by the homophobia of their family, community, and culture, Bindi and Rimli will need to fight for a chance at love. (978-1-63679-204-0)

Perfectly Matched by Toni Logan. A beautiful Cupid named Hannah, a runaway arrow, and just seventy-two hours to fix a mishap that could be the best mistake she has ever made. (978-1-63679-120-3)

Royal Exposé by Jenny Frame. When they're grouped together for a class assignment, Poppy's enthusiasm for life and love may just save Casey's soul, but will she ever forgive Casey for using her to expose royal secrets? (978-1-63679-165-4)

Slow Burn by Missouri Vaun. A wounded wildland firefighter from California and a struggling artist find solace and love in a small southern town. (978-1-63679-098-5)

The Artist by Sheri Lewis Wohl. Detective Casey Wilson and reclusive artist Tula Crane are drawn together in a web of passion, intrigue, and art that might just hold the key to stopping a killer. (978-1-63679-150-0)

The Inconvenient Heiress by Jane Walsh. An unlikely heiress and a spinster evade the Marriage Mart only to discover true love together. (978-1-63679-173-9)

A Champion for Tinker Creek by D.C. Robeline. Lyle James has rescued his dad's auto repair business, but when city hall condemns his neighborhood, Lyle learns only trusting will save his life and help him find love. (978-1-63679-213-2)

Closed-Door Policy by Erin Zak. Going back to college is never easy, but Caroline Stevens is prepared to work hard and change her life for the better. What she's not prepared for is Dr. Atlanta Morris, her gorgeous new professor. (978-1-63679-181-4)

Homeworld by Gun Brooke. Headed by Captain Holly Crowe, the spaceship Velocity's crew journeys toward their alien ancestors' homeworld, and what they find is completely unexpected—and they're not safe. (978-1-63679-177-7)

Outland by Kristin Keppler & Allisa Bahney. Danielle Clark and Katelyn Turner can't seem to stay away from one another even as the war for the wastelands tests their loyalty to each other and to their people. (978-1-63679-154-8)

Secret Sanctuary by Nance Sparks. US Deputy Marshal Alex Trenton specializes in protecting those awaiting trial, but when danger threatens the woman she's falling for, Alex is in for the fight of her life. (978-1-63679-148-7)

Stranded Hearts by Kris Bryant, Amanda Radley, Emily Smith. In these novellas from award winning authors, fate intervenes on behalf of love when characters are unexpectedly stuck together. With too much time and an irresistible attraction, anything could happen. (978-1-63679-182-1)

The Last Lavender Sister by Melissa Brayden. Aster Lavender sells her gourmet doughnuts and keeps a low profile; she never plans on the town's temporary veterinarian swooping in and making her feel like anything but a wallflower. (978-1-63679-130-2)

The Probability of Love by Dena Blake. As Blair and Rachel keep ending up in the same place despite the odds, can a one-night stand turn into forever? Or will the bet Blair never intended to make ruin their happily ever after? (978-1-63679-188-3)

Worth a Fortune by Sam Ledel. After placing a want ad for a personal secretary, a New York heiress is surprised when the woman who got away is the one interested in the position. (978-1-63679-175-3)

A Fox in Shadow by Jane Fletcher. Cassie's mission is to add new territory to the Kavillian empire—murder, betrayal, war, and the clash of cultures ensue. (978-1-63679-142-5)

Embracing the Moon by Jeannie Levig. Just as Gwen and Taylor are exploring the new love they've found, the present and past collide, threatening the future they long to share. (978-1-63555-462-5)

Forever Comes in Threes by D. Jackson Leigh. Efficiency expert Perry Chandler's ordered life is upended when she inherits three busy terriers, and the woman she's referred to for help turns out to be her bitter podcast rival, the very sexy Dr. Ming Lee. (978-1-63679-169-2)

Heckin' Lewd: Trans and Nonbinary Erotica by Mx. Nillin Lore. If you want smutty, fearless, gender-diverse erotica written by affirming own-voices folks who get it, then this is the book you've been looking for! (978-1-63679-240-8)

Missed Conception by Joy Argento. Maggie Walsh wants a relationship with Cassidy, the daughter she's only just discovered she has due to an in vitro mix-up. Heat kindles between Maggie and Cassidy's mother in a way neither expects. (978-1-63679-146-3)

Private Equity by Elle Spencer. Cassidy Bennett spends an unexpected evening at a lesbian nightclub with her notoriously reserved and demanding boss, Julia. After seeing a different side of Julia, Cassidy can't seem to shake her desire to know more. (978-1-63679-180-7)

Racing the Dawn by Sandra Barret. After narrowly escaping a house fire, vampire Jade Murphy is unexpectedly intrigued by gorgeous firefighter Beth Jenssen, and her undead existence might just be perking up a bit. (978-1-63679-271-2)

Reclaiming Love by Amanda Radley. Sarah's tiny white lie means somehow convincing Pippa to pretend to be her girlfriend. Only the more time they spend faking it, the more real it feels. (978-1-63679-144-9)

Sol Cycle by Kimberly Cooper Griffin. An encounter in a park brings Ang and Krista together, but when Ang's attempts to help Krista go spectacularly wrong, their passion for each other might not be enough. (978-1-63679-137-1)

Trial and Error by Carsen Taite. Attorney Franco Rossi and Judge Nina Aguilar's reunion is fraught with courtroom conflict, undeniable chemistry, and danger. (978-1-63555-863-0)